Ash
&
Bone

Also by John Harvey
in Large Print:

Last Rites

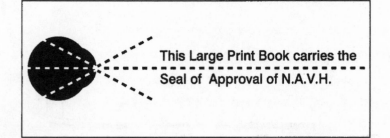

This Large Print Book carries the
Seal of Approval of N.A.V.H.

Ash
&
Bone

JOHN HARVEY

Thorndike Press • Waterville, Maine

Published in 2006 by arrangement with Harcourt, Inc.

Thorndike Press® Large Print Reviewers' Choice.

The tree indicium is a trademark of Thorndike Press.

The text of this Large Print edition is unabridged.
Other aspects of the book may vary from the original edition.

Set in 16 pt. Plantin by Elena Picard.

Printed in the United States on permanent paper.

Library of Congress Cataloging-in-Publication Data

Harvey, John, 1938–
   Ash & bone / by John Harvey.
      p. cm.
   "A Frank Elder mystery."
   ISBN 0-7862-8565-6 (lg. print : hc : alk. paper)
   1. Retirees — Fiction. 2. Ex-police officers — Fiction.
3. Cornwall (England : County) — Fiction. 4. Teenage
girls — Crimes against — Fiction. 5. London (England)
— Fiction. 6. Policewomen — Fiction. 7. Large type
books. I. Title: Ash and bone. II. Title.
PR6058.A6989A94 2006
  823'.914—dc22   2006002852

For Graham
Good friend and sound adviser
for more than twenty years

As the Founder/CEO of NAVH, the only national health agency solely devoted to those who, although not totally blind, have an eye disease which could lead to serious visual impairment, I am pleased to recognize Thorndike Press* as one of the leading publishers in the large print field.

Founded in 1954 in San Francisco to prepare large print textbooks for partially seeing children, NAVH became the pioneer and standard setting agency in the preparation of large type.

Today, those publishers who meet our standards carry the prestigious "Seal of Approval" indicating high quality large print. We are delighted that Thorndike Press is one of the publishers whose titles meet these standards. We are also pleased to recognize the significant contribution Thorndike Press is making in this important and growing field.

Lorraine H. Marchi, L.H.D.
Founder/CEO
NAVH

* Thorndike Press encompasses the following imprints: Thorndike, Wheeler, Walker and Large Print Press.

Don't come round reminding me again
How brittle bone is.

— Billy Bragg,
Valentine's Day Is Over

By your late thirties the ground
has begun to grow hard.
It grows harder and harder until
the day that it admits you.

— Thomas McGuane,
Nobody's Angel

The first girl dead, there wasn't any choice.

Her friend — her sister, or was that all part of the pretense? — standing in the corner of the room, naked, one arm across her breasts.

Wanting to know what she'd seen but knowing. Reading it in her eyes. The thin stream of urine that ran down her leg.

"Oh, Christ!" he'd said.

Then someone, "I'll take care of it."

And when he looked again she wasn't there. Neither of them were there.

Chapter 1

Maddy Birch would never see thirty again. Nor forty either. Stepping back from the mirror, she scowled at the wrinkles that were beginning to show at the edges of her mouth and the corners of her eyes; the gray infiltrating her otherwise dark brown, almost chestnut, hair. Next birthday she would be forty-four. Forty-four and a detective sergeant attached to SO7, Serious and Organized Crime. A few hundred in the bank and a mortgaged flat in the part of Upper Holloway that North London estate agents got away with calling Highgate Borders. Not a lot to show for half a lifetime on the force. Wrinkles aside.

Slipping a scarlet band from her pocket, she pulled her hair sharply back and twisted the band into place. Taking a step away, she glanced quickly down at her boots and the front of her jeans, secured the Velcro straps of her bulletproof vest, gave the ponytail a final tug, and walked back into the main room.

To accommodate all the personnel involved, the briefing had been held in the hall of an abandoned school, Detective Superintendent George Mallory, in charge of the operation, addressing the troops from the small stage on which head teachers since Victorian times had, each autumn, admonished generations of small children to plough the fields and scatter. The fields, that would be, of Green Lanes and Finsbury Park.

Wall bars, worn and filmed with gray dust, were still attached to the walls. New flip charts, freshly marked in bright colors, stood at either side of a now blank screen. Officers from the tactical firearms unit, SO19, stood in clusters of three or four, heads down, or sat at trestle tables, mostly silent, with Birch's new colleagues from Serious Crime. She had been with her particular unit three weeks and two days.

Moving alongside Birch, Paul Draper gestured toward the watch on his wrist. Ten minutes shy of five-thirty. "Waiting. Worst bloody time."

Birch nodded.

Draper was a young detective constable who'd moved down from Manchester a month before, a wife and kid and still not twenty-five; he and Birch had reported for duty at Hendon on the same day.

"Why the hell can't we get on with it?"

Birch nodded again.

The hall was thick with the smell of sweat and aftershave and the oil that clung to recently cleaned nine-millimeter Brownings, Glock semiautomatic pistols, Heckler and Koch MP5 carbines. Though she'd taken the firearms training course at Lippetts Hill, Birch herself, like roughly half the officers present, was unarmed.

"All this for one bloke," Draper said.

This time Birch didn't even bother to nod. She could sense the fear coming off Draper's body, read it in his eyes.

From his position near the door, the superintendent cast an eye across the hall, then spoke to Maurice Repton, his detective chief inspector.

Repton smiled and checked his watch. "All right, gentlemen," he said. "And ladies. Let's nail the bastard."

Outside, the light was just beginning to clear.

Birch found herself sitting across from Draper inside the van, their knees almost touching. To her right sat an officer from

SO19, ginger mustache curling around his reddish mouth; whenever she looked away, Birch could feel his eyes following her. When the van went too fast over a speed bump and he jolted against her, his hand, for an instant, rested on her thigh. "Sorry," he said and grinned.

Birch stared straight ahead and for several minutes closed her eyes, willing the image of their target to reappear as it had on the screen. James William Grant. Born Hainault, Essex, October 20, 1952. Not so far then, Birch thought, from his fifty-second birthday. Birthdays were on her mind.

Armed robbery, money laundering, drug dealing, extortion, conspiracy to murder, more than a dozen arrests and only one conviction: Grant had been a target for years. Phone taps, surveillance, the meticulous unraveling of his financial dealings, here and abroad. The closer they got, the more likely it was that Grant would catch wind and flee to where the extradition laws rendered him untouchable.

"It's time we took this one down," Mallory had said at the end of his briefing. "Way past time."

Five years before, an associate of Grant's, ambitious enough to try and freelance some Colombian cocaine conveniently mislaid between Amsterdam and the Sussex coast, had been shot dead at the traffic lights midway along Pentonville Road, smack in the middle of the London rush hour. After a trial lasting seven weeks and costing three-quarters of a million pounds, one of Grant's lieutenants had eventually been convicted of the killing, while Grant had slipped away scot-free.

"What d'you think?" Draper asked, leaning forward. "You think he'll be there? Grant?"

Birch shrugged her head.

"He fuckin' better be," the Firearms officer said, touching the barrel of his carbine much as earlier he had touched Birch's leg. "Feather in our fuckin' cap, landing a bastard like him." He grinned. "All I hope is he don't bottle out and give it up, come walking out with his hands behind his fuckin' head."

As the van veered left off Liverpool Road, someone toward the rear of the vehicle started humming tunelessly; heads turned sharply in his direction and he ceased as abruptly as he'd begun. Sweat gathered in the palms of Birch's hands.

"There pretty soon," Draper said to nobody in particular. "Got to be."

15

Conscious that the man next to her was staring more openly, Birch turned to face him. "What?" she said. "What?"

The man looked away.

Once, after a successful operation in Lincoln, her old beat, a good result, she and an officer who'd been eyeing her all evening had ended up with a quick grope in a doorway. His hand on her breast. What in God's name had made her think about that now?

"We're getting close," the driver said over his shoulder.

One side of York Way was derelict, half-hidden behind blackened walls and wire fencing; on the other, old warehouses and small factories were in the process of being converted into loft apartments. Underground parking, twenty-four-hour doormen, fifteen-year-old prostitutes with festering sores down their legs and arms a convenient ten-minute stroll away.

From the front the building seemed little changed, a high-arched wooden door held fast with double padlock and chain, its paintwork blistered and chipped. Small windows whose cobwebbed glass was barred across. Birch knew from the briefing that the guts of the place had already been torn out and restoration was

16

well in hand. A light showed dimly behind one of the windows on the upper floor.

Either side of her, armed officers in black coveralls, the single word POLICE stenciled in white at the front of their vests, were moving silently into position.

No sweat in her palms now and her throat was dry.

"You bastard!" Laughing.

"What?"

"You know."

"No. What?"

Wary, Vicki walked over to where Grant was stretched out on the bed, cotton sheet folded down below his waist. For a man of his years, she thought, not for the first time, he was in good shape. Trim. Lithe. He worked out. And when he'd grabbed her just now, fingers tightening about her wrist, it had been like being locked into a vise.

"C'mere a minute," he said. "Come on." A smile snaking across his face. "Not gonna do anythin', am I? So soon after the last time. My age."

She knew he was lying, of course, but complied. Vicki standing there in a silver thong and a tight white T-shirt ending well above the stainless steel ring in her navel.

What else was it about but this?

When she'd first met him, a month or so before, it had been at the Motor Show, Birmingham. Vicki not wearing a whole lot more than she was now, truth be told, a couple of hundred quid a day to draw attention to the virtues of a 3.2-liter direct-injection diesel engine, climate control, and all-leather interior.

He'd practically bought the vehicle out from under her and later screwed her on the backseat at a rest stop off the A6. "Christen the upholstery," he'd said with a wink, tucking a couple of fifty-pound notes inside her dress. She'd balled them up and thrown them back in his face. He'd paid more attention to her after that.

"I've got this place in London," he'd said. "Why don't you come and stay for a bit."

"A bit of what?"

The first time he'd seen her naked it had stopped him in his tracks: he'd had more beautiful women before, but none with buttocks so round and tight and high.

"Jesus!" he'd said.

"What?"

"You've got a gorgeous arse."

She'd laughed. "Just don't think you're getting any of it, that's all."

"We'll see about that," he'd said.

Fingers resting lightly just below her hips, he'd planted a careful kiss in the small of her back. "Who was it?" he'd said, hands sliding down. "Pushed in his thumb and pulled out a plum? Little Jack Horner? Little Tommy Tucker?"

After that he'd taken her facedown on the polished wood floor, bruises on her knees and breasts that smelled of linseed oil.

"Will, don't," she said now, shaking herself free. "Not now. I have to go and pee."

"What's wrong with here?" Pointing at his chest.

"Over you, you mean?"

"Why not? Wouldn't be the first time."

"You're disgusting."

"You don't know the half of it." He reached for her but she skipped away.

"Don't be long," he said, leaning back against the pillows and watching her as she walked toward the door.

There was access from a courtyard at the rear, stairs leading past three balconies to the upper floor. The loft apartment where Grant lived was entered through double doors, a single emergency exit leading to a fire escape at the farthest end.

Draper close behind her, Birch turned a corner into the courtyard and flattened herself against the wall. Weapons angled upward, armed officers were in position at the corners of the square, others scurrying toward the first and second balconies, and she waited for the signal to proceed. When it came moments later, she sprinted for the stairs.

The walls were exposed brick, furnishings tasteful and sparse. Shifting his position, Grant poured himself another glass of wine. Dusty was still in the CD player and he clicked the remote.

"Why do you listen to that old stuff?" Vicki asked from the far end of the room.

"Greatest white soul singer ever was," Grant said.

"History," Vicki replied.

Grant grinned. "Like me you mean?"

"If you like."

One knee on the bed, she ran her fingers up through the graying hairs on his chest and, reaching up, he kissed her on the mouth.

At the head of the stairs, Birch waited, catching her breath, Draper on the landing below. The outer door to Grant's apart-

20

ment was in clear sight. Mallory appeared level with Draper and then went on past. There was armament everywhere.

"After a little glory?" the superintendent whispered in Birch's ear.

"No, sir."

He smiled, and there were mint and garlic on his breath. "Second fiddle this time, Birch. Sweeping up the odds and ends."

"Yes, sir."

"You and your pal Draper. Down a floor. Just in case."

Mallory moved on toward the door, Repton at his back, two officers wielding sledgehammers in their wake.

Volume high, the interior of the loft pulsated with sound: French horn, strings, piano, and then the voice. Unmistakable.

Vicki reached down and touched Grant's face, straddling him. Arching his back, eyes closed, Grant found her nipples with his fingertips.

Dusty swooped and soared and swooped again.

At the first crash, Grant swung Vicki onto her side and sprang clear, one hand clawing at a pair of chinos alongside the bed, the other reaching past Vicki's head.

21

The outer door splintered inward off its hinges.

Fear flooded Vicki's face and she began to scream.

The pistol was tight in Grant's grasp as he turned away.

From the landing below, Birch heard music, shouts, feet moving fast across bare boards, the slamming of doors.

"What the fuck?" Draper said.

"Move," Birch said, pushing him aside. "Now."

Positioned on the balcony opposite, one of the police marksmen had Grant in his sights for several seconds, a clear shot through plate glass as he raced down the emergency stairs, but without the order to fire the moment passed and Grant was lost to sight.

"In here," Birch said, kicking open the door and ducking low.

Draper followed, swerving left.

Birch could feel the blood jolting through her veins, her heart pumping fast against her ribs. The room they were in ran the length of the building, iron supports strategically placed floor to ceiling. Some of the floorboards had been removed prior to being replaced. Building materials were stacked against the back wall, work begun and then abandoned. Low-level light seeped through windows smeared with grease and dust.

Birch reached for the switch to her left with no result.

Voices from the stairs, urgent and loud, descending; more shouts, muffled, from the courtyard outside.

"Come on," Draper said. "Let's go."

Birch was almost through the door when she stopped, alerted by the smallest of sounds. She swung back into the room as Grant eased open the door at the far end and stepped through. Bare-chested, barefoot, pistol held down at his side.

Birch's voice wedged, immovable, in her throat.

"Police!" Draper shouted. "Put your weapon on the ground now."

She would wonder afterward if Grant had truly smiled as he raised his gun and fired.

Draper collapsed back through the doorway, clutching his neck. Instinctively, Birch turned toward him and, as she did so, Grant ran forward, jumping through a gap in the boards to the floor below. With barely a moment's hesitation she raced after him; when she braced herself, legs hanging through a gap a meter wide, the boards on either side gave way and she was down.

Grant had landed badly, twisting his ankle, and was scrabbling, crablike, across the floor, seeking the pistol that had been jarred from his grasp. A nine-millimeter Beretta, hard up against the wall. As he pushed himself up and hopped toward it, Birch launched herself at him, one hand seizing his ankle and bringing him down. Flailing, his hand struck the squared-off butt of the pistol and sent it spinning beyond reach.

"Bitch!"

He kicked out at her and she stumbled back.

"Fucking bitch!"

Grant was on his feet and moving toward her. No smiling now.

Birch heard movement behind her and then the sound of a weapon being discharged close to her ear. Once and then once again. As she watched, Grant skidded backward, then crumpled to his knees, his face all but disappearing in a welter of blood.

"Textbook," Mallory said softly. "Head and heart."

Birch's skin was cold; her body shook.

"You or him, of course. Didn't give me any choice."

Vomit caught in the back of Birch's throat. Her eyes fastened on Grant's pistol, still some meters away across the floor.

The superintendent bent low toward the body. "Ambulance, I dare say. Not that it'll do a scrap of good. He's bleeding out."

When he stood up, a second weapon, a .22 derringer, was close by Grant's turned-in leg, small enough to hide inside a fist. *Now you see it, now you don't.* No matter how many times Birch would run it through in her mind, she would never be sure.

"Trouser pocket," Mallory was saying conversationally. "Small of the back." He shrugged. "There'll be an enquiry, routine." His hand on her shoulder was light, almost no pressure at all. "You'll be a good witness, I know."

Armed officers were standing at both doors, weapons angled toward the ground.

Chapter 2

Birch stood on the cobbled stones outside, drivers slowing down to gawk through misted windows as they passed. The rain fell in thin, seamless lines, giving the road a dull sheen. She didn't smoke, never really had, but there seemed to be a cigarette in her hand.

Without her hearing him approach, Mallory was at her side.

"You okay?"

"Yes, I think so."

"Holding up, that's good, that's good."

Birch opened her fingers and watched the cigarette fall to the ground.

"You'll be coming with us for a drink. Later. A wee celebration."

"I don't know."

"It's expected." His fingers grazed her arm. "No need to stay long. Show your face. That's all."

She stared at him, not knowing what to

say. The hair on his head was iron gray, matted down by the rain.

"That's settled then." With a brief smile, he turned and walked away.

Behind them, the business of recording and cleaning up went on. Grant's girlfriend was sitting in the backseat of a police car with one of the officers, someone's coat around her shoulders, tea from a thermos in both hands. An ambulance stood waiting to take Grant's body to the mortuary once the preliminary examinations had been carried out. Paul Draper was in one of the intensive care wards at University College Hospital, fighting for his life.

A celebration, Birch thought . . .

The club was on Gray's Inn Road, the far side of King's Cross, the function room on the first floor. A shield bearing the coat of arms of St. David was on the wall above the long bar, Van Morrison and Rod Stewart rasping alternately through the speakers at either end, barely holding their own against the noise. Forty or fifty people and, for the next hour or so, free booze.

Two of the snooker tables had been covered over and were already crowded with discarded glasses, large and small. At the third table Maurice Repton stood repetitiously chalking his cue, watching as the young Asian DC he was playing potted the last red and lined up the pink. He saw Birch glance in his direction and acknowledged her with a nod.

"Buy you a drink?" The SO19 officer from the van, ginger mustache, was alongside her, smiling hopefully.

"I thought the boss had put his card behind the bar."

"So he has. Stupid, really, something to say."

Birch said nothing and hoped he'd go away.

"Graeme Loftus," he said, holding out his hand.

"Maddy Birch."

Loftus made a signal toward the bartender and pushed an empty pint glass in his direction.

"You?"

Birch shook her head.

"In the thick of it, what I hear."

"You could say that."

"Lucky bastard."

"You think so?"

Loftus lifted his fresh pint, spilling beer down the back of his hand. "Never got a look-in where we were."

"Ask Paul Draper where he'd rather've

been," Birch said. "Ask his wife."

"Paul . . . ? Oh, yes, him. Poor sod. Still hanging on, isn't he?"

"Last I heard."

"Look," Loftus said, "when we're through here, you wouldn't fancy . . ."

"No," Birch said.

"Okay, suit yourself." There was an edge to Loftus's voice as he turned and shouldered his way back into the fray.

Standing a little apart, George Mallory seemed to be warming up to make a speech, his voice, now and again, sawing through the general cacophony.

Whenever Birch closed her eyes, she saw Grant's head imploding like a bloodied rose. She drained her glass and headed for the stairs.

Repton was just exiting the Gents, still zipping up his fly.

"Not going?"

"No," she lied.

"Good. Come and have a drink with me." Taking her by the elbow, he steered her back toward the bar. "What'll it be?"

"Tonic water'll be fine."

"Gin and tonic for the lady," Repton called. "Scotch for me."

Birch knew better than to protest.

Five or so years younger than Mallory,

slightly built, Repton was wearing a gray suit with a faint stripe, a dark blue tie with silver fleurs-de-lis. His fingernails looked to have been trimmed and buffed. Dapper, was that the word? Once upon a time it probably was.

Repton downed his whiskey at a single swallow. "There," he said, "that's my bit for race relations. Letting one of our brown-skinned brethren get the better of me, eighty-seven points to thirteen." He winked. "Hubris. The Atkins diet of the soul. And you. No aftereffects from this morning, I see. Still looking like the proverbial million, give or take."

Birch had deliberately chosen a green corduroy skirt that was full and ended well below the knee, a loose cotton top the color of cold oatmeal, tights and shoes with a low heel. "I look like shit," she said.

"Young Loftus didn't seem to think so. Practically coming in his pants just standing next to you."

Color flared in Birch's cheeks.

"Sorry," Repton said. "Nothing out of line, I trust. Not going to haul me up before some board or other? Sexual fucking harassment." He winked again. "Load of bollocks, don't you think? Empirically speaking."

"I've heard worse, sir," Birch said.

"I'm pleased to hear it."

Birch sipped her drink.

"Oh, oh," Repton said, nudging her arm. "Here comes George's speech." He gave her flesh a generous squeeze. "Mentioned in despatches, I'd not be surprised."

She left as soon as she possibly could, pulling the need-the-restroom trick and grabbing her coat from the pile in the cloakroom below; a brisk stride to King's Cross and then the Northern Line to Archway. She could walk from there in ten minutes or less.

When she'd first transferred down from Lincoln, three years ago now, she'd stayed in a hostel: forever taking other women's hair out of the bath; hearing their war stories in the corridors, Saturday nights when they'd been out on the prowl; cleaning them up after they'd been sick in the sink, wiping their sorry faces and listening to their woes. Everyone's favorite auntie.

As soon as she could she'd moved out, rented a room, and looked around for something to buy, something she could afford. She'd been lucky to get the flat when she did, prices about to take a hike and families with young kids starting to colo-

31

nize what had previously been the province of single moms on welfare, economic migrants, laborers sharing three to a room, and old geezers who'd been there long enough to remember the Blitz.

Compared to what she'd had in Lincoln, a newly built condominium just a bus ride from the city center, it wasn't much. Three rooms and a bathroom on the ground floor; the kitchen no bigger than a cupboard; French windows leading out to the strip of garden she shared with the people upstairs. Whoever had lived there before had had a love affair with red paint; when she woke up in the mornings, it vibrated behind her eyes.

Gradually, when her shifts didn't leave her too tired, she brought the place into line, made it feel more her own. Two layers of undercoat in both bedroom and living room and then a quiet pale green on top. Doing the same to the kitchen would have meant taking down too many shelves, and she resorted to covering as much as she could with postcards and old photographs: those sunflowers in garish reproduction; the village outside Louth where her parents used to live.

Coming in this evening, she threw her coat down on the bed, kicked off her shoes, and wandered into the living room, flicking through the TV channels before switching the set off again. She'd missed the news.

She thought she'd make a cup of tea.

Waiting for the kettle to boil, she phoned the hospital where they'd taken Paul Draper.

"Are you a relative?"

"A colleague. I was with him when . . ."

"I'm sorry. We can only pass on information to the immediate family."

What the hell did that mean? Birch wondered. Did it mean he was still in the middle of some bloody operation? Did it mean he was dead?

She took her tea back into the living room and, without switching on the light, sat, legs curled up beneath her, on the settee she'd bought from an auction room near the Angel.

The look on Graeme Loftus's face came back to her, the scarcely veiled anger in his voice when she'd turned him down; Maurice Repton's fingers hard and quick against her arm. Was there ever a situation, she thought, when men, most men, didn't feel it their right to test the waters, chat the chat, rub up against you like dogs in heat?

She closed her eyes, and, when she did so, she saw Grant in the converted warehouse, scrambling to his feet.

"Fucking bitch!"

As he moves toward her, his hands . . . what are his hands doing? . . . the left one reaching out toward her, fingers spread, the right . . . where is the right? . . . is it curving low, low and out of sight, reaching for something perhaps . . . ?

The gun in Mallory's hand fires twice, the barest of intervals between the shots, and when she opens her eyes again, Grant is no more.

The pistol on the floor. A derringer, no bigger than the span of a man's hand: a weapon that, once upon a time, was only seen in Western movies on rainy Sunday afternoons, emerging from the sleeve of some two-bit gambler caught dealing from a crooked deck.

Now you see it, now you don't.

Birch shivered.

Her tea was cold.

Setting it down, she glanced toward the French windows and, for an instant, behind the faint reflection of her own face, something moved.

Birch froze.

Two seconds, maybe four, no more. Swiftly on her feet, she turned the key in the door, slipped back both bolts, and stepped outside. Leaves from next door's fruitless pear tree were sprinkled on the grass. Shrubs and faded flowers in the borders to each side. At the garden end a thick mesh of buddleia, interspersed with holly, stood head high and dark, enough of a breeze to turn the spear-shaped leaves.

Birch stood quite still.

Other than the sounds of the city shifting about her, nothing stirred.

Her heart slowed to a normal beat.

That's all it had been, then, only something moving in the wind.

Back inside, she locked the door, drew the curtains, and went carefully to bed.

Chapter 3

The office of the Assistant Commissioner in charge of the Specialist Crime Directorate was on the seventh floor; along with a number of other units, SO7 came within his overall command. Just about the only things above him, ran the tale, were God and all His angels. Birch hoped they were on her side.

She gave her name to the civilian clerk in the outer office and declined the invitation to take a seat. When the clerk gave her the once-over she pretended not to notice. Ten minutes she'd spent that morning, polishing the black boots she was wearing with her navy blue trouser suit, bought over a year ago at M & S and already showing some signs of wear.

A buzzer sounded on the clerk's desk.

"You can go through."

Birch knocked, took a breath, and entered. Lean, bespectacled, nicely balding,

Assistant Commissioner Harkin smiled from behind his desk. His tie knotted neatly and clipped, he was in shirtsleeves, cuffs turned back. Younger than quite a few of the officers below him, Mallory included, he was not so many years older than Birch herself.

"Detective Sergeant. Maddy. You'd rather sit or stand?"

"Stand, sir, if that's all right."

"Of course, whatever you're comfortable with. I'm sure this won't take long."

The room was airless but not unpleasant, a faint background odor of antiseptic and flowers. Anonymous paintings on the walls. A water carafe and glasses on a narrow table to one side. It reminded Birch of the lounge at Gatwick Airport, the one time she'd been bumped up to business class.

Harkin tapped papers on his desk. "You've not been in the unit long."

"No, sir."

"Settling down?"

"Yes, sir. I think so."

"Yesterday," he said. "First thing that has to be made clear, the manner in which you acquitted yourself, first rate. Absolutely first rate." He beamed as though he had been praising himself. "Everything

37

I've heard, the detective superintendent's report — well, you heard him last night, of course, extolling your virtues at great length — it all points to a good job well done. Initiative. Steady head. Guts. Above all, guts. Going up against an armed man. Commendation material, I'd not be surprised."

"Thank you, sir."

"Do you no harm when it comes to promotion. None at all. You've taken the inspector's examination, I dare say?"

"Twice, sir."

"Hmm. Well, qualities will out. Eventually. Your kind of quality. In the field." He coughed into the back of his hand. "There'll be an enquiry, of course. Fatal shooting. Officers from another force. Standard procedure."

"Yes, sir, I understand."

"And you've no concerns, I take it?"

"Concerns, sir?"

"Regarding the enquiry. Sequence of events and so on."

"Sir?"

"No doubt in your mind as to how it all played out?"

Birch could feel the sweat prickling beneath her arms. "No, sir."

Harkin nodded and glanced toward the

window as if something outside had suddenly claimed his interest. "DS Mallory's actions, appropriate, you'd say, to the situation?"

"Yes, sir."

"Good. Excellent."

After noticing a slight tic in the commissioner's left eye, Birch was finding it difficult not to stare; she looked at the floor instead.

"You, personally," Harkin said. "Incidents like these, violent death, sometimes takes a little while for them to settle in the mind."

"Yes, sir, I'm sure."

"If there's any help you feel that we can offer . . . a little personal time, maybe. A chat with someone versed in these things, someone professional . . ."

"A psychiatrist, sir?"

"That sort of thing."

"I don't think there's any need. Really. I'm fine."

"Yes, yes. I'm sure you are." Harkin rearranged papers on his desk. "If there's nothing else then . . ."

"DC Draper, sir, I was wondering if there was any news?"

"Ah." Harkin removed his glasses and pinched the bridge of his nose between forefinger and thumb. "A shame about DC Draper. Great shame."

One of the first things Paul Draper had done, he and Maddy chatting together on their first day in the squad, was to show her a photograph of his wife and kid. Alice and Ben. On holiday somewhere in the northwest. Blackpool. Morecambe. A faint suggestion of sea on the horizon. Alice in a two-piece swimsuit, not a bikini exactly, her figure not yet back to what it once had been, Ben in a little Onesie on her knee. Alice having to narrow her eyes slightly against the light, but smiling nonetheless, her skin pale, as if unused to the sun.

"You must come round," he'd said. "We'll get a takeaway, eat in. Alice'd be chuffed with the company."

Birch never had.

Now she sat awkwardly on the edge of a chair, backs of her legs going numb. Alice was slumped back on the love seat opposite, the child fretting at her breast. Cups of tea on the table, half-cold. Biscuits, some broken fragments of biscotti. There'd been photographers outside, a few; one reporter, insistent, from the local whatever-it-was, *Journal* or *Gazette*.

"Alice . . ."

At the sound of Birch's voice, tears appeared again on Alice Draper's face. How could she not cry? Birch thought. Twenty-three and a wee boy of no more than six or seven months and then this . . .

Birch forced herself to her feet. Through the partly drawn curtains she could see the flats opposite, identical to the one in which she was standing: balcony upon balcony busy with tubs of flowers, rusting bicycles, washing twisting in the late afternoon breeze. The dark already falling into place.

"It's not bad," Draper had said. "Not bad at all. Ex-council, couldn't afford it else. But okay. You wait till you see."

He looked a little like that guitarist, Birch had thought, the one who used to play with Morrissey.

Alice had said very little. Before finally being pronounced dead, her young husband had said nothing at all. Flowers from the Metropolitan Police Commissioner lay by the sink, waiting to be put in water. *I'll do it before I go,* Birch thought. Wash these cups, make a fresh pot of tea. See if I can't persuade Alice to eat something, a sandwich at least.

While she was waiting for the kettle to boil, Alice switched on the television news.

41

"Alice," Birch said, "are you sure this is a good idea?"

Colors unnaturally bright, Paul Draper's face flickered for a moment on the screen, then disappeared.

"Alice . . ."

Seated behind a bank of microphones, the assistant commissioner looked somber yet purposeful.

"From all the information available to me, I have no doubt that the operation was carefully and professionally planned and executed with a high level of competence that does credit to all the officers involved. With regard to the tragic death of a young detective constable . . ."

Regardless of Alice's wishes, Birch leaned forward and switched off the set.

Ben was wriggling in his mother's lap, whimpering against her chest.

"Alice, Alice. I think you might be holding him too tight. Do you want me to take him for a minute? Here. That's it. Just while you drink your tea."

The baby's pale eyes looked at her in wonder when she lifted him toward her and Birch felt something kick, hard, against the hollow of her insides. When Alice picked up the cup it slipped between her fingers, spilling tea across the table and the floor.

"Never mind," Birch said. "I'll clean it up."

Alice looked back at her blankly. "Paul," she said. "Paul, Paul."

"Poor cow." Vanessa Taylor broke off a piece of chapati and used it to wipe up what remained of the chicken masala. "What kind of life's she got now?"

A good year they'd been doing this, Taylor and Birch, meeting up every week or so, when shifts allowed, a drink or two first and then some curry. A good talk. Bit of a bitching session, sometimes. Rules and regs. Pay. All that dyke or slut innuendo that was supposed to have been knocked on the head once and for all.

At twenty-nine, Taylor was not only younger than Birch but shorter and broader too, a figure on her and she didn't care who knew it. Before joining the force, she'd tried secretarial work, then nursing, but not for long. Glorified bloody chambermaids, that's all you were, she said. More blood and piss than the pubs in Kentish Town, which was where she was currently stationed. Three years as a uniformed constable and she still wasn't certain she'd stick with it.

Birch had met her on a training course

soon after moving down to London: *Integrating Police Work with the Ethnic Community.* Taylor sizing up the Asian community worker who was leading the afternoon session. "Wouldn't mind integrating with that," she'd winked. "Given half the chance." It turned out Taylor lived no more than a few streets away from Birch, Upper Holloway.

This evening, eyeing one of the waiters whenever he passed their table, Taylor reminded Birch of that first occasion and asked her had she ever, you know, been with anyone Indian, Pakistani?

Birch said she didn't think she had.

"I had this lad once . . . ," Taylor said, lowering her voice as she leaned forward. "Student nurse at the hospital. Great big eyes."

"Just the eyes?"

"Stop." Laughing. "Lovely-looking he was, beautiful skin."

"You'll be telling me next you had him in the storeroom cupboard amongst the bandages and bedpans."

"Better than that. Upstairs, on one of the empty beds. Ward was temporarily closed down because of the cuts." Her face was flushed, but it was probably due to the curry.

"What happened?" Birch said.

"What d'you mean what happened?" Taylor laughed again, louder than before. "Too long ago to remember? Draw you a diagram if you like."

"Not that, you idiot. I mean what happened to the bloke?"

"Oh, him. I dunno. Next week he'd moved on to Obstetrics. Good, though. Top ten, I'd say." She grinned. "How about you? Top ten shags of all time."

Birch looked warily around, prepared to be embarrassed. "Don't joke. I'd be scraping the barrel to come up with five or six."

"You're kidding."

"You should try getting married before you're twenty-one. Trims your sails a bit, I'm telling you."

Taylor crossed her knife and fork across her plate. "You never were! Married that young?"

"Wasn't I?"

"How come you never said?"

"I don't know. Don't much like talking about it, I suppose."

"Well, who was he? At least tell us that. What was his name?"

"Terry, his name was Terry. Okay? Satisfied? He was this bloke, older, a bit older,

45

and I was just a kid, still living at home, and I thought he was God's gift. Now let's just leave it, right?"

"Right." Taylor shrugged and ordered two more bottles of Kingfisher. No point in pushing it further, she could see that. Not unless she fancied trolling along to the karaoke session in the pub later on her own.

"I keep thinking," Birch said a few minutes later, "that poor little lad, Paul Draper's boy, growing up without a dad."

"She'll find someone else, won't she? If she's any gumption. Kid'll not remember."

Birch shook her head. "You really think it's that simple?"

"Yes. If you want it to be."

"Sometimes I wonder," Birch said, "if you know you're even born."

"Fuck off," Taylor said, laughing. "And pass us over that aubergine thingy if you're done with it."

Shortly after midnight, the two women emerged from the raucous glitter of a late night extension and set off, arm in arm, along the Holloway Road. Taylor had talked Birch into a duet version of "Dancing Queen," which had been fine until Birch lost it two-thirds of the way through and faltered to a halt.

"What got into you?" Taylor asked. "We were going great."

"I don't know. Suddenly realized what I was doing, I suppose. Up there in front of everyone. Looking a right prat."

"Come on," Taylor said, "I'll walk you to the end of your street."

"You're sure? No need."

"No, do me good. Walk off some of that beer. Nothing worse'n waking up of a morning, feeling bloated." She laughed. "Less it's not waking up at all."

"Not funny, Nessa."

"Sorry." Taylor gave her arm a squeeze. "Really got to you, hasn't it? What happened."

"Last night," Birch said, "when I got home, getting ready for bed, I saw these specks of mascara here, alongside my eye. Except it wasn't mascara, it was blood."

Taylor didn't say anything else until they reached the corner of Birch's road. "Take care," she said, giving Birch's arm a squeeze. "Get some sleep, eh? Try not to think about it too much. And give me a call tomorrow."

"Okay," Birch said, "if I can. You take care, too."

Birch watched for a moment as Taylor quickened her pace, and then turned toward home. The click of her low heels on the pavement as she walked. Here and there, lights faint behind drawn curtains or lowered blinds. Of course what had happened had got her rattled. Grant, Draper. It stood to reason. Only now that wasn't all. Her key stiffened for a moment in the lock, then turned. She knew she should never have said anything to Taylor about being married, about Terry, fetching all that up from where it lay buried, starting herself thinking about him after all this time. Terry. All abs and promises. She allowed herself a rueful smile. North Wales, the last she'd heard from him. Married again and good luck to the pair of them.

Birch poured the last of the orange juice into a glass and carried it into the living room. No way that would have been him, skulking midweek around a North London boozer, staring at her from the back of the crowd. His face stopping her in her tracks, mid-chorus. Everyone clapping, laughing. "Dancing Queen." Just someone who looked a bit like him, that was all.

The curtains were drawn fast across the French windows to the garden, shutting out the night. The glass was cold in her hand. She sat there until her legs had begun to numb, willing her eyes to close, her mind to still.

Chapter 4

At first, Elder had wondered if he would ever get used to the weather in this part of Cornwall. Mostly, like a delinquent five-year-old, it was unable to make up its mind five minutes at a time. Sunshine followed by fierce lashings of near-horizontal rain and then sunshine again, and through it all, sun and rain, the inevitable wind. "Keeps you on your toes," the locals said when he complained. When they said anything at all.

Then, one late, dark afternoon toward the end of October, he realized there'd been three days solid in which the fog had rolled in off the Atlantic, met and mingled with the mist veiling down off the hills, and never lifted, pressing down an immovable gray, and through it the rain had continued to fall, harsh and unyielding, and he had barely noticed.

Sitting in the deep corner of the kitchen

illuminated by a single bulb, he had read steadily — Priestley currently, a threadbare edition of *The Good Companions* — rising occasionally to make tea or switch on the radio for the sound of a voice. Sometimes, setting Priestley aside, he closed his eyes and listened to one of the few pieces of music he possessed, a cassette of string quartets he had picked up at the local village swap meet. Local meant a good two miles across fields by hedge and stile.

He had moved twice since early summer, when the owner of the place he'd rented for close to two years had decided to put it up for sale. First, and briefly, he took a third-floor flat in a tall Victorian house in Penzance, with views across the harbor toward St. Michael's Mount. It was not a success. Small, scarcely metropolitan, Penzance was just enough of a town to remind him of what he'd willingly left behind: Lincoln, Leeds, Mansfield, Nottingham. After that, he'd gone back across the peninsula to where he was now, a former farm laborer's cottage between moor and sea.

The downstairs was warmed by an oil-fired stove, which heated the water when it had a mind, and on which Elder gradually retaught himself to cook. Nothing spectacular: stews, casseroles, pasta, fish. What was the point of living so close to the sea if you didn't eat fish? Mackerel, red mullet, megrim, sea bass, lemon sole, occasionally shark. His favorite, mackerel, was, providentially, the cheapest by far.

The walls of the room in which Elder slept were bare stone save for one section on which plaster had been unevenly slapped. A second, smaller room held clothes he now rarely wore, boxes and bags, dribs and drabs of a life he scarcely chose to recognize. At some stage a bathroom had been added to the rear of the building: the toilet seat rocked precariously when touched, the fittings bought cheaply second- or thirdhand; the bath itself, below its wide old-fashioned taps, was ringed with generations of overlapping reddish stains.

A short distance along a narrow lane was the farm to which the cottage had formerly belonged, now dilapidated and abandoned. Sacking at the windows, rough hasps and padlocks at the doors. Some story Elder had part overheard, a family feud that had turned son against father, father against son. Other farmers pastured their cattle on the fields, paying dues. Stray walkers aside,

51

Elder scarcely saw a soul from one week's end to the next.

It suited him to a tee.

Three years now since his marriage to Joanne had imploded and he had retired from the Nottinghamshire Force, off with his tail between his legs, almost as far west as it was possible to go. More than a year since his daughter Katherine had been abducted by Adam Keach. Abducted, raped, and almost killed. Katherine, sixteen.

What happened to her, Frank, it's your fault. You nearly killed her. You. Not him.

Joanne's words.

Because you had to get involved, you couldn't let things be. You always knew better than anybody else, that's why.

Of course, he had dreams.

But none so bad as Katherine's.

You'll get over this, Frank. You'll come to terms, find a way. But Katherine, she never will.

In the spring, before the trial, she had come to visit him, Katherine. They had talked, walked, sat drinking wine. In the night, he had been woken by her screams.

"These dreams," she'd said, "they will go, won't they? I mean, with time."

"Yes," Elder had replied. "Yes, I'm sure they will."

Wanting to protect her, he'd lied.

Now she refused to speak to him, broke the connection at the sound of his voice. Changed the number of her cell phone. Didn't, wouldn't write.

Your fault, Frank . . .

Well, of course, in a way it was true.

Adam Keach had killed another girl, a young woman, Emma Harrison, only weeks before taking Katherine. Elder had been back working for the Major Crime Unit at the time, a civilian consultant attached to the investigation. Found fit to stand trial and hoping for a lighter sentence, Keach had pleaded guilty and Elder had breathed a sigh of relief. It saved Katherine from going onto the stand and giving evidence, being cross-examined.

In the matter of abduction and serious sexual assault, the judge handed down sixteen years. For the murder of Emma Harrison, life.

"Life doesn't mean life though, does it?" Katherine had said. "Not anymore."

It was just about the last conversation they had had.

The Notts Force had contacted him since about another case in which they thought Elder's experience and expertise might be of use.

"After Keach," Elder had said, "I'd've thought you'd've had all the help out of me you'd want."

"Don't come down so hard on yourself, Frank," the senior officer had replied. "You're the one as caught him. Brought him in. Saved your lass's life."

Elder had been polite but firm. Retirement suited him fine.

"You'll go crazy down there, Frank. End up topping yourself, like as not."

Elder had thanked him for the thought and hung up the phone.

The day had begun with a faint mist across the hills and then a soft rain that scarcely seemed to dampen the ground. By noon it was bright and clear, with only a scattering of off-white clouds strung out across the sky to the west. Elder stuffed his book into one pocket of his waterproof coat, an apple and a wedge of cheese into the other, and set out toward the coast path at River Cove, just short of Towednack Head. For thirty minutes or so he sat on a boulder opposite Seal Island, eating his bit of lunch and alternately reading or gazing out at the water tumbling up, then falling back. Usually there were seals stretched out on the rocks or swimming near the shore, rounded heads fast disappearing as they dived for fish, but not today.

Walking back he noticed the bracken facing up the moor had turned an almost uniform rusted brown, patched through here and there with yellow-flowering gorse. Late autumn and the nights drawing ever closer in.

As he entered the house, he had only time to pull off his coat and unlace his boots before the phone startled him.

"Hello?"

"Frank?"

"Yes."

"It's Joanne."

He knew; you didn't live with someone for twenty years without recognizing each turn and intonation of her voice, even the breath drawn before speaking, the weight of a pause.

"What's wrong?" Elder said.

"Does it have to be something wrong?"

"Probably."

The breath there, head turning aside. A glass of wine? A cigarette?

"It's Katherine," Joanne said.

Of course it was. The adrenaline had started to pulse in his veins. "What about her?" he said.

"It's difficult."

"Just tell me."

Another pause. Longer.

"I'm worried. Worried about her. The way she's been behaving lately."

"Behaving? How? What do you mean?"

"Oh, staying out late, getting drunk. Not coming home till three or four in the morning. Not coming home at all."

"You've spoken to her?"

"Frank, she's seventeen . . ."

"I know how old she is."

"I say anything, she tells me to mind my own business."

"And Martyn?"

"Martyn's got nothing to do with this."

Elder sighed. "She won't talk to me, you know that."

"She's your daughter, Frank."

As if he'd forgotten.

"When she stays out," Elder said, "d'you know where?"

"She's seeing someone, I know that. I think sometimes she stays there."

"You think?"

"Frank, I just don't know."

He sighed again. "All right, I'll come up. Tomorrow. The day after. I'll get the train."

"Thank you, Frank."

She's your daughter.

He set down the receiver, walked to the window, and stared out. Mist plaiting itself between blackened filaments of hedge. The coming dark. Images of what Adam Keach had done to Katherine kept forcing themselves under the edges of his mind and he struggled to will them away.

When she had been seven, possibly eight, one of the last times she let him walk her all the way to school, right up to the gates — London it would have been, Shepherd's Bush, green school cardigan, gray pleated skirt, green tights, black shoes he'd shined the night before, book bag in her hand — he'd ducked his head toward her and she'd thrown up an arm — "Don't kiss me now!" — and run toward her friends. Shutting him out.

Not coming home till three or four in the morning. Not coming home at all.

Seventeen.

Stupid, he felt, standing there. Stupid, helpless, and old.

The bottle of Jameson was in the drawer.

It wouldn't help, he knew that, but what else was he supposed to do?

Chapter 5

The official enquiry into the shootings of James William Grant and Paul Draper was opened within two weeks of the incidents taking place. The Police Complaints Authority, which routinely managed such matters, asked Detective Superintendent Trevor Ashley from the Hertfordshire Force to conduct the investigation, and, as his number two, Ashley chose a newly promoted chief inspector, Linda Mills. Chalk and cheese. Ashley wore muted tweed jackets with leather patches on the arms and affected a voice that was slower and more up-country than his home, less than forty minutes' drive north from London, warranted. Mills had the lean and driven look of someone who began the day with a bracing cold shower and an energetic fifteen or twenty laps in the pool.

Assisted by three other officers and two civilian clerks, Ashley and Mills were allocated a Portakabin in the car park as their base, together with a pair of interview rooms in the main building. One of the first officers called in for questioning was Birch.

Taking his time, the superintendent took her through her written deposition, step by step, stage by stage, Mills watching her closely, not aggressively, occasionally making a neatly written note. Birch wearing the same blue suit: weddings, interviews, and funerals.

"Since making this statement," Ashley said. "When was it? The morning after the incident? You've had no further thoughts? There's nothing you'd like to add?"

"No, sir. I don't think so."

"Sometimes, you know, on reflection . . ."

"Thank you, sir, but no."

"Good, good." With a glance toward his number two, Ashley settled back in his chair.

Linda Mills took her time. "DC Draper and yourself, if I understand rightly, you were among the first officers to arrive at the entrance to Grant's flat?"

"Yes, ma'am."

"And this was by design?"

"I'm sorry, I . . ."

"Part of the plan outlined at the briefing

59

that you and DC Draper . . ."

"No. Not exactly."

"It was what, then? Accident? Chance?"

"Yes, ma'am."

"Which?"

Birch hesitated. "Chance, I suppose."

The chief inspector glanced down at the papers in front of her. "Not entirely."

"I'm sorry, I don't quite . . ."

"According to your statement, it was Superintendent Mallory who ordered you to move back down the stairs."

"Yes. Yes, that's correct."

Mills looked at her squarely. "Why, in your estimation, did he do that?"

Birch took her time; her head was starting to buzz. "I think he was concerned for our safety."

"And that was the only reason?"

"I believe he wanted us to cover any possible escape."

"Even though you were still unarmed?"

"There were armed officers on the stairs. Everywhere."

"With orders to fire if necessary?"

"I assume so, yes."

"And yet, in the event, it was Superintendent Mallory who did the actual firing."

Birch hesitated slightly, without knowing why. "Yes, ma'am."

"And the reason Superintendent Mallory discharged his weapon when he did?"

"As I've said in my report . . ."

"The reason was?"

"In my report, it's . . ."

"The reason, Sergeant?"

"My colleague had already been shot. Grant had shot him."

"And the superintendent knew this?"

"I assume so, yes."

Mills sighed and sat back. Though it wasn't especially hot in the room, a slick line of sweat was making its way slowly down Birch's back. Her hands were sticking to the sides of the chair. Superintendent Ashley slid one of the papers around at an angle. "According to this diagram, the weapon Grant had used to shoot DC Draper was out of his reach here when Superintendent Mallory entered the room."

"Yes. That's right. But he had another weapon."

"Grant was carrying a second gun?"

"Yes."

"That would be the derringer .22?"

"Yes, sir."

"And where was he carrying this backup gun?"

Birch faltered. "I don't know. I mean, I'm not sure."

"But you did see it? The second gun?"

Christ! Why was this so difficult? "Not at first, no."

"How do you explain that?"

"He was carrying it out of sight. Concealed."

"But I thought he had just jumped out of bed naked," Mills said, taking over. "Next to naked."

"He was wearing trousers."

"Trousers?"

"Yes."

"Just trousers?"

"Yes."

"So where was the gun?"

Birch could feel the sweat now beneath her arms. "I don't know. In the waistband, possibly. At the back. In one of the pockets. I'm sorry, I just don't know."

Mills and Ashley exchanged a look.

"So," Ashley said, "just to be clear, you did see Grant reaching for the second gun?"

"I saw him reaching down, yes."

"Reaching down?"

"Yes."

"Reaching for the derringer?"

"I assume so, yes."

"And you felt under threat?"

"Of course."

"From Grant?"

"Yes."

"Because you saw the weapon in his hand?"

"I'd just seen him shoot DC Draper. I thought he would kill me if he could."

"So Superintendent Mallory's action was entirely justified? In your eyes?"

"Yes."

"Even though," Mills said, her voice sharper than before, "you never saw the weapon in Grant's hand?"

"I saw it on the floor, beside him when he fell."

"But not actually in his hand?"

Birch hesitated, longer this time. "No, ma'am, not actually in his hand."

Linda Mills closed her eyes. Trevor Ashley smiled.

"Good," Ashley said. "That's all, I think, for now. Thank you, Sergeant, for your time."

Birch felt slightly dizzy as she stood.

"I should try and avoid discussing this with your colleagues," Mills said. "In all probability we will want to talk to you again."

Back outside, Birch could smell the perspiration rising off her in waves.

Maurice Repton intercepted her in the

corridor downstairs, hair carefully combed, giving off a faint smell of cologne.

"How did it go in there, anyway?" Repton asked. "The interview. Rubber truncheons and thumbscrews?"

Birch managed a smile. "No, sir. Nothing like that."

"Nothing tricky?"

"No, sir, not really."

"No awkward questions? About the shooting?"

Birch shook her head.

"Give you a tough time, did she?"

"Sir?"

"The Mills woman. Always come down hardest on their own kind."

"Not too bad, sir."

"She'll have Ashley's job while he still thinks pension is just a seven-letter word on *Countdown*, poor sod. Assistant chief constable in ten years. Equal opportunities advertisement, pictures in the press." He took a small step back, sardonic grin in place. "Shame she's not blessed with a touch of the tar brush, be ACC already."

When Birch reached the main door, she stood fully five minutes, breathing in what air she could.

Chapter 6

The onset of winter always affected Maddy Birch badly, the putting back of the clocks rocking her body in the same hormonal way as her monthly periods, sending her in search of Nurofen and curling her up beneath the quilt with a hot water bottle held fast against her stomach.

As she hurried home on newly dark nights like tonight, the wind funneling along the warren of streets between Holloway Road and Hornsey Rise, even the scarf tucked down inside her coat didn't keep out the chill. If she could have afforded to keep the heat on in her flat throughout the day, she would. Anything to avoid opening the door into the cold ground-floor rooms that, now November was nigh, smelled forever damp.

The first thing she usually did, even before taking off her coat, was set a match to the gas fire in the hearth; then she would fill the kettle and press down the switch, a mug of tea to warm her hands. If it were really cold, hot buttered toast. What she'd be like come February didn't bear thinking about.

"It can't be as bad down here as where you come from," Taylor had said once when Birch had complained. "Bloody Lincolnshire! Wind blows straight across from Siberia up there. Hear the wolves howling in the bloody night."

On this particular night, however, there were things on Birch's mind other than the wind: DCI Repton waiting to ask her about her session with the enquiry team, his concern all but shielded behind his bigotry, real or assumed; the superintendent's "So, just to be clear, you did see Grant reaching for the second gun?" — casual enough to be almost an afterthought. "In all probability we will want to talk to you again."

Birch pushed open the narrow gate and lifted her keys from her bag; someone had used her small square of front garden as a dumping ground for a half-empty tray of chips and mushy peas.

Stepping into her flat, in the instant between pushing back the door and switching on the light, she froze, a wave of cold like electricity along the backs of her legs and arms. For that moment, her heart seemed to stop.

The doors to the living room and bathroom, both leading off the hall, stood wide open, and at that time of the year she always kept them closed.

"Hello?"

Her voice sounded strange, unnaturally thin.

There was time to step back outside, relock the door. But what then?

Instead she went quickly forward into the living room, flicking on the light.

Nothing stirred, nothing moved.

Bedroom, bathroom, kitchen the same.

Birch's breathing steadied; the adrenaline ceased to flow through her veins. What little she possessed of value was still in the flat. A glass sat on the draining board, one she seldom if ever used. The bolt across the top of the French windows was unfastened, and when she put pressure on the curved handle, it sprang open, unlocked. There were slight circular marks on the outside she couldn't remember seeing there before.

The skin prickled along her arms.

After locking the windows correctly, she went through each room carefully again.

Her watch said ten past eight and she was due to meet Taylor at nine. Birch was at the point of phoning to cancel, had the telephone in her hand, when she changed her mind.

Their favorite curry house, on Kentish Town Road, had undergone a makeover, stripping out the flock wallpaper and remarketing itself as hyper-cool, so that it now resembled an expensive canteen with discreet lighting and Egyptian cotton napkins in pale lavender. This place, in the hinterland between Tufnell Park and Archway, was more their kind of thing, nothing fancy, fine until after pub closing time, when the atmosphere would become edgily raucous and papadoms were liable to be sent skimming like Frisbees through the gaseous air.

"Nothing was stolen, right?" Taylor said. "Missing?"

Birch shook her head.

"But things had been moved around, you said? Disturbed?"

"One or two. I think so. I'm not sure."

"And the doors out into the garden, you couldn't have left them unlocked?"

"No."

"You're positive?"

"Yes. No. I mean, I'm always careful about things like that. But, no, I can't swear to it, no."

Taylor angled her head to one side. "You're not getting weird on me, are you? Freaking out?"

"It's all very well for you," Birch said. "Taking the piss."

"I'm not," Taylor said. "Here, have a piece of my chicken tikka. Cheer yourself up."

"It's not funny." Birch surprised herself with the force of her voice. "It's not some bloody joke."

"Then report it," Taylor said.

"There's no point."

"Why not?"

"Because whoever I reported it to, their reaction would be just like yours."

"I'm sorry."

"It's okay." Forcing a smile, Birch took some of Taylor's chicken tikka. "It's just with this other business as well, the enquiry. They had me in this afternoon."

"How was it?"

"Like I was in the dock for something I didn't know I'd done."

"Bastards."

"Doing their job, I suppose."

"That's it now, though?"

Birch shook her head. "They'll more than likely want to talk to me again."

They were drinking coffee — almost certainly instant, but it did come with After Eights — when Birch said, "That other night, the karaoke, remember? When it all went wrong. There was something I didn't tell you."

Taylor stopped stirring her two sugars. "Go on."

"I thought I saw someone I knew."

"In the pub?"

"Yes. Standing near the back, watching."

"Who?"

"My ex-husband, Terry."

"And was it?"

"No, I don't think so. Someone who looked like him, that's all. Far as I know Terry's in North Wales and good riddance."

Taylor smiled. "You've not forgiven him then?"

"What for?"

"I don't know, do I? Last time I asked about him, you practically jumped down my throat."

"I'm sorry."

Taylor shrugged. "Your business, not mine."

"It's not that, it's just . . . you know . . ."

70

"Not still nursing a crush for him, are you?"

"Christ, no!"

"Then what's the big mystery?"

"There's no mystery."

"You just don't want to confide in your best friend, that's all."

Birch laughed. "You don't give up, do you?"

"Not usually, no."

"All right, but I'm going to need a drink."

"Here, or the pub?"

"The pub."

Taylor turned around and signaled to the young waiter who was leaning against the wall, texting someone on his cell phone, to bring them the bill.

It was quite dark outside, a few people walking by, cars, the occasional bus. The pub was quiet, mostly regulars, one pool table, a television above the bar. They took their drinks to a quiet corner near the window. When Birch started telling her story, she thought how mundane it sounded, how everyday.

Terry had been working just up the street from where she'd been living with her parents when she first met him, a builder, plasterer to be more exact, most of the houses in that part of Stevenage being renovated, made good. Birch had taken a shine right off. Cheeky bugger, Terry, but not as bad as some of them, not crude. Nice body without his shirt, she'd noticed that. Nice hands, considering the work he did, not too rough.

After a week of hints and innuendo, he'd come out with it, asked her to meet him for a drink Friday night and she'd thought yes, why not? She'd been working in London then, Capital Radio, in reception, taking the train in every day to King's Cross, then the Piccadilly Line to Leicester Square. Exciting at first, all that buzz and noise.

They'd gone on holiday together, that first summer, Majorca, and he'd proposed, not down on one knee but as good as, rolling around on the sand outside their hotel. She'd thought it was the drink talking, that he'd try to pass it off the next day as some kind of a joke, but that wasn't the way it was at all. Three months later there they were outside the registry office, Birch in a nice little suit from Next, new shoes that were killing her, the look on her mum's face sour enough to turn milk. Whatever expectations she'd been nurturing about a future son-in-law, it was clear Terry didn't live up to them.

What she did say was: "You watch out, my girl, he'll have you pregnant this side of Christmas and where's your independence then? Where's your bloody life?"

It hadn't worked out like that, but not for lack of trying.

Birch had thought the problem might lie with Terry, but it turned out it was with her. Terry had one kid already, a boy, four years old, living in Milton Keynes with his mother, a part-time hairstylist called Bethan. Birch found out quite by chance.

It turned out that when she'd thought Terry was away working on some housing project in Northampton, he was in a two-bedroom flat in Milton Keynes with Bethan and the boy, playing happy families.

"None of your fucking business, is it?" Terry said when she confronted him.

Birch told him he had to choose, her or Bethan, and he began packing his bag.

"What the hell did you marry me for?" Birch asked.

"Fuck knows!"

When she said she wanted a divorce, he said fine.

When she got home from work that evening, he'd gone. She hadn't been married much more than two years and, in retrospect, she was amazed it had held together that long.

"Was that when you joined the police?" Taylor asked, as Birch reached for her glass.

Birch nodded. "I was bored, wanted to get away. The look on my mum's face whenever I came in, a mixture of pity and I-told-you-so." She laughed. "We'd been to Lincoln a few times, when we were up in Skegness on holiday, driven over to look at the cathedral, mooch around. I thought it was a nice enough place." She laughed again. "At least it wasn't Stevenage."

"What made you leave Lincoln and come down here, to the Met?"

"Bored again, I suppose."

"And now this Grant business, the enquiry. It's getting you all stressed out. No wonder you're seeing things."

"Thank you, doctor."

"I used to be a nurse, you know."

"I know."

"You know what you ought to do," Taylor said. "The perfect solution."

"Go back to Lincolnshire?"

"Nothing that extreme. Take up yoga instead."

"Me? Yoga? You're joking."

"I don't see why."

"Can you see me sitting cross-legged in some draughty room like a Buddha in tights?"

"It's not like that. That's meditation if it's anything. Yoga's brilliant. Helps you relax. And it's really good exercise." She grinned. "Look at me."

"I don't know."

"Go on. There's a new class just started. Where I go, that community center by Crouch Hill. Introduction to Yoga. Give it a try."

"I'll see. No promises, mind."

"Okay. Now drink up and I'll walk you home. Make sure there's no bogeymen under the bed."

The first evening Birch went she almost packed it in during the warm-up. All these women — they were all women — taking turns standing with their back to the wall with one leg outstretched and raised as high as possible, their partner holding it by the ankle. One or two actually got their legs high enough to rest their ankles on their partners' shoulders, while it was all Birch could do to manage forty-five degrees for seconds at a time.

It didn't seem to get any easier. Reaching the required position was difficult enough — Downward Dog or Child's Pose — but holding it was even harder. Birch was acutely conscious of her muscles stretching, legs and arms quivering, the instructor bending over her from time to time and moving her gently but firmly into position. "That's it, Maddy. Wider, wider. Wider still."

When it was over she limped home and into a hot bath and vowed never to return. But she did. The next Wednesday and the next and the Wednesday after that. By then it had even stopped hurting.

Chapter 7

Miracle of miracles, his connection pulled into Nottingham station no more than twenty minutes late. The young taxi driver chatted amiably as he drove, apologizing for the detour necessitated by the tram tracks along Canal Street and up Maid Marian Way. "Testing 'em, know what I mean? Putting 'em down, pulling 'em up, putting 'em down. Trams they got goin' round, five mile an hour you're lucky. First ones 'posed to be startin' next year. Same they said last year, i'n it?"

The house was in the Park, a large and rambling private estate near the castle. Victorian mansions originally built for those who had profited from mining and manufacturing, the sweat and labor of others. Now it was barristers and retired CEOs, new heroes of IT and dot-com.

Martyn Miles had made his money from women's fashion and a chain of hair and beauty salons, in one of which Elder's wife, Joanne, had been working when her affair with Miles began.

Miles had bought a tract of land near the northern edge of the estate, carved out of some burgher's tennis courts and grounds, and commissioned an architect friend to design something modern yet self-effacing, a curve of concrete frontage borrowed from Frank Lloyd Wright and the New York Guggenheim. The emphasis inside was on space and light, everything arranged around a living room of double height, separated from the stone patio and garden by a wall of glass.

When Joanne's marriage to Elder had broken down, Miles had moved her in. Since then, things between them had been rocky: the last Elder had heard, Miles, after moving out and magnanimously leaving Joanne with the keys, had thought better of it and moved back in. But since then things might have changed again.

Joanne's Freelander was parked at the curb outside. No sign of whatever Miles might currently be driving, but there he was, stretched out on the sofa, legs crossed at the ankles, pale blue linen shirt complementing the blue-gray of the room.

"Hello, Frank." He swung his legs

around slowly and smiled. Something colorless with tonic sat within reach on the floor. "Just holding down the fort till you arrived."

Elder said nothing. Brittle, anonymous jazz played faintly through unseen speakers.

Joanne stood close by the glass, smoking a cigarette.

Opening the front door to him, she had turned her head from the kiss Elder had maladroitly aimed at her cheek.

"Can I get you anything, Frank?" she said.

He shook his head.

She was wearing a silver-gray metallic dress that shivered when she moved. Makeup, even expertly applied, hadn't been able to disguise the dark skin below her eyes.

"It's a good thing you came, Frank," Miles said. "A good thing. Get this sorted before it goes too far."

How far was that? Elder wondered.

"These past weeks," Miles said, "she's been out of control. Running wild."

"Don't exaggerate," Joanne said.

"You wouldn't know, Frank," Miles continued, ignoring her. "No way you could, not living where you do. But she's been doing just as she likes, out all hours. Seventeen, I know, Frank, a young woman, but even so. Rolled up here drunk more than a few times, smelling like I-don't-know-what, some poor sod of a taxi driver outside waiting to get paid. I've tried talking to her, but she won't listen. And, besides, you might not think it's my place."

"All that happens," Joanne said, "you end up losing your temper."

"Sometimes she's enough to make a saint lose his temper."

"You would know."

"Okay, okay." Miles raised both hands in resignation. "I'll off out and get a drink, let you two talk amongst yourselves. Good to see you, Frank."

Elder nodded.

Whistling softly, Martyn Miles slipped his feet into a pair of soft leather shoes, pulled on his leather coat, expensive and black, and left the room.

Neither of them spoke until they heard the front door close.

"Sit down, Frank. Are you sure you won't have a drink? I'm having one."

"Okay, a small Scotch'll be fine."

"I'll see what there is."

"Anything."

She poured herself a large white wine,

Elder a more than decent measure of good malt.

"She's not here, then?" Elder said. "Katherine?"

"She came in an hour ago, changed her clothes, and went out again."

"She knew I was going to be here?"

"I told her."

"And you don't know where she went?"

Joanne shook her head.

Elder sipped his Scotch. "You said she was seeing someone."

"Rob Summers."

"Someone she knew from school, or . . . ?"

"He's not a boy, Frank. In his twenties, maybe more."

"You've met him, then?"

"Not met exactly."

"And the two of them, it's serious?"

"If it was, it wouldn't be so bad. It's more casual than that, as far as I can tell. His whim, I dare say. When she's not with him, she's hanging round with all manner of riffraff. Punks and Goths and God knows what. The kind you see lolling around the Old Market Square."

"Jesus," Elder said.

"I am worried about her, Frank. You know, drugs and everything."

"She's got a level head on her."

"You think so?"

Elder got up and paced from wall to wall. "That psychiatrist she was seeing . . ."

"Psychotherapist."

"You haven't talked to her, I suppose?"

"Katherine stopped going to her a good few months ago."

Elder stopped close to where she was sitting on the sofa. "It's a mess, isn't it? A fucking mess."

Reaching up, she took hold of his hand and, for a moment, until he pulled it away, rested her head against his arm.

Elder spent the night in one of the small hotels on Mansfield Road. In the morning he took one look at the breakfast and opted instead for a brisk walk into the city center and a cup of coffee sitting hunched up against the window in Caffè Nero, scanning the front page of the paper someone had left behind.

The Old Market Square had been spruced up since Elder had seen it last. The grassed areas toward the Beastmarket end had been landscaped and some of the old benches had been replaced. Katherine was sitting at the northern edge of the Square, and not alone. Either side of her, two men of indeterminate age, bearded, shaggy-haired, and scruffily dressed, sat with cans of cheap lager in their hands. It was not yet ten in the morning.

A girl in a beaded halter top and skin-tight jeans, her face festooned with studs and rings, sat cross-legged on the ground.

A tall man with a blond ponytail, wearing jeans and a stained Stone Roses sweatshirt, stood with one foot balanced on the end of the bench, watching Elder as he approached.

Elder stopped a short distance away.

"Kate . . ."

Not looking up, Katherine continued, carefully, to roll a cigarette.

"Katherine, we have to talk."

"Sod off," one of the seated men said.

Katherine brought the roll-up to her mouth and licked along the edge; pulling clear a few stray strands of tobacco, she took a disposable lighter from her pocket and lit the cigarette, drawing the smoke down into her lungs. One more drag and she passed it to the man on her left.

"Katherine," Elder said again, his voice raised and impatient.

"Leave me alone."

"I can't."

Elder moved closer and the ponytailed

man swung his foot down from the bench and stood in his way.

"He's police," one of the men on the bench said. "Fuckin' law."

"Not anymore," Katherine said.

"Who is he then?"

"My father. He thinks he's my father."

"Katherine . . ."

"She doesn't want to talk to you," the ponytailed man said. "Can't you see?"

"Get out of the way," Elder said.

The man grinned and stood his ground. "Make me."

Fists clenched tight at his sides, Elder wanted to punch the sneering face as hard as he could. Instead, with one last glance at Katherine, he walked away to the sound of their jeers.

What the fuck, Elder thought, as he crossed South Parade and walked on to Wheeler Gate, what the fuck am I doing here? What's the point of all this? A waste of fucking time. He was a stone's throw from the railway station before he stopped and turned around.

For the next two hours, he stood in shop doorways, sat on the stone steps in front of the Council House, shared a desultory conversation with the *Post* seller near the corner of King Street and Long Row. He bought a sandwich and a cup of coffee in Prêt à Manger and sipped the coffee slowly through the lid.

The way Katherine was sitting now, arms tight across her chest and wearing only a thin sweater, he thought she must be cold. Perhaps if he bought coffee for her, some hot tea or soup . . . but he did neither, continued instead to watch and wait, knowing that she didn't want him anywhere near but unable now to drag himself away.

He remembered her as a young girl, a child, tears flooding her eyes, screaming "I hate you!" at the top of her lungs and then, moments later, allowing him to fold her inside his arms and kiss the top of her head, the warmth of her hair.

As the bells chimed the quarter hour, a man crossed toward where Katherine was sitting.

Instinct prickled the skin on Elder's wrists and the backs of his hands.

He was not a big man, around five-seven, slightly built, denim jacket, jeans, checked shirt, high-tops, fair hair flopping forward over his face. He spoke to several of the small group gathered around the bench, stepping back a step or two to talk

85

to the ponytailed man, who had wandered off earlier and then returned. Katherine he ignored, but Elder had noticed the way she became more alert at his approach, her back more upright, fingers combing through her rough shag of unkempt hair.

Five minutes, more, as if noticing her for the first time, he offered Katherine a cigarette and lit it from his own. Another few minutes and she was standing at his side, both of them talking now, quite animatedly. Three buses went past in slow convoy, hiding them temporarily from Elder's view, and when he saw them again they were walking toward the fountains, passing in between, his hand coming to rest across the top of her shoulders as they moved past one of the stone lions guarding the Council House before turning right into Exchange Arcade.

Elder picked them up again as they emerged.

At the foot of Victoria Street, the man reached for her hand and she pulled it away. Down through Hockley, not touching, side by side. Coffee shops, bars, hairdressers, retro clothing, Indian restaurants. Goose Gate into Gedling. Waiting for a gap in the traffic on Carlton Road, his arm went around her shoulders again and she did nothing to resist.

Now they were in Sneinton, short rows of narrow streets, terraced houses, back-to-backs, some with brightly painted front doors and patterned blinds, others with makeshift curtains at the windows, broken glass. The house they stopped outside was midway along, a fading NOT IN MY NAME poster alongside one more recent, WAR CRIMINAL! writ large above a photograph of George W. Bush.

A cat, ginger and white with a white-tipped tail, jumped up onto the window ledge and rubbed its head against Katherine's arm as she stood waiting for the man to unlock the door. Running between their legs, the animal followed them into the house and the door closed behind them. Elder glimpsed Katherine for a moment, standing at the downstairs window, before she pulled the curtains closed. Whether she saw him or not, he did not know.

Chapter 8

He stood there for five minutes, ten, fifteen. *My father. He thinks he's my father.* There was still time to walk away. Elder walked, instead, across the street and, seeing no bell, knocked on the door.

The music playing as the door opened was loud, rhythmic, and fast, nothing he recognized.

"Yes?"

"Rob Summers?"

"Depends."

"On what?"

Summers smiled. The checked pattern on his shirt was mostly shades of green and gray; his eyes a pale, watery blue.

Elder looked past him into the narrow hall. Coats hung, bunched, along one wall; a strip of carpet, worn but clean, ran along the floor.

"Police, right?" Summers said. "You're not selling something, not religious.

You must be the police."

"Not exactly."

A smile of understanding passed across Summers's face and, relaxing his shoulders, he leaned sideways against the wall. "Katie," he called, putting a little singsong into his voice. "Your old man's here."

After a moment, Katherine appeared at the end of the hall, waited long enough to recognize her father's face, then turned away.

"I suppose you'd better come in," Summers said.

The room was small and dimly lit, a small couch and two unmatched armchairs taking up much of the space. Shelves either side of the empty fireplace were filled with books, videos, and DVDs, crammed in this way and that. More books and magazines lay in piles on the floor. In one corner was a small TV, VCR alongside it, DVD player on top. More shelving stretched along the back wall, what had to be several hundred vinyl albums below the different elements of the stereo system, CDs in profusion above.

The smell of dope hung, faint but sweet, upon the air.

Summers lowered himself into one of the chairs and motioned for Elder to do the same. The bass beat from the speakers was repetitive and insistent.

"Get you anything?" Summers asked. "Coffee, anything?"

"You think you could turn the music down a little?"

"Sure." Summers pressed the remote on the arm of his chair.

"I want to talk to Katherine," Elder said.

"That's up to her."

"I've come a long way."

"Cornwall, isn't it?"

"Yes," Elder said, surprised that he knew, that she had bothered to tell him.

"Your choice, wasn't it?"

"Look." Elder leaned forward. "You can see the state she's in."

"State?"

"You know what I mean."

"I'm not sure I do."

"Those people in the Square . . ."

"What about them?"

Elder shook his head.

"They look out for her," Summers said. "Leave her alone."

"And you?"

Summers pushed himself up from his chair. "Back in a minute, okay? I'll see what she says."

Alone in the room, Elder looked around.

White Stripes. Four Tet. The People's Music. Diane di Prima. Ginsberg. Dylan. Drop City. Neil Young. Several copies of the same pale green booklet on top of a stack of magazines. *Scar: Poems by Rob Summers.* Elder lifted one clear and flicked through the pages.

> the snap of his cuff
> a blade's edge
> brilliant threads
> vermillion wings
>
> sweat coils
> slow and sure
> violet rope
> around your neck
>
> face blinded
> I brace my back
> against a sudden
> blaze of light

"You read poetry?" Summers said, coming back into the room.

Elder let the booklet fall closed on his lap. "No, not really."

Summers sat back down.

"You write a lot?" Elder asked.

"A lot?" Summers smiled. "I don't know

about that. But, yes, when I can. Poetry mostly. The occasional short story."

"And you can earn a living doing that?"

"I wish."

"What do you do?"

Summers smiled again. He smiled a lot. "Teach, what else? Class at the university. Adult Ed. Bits and pieces here and there."

"I do want to talk to Katherine," Elder said. "Then I'll go."

"She knows you're here. It's up to her."

"If you asked her," Elder said.

Smiling, Summers shook his head. "That's not the way it works."

"Rob," Katherine said from the doorway, "it's all right." How long she had been standing there, Elder wasn't sure.

"You want me to stay?" Summers asked her.

"No, it's all right." Her face was pale, tiredness darkening her eyes.

Summers touched Katherine lightly as he went past.

Elder waited for her to come and sit down, but instead she walked to the window and opened the curtains enough to be able to look out. The music came to an end and voices could be heard, faint and indistinct, through the neighboring wall. In the kitchen, Rob Summers was washing pots, putting them away.

"I'm sorry," Elder said finally.

"What for?" He had to strain to make out the words.

"Whatever I've done to make you this upset. Angry."

When she turned to look at him there were tears he hadn't suspected on her face.

"I don't know what you expect from me," Elder said. "I don't know what you expect me to do."

"Nothing."

"You're hurting yourself, you must realize that."

Slowly, Katherine shook her head. "You saved me. From Keach. After he did all that stuff to me. He was going to kill me and you saved me."

"Yes."

"And now you wish you hadn't."

"That's ridiculous."

"Is it?"

"Yes."

"You don't like me like this."

Elder paused. "No. No, of course I don't."

"You want me to be like I was before."

"Yes."

She slid her hands across her face. "Dad, I'm never going to be like I was before."

How long he sat there he wasn't sure. Summers didn't reappear. Katherine left the room and then returned, and the next thing he knew he was standing next to her at the front door.

"You'll be careful," he said.

"Yes, of course." A smile fading in her eyes, she seemed young again, young and old beyond her years. *You're seventeen,* he wanted to say. *Seventeen. What are you going to do with your life?*

"If . . . if I need to get in touch?"

"Call me at Mum's."

"Not here?"

"Bye, Dad." Fleetingly, she kissed him on the cheek. Her hand touched his. She stepped back into the house and closed the door. A moment later, maybe two, the curtains were pulled closed.

Beyond Plymouth the train slowed its pace, stopping every twenty minutes or so at this small town or that. Countless times, Elder picked up his book only to set it back down. Staring out of the window into the passing dark, there was only his own face staring back. Six miniatures of Scotch lined up, empty, on the table before him: the slow but steady application of alcohol to the wound, the plastering over of helplessness and guilt. Should he have stayed? With a sweep of his hand, he sent the bottles flying, ricocheting from seat to empty seat and skittering along the floor. The few people still in the carriage tightened their faces and made themselves as small as they could.

By the time the train drew, finally, into Penzance, there were no more than a dozen passengers left. From the platform he could hear the sea, the waves splashing up against the concrete wall.

The taxi driver bridled when Elder told him the address. "It's gonna cost 'e. Hole through my exhaust goin' down that lane, had that happen before."

Ignoring him, Elder slumped into the back.

Come morning, he knew, his head would feel like a heavy ball that had been bounced too many times. The cottage was a darkened shell. He gave the taxi driver five pounds over the fare and stood watching him drive away, red taillights visible between the dark outlines of bracken and stone that lined the lane, and then not visible at all. Inside, he drank water, swallowed two aspirin, and went to bed.

Rain, hard against the windows, woke

him at three; by five he was sitting in the kitchen below, leafing through a week-old issue of the *Cornishman* and drinking tea. When eventually he stepped outside, purple light was already bruising the crest of the moor and all he could see was Katherine's face.

But within an hour the rain had dispersed and there was freshness in the air. In a short while, he would set off on a walk, possibly along the Tinner's Way, past Mulva Quoit to Chun Castle and beyond, allow his head the chance to clear. Later, he might take the car into town, spend some time in the gym; stock up on food, call in at the library, see about, perhaps, signing on for that woodworking course he'd been thinking of. Settle back into a routine. So far away, it was almost possible to forget the rest of the world existed.

Family. Friends. Responsibilities.

Chapter 9

Maddy Birch's body was found near Crouch Hill, at the bottom of a steep path leading down to the disused railway line. A woman walking her dog, early morning, saw something flesh-colored sticking up from between the leaves. Her 999 emergency call was classified urgent and a patrol car arrived minutes later, driving in along the narrow lane leading past the adventure playground and children's nursery toward the community center at the farthest end.

The body had fallen or been thrown some forty feet down the muddied bank into a tangle of blackberry bush and bracken.

The first officers at the scene called for reinforcements and began moving back the scattering of spectators that had already started to gather. Soon the area would be secured and properly cordoned off by officers from Forensic Science Services, the body shielded by a canopy until the medical examiner had finished his preliminary investigation. Diagrams would be drawn, the scene examined in scrupulous detail, numerous Polaroids taken, measurements noted down: the whole operation captured on video.

The first two detectives from SCD1, Homicide, arrived some twenty minutes later. Lee Furness and Paul Denison, both DCs, showed their IDs and spoke briefly to the uniformed officers before pulling on protective clothing. Not wanting to obliterate anything Forensics might find on the path, they scrambled down through the bracken some twenty meters away.

Losing his footing midway, Furness cursed as dark mud smeared the leg of his coveralls.

Denison reached the bottom first.

"Jesus," he said and crossed himself instinctively. The dead woman's eyes were open and he wished that they were closed. Curly-haired and round of face, at twenty-seven Denison was the youngest in the team, younger than Furness by a full year.

The woman's skin was the color of day-old putty, save where it had been sliced and torn.

Careful not to contaminate the scene,

Furness, wearing a pair of latex gloves, pried a pair of white cotton knickers from the brambles on which they had snagged, dropped them into a plastic evidence bag, and sealed the bag along the top.

When they looked up, their detective sergeant, Mike Ramsden, had arrived and was standing at the top of the bank, looking down. Burly, broad-shouldered, tall, wearing a scuffed leather jacket and tan chinos, tie loose at his neck, Ramsden epitomized the public's image, post-TV, of what a police detective should look like.

"Boss here?" Ramsden called.

"Not yet," Denison said.

"Forensics?"

"On their way."

"Time for you two to get it sorted," Ramsden said. "Make a name for yourselves. Just don't go trampling over everything."

His breath hung visible on the morning air.

Karen Shields, promoted to detective chief inspector some twelve months before, was on her way to Hendon and a weekly meeting at Homicide West when the call came through. Why, when it was based in north London, it wasn't called Homicide

North, Shields had never quite figured out. And besides, in a year or so, after yet another reorganization, it would be called something else. It hardly mattered. Over an excess of instant coffee and without too much rancor, she and other senior officers would review progress in the various investigations under way, pool information, prioritize.

The murder of an Afghan shopkeeper, attacked at Stroud Green by a gang of youths armed with blades and iron bars, was foundering amid a welter of denial, false alibis, and barefaced lies. The two fourteen-year-olds they were certain had been responsible for setting fire to an eighty-six-year-old woman after breaking into her flat had been arrested, and then grudgingly released for lack of evidence. The week before, a family in Wembley, a mother and three children under ten, had been found bludgeoned to death, two of the children in their beds, one on the stairs, the mother in the garden as she tried to raise the alarm. The father had hanged himself from the top of a brightly colored jungle gym in the kids' playground of the local park.

And then there were the young black men: investigations undertaken with

DCC4, Racial and Violent Crimes. One man shot dead as he sat drinking coffee at a sidewalk café in Camden Town; another, possibly as a reprisal, gunned down as he came up the steps from Willesden Green station; a third, no more than seventeen, knifed outside the bowling alley in Finsbury Park. On and on.

Shields knew the figures: the murder rate in England and Wales for the previous year was the highest ever, with shooting-related deaths up by some thirty-two percent. The highest overall recorded crime rate was in Nottinghamshire, though violent crime per capita was more prevalent in London, with men under the age of twenty-six the most frequent victims. Gun crime aside, the biggest increases were in stranger violence, harassment, and rape. And despite the growing prevalence of guns on the streets, the most popular murder weapon by far was still some form of sharp implement. Knife. Machete. Razor. Sharpened spade.

She thought of this as, having turned her car around, she fought her way back through the rush hour traffic; single men in suits steering one-handed as they smoked cigarette after cigarette and snapped, illegally, into their cell phones; good-looking young moms ferrying their children to school in SUVs.

"When you goin' to settle down, girl?" her grandmother had asked when she made her regular Christmas visit home. "Have some babies of your own?"

Home was Spanish Town in Jamaica, the progeny of sisters and cousins swarming around her like an accusation.

"Girl, you not gettin' any younger." The cataracts in her grandmother's eyes preventing her from seeing how old — how hard — she had become.

At Crouch End Broadway, Shields steered wide past a car hesitating at the pedestrian lights, slid into the left-hand lane, and accelerated up the hill. Incongruous, a giant totem pole outside the playground signaled the entrance to the lane, and she slowed almost to a halt before pulling in behind Mike Ramsden's Sierra.

A quick glance in the rearview mirror, a hand pushed up through her short tousled hair; her lipstick could do with replenishing, but for now it would have to do. She was wearing a dark brown pantsuit and boots with a solid heel that brought her as close as damn-it to six foot. Well, five-ten. Her Don't Mess With Me look, as she liked to think.

Removing his hands from his pockets,

Ramsden walked toward her. Down below, she could see Forensics already at work, shielding the body from sight.

"What have we got?" Shields said.

Ramsden coughed into the back of his hand. "White female, thirty-five to forty-five, multiple stab wounds; dead some little time. Last night at a guess."

"ME not here yet?"

"Stuck in traffic."

"Tell me about it." Shields moved closer to the edge and looked down. "That where it happened?"

"My guess, she was attacked somewhere up here and then pushed."

Shields looked along the area to their left that had now been cordoned off, the muddied slope leading steeply down.

"Marks you can see," Ramsden said. "That and the angle of the body." He shrugged. "Maybe he finished her off down there, who knows?"

"Any ID yet?"

"Not so far."

"No one similar reported missing?"

"Early days."

Shields sighed and patted her coat pocket, hoping for a mint; since she'd stopped smoking on New Year's Day, she'd been committing dental suicide.

"Any idea yet what she was doing here?"

Ramsden told her so far they'd found a gray sports bra and matching sweatshirt, the sweatshirt dark with mud and what was almost certainly blood. A pair of gray jogging pants had lain nearby. One blue and white Puma running shoe had been discovered close to the body, the other among the trees at the far side of the old railway track, where presumably it had been hurled.

"Out running," Shields said. "Chances are she'll live close."

Earlier in the year a woman had been attacked and killed while jogging in east London, Hackney. Stabbed. The investigation was still ongoing.

Shields glanced around at the flats that ranged below. At the end of the lane, she knew, a path led down to a crescent of Victorian houses and the sprawl of another low-rise council estate at the far side of Hornsey Road. Before being assigned to SCD1, she'd run a missing person investigation here, a three-year-old boy who'd gone missing from the nursery and been found forty-eight hours later, safe but cold, asleep in someone's garden shed.

"Who found the body?"

Ramsden pointed toward a thirtyish

woman in a yellow puffy jacket, standing with two other women of similar age. All with cigarettes on the go.

"Who talked to her?"

"Furness and Denison."

"Talk to her again."

"But . . ."

"Again, Mike. Do it yourself. I'm going down to take a look."

Her protective clothing was in the boot of the car. Changed, she made her way carefully down, not wanting to make a fool of herself by slipping. The DI in charge of the Forensic team was someone she'd worked with before.

Inside the canopy, Shields bent toward the body. Some of the cuts looked superficial; others, she guessed, ran deep. There was bruising to the neck and face, another bruise — the result of a kick? — above the pelvis on the left-hand side. A fine spray of dried blood speckled the inner thigh, and something silver and crystalline trailed, snail-like, across the curve of her stomach.

Sexual assault?

Until the postmortem there was no way to know for sure.

She stepped back outside and turned in a slow circle, trying to get a sense of what had happened, taking her time.

Ramsden was on his way toward her, having taken the long way around.

"The woman," Ramsden said. "Nothing she didn't say first time round." He took a stick of chewing gum from his top pocket, removed the wrapping, and put it in his mouth.

Shields held out her hand.

"Sorry," Ramsden said. "Last one."

She didn't know whether to believe him or not.

"She recognize the victim?" Shields asked.

"Not from what she saw."

"Get her to look at one of the Polaroids. Good chance, if they both use this place a lot, she'll have seen her before."

But now Denison was shouting something from above, altar-boy face shining and a canvas sports bag held high in one gloved hand.

"Lucky bollocks," Ramsden said, half beneath his breath. "Fall in shit and he'd come up with a five-pound note."

They climbed back up.

"It was back there," Denison said, pointing. "Community center. Pushed down below the steps by the door."

"You've checked inside?" Shields asked.

Denison shook his head. "Just a quick look. Sweatshirt. Towel. Socks."

"Then we don't know it's hers," Ramsden said.

"Let's see," Shields said, reaching into the bag with gloved hands.

The wallet was safe in an inner pocket, square and dark, the leather soft with use. She lifted it out and let it fall open in her hand.

"Oh, shit," she said softly. "Shit, shit, shit."

"What?" Ramsden said.

Shields held out toward him the warrant card with its small square photograph: Maddy Birch, Detective Sergeant, CID.

"She's one of ours."

Chapter 10

The press conference was packed to the gills. Television cameras, tape recorders, a smattering of old-fashioned spiral-bound notebooks, ballpoints at the ready. On the raised platform, a technician made a last-minute check of the microphones. The noise in the hall ebbed and flowed. Out front, a Press and Public Relations officer had a quick word with the reporter from Sky News. Barring a terrorist attack or a celebrity scandal, the timing should guarantee blanket coverage on all the terrestrial channels, plus satellite and cable. BBC Radio was taking a live feed into its five o'clock news. A curtain twitched to one side, a door opened, and, stern-faced, they shuffled in.

The platform was rich in seniority and rank. Assistant Commissioner Harkin took center stage, to his right the detective chief superintendent in command of Homicide West. Seated at the far left, Karen Shields was the only woman, the only black face among all those sober-faced and somber-suited white men.

Arguments that she'd be better occupied elsewhere had been brushed aside: Public Relations liked to get her on camera as often as they could.

In her absence, Lee Furness was busy liaising with Forensics and overseeing the local area enquiries, while Mike Ramsden had traveled north to interview Maddy Birch's mother. Alan Sheridan, Shields's office manager, was accessing the Sex Offenders Register, searching through computerized records of similar crimes. Only Paul Denison was temporarily idle, twiddling his thumbs in the car park waiting for Shields while she was stuck, unhappily, behind a microphone.

Bald head shining a little in the lights, the assistant commissioner began his statement: "We are, all of us, shocked and saddened by the death of a colleague in this tragic and senseless way." Using his notes sparingly, he spoke of Maddy Birch as a resourceful and dedicated officer who had shown extreme bravery only recently in going up against an armed and dangerous criminal when she herself was unarmed. "All of us within the Metropolitan Police

Service," he concluded, "have a grim determination to bring Maddy's killer or killers to justice as soon as possible."

Flashbulbs popped.

Harkin gave brief details of the circumstances of Birch's death and went on to give assurances that the Homicide officers leading the investigation would be able to call on the support, as necessary, of other Operational Crime Units, as well as the facilities of the National Crime Intelligence Service. Shields, finally, was introduced as one of the officers who were, as he put it, dealing with the minute-by-minute, the day-to-day, the real nitty-gritty. No one, least of all Shields, had warned him it might no longer be politically correct to say nitty-gritty.

The first question was hurled almost before Harkin had finished speaking: was it true that Maddy Birch had been sexually assaulted prior to her death?

"Until the postmortem has been carried out by the Home Office pathologist," he said, "any such assumptions are purely speculation." It was an answer guaranteed to increase speculation tenfold.

Numerous questions followed about the exact nature of the attack, most of which were deflected.

"Given the similarity of circumstances," asked the reporter from CNN, "do the police think there is a connection between this murder and that of the woman killed while jogging in Hackney in February?"

They'd been expecting that one.

"Be assured," Harkin responded, "there will be the closest contact with officers conducting that investigation."

He did think, then, there was a connection?

"As I say, we are exploring that avenue alongside several others."

"Nobody has yet been charged with the Victoria Park murder, is that correct?"

That was correct.

"And all three men arrested in connection with the murder have since been released?"

That was so.

Harkin sighed. "If we could concentrate our attentions on the tragic death of Detective Sergeant Birch . . ."

But the crime correspondent for the *Guardian* was already on his feet. "The assistant commissioner alluded to the police operation in which Detective Sergeant Birch was involved, and which resulted in the death of a fellow officer and the fatal shooting by the police of James William

Grant — I wonder, can he tell us what progress is being made in the enquiry into those events presently being carried out by the Hertfordshire Force?"

"I'm afraid I don't see that has any relevance here."

"But the enquiry is ongoing?"

"You have my answer." Harkin's face was set in stone.

"I think," the Public Relations officer began, "if there are no further questions . . ."

"I have a question for Detective Chief Inspector Shields." Eyes turned toward the Home Affairs correspondent from the BBC. "As a woman officer, does this case have a special resonance for you?"

Fuck, Shields said inside her head.

Twenty cameras flashed in her direction.

"As a police officer," she said, "all cases of this seriousness, especially where the deaths of fellow officers are involved, resonate equally."

Off to one side, the PR officer nearly wet himself with joy.

"Gentlemen," said Assistant Commissioner Harkin, rising to his feet. "Ladies. Thank you for your time."

Seeing Karen Shields approach across the car park in his rearview mirror,

Denison turned the key in the ignition.

"How did it go, ma'am?"

Shields slammed the car door closed. "Stop ma'aming me and drive the fucking car."

Not too well, then, Denison thought.

Shields buckled herself in and stared straight ahead. Hendon to Kentish Town, half an hour if they were lucky, three-quarters if not.

Taylor's commanding officer was waiting for them in reception. "PC Taylor's in my office. You can talk to her there."

"Thank you."

Taylor jumped to her feet when the door opened. She was wearing her police uniform, the top button of her tunic fastened tight at her neck; there was a slight but unmistakable smell of perspiration in the room.

Awkwardly, Taylor held out her hand and then, before Shields could respond, let it fall by her side.

Sitting, Shields introduced Denison and herself.

"Maddy Birch," Shields said, "you knew her. You've got some information, I believe."

"Yes. As soon as I heard what had happened — I'm sorry, I still can't believe it

— as soon as I heard, I went to my inspector here and asked to be put in touch."

Shields nodded. "I'd like to record this conversation. I take it you've no objection?"

"No, of course not."

Denison placed the pocket recorder on the desk between them and switched it on.

"Very well, then, in your own time."

Taylor told them about Birch's growing fears that she had been watched and followed; her feeling that someone had been inside her flat.

"She didn't report any of this?"

"No."

"Do you know why?"

Taylor wriggled a little in her seat. "It wasn't as if she had any proof. I think she was worried she might not be believed. That people might think she was, you know, imagining things."

"And you? What did you think?"

"Did I believe her?"

"Yes."

"Not at first. Not if I'm to be honest, no. Ever since the Grant business, that young officer getting killed, it had really shaken her up. You could tell. I thought maybe it was a reaction to that. Nervous, you know. But then, when she said someone had broken into her flat, I believed her then."

"And she didn't have any idea who this person — if it was one person — might have been?"

"No, not really."

"You don't seem sure."

Taylor fidgeted with her hair. "Well, there was this one time we were in the pub and Maddy thought she saw someone she knew. Her ex."

"Ex-husband, lover, what?"

"Husband. Terry."

"And how did she react?"

"She didn't say anything at first, not to me. But you could tell, yes, she was surprised. Thinking she'd seen him."

"They weren't in touch?"

"No. Not at all. Quite a while, at least. He'd moved away. North Wales, I think she said."

"And when she saw him, her reaction, was it just surprise?"

Taylor took her time, wanting to be clear. "No. I think it was more than that. More as if she was afraid, you know?"

Mugs of tea sat on a metal tray, untouched. Paper packets of sugar and plastic spoons. Shields noticed the low background hum from the central heating for the first time. Mike Ramsden was up in

Lincolnshire talking to Birch's mother. Where was it? Louth? Surname Birch, she remembered. Maddy must have taken her own name after the divorce.

"When she told you about her flat being broken into, she didn't say she thought it might have been him? Terry?"

"No. And by then she was saying it probably hadn't been him at the pub at all. Just someone who looked a bit like him, that's all."

"Enough like him to make her afraid."

"Yes. Yes, I suppose so."

Shields could feel her nerve ends tightening, a scenario beginning to play out in her mind, and had to will herself not to let it race too far ahead.

"That night, after the pub, you didn't notice anyone hanging around, acting suspiciously at all? Anyone who might have been him?"

"No. I've been thinking about it, but no." Taylor looked bereft, on the verge of tears.

"Here." Shields tore open two packets of sugar and emptied them into one of the mugs of tea. "Drink some of that."

"Do I have to?" Taylor smiling despite everything.

"God, no." Leaning forward, she

switched off the tape. "Where's the nearest pub?"

"End of the street."

"How long will it take you to get out of that uniform?"

Pocketing the recorder, Shields got to her feet. "Paul, get through to the office, have somebody check on Maddy Birch's file. Her married name might be somewhere there and I missed it. And see if you can raise Mike, tell him to give me a call."

Shields bought a screwdriver for Taylor, Coke with ice and lemon for herself, tonic water for Denison.

"Paul here's not old enough to drink anyway," she said.

Denison blushed.

When Taylor asked how the investigation was going, Shields shrugged and shook her head. "Ask me in a couple of days."

The television over the bar seemed to be showing a rerun of some soccer game or other; at least it wasn't the news. A brace of gaudy machines at the far end of the room were vying with one another for the most annoying electronic jingle. Most of the tables were taken by solitary drinkers, men nursing pints of whatever bitter was on special.

"You liked her, didn't you? Maddy."

"She was great. A laugh, you know. But not silly, like some. Sensible. And straight, no side to her, you know what I mean? Said what she felt. She . . ." Taylor's face wobbled and she fumbled for a tissue in her bag. "It was all getting to her, you know? That's why . . ." She gulped air and brought her hands to her mouth. "That's why I suggested yoga. I thought it would help, make her less stressed out." She was unable now to hold back the tears. "That bloody place. If it hadn't been for me, she'd never have gone. Never have been there. Never have got herself bloody killed."

Shields leaned closer and put her arm around the other woman's shoulders.

Denison looked more embarrassed than usual.

"Listen," Shields said. "Vanessa. If she was right, if someone was following her, intending to harm her, it would have happened anyway. And if it was something else, pure chance, there's nothing you or anyone else could have done. Okay?"

"Yes. Yes, I suppose so."

"Good."

Taylor blew her nose loudly.

"Here," Shields said. "Drink up."

At which moment Shields's cell phone started to ring and she stepped out to the street.

Mike Ramsden's voice was indistinct.

"Is this a crap line or are you whispering?"

"It's a crap line."

"Listen, Mike. I want to know the name of Maddy Birch's ex. Address too, if you can get one. Anything else about him. How things were between them. Threats. Animosity. Anything. All right?"

"Do what I can."

"Okay, soon as you get a name, call me back."

Shields hung up.

In the hallway of the small terraced house in Louth, Mike Ramsden slipped his phone back into his pocket and looked for a moment at the photograph, framed and hanging on the wall, of a young Maddy Birch at her graduation ceremony. Behind him, in the living room, there were more photographs and a scrapbook full to overflowing open on the low table beside Carol Birch's chair. For the better part of an hour he had been sitting opposite her, balancing an empty cup and saucer in the palm of one hand, pretending to listen. "I only moved up here to be near her and then she up and moved to London."

Ramsden sighed and turned back into the room.

"What about boyfriends?" Shields was asking Taylor. "Good-looking woman, not old, there must have been someone?"

"I don't think so. No one special. I mean, if we were out, blokes would try it on, you know, giving her the chat, but she didn't seem interested. It was more like, if anything was going to happen, she wanted it to be more than just a one-night stand, you know?"

Shields knew only too well.

"So, no one at all?"

"Oh, one guy maybe. This roofer she met."

"Roofer?"

"Yes, you know." Taylor gestured vaguely upward. "One of those blokes always up scaffolding, doing a lot of shouting, re-placing tiles. Steve was his name. Steve Kennet."

"How long ago was this?"

"Few months back, maybe more."

"And this was serious?"

"Not really."

"You know where he lives, this Steve?"

Taylor shook her head. "Archway somewhere."

Shields made a note of the name; if it came to it, he shouldn't be all that difficult to find.

Less than ten minutes later Ramsden rang her back. "Name's Patrick. Terence Patrick. I've got an address in Prestatyn. Fifteen Sea View Terrace."

"Current?"

"I'm not sure."

"Shouldn't be too hard to check. Listen, Mike, if I don't get back to you inside the hour, I want you to meet me there tomorrow morning. Prestatyn. Eight. Eight-thirty. I'll catch an early flight from Stansted. Liverpool or Manchester."

"And how am I supposed to get there from the wilds of fucking Lincolnshire?"

"Leave early."

Shields pressed DISCONNECT and looked at her watch. She needed to get back to the office, make some calls. She thought they'd got as much out of Vanessa Taylor as they were going to get for now. They could always talk to her again. She was thinking about Terry Patrick, how he might have heard the news of his ex-wife's death. If and when and what he'd felt. If he hadn't known already.

Thinking about Birch's mother, trying to imagine how you began to come to terms with what had happened. If you ever did. Children were supposed to outlive their parents, wasn't that the way it was supposed to be?

Chapter 11

Whoever had named Sea View Terrace had either an ironic sense of humor or a very tall ladder. It wasn't even a terrace anymore, but a street of 1970s semi-detacheds, each with its own garage, right or left. The pebble-dash facade of number fifteen, once white, was now a sour, yellowing cream. Wooden planks and sundry pieces of scaffolding littered the front yard. The garage door was partway open.

Shields drove slowly past in the rental car she'd picked up at the airport, reversed into a three-point turn, and stopped several doors down. Mike Ramsden's Ford Sierra, showing every sign of having battered along the M6 in heavy rain, was parked farther along on the opposite side, Ramsden catnapping behind the wheel.

Shields got out of the car, wearing a faded green suit, almost certainly a mistake she thought, popped a mint into her mouth, and turned up the collar of her coat; the rain had dwindled to a steady drizzle, gray out of a gray sky.

She rapped her keys against the Sierra's window and Ramsden was instantly awake. Several lidded coffee cups and an empty Burger King box were on the passenger seat alongside him, an orange juice carton on the floor.

"I thought you said eight," he said, winding down the window. "Eight-thirty?"

"I did."

Ramsden looked at his watch and grunted. It was close to twenty past the hour.

"What time did you get here?" Shields asked.

"Round seven."

Shields nodded in the direction of the house. "Anything happening?"

"Patrick's been in and out the garage a couple of times, fiddling with stuff in his van. Had on his white overalls second time, off to work soon I don't doubt."

"Anyone else around?"

"Face at the window. Wife, girlfriend, someone."

"Well," Shields said, "let's go and introduce ourselves."

The woman who came to the door was plumpish, shortish, a smoker's mouth and mid-length straw-colored hair, and breasts that, underneath a pale cotton top, seemed to have a life of their own.

"Mrs. Patrick . . . ?"

Her glance moved from one face to the other and back again. "Sorry, I'm afraid I don't have time . . ."

But Shields was holding up her badge. "We're police officers," she said.

The woman looked past them to the empty street outside. "Terry," she called over her shoulder. Then, stepping back into the hallway, "You'd best come in."

The central heating was turned up high. A radio was playing in another room, the cajoling voice of some near-desperate DJ. Terry Patrick appeared at the end of the hall. His fair, almost sandy hair was in need of a comb; dried patches of plaster and specks of old paint clung to his overalls and the work boots on his feet. Fifty, Karen thought, if he was a day. Around the same height as herself. One of those men who become more wiry with age, rather than gaining weight.

"What's all this then?"

But from his eyes he already knew.

"It's about Maddy, isn't it?"

"Just a few things," Shields said. "Routine, really."

"Come on through," he said. And then, "Tina, get the kettle on, will you?"

The sigh was practiced, automatic. "Tea?"

"If there's any chance of coffee?" Shields said.

"It'll be instant."

"That's fine."

"That'll be for the both of you, then?"

Ramsden nodded.

"Suit yourselves."

The living room was dark and overburdened by furniture. Wherever the radio was playing, it wasn't here. The kitchen, probably. Shields could just recognize the Delfonics, "Didn't I Blow Your Mind This Time?" Going back.

"Sit yourselves down," Patrick said.

Shields sat at one end of a sofa that had seen better days, Ramsden on a high-backed chair near the window. Patrick settled himself into what was obviously his chair, creased leather, opposite a large-screen TV.

"It must have come as a shock," Shields said, "what happened."

"Course it bloody did. All over the news, like. Couldn't believe it at first." He made a small derisive sound, somewhere between a snort and a laugh. "What they say,

126

isn't it? When something happens. Couldn't believe it. But it's true. Someone gets, you know, killed — accident, whatever — you never expect it to be someone you know."

Leaning back, he lifted his feet onto a low wooden table that seemed to have been put there for the purpose. Keeping his boots off the shag carpet.

"Poor silly cow," he said. "Out jogging, that's what they said." He shook his head. "London. Late at night, some park or other. You'd've thought she'd have known better."

Coffee and tea were carried in on a metal tray, sugar still in its packet, a solitary spoon.

"Thanks, Tina, love."

Patrick's hands, Shields thought, watching him stir two sugars into his tea, were broad across the knuckles, lightly etched with paint.

"Maddy," she said, "when did you last see her?"

Patrick smiled a quick, lopsided smile and, for the first time, Shields caught a sense of how he might have been an attractive man, fifteen or more years before.

"Been thinking about that, haven't I? Tina asked me the same thing. 'Eighty-six, it must have been. The divorce. Year after it all, you know, went pear-shaped." He picked a small circle of paint from the leg of his overalls and flicked it toward the empty fireplace. "Seventeen years."

His wife was still standing in the doorway, watching him, her face impossible to read.

"You've not seen her in all that time?" Shields said.

"Not the once."

"But you'd kept in touch?"

"Not really, no. Her folks, they were always pretty decent, sent a card at Christmas, that kind of thing. Leastways, till her father died. Four or five years back now, that'd be. Maybe more."

"And you didn't see Maddy, no communication, nothing?"

"I said no, didn't I?"

"Mr. Patrick, you're sure?"

"Tell them, Terry," his wife said. "For Christ's sake, tell them." Stepping back into the hall, she closed the door slowly but firmly behind her.

Patrick picked up his mug, held it in both hands for a moment without drinking, then set it back down.

"Seven or eight years back . . ."

"Which?"

"Seven, seven. Me and Tina, we were

going through a bad patch. It happens. Things get out of hand, slip gear." He looked quickly across at Ramsden, as if for affirmation. "I moved out for a while, bunked up with a pal. After a bit, I got in touch with Maddy. Tried to. I don't know, I suppose I had this daft idea we might get back together. Got her address and that from her mum. Phoned and it was like talking to the bloody clock. Just didn't want to know, did she? I wrote a few times after that, asking, you know, couldn't we meet? Stupid, really. Plain bloody stupid. She never replied, of course, not a bloody word." He lifted his head and gave a sour little smile. "Tina and I, we got things sorted." He shrugged. "Maybe it's not perfect, but then you tell me, what is?"

The radio, already indistinct, was lost to the sound of a vacuum cleaner, as it banged against the baseboard in the hall.

"This was all seven years ago," Shields said.

Patrick nodded.

"And there was no contact between you since?"

A shake of the head.

"Nothing. You'd not spoken, set eyes on her?"

"No, I said."

"How about October?"

"Sorry?"

"October of this year."

Patrick leaned forward, leaned back, looked toward the door. The vacuuming stopped, then started up again. Shields watched as, fingers spread, his hands pushed hard along the tops of his thighs. His voice when he spoke was choked, deliberately low.

"It was an accident, right? No. Coincidence. That's it, coincidence. I'd been down there on a job, London. Well, the money's good, better than you can expect up here and you can always doss down a couple of nights in the van. Anyway, this night, after working, right, we go out for a few beers, just the three of us, me and these two other blokes, one pub and then another and all of a sudden there she is, her and this other bird, up on stage singing some bloody song." Patrick wiped the back of his hand across his mouth before carrying on. "Couldn't believe it. Just stood and fucking stared. 'What's up?' one of these blokes said. 'Fancy it, do you?' I wanted to thump him, didn't I? Bury my fist in his fucking face. Just turned round and left instead. Couldn't wait to get out of there. Walked for fucking miles, must

130

have done. Fucking miles. Don't ask me why." Another glance toward the door. "I don't want her to know."

Shields waited, watching his face, the spots of anger slow to fade from his cheeks.

"Why didn't you wait, go and talk to her, say hello?"

"I don't know."

"All the effort you'd made before . . ."

"I know, I know. It was just — I don't know — the surprise, I suppose. The shock. Pathetic, isn't it? And now . . ." He looked into Shields's face. "You don't know who it was? Who killed her?"

"Not yet," she said. "Not for definite."

His eyes were a pale greeny-gray and they scarcely wavered under her gaze.

"The bastard," Patrick said. "Hanging's not good enough for him, whoever he is."

"Where were you two nights ago?" Shields asked, much as she might have asked for a refill for her coffee.

Patrick blinked. "Here. Why?" And then, "Oh, yes, of course. I suppose you have to ask."

"Here at home with your wife?" Shields said.

"More or less. Knocked off work around four-thirty, five. New development the other side of town, been there a couple of weeks now, plastering, helping out. Anyway, left there, stopped off at the bookie's, quick pint across the street from there, back here no later than seven. Bit of supper, watched the box. Don't ask me what. Early night. Tina, she likes to read a bit in bed but not me. Spark out before eleven, I shouldn't wonder."

"Apart from your wife," Ramsden said, speaking for the first time, "there are people who'd back this up?"

"I daresay, yes. Bookmaker's for certain, one or two in the pub."

"You can give us the details?"

"Yes, of course."

Ten minutes later, they were back out in the street, standing alongside Mike Ramsden's car, Ramsden smoking a rare cigarette and Shields standing close enough to inhale the smoke.

"What do you think?" he asked.

"When he started talking about her, the way she ignored him when he tried to get in touch, you could see the veins standing out in his wrists."

Ramsden nodded. "You think he's telling the truth?"

"Here and there."

"You want me to check out some of these names?"

"Do that. I think I'll wait around till he's gone off to work, go back and have a word with the wife."

"None too crazy about the idea of him and Maddy, is she?"

"Maybe she's got good reason."

"My missus thought I had the hots for somebody else, she'd help pack my bag, give me her blessing."

Shields laughed. "Mike, there's exceptions to everything."

"He hit me once," Tina said. "Few years ago now. I can't even remember what over, most likely nothing, nothing important, but I can remember it happening. Crack, hard round the side of the face. Somewhere between a punch and a slap. This come up all black, didn't it? Black, purple, yellow."

"What did you do?" Shields said.

They were sitting at a small table in the kitchen, more Nescafé, the radio turned low. Shields knew there was some reason, other than taste, she shouldn't be drinking anything made by Nestlé, something to do with children in Africa, babies, but she couldn't remember exactly what.

Tina shook a cigarette out from the pack and picked up a disposable lighter.

"I waited, didn't I? Waited till I was doing the ironing. Oh, not when it was hot. Just, you know, handy. Caught him one on the back of his hand while he was sitting where you are now, reading the paper. Hollerin' and screamin' something dreadful, wasn't he? Swelled up like a half-pound of sausage; couldn't work for a week. 'Lay that hand on me again,' I told him, 'and I'll take the bread knife to it when you're asleep.' "

"He didn't try and get you back?"

Tina laughed. "Too busy sitting there feeling sorry for himself, wasn't he? 'What the hell you have to do that for?' over and over."

"He has got a temper, though."

"Two of us, that is."

"He said you went through a bad patch some years ago, came close to breaking up."

"God! Confession time in there, was it? Some kind of therapy session."

Shields smiled. "Maybe."

"He'd been seeing this woman, hadn't he? Some slag he'd met, God knows where. Pathetic. I told him if that was what he wanted he could piss off and get on with it. Soon come back with his tail between his legs, didn't he? Begging me to take him back."

"And you did."

Lifting a hand, Tina pushed her hair back off her face. "Look at me, not exactly going to be mistaken for Miss Prestatyn, am I? Just some dumpy little tart with a fat arse and half a brain. Learn to take what you can get. And besides, he's not so bad, earns good money most of the time and not mean with it, like some." She drew hard on her cigarette. "You could do worse, believe me. A lot worse. I know."

Shields sipped at the lukewarm coffee to the faint strains of "Rocket Man."

"Ooh, I love this," Tina said, reaching toward the radio. "You mind if I turn it up?"

Shields always thought listening to Elton John was like a quick fuck in the dark: okay till you turned on the light.

"Were you here," Shields asked, "when he heard about his ex-wife, what had happened?"

"Both watching the news, weren't we? Half-watching, anyway. All of a sudden Terry's shouting out 'cause he's heard her name and then there's this picture of her on the screen. Someone saying how she'd been murdered. Terry, he sort of froze. Stunned, like. As if he couldn't believe it. Ages before I could get him to say a word. Really got to him, you know." She stubbed out her cigarette. "Made me think twice about going out at night, even round here, on your own. Always some bastard man, out there, waiting for you."

She turned the radio back down.

"He wrote to her, you know. Maddy. More than a few times. I'm not supposed to know. Found one of the letters in his coat pocket. Steamed it open. All this bollocks about how she was the love of his life and that. Burned it, didn't I? Tore it into little pieces and set fucking light to it. Never said anything; soft sod must've thought he'd posted it."

She lit another cigarette.

"Maybe she was, you know? Love of his life? Least someone thought that of her, eh?"

Chapter 12

Elder had finished J. B. Priestley and gone back to Patrick O'Brian. Each morning he listened to the coastal reports on Radio Cornwall: NCI St. Ives, NCI Gwennap Head, NCI Bass Point. One blustery day, returning from a tramp across the fields, a beast lay dead in the otherwise deserted farmyard along the lane, legs poking stiff from either side of its distended belly, plastic sheet flapping loose about its head. When he went out again toward dusk, it had disappeared, leaving just the trail through the mud where it had been dragged.

Since returning from Nottingham, he had phoned Joanne with some regularity and asked after Katherine; every few days at first, then less often. Sometimes his daughter was there, sometimes not. She's seems to have settled down, Joanne assured him. Stays home more. She's even talking about going to college, finishing her AS exams. Whoever Katherine was talking to, it wasn't him.

Elder sent her a letter, drafted carefully beforehand, trying to explain how he felt, how he felt about her. Not expecting a reply, he still checked the mailbox each day, still felt the same twinge of hurt. He thought of going up again to see her, but rationalized it would only serve to make things worse. Katherine might have settled down, as Joanne had suggested, but he had not.

With the winds lashing more and more fiercely in from the Atlantic, Elder ordered another load of logs and stacked them in the lean-to at the side of the cottage, splitting some with an ax for kindling. The bottle of Jameson in the kitchen went down a little more each evening, slow but steady.

And then, the first week in December, a Monday, he opened a three-day-old paper and read the news: the body of a police officer had been found near a disused railway line in north London, sexually assaulted and left for dead. As soon as he saw the name, he knew who she was.

It had been sixteen years ago. Elder had

been based in Lincoln, CID, established, not so many months from turning forty. The big four-O. Katherine was barely two, a toddler, agile enough at night to insert herself between Joanne and him in their bed. He had noticed Maddy Birch around the station, the odd word exchanged in passing, nodded greetings in the canteen: enough to notice the color of her eyes, the same shade as Joanne's, the absence of rings on her left hand. Late twenties, he supposed, maybe younger.

One evening, late, at a going-away party for someone in Traffic neither of them really knew, they bumped up against each other in the crush at the bar, her hand resting for a moment on his arm as she steadied herself, the second time surely no mistake. When he'd smiled what was intended as an inviting smile, she'd looked away. Which of them had contrived that they leave together, he was never sure; maybe neither, maybe both. The cobblestones outside were slippery and wet, the street narrow and steep. Only natural to reach out a hand, steady her against a fall. Above and behind, lights picked out the west front of the cathedral, the stonework of the castle opposite. His fingers touched her cheek and neck. The doorway into which they half-stumbled, half-stepped was barely deep enough to hold them both. His mouth found hers, her mouth found his. She said his name. Clumsily unbuttoning her coat, his hand closed on her breast. She fumbled with the front of his clothes, gave up, gripped hard instead. The flesh of her neck was warm and soft and when he kissed her there, low in the dip between muscle and bone, she moaned and squeezed tighter and he came, standing there, came against her hand.

Oh, Christ!

She kissed him near the side of his mouth and, after a moment, when she stepped away, there was light enough to see the rueful smile upon her face.

"I'm sorry," he said.

"Don't be." Her finger to his lips. And then, "Come on, let's walk," linking her arm through his.

At the foot of the hill, they went their separate ways, she a short walk to the place she'd recently bought, he in a taxi to the home where wife and child would doubtless be sleeping, somehow managing to take up, between them, most of the bed.

The central heating had switched itself off automatically and, still wearing his coat, he sat in the kitchen with both hands around a glass of whiskey, taking his mind as slowly as he could through what had happened, moments that were already uncertain, half-imagined.

Neither of them spoke of it again; nothing else happened.

It was the only time, in all the years of his marriage, that Elder had strayed.

Yet he found himself from time to time remembering, images appearing from nowhere, a kaleidoscope of touch and warmth and breath.

And now she was dead.

He read the report again.

Maddy had been at a yoga class that evening and had left alone; it was assumed she'd been attacked shortly afterward. As yet the police were uncertain as to the exact sequence of events. What was certain was that at some point after finishing her class, getting changed, and leaving the center, Maddy Birch had been attacked, most probably raped, beaten, cut, and left for dead.

Elder knew that Robert Framlingham was now based with the Murder Review Unit at Trenchard House; not so many months ago he had been in touch, eager to persuade Elder to join his team of recently retired detectives who were being increasingly used to reexamine cold cases or review investigations that had stalled. As he had with the earlier approach from Nottinghamshire, Elder had politely yet firmly declined.

Framlingham's voice, as ever, was rich and full, unlike the man himself, who was whippet-thin and tall enough to make Elder crane his neck whenever they met.

"Frank, changed your mind, I'll be bound."

"Afraid not," Elder said.

Framlingham chuckled. "Well, if it's about a loan . . ."

"Don't worry, not that."

"Then shoot."

"The DS who was murdered at Crouch Hill, Maddy Birch . . ."

"Not idle curiosity . . ."

"Not really. I knew her. I mean, we worked together. A while back. Lincolnshire."

"Personal, then?"

"If you like."

"What's your interest, Frank? I mean, exactly?"

"I'm not sure. Just wondering who was handling the investigation, how it was going?"

"Not my department, Frank. Not yet. Nothing breaks, they'll bring us in soon enough."

"There's no one I could talk to, just informally?"

Framlingham seemed to hesitate. "Let me have your number again, Frank, I'll get back to you."

When he did, Elder was raking out the ash from the wood-burning stove, prior to setting it for the evening. Not quite dark, the light toward the sea was rimmed with pinkish red. The temperature seemed to have dropped some five degrees.

"I've spoken to the head of the Murder Squad," Framlingham said. "Explained the situation. He gave me the name of one of his DCIs. Shields. Karen Shields. Mean anything to you?"

"Can't say that it does."

"You could do worse than chance your arm, give her a call. Say you've had a word with me first, if you think it'll help. If she thinks you might have something useful to throw into the pot, background, that sort of thing, she might be willing to talk."

"It was a long time ago, Robert."

"Well, you'll know best. But here's her office number anyhow."

Elder found a pen and wrote it on the back of his hand.

"And Frank . . ."

"Yes?"

"You know what I'm going to say, don't you? Anytime you do change your mind . . ."

"Thanks for the number, Robert," Elder said.

Shields could feel things slipping irrevocably away.

Patrick's alibis for the night in question had proved near-perfect. Tina aside, five other witnesses were prepared to swear he was in North Wales and not in London.

Stone wall. Try again.

So far Forensics had given them little or nothing. No skin beneath the victim's fingernails, no saliva, no semen; what resembled a snail's slow trail across her body had proved to be exactly that. The only blood was Birch's own. All the indications were that she had been raped; penetration had certainly taken place. A condom had presumably been used, though one had not been found at or near the scene. Shoe prints and boot prints were too confused, too partial to be of any direct use. Of any possible weapon there was no sign.

The other members of Birch's yoga class had all been interviewed; Birch had chatted with one or two of the students before the session started, a few more once it was over, nothing consequential. She had been among the last to leave. The café in the center had closed at seven and there had been few other people still on the premises, all of them tracked down and spoken to. Occupants of the properties backing the center had been canvassed; appeals had been made for anyone who might have been using the lane or the old railway line as a shortcut or to walk their dogs to come forward.

The caretaker remembered seeing someone, almost certainly Birch, heading off along the lane toward Crouch Hill, the opposite direction to the one she would have taken if she were going directly home. But then Crouch Hill would have quickly led to the Broadway and bars, restaurants, and cafés aplenty, where she could either have been meeting someone by arrangement or meaning to have supper or a drink alone. Except that none of the waiters or bar staff recognized Birch as having been among their customers that evening.

So had she been attacked almost immediately after leaving the center — risky, with others still presumably within earshot — or had she, indeed, walked down to the Broadway and later returned by the same route? And was her attacker some stalker, as yet unknown, someone waiting for her in the shadows, waiting for his chance? Or had it been a random act, Birch's misfortune to be in the wrong place at the wrong time?

Too many questions still unanswered.

"Phone, ma'am," said one of the office staff, interrupting her train of thought. "For you."

"Who is it?"

"A Frank Elder? He's called several times before. Something about Maddy Birch, apparently."

Shields sighed. It was way past seven already. Staff pulling in overtime. What she wanted was to go home, open a bottle of red, and drink the first glass while she soaked in a warm bath.

"Okay."

She perched on the end of a desk, one foot resting on the seat of a chair. Across the room she could see Lee Furness slowly scrolling through a list of names on the computer.

"Hello, this is DCI Shields."

"Frank Elder."

"I believe you've got some information about Maddy Birch."

"Not information exactly."

"What then?"

"I worked with her. Maddy. In Lincolnshire."

"How long ago?"

A pause. "Eighty-seven, eighty-eight."

"And you were what? Close? Close colleagues? What?"

"Close, I don't know. Not really. We worked together, that's all. I was just wondering how things were going. The investigation."

"How things are going? What do you think this is? *Crime Watch*?"

"I'm sorry, I was given your name . . ."

"Look, maybe you should talk to the press office. If anyone. Just hold on and I'll get you transferred."

"No, it's okay. It doesn't matter. I'm sorry to have taken your time."

Shields heard a click as the phone was replaced.

Just about the last thing she needed, some old geezer with too much time on his hands.

Chapter 13

"Bloody shame," Linda Mills had said, when she heard of Birch's death.

"Shocking," Trevor Ashley agreed.

"Now we'll never get the chance to talk to her again."

Ashley looked at her sharply, but held his tongue.

Things moved slowly on. It was the second week of December, some eight weeks since the enquiry into the Grant shooting had opened; three, give or take, since Maddy Birch's body had been found off Crouch Hill.

Despite the often open hostility of many of those who were interviewed, the enquiry had kept, doggedly, to the rails. Mills, frustrated by their lack of progress, had become grimmer and more short-tempered even as her superior seemed to become more avuncular and benign. But for all of their probing, questioning, and reconstructing, after almost two months there was no proof of any wrongdoing, no reprimand, no charge.

That Grant was a major villain was beyond doubt, the presumption that he was close to fleeing the country well-founded, as was the supposition that he would be armed. The logistics of the raid left something to be desired and a recommendation to review planning procedures would be attached as a codicil to the final report. At base, however, the facts spoke for themselves: Grant had fatally wounded one officer and if Mallory had not acted as he had, there was every reason to believe Grant would have killed another.

End of story.

Wrap it up, dot the i's and cross the t's, sign your name, and leave.

Honor satisfied and justice seen to be done.

When it came down to it, whatever her lingering doubts, Linda Mills would be glad to shake the dust of London off her feet. Ashley had warned her what it would be like, that she would feel isolated and embattled and regarded as the enemy, and he'd been right. The experience, though, had been something she wanted, something to add to her profile, broaden her CV.

"I owe you both a vote of thanks," the assistant commissioner said in his office. "A difficult task professionally executed."

"I owe you a slap-up dinner," Ashley said later, broad grin on his face. "Prawn cocktail, steak and chips, Black Forest gateaux, the whole bit."

"You owe me," Mills told him, "a sight more than that."

The day after the final report had been delivered to the printer, the day before the bound copy was delivered to the assistant commissioner, she had been sitting on the low steps outside the Portakabin that had remained their temporary home, smoking a longed-for cigarette.

She had scarcely heard Mallory as he crossed the car park, light of foot, only glancing up at the last moment and dropping her cigarette hastily, like a fourth-former caught behind the bike sheds.

"Don't worry," Mallory said. "Your secret's safe with me."

As she stood up, Mills squashed the smoldering butt beneath her foot.

"We're all guilty of something, big or small," Mallory said. "Wouldn't be human, else." The smile lingered in his eyes. "Here," he said, taking a packet of Benson and Hedges from the side pocket of his blazer. Blue blazer and brown trousers. Highly polished shoes. "Have one of mine."

"No, thank you, sir."

Mallory shrugged and produced a lighter. "I was hoping I might bump into you," he said, the smoke drifting toward Mills's face.

"Sir?"

"Before you shut up shop and turn tail for Hatfield . . ."

"Hertford, sir. It's Hertford, actually."

"Hartford, Hatfield, Hitchin — all the same. Penny-ante little market towns with scarce a pot to piss in. Low-grade drug dealing and a handful of public order offenses of a weekend the best you can hope for."

Mills nodded noncommittally.

"Always the worry," Mallory said, "let one of your kind out of the box and you never know which way they'll jump. Chancy, that. Like letting off a firework in the middle of the bonfire, Guy Fawkes Night. Any bloody thing could happen." Almost imperceptibly, he moved closer toward her. "Someone could even get burned."

For a moment, maybe more, his eyes

bore into her, before, with a deft smile, he stepped away.

"But you now," he said, "no need to worry by all accounts. Everything by the rules. Light the blue touch paper and stand well clear."

"You've seen the report," Mills said, challenging.

"Place like this, difficult to keep things under wraps."

"But you have seen it. A copy at least."

"You think so?"

She knew it. He'd read it, relished it, and relaxed. Exonerated in Times New Roman, double-spaced. Her signature at the bottom.

"You may think," Mallory said, "I owe you a favor."

"Not at all, sir. We did our job, that's all. Just like you said. And I was only the junior officer, after all."

"Junior, maybe, but always pushing hardest, eager for the truth. Gave poor Maddy Birch a rough ride, from what I hear. Had her up against the ropes. To mix a metaphor or two. Still, no gain having your card marked by a fool, and you're no fool."

A wink and a smile and he was on his way, leaving Mills wondering if there wasn't something crucial that they'd missed.

"Cocky bastard," Ashley said when she told him. "Not enough to be ahead of the game, he has to let you know."

"Why me, though? Why not you? You're in charge."

Ashley laughed. "Mallory's way of thinking, not worth getting out of bed to put one over on old jossers like me. But you. You're sharp, bright, on the way up. A woman, too. If he can intimidate you a little, then he will."

"I don't see what he stands to gain."

"Right now? Aside from pumping up his vanity? Control. Leverage, sometime in the future. Who knows?"

She looked at him keenly. "You think we've let him get away with something, don't you?"

Ashley shrugged. "This time, I honestly don't know. But I did my time in the Met, before opting for a quieter life. Coppers like Mallory, old school, they've been getting away with stuff for years. Big, small, more often than not just to prove they can. It's what gives them a buzz."

Thinking about the way Mallory had materialized almost silently alongside her and the sly superiority of his smile, Mills shuddered as if someone had just stepped close to the corners of her grave.

Chapter 14

It bit into him, like a tick that had infiltrated beneath his skin. No matter where he went, what he did. The routines with which he'd bolstered up his life since moving west no longer seemed enough. Each day he made a point of listening to the radio, scouring the papers for news.

On page two of the *Telegraph*, mid-December, something caught his eye: the investigation into two deaths in a police raid carried out a little over two months before. The paper's crime correspondent, claiming to have seen a leaked copy of the report, forecast a positive outcome to the official enquiry carried out by Superintendent Trevor Ashley and officers from the Hertfordshire force.

Alongside the article, two columns wide, was a photograph of a smiling Detective Superintendent George Mallory, taken outside the Old Bailey, with his DCI,

Maurice Repton, standing several paces behind, almost squeezed out of the frame. At the time, readers were reminded, Mallory's commanding officer had been quick to attest to the professionalism with which the raid had been planned and carried out. A further paragraph referred to the tragic death of Detective Constable Paul Draper, a small head-and-shoulder shot rendering him almost impossibly young. *If it had not been for Superintendent Mallory's quick thinking and resolute action, more lives might have been lost.*

Two pages on, a single paragraph near the foot of the page attested to the fact that the investigation into the death of Detective Sergeant Maddy Birch was still ongoing and that no arrests had so far been made.

Let it alone, Frank, he told himself. *Let it be.*

After yet another restless night he rose early, made coffee, walked down to the coast path to clear his head, rang Robert Framlingham, and caught the London train.

Paddington Station was thick with travelers, the natural hubbub and bustle overlaid with the saccharine wail of poorly amplified voices wishing them all a merry little Christmas. As Elder crossed the lobby, a *Big Issue* seller with tinsel in his hair and two extravagant sprigs of mistletoe tied to either side of his head like horns lurched toward him, puckering up rouged lips.

The underground platform was dangerously crowded — delays on the District, Circle, and Bakerloo lines — and, when it arrived, the first train was nearly impossible to board. At Oxford Circus there was a five-minute queue to get out of the station.

In daylight, the skeletal snowflakes and reindeer that hung high above the street looked ugly and incomplete. Shop windows burgeoned with tawdry and expensive imprecations to buy, and Elder, hating it, hating every bit of it, felt nonetheless guilty that he had neither bought a present for Katherine nor thought of one; had, in fact, bought nothing for anyone.

The restaurant was on one of the narrow streets that ran between Regent Street and Great Portland Street, home, for the most part, to small clothing wholesalers, their windows sprayed with fake snow. A sign on the door wished Elder a Merry Christmas in Italian, and inside, red and green streamers looped cheerily along the walls.

Framlingham was already seated at a corner table, tucking into an antipasto of tuna and fagiolini. He was wearing a tweed suit that reminded Elder of damp heather, a cream shirt, and a mustard tie.

Levering his tall frame out of his chair, the chief superintendent held out his hand. "Frank, how long?"

"Seven years, eight?"

"And since you and I were the scourge of every bully boy and malefactor in Shepherd's Bush?"

Elder smiled. "Thirteen or so."

A waiter took his coat and pulled out his chair.

When Elder had first moved down to London with Joanne, Robert Framlingham had been his immediate superior. Now, after one or two high-profile successes, his profile as head of the Murder Review Unit was growing. He had a house in Chiswick that he'd had the foresight to buy before the boom, and a cottage in Dorset, near the coast. Sailing was his passion.

There was a wife whom Elder had met no more than once or twice; three children, the youngest still at university, the others out in the world, paying back, no doubt, their student loans.

"You and Joanne," Framlingham said once they'd settled. "I was sorry to hear things didn't work out."

Elder shrugged.

"Still see much of her?"

"Not a lot."

"And the girl — Katherine, is it? — Frank, that was a terrible business. Nothing worse." He broke off a piece of bread and wiped it around his plate. "Coping, is she?"

"I'm not sure."

"And you?"

Elder said nothing.

Framlingham leaned forward. "All this kowtowing to civilized values and decency is all very well, but, cases like that, left to me, the bastard would've been given a taste of his own medicine and then sent for the long drop off some nice corded rope."

The waiter, a sprig of holly pinned to his red vest, had reappeared, smiling, at the table.

Oil ran down between Framlingham's fingers. "Calves' liver's good, Frank. Sage and butter, nice and simple."

Elder nodded, looked quickly down the menu, and ordered lamb cutlets with rosemary, sautéed potatoes, and spinach.

"You'll have some wine, Frank? Red or white?"

"Red?"

Framlingham ordered a bottle of Da Luca Primitivo and some mineral water, and for ten or so minutes they allowed themselves to gossip about half-remembered colleagues. Framlingham's liver leaked blood, pink across the plate.

"What I have to wonder, Frank, this current business, Maddy Birch, why it matters so much? To you, I mean."

"I've told you, we worked together."

"Come on, Frank, it's got to be more than that."

Elder shook his head. "I knew her, liked her. That was all."

Framlingham poured more wine. "More than fifteen years ago. Around the time Katherine was born, a little after? You were tupping her, Frank, no great disgrace. Times like that, it happens. Feeling a little trapped, I shouldn't wonder. You looked around and there she was. Young, available I daresay."

"It wasn't like that."

Framlingham laughed. "For Christ's sake, Frank, spare us the holier-than-thou. We've all been there. If we're lucky, seen it slip between the sheets and out of

160

sight, no one any the wiser."

Elder bit into a piece of lamb. Well-done was what he'd asked for and well-done was what he'd got.

"Admit it, Frank. You had her. Once, twice, half a hundred times. That doesn't matter."

"No."

Framlingham read the seriousness in his face.

"It's worse then. You didn't have her, Frank. Just wanted to. Fancied her and most likely she fancied you. But somehow you let her get stuck inside your head. She was the one you pictured when you were screwing your wife or jerking off in the shower."

Elder reached for the bottle and refilled his glass. "She's dead and I want to know why. I want whoever was responsible to be caught. Is that so wrong?"

"No, it's not wrong."

"Then can you help?"

"Can *you*, that's the thing." Framlingham steepled his fingers. "Come on, Frank, you'd not have come up to see me if you'd wanted nothing more than a fair-to-middling lunch, a few questions asked and maybe answered. You might not want to sign back on full-time, but you'd not mind a bite at this. Am I right?"

"I suppose so."

"Is that a yes?"

"All right. Yes."

"It'll not be easy, Frank, not this one. It's not just that she's a woman, Frank, Detective Chief Inspector Karen Shields, enough of them in high places nowadays for that scarcely to be an issue. But into the bargain she's black." He set down his glass. "Politics, Frank. On the one hand we're instigating anti-racist policies left, right, and center, practically dragging ethnic minorities off the streets and begging them into uniform, and at the same time, we'll spend half a million pounds to prove some member of the Black Police Association has been fiddling his expenses. It beggars bloody belief."

"And because of this," Elder said, "Karen Shields gets treated with kid gloves."

Framlingham ordered coffee, poured the last of the wine.

"This investigation, Homicide gave it everything. She was one of ours, after all. Overtime, technical support staff, everything. Then, when there was no early breakthrough, things were scaled down. You know the way it goes. Normally, by now, some of my lot would be moving in, putting the whole thing under review. Starting from scratch if need be."

"And that's not happening?"

"Not yet. Could be someone's frightened if she's knocked off the case, Shields will start waving the race card, claiming discrimination."

"And would she?"

"I don't think so. Not from what little I know of her, but . . ." Framlingham waved a hand. "I daresay she's got pressures of her own. When it comes down to it, who's to say?"

"You think you will get called in though? Whatever happens?"

"Unless there's a result, yes."

Elder sat back in his chair.

Glancing at the bill the waiter had quietly left, Framlingham took out one of his credit cards and dropped it on the table. "Go home, Frank, relax. It's nearly Christmas. I'll be in touch."

Chapter 15

Karen Shields began her day at five-thirty-five with a sore throat, a thick head, and a brace of Paracetamol. Just what she needed, coming down with some bug the morning she had to explain to her superior why it was that after almost four weeks, not only had no arrests been made, the only serious suspect they'd had had come up pure as the driven snow. She could already see the look on her boss's face as he offered her a Kleenex for her cold and shuffled her aside.

Not only was Birch's ex-husband Terry no longer a viable suspect, but any link with the Hackney murder now seemed more tenuous than before. A second attack, not fatal, but similar, had been carried out on a woman jogging in parkland no more than two miles away from the first incident, and two men had been arrested for both crimes and were being questioned. No links with Birch's death had yet come to light.

In the kitchen Shields made coffee in a stove-top pot and slipped bread into the toaster. Everyone who'd been close to Maddy Birch in any way in recent years, from a cousin who lived in Esher to the roofer she'd haphazardly dated over a four-month period, had been interviewed, in some cases twice, and, where necessary, alibis had been checked.

"One thing you'd have to say about her," Shields's sergeant, Mike Ramsden, had observed, "she had a taste for blokes who worked with their hands."

"Liked a bit of rough," Lee Furness had said, the look on Shields's face, remembering how Birch had been found, stopping him like a slap.

It nagged at her regardless: the possibility that the killer had been someone with whom Birch had been involved, someone of whose identity they were still unaware.

She had gone back to Birch's friend Vanessa Taylor, probing for some forgotten reference, some chance remark; she'd talked to other officers with whom Birch had shared the occasional confidence and come up blank. Every square inch of where

Birch had lived had been pored over, every name jotted down, every number traced.

Nothing. No one.

Shields spread butter on her toast.

Could there have been someone nevertheless?

Someone who, as Birch had feared, had taken to following her, watching her, slipping, unseen, into the security of her home?

More information, that was what Shields wanted, and she couldn't see where it might come from. If there had been a laptop, or even an e-mail address, they might have found hits on some site or other that would lay open some secret predilection. Cross-dressing, water sports, rubber — it wasn't beyond the edge of possibility that Furness had been right, Birch had liked an element of pain, loss of control, a bit of rough . . .

Outside it was still dark, the cars moving evenly along Essex Road behind dipped headlights. Another half hour or so before the traffic would start to snarl up, north toward Commercial Road, south to the Angel.

The roofer, Kennet, when they brought him in, had been politeness itself, due deference in his manner and calluses on his

166

hands. In all the time he'd been seeing Birch, he doubted if they'd met more than once or twice a week. "You know how it is," he'd said, smiling at Shields open-faced. "Shift work. Overtime."

Could she imagine him . . . ? She'd been doing the job long enough to be able to imagine anyone doing anything.

She'd allowed the coffee to bubble for too long and it tasted slightly burnt. Opening the fridge, she took out some jam for her second piece of toast. Maybe she should be having porridge these mornings? Shredded Wheat? Start snarfing down vitamins and those seeds she kept reading about. Linseed? Sesame?

If Birch had been right and she was being stalked, Shields realized it need not have been anyone she knew, but someone she had come into contact with accidentally and who had become somehow infatuated. Shit, it could have been anyone. Possible suspects on the Sex Offenders Register were still being checked, but with nothing from Forensics to help narrow the field, chances were slim. The same with information from National Records, the Holmes2 computer. Shields certainly wasn't holding her breath.

Six o'clock and she switched on the

radio for the news. Another American soldier ambushed in Iraq, a few more Palestinian children killed. With only six more shopping days to Christmas, retailers were cautiously optimistic of a record year. Shields had bought presents for her family in Jamaica, wrapped them up but not actually taken them to the post office. They would arrive late, of course. There was still her father to think of and nieces and nephews by the score. Her first few Christmas cards stood on the shelf beside the stereo, as yet unopened. Last year she had managed to sign and send her own just before New Year's.

Come and spend Christmas Day with us, said her brother in West Bromwich, her baby sister in Stockwell. The children would love to see you, wrote her other sister from Southend.

She didn't know if she could take so much turkey, so much screaming, so much apparent happiness. Pouring the last of the coffee, she picked up her cup and went back into the bedroom to finish getting dressed.

Chapter 16

Mindful of the season, and remembering Katherine sitting open to the elements on a city-center bench, Elder bought her a double-weight wool scarf, long enough to wind around her neck more than once and then tuck snugly down. When she had first visited him in Cornwall, almost two years before, he had pointed out Eagle's Nest, the house where the artist Patrick Heron had lived, which dominated the landscape where Elder had then been staying; now he bought her a slim book with reproductions of the paintings Heron had made of the shrubs and flowers in his granite-bordered garden. He added a box of dark Belgian chocolates and, at the last minute, a pair of blue Polartec gloves, wrapped them up, and sent them, along with a card, to Nottingham, first-class.

Several days later, uncertain, he bought a card for Joanne, simple, nothing fancy, quickly wrote *Happy Christmas, Love Frank,* sealed it, and slipped it into an already crowded mailbox.

That was it.

He had cousins somewhere, and when he had lived in London and later in Nottingham they had exchanged greetings at Christmas and, sporadically, on birthdays, but since his move west, they had lost touch.

Instead of a turkey, he ordered a prime leg of lamb from the butcher's on Fore Street and, having grown up in the days when most shops had closed for several days over the holiday, stocked up on vegetables and milk and bread. For some minutes he lingered over a small Christmas pudding before settling for a pack of mince pies and a carton of double cream.

The last weekend before Christmas, he drove up-country and watched Plymouth Argyle outmaneuver and outplay Notts County by three goals to none. It was his first live match in years and was watched in a mixture of blinding sunshine and driving rain, County willing and eager but lacking purpose or plan, the phrase "headless chickens" coming easily to mind.

On Christmas Day, he put the lamb in the oven on low and set out for a walk that would take him almost to the opposite coast, certainly well within sight of St. Michael's Mount, before turning back. Despite forecasts of heavy rain and high winds, he was rewarded with clear skies and no more than a single shower. A long, slow bath and a glass of whiskey on his return and lamb that fell away from the bone at a glance.

Joanne's card, as spare and functional as his own, stood on the kitchen shelf between a large jar of Branston pickle and a bottle of HP sauce. Though he'd willed himself, without success, not to listen for the mail van on the lane, persuaded himself, as best he could, there was no likelihood that she would send him anything, the absence of an envelope bearing Katherine's writing, a card with her name, cast a pall, longer and deeper, over each and every day.

For Elder, as for Karen Shields, the new year started early, a gray Monday at the nub end of December, at the north London headquarters of Homicide West.

Elder was in the room when Shields arrived, together with a tall man wearing a Barbour jacket and twill trousers, whom she recognized as Robert Framlingham,

171

head of the Murder Review Unit.

"Karen," Framlingham said, extending his hand. "Good to meet you at last."

So that was the way it was going to be. She was surprised it had taken this long.

Introduced, she shook hands with Elder. His grip was dry and strong and no more lingering than her own.

"The Maddy Birch case," Framlingham said. "I've asked Frank here to take a look, see if he can't lend a hand."

Elder was dressed in a dark suit that had seen somewhat better days, a pale blue shirt and an inoffensive tie, and shoes that, though recently shined, were as creased as the lines around his eyes. Shields wondered how he had got the scar on his face.

"You're shunting me aside," Shields said.

"Not at all," Framlingham replied. "That's not the way we work at all."

"Oh?"

"No. Frank will sit down with you and your team, review the progress in the investigation so far . . ."

"Mark my card."

"Not in any way. What Frank will do, in full consultation with you, is try to point up areas which will open up the enquiry to new ground."

"But it's still my investigation?"

"You are the lead officer, yes."

"In charge."

"Absolutely."

Bullshit, Shields thought. Bullshit.

"Frank here knew Maddy Birch," Framlingham said. "Worked with her in Lincoln."

Shields looked across at Elder, his face giving nothing away.

"Well," Framlingham said cheerily, "the sooner you and Frank sit down and talk, the better."

After raising an imaginary glass, he walked away.

"You want to get some coffee?" Shields asked. "Talk things through."

"What I'd like to do," Elder said, "is read through the log, the pathologist's report. Familiarize myself with what's been done. Tapes of any interviews. And then I'd like to drive out to where she was killed. Look around. We can talk after that."

Shields looked at him through narrowed eyes. "Whatever you say."

"I'm sorry," Elder said.

"No. No, you're not."

DS Sheridan was the office manager: cheery, somewhat portly, still possessed of a Potteries accent, which flourished after standing with the home supporters at the Britannia Stadium, which he did most Saturdays Stoke City were at home.

"Call me Sherry, everyone else does."

Elder explained what he needed and found himself set up with a corner desk, a tape player with headphones, a rackety but still functioning PC, and, until the files began arriving in profusion, plenty of elbow room.

Shutting out the rise and fall of background noise as well as he could, Elder read and listened and read some more, only stopping when his vision blurred and his head began to throb. How much longer he thought he could ignore the fact that he needed glasses was between him and his self-esteem.

Toward the end of the morning, Mike Ramsden came over and introduced himself, the pair of them discovering a few acquaintances in the Met in common.

"Fancy a bite in the canteen?" Ramsden said.

"Later in the week definitely," Elder said. "Right now, I'd better push on."

Ramsden gave Elder a "suit yourself" look and moved away. How to win friends and influence people, Elder thought; second time today. By four-thirty, he realized he had read the same page on the screen three times without taking in more than a few words.

One of Elder's main concerns about coming up to London had been where he would stay and what it would cost; but Framlingham had assured him something would be arranged and, on arrival, had handed him a cell phone and two sets of keys: one to a no-longer-new maroon Vauxhall Astra and the other to a flat in a short block near the top of Hendon Lane, near Finchley Central Station.

The car ran better than its looks suggested it might; the flat, presumably maintained as a safe house for the witness protection program and such, was well equipped, recently cleaned, and totally anonymous. Kitchen, living room, bathroom, bedroom. Radio in the kitchen; TV and VCR in the living room. With the windows closed it was almost possible to shut out the sound of traffic from the nearby North Circular Road. There were butter and a pint of milk in the fridge, a sliced loaf in its wrapping, biscuits, a jar of instant coffee, a packet of PG Tips, and some strawberry jam.

Elder walked past the tube station to

Ballards Lane and bought a hearty chunk of cheddar cheese, a packet of bacon, eggs, oranges and bananas, a bottle of Jameson, and some dark Nicaraguan ground coffee. Not all in the same shop.

When she had stayed with him in Cornwall, Katherine had teased him about the way in which, having drunk nothing but tea for years, he had become a coffee snob. Well, he had reasoned, there were worse things to be snobbish about.

Back at the flat, he spooned coffee into a plain white china jug, and, while it was standing, cracked the seal on the Jameson and poured himself a small glass. Reading through the files, he could see why Maddy Birch's former husband, Terry Patrick, had seemed an almost irresistible suspect and could read Karen Shields's anger and disappointment between the lines.

Cross-checking the records of the Sex Offenders Register and the National Criminal Intelligence Service, the computer had flagged some twenty names, all but three of whom had so far been checked and eliminated. Elder wondered how many of these warranted looking at again.

As for the forensics, he couldn't think of many cases he'd worked where the evidence amounted to so little. No blood save for the victim's own. No stray hair, no shred of skin. It was hard to believe: so hard it had to be worth persuading Forensic Services to look again, reexamine the clothes and the body.

And he wanted to talk to — who was it? — sliding his glass to one side, he fumbled through his notes — Vanessa Taylor, Birch's best friend. Maybe this guy, as well. The roofer. Kensit? Kendrick? Kennet. Came over as so reasonable on the tape, talking about the times Maddy had stood him up at the last moment, evenings canceled whenever she had been thrown some unexpected overtime. Like a south London boy who'd somewhere picked up a few lessons in gender and the negotiation of personal space. Elder slipped the headphones free. Maybe Kennet had never been that involved, not enough to really care. Maybe he was just a nice bloke. There were still some around.

Stretching, Elder walked to the window. The taillights of vehicles sparkled and blurred as they moved in slow procession toward Finchley Lane, the Great North Way, the M1. Men and women, mostly men, hurried home from the station, backs bowed, heads bent into the wind. Here and there, umbrellas sprouted; spots of rain against the glass. He should phone Joanne and tell her where he was, let her have this number just in case. In case of what?

Dad, I'm never going to be like I was before.

On impulse, he called Maureen Prior first.

He and Prior had worked closely together for three years in Nottinghamshire, right up to the time of his retirement, and then again last year, when Katherine had been abducted. As an officer, she was efficient and perceptive, her judgment fair but unyielding. At work, she was intolerant of fools, timeservers, anyone who stepped outside the line. But Elder knew next to nothing about her as a person, as a woman. She had never divulged anything about her private life, and all of the speculation that usually arose around unmarried women officers had simply evaporated. Elder knew where she lived and nothing more; he had never been invited past the front door.

"I thought you'd turned your back on all that," Prior said, when he outlined what he was doing in London.

"So I had."

"But this was different?"

"Something like that."

"I'd like to think you'd do the same for

178

me, Frank, if the circumstances were the same."

"What's that?"

"Saddle up that white horse of yours and ride up out of the west."

"Bollocks, Maureen."

She laughed, a low chuckle. "Hope you'll be all right, Frank. Working with a woman."

"Shouldn't I be?"

"Depends."

"I worked with you."

She laughed again, more open this time. "That was easy, Frank. You scarcely thought of me as a woman at all."

Joanne, when he spoke to her, was taciturn, distracted, her mind elsewhere.

"How's Katherine?"

"Oh, you know, much the same."

"I don't suppose she's there?"

He could hear voices, muffled, Joanne with her hand, he imagined, not quite covering the phone.

"No, Frank, I'm sorry, no."

Which, in the circumstances, probably meant yes. Joanne currying favor. He didn't push it.

They exchanged a few words about Christmas, Joanne's plans for New Year's

Eve, and that was that. As soon as the call was over, suddenly hungry, Elder made himself bacon and eggs, slices of soft white bread buttered and folded over, more coffee. Switching on the radio, he worked his way through the dials: a low rumble from down near the bootstraps which the DJ informed him came from the late, great Johnny Cash; something languidly classical; someone with a faint Scottish accent explaining the intricacies of European Union budgeting; fevered commentary on Coventry versus West Ham; a jolt of violent, acerbic sound, like the contents of an old-fashioned kitchen being demolished around someone playing electric guitar — the thrash metal he'd read about somewhere?

Opting for the orchestral concert, he angled his legs around on the couch. Birch's killer: had she known him, or had she been taken by surprise? Opening the envelope, he looked at the photographs of the wounds. Vicious and deep. Vicious, and yet whoever had delivered them had retained a degree of control, of calm; calm enough not to have left any apparent clues, to have taken scrupulous care. Controlled anger: anger and control.

Training, then?

Elder closed his eyes.

Army? SAS?

Under the wash of music, he drifted off.

All that coffee, he thought, waking fifteen minutes later to the sound of the announcer's voice and bright applause, *how could I fall asleep?*

He tried the TV. On one channel, a disparate group of men and women were clambering their way, laboriously, through the jungle; on another, the same people, or others that looked just like them, were sitting around on couches, not speaking, doing nothing at all. So easy to switch off.

The volume of traffic had eased. High up where he was, he could see the strange, muted glow thrown up by the city, a false, unchanging day for night. Back down in Cornwall the sky would be close to black and scored through with stars, Cassiopeia, Pegasus, the Plough.

He pictured Birch walking — running? — through a dark space he had not yet seen, except in photographs. The movement of branches in the wind. Foxes following a trail across back gardens; the cry, unworldly, of cats in heat. Clouds across the moon.

Something moving in the thickets of

shrub and bush down by the old railway line.

A voice.

Did he call out?

Maddy. Her name.

Trying to conjure her face as she turned toward the sound, Elder could only see her eyes picked out green in the shadow of the cathedral light, her mouth broadening into a smile and then closing around his in a kiss.

You didn't have her, Frank. Just wanted to. But you let her get stuck inside your head.

Freeing the cord from the hook around which it had been looped, Elder lowered the blind. Another small whiskey before turning in. The sheets unwelcoming and cold. After catnapping as he had, he thought it would be hard to get to sleep, but not so. A few small shifts of position and the next thing he knew he was stretching awake by habit, the hands on his watch showing six o'clock.

Chapter 17

Shaded green, the narrow swath of designated parkland stretched east to west across page twenty-nine in the *London A to Z*, Highgate to Stroud Green. The best approach to the particular section he wanted was unclear from the map, and Elder drove into a crescent off the main road and parked between a Dumpster and a long-abandoned Nissan with its windows smashed and the engine half removed. From there, following a sign, he walked along a narrow alley between houses, bypassing both a discarded fridge and a dismembered supermarket cart, before finding himself on a track leading to a two-story wooden building he assumed to be the community center.

Broadening out, the path led toward a children's nursery on the right, a five-a-side pitch-and-play center farther along; a fence, broken down in several places, separated it from the slope, tangled and over-grown, that angled steeply toward the muddy track below.

Elder stood quite still, tuning out, as best he could, the faint morning discord from the nearby flats, the traffic sounds from either side. Some twenty meters off, a female blackbird scuffled through dry leaves before flying away into the far trees. The sky was a watery blue, shaded over, here and there, with gray. Elder could see his breath, off-white, on the air.

She had walked here, Maddy; stopped for a moment, alerted by a sound.

Or, jogging, had she paused and bent forward, hands on hips, catching her breath?

Elder turned through a slow circle: how close, even at night, could someone get without being heard or seen?

In his imagination, he saw a shadow stepping silently out of the dark.

Why didn't Maddy run? And if she did, why, fit and strong as she was, did she not get away?

Because she knew him, surely.

Close. Her breath upon his face. Laughing, as they stumbled out from the doorway onto the cobbled street. Did she take his hand or slip her arm through his?

Carefully, Elder made his way down toward the old railway track, while above him, whistling cheerfully, a man pushed a stroller containing a well-wrapped toddler toward the nursery. Walking briskly, a woman appeared with her dog and then, as quickly, disappeared. From the reports he had read, the diagrams, Birch had been attacked above and then been pushed or fallen, the last, the fatal blows most likely delivered near where he now stood.

In all probability, her assailant had continued to stab her after she was dead. No weapon found. Remembering the severity and extent of the wounds, Elder saw him wiping the excess of blood off on the grass, the ground.

How long had it taken?

How long?

Longer, possibly, to have cleared away all telltale traces than to have committed the crime itself.

How long had it been before someone else had come along, stopped perhaps, thinking he had heard something, and looked down, but, seeing nothing, continued on his way?

And the murderer, which way had he gone?

To the east, the track ran on below

Crouch Hill and almost all the way to Finsbury Park, a myriad of small side roads with easy access leading off on either side; westward, it opened out onto Shepherd's Hill, adjacent to the main road leading north toward the A1 and the motorway. A car conveniently parked. Light traffic flow. Birch's killer could have been tucked in by midnight, leaving her body to the elements, the foxes and the rodents, small insects, crows.

Elder saw again the postmortem photographs of her face, the wounds, open, not quite scabbed over, to her torso and along the insides of her arms.

Climbing back up, he turned up the collar of his coat against the freshness of the wind; mud clung to the cuffs of his pants, the soles of his shoes.

Back in the street where he had parked, a pair of thirteen-year-olds were considering the possibility of liberating the Astra's radio; seeing Elder approach, they spat thoughtfully at the ground and strolled, hands in pockets, nonchalantly away.

Off duty, Taylor was wearing a denim skirt and black woolen tights, calf-length reddish leather boots, and a denim jacket over a high-necked purple sweater that seemed to have shrunk in the wash. Her dark hair was curly and closely framed her face; her lipstick, newly applied, was a vivid shade of red.

The café where she had suggested meeting was close to the Holmes Road police station. Most of the tables were taken and the buzz of conversation and the occasional hiss of the coffee machine were underscored by music, Middle Eastern, Elder thought, coming from a radio cassette player on the counter.

Elder made his way to where Taylor was sitting and introduced himself.

"Managed to pick me out okay, then?" she said with a grin.

Most of the other customers either had small children clamoring around them or were well above retirement age.

The waiter appeared at Elder's elbow almost as soon as he'd sat down, and he asked for an espresso and a glass of water. Taylor was tucking into a wedge of sticky straw-colored pastry and drinking what looked like Coke.

"So what do I call you?" Taylor asked.

"Frank?"

"No rank or anything?"

"Not anymore."

Taylor looked at him appraisingly. "And they've dragged you out of retirement to help out?"

"Something like that."

"Long as the bastard gets caught."

"Yes."

"Well, whatever I can do." Her pastry not quite finished, she pushed her plate aside with an air of martyrdom.

"I knew Maddy a little back in Lincoln," Elder said. "But that was a long time ago. You can probably give me a better picture of what she was like than anyone."

"Where do you want me to start?"

"Wherever you like."

For the next fifteen minutes, Elder listened, prompting Taylor occasionally, but in the main content to sit and take occasional sips from his espresso while she talked.

"Tell me a bit more about this Kennet," Elder said, when she'd finished. "Maddy seems to have gone out with him for quite a while."

"I don't know if there's a lot more to say. I met him a few times, seemed nice enough. Good-looking bloke, I'll give him that. Bit cocky, maybe." She smiled. "Not as bad as some."

"She liked him though?"

"I suppose so, yes. She'd never have gone with him otherwise." Taylor reached over and speared a piece of pastry with her fork. "To be honest, I think it was the sex as much as anything. I don't mean it was so great, not according to Maddy anyway; nothing earth-shattering, not like Meg Ryan in that film, but, well, she'd not been with anyone in ages and I suppose . . ." she laughed. "Well, I suppose it made it a bit of a change. Made her feel good about herself, you know?"

Elder thought he might.

"And, from what you say, it just petered out?"

"In a manner of speaking." There was a broad grin on Taylor's face.

"You know how Kennet felt about that?"

"He was fine about it, far as I know. No big scene or anything." She shrugged. "I don't think it was such a deal for either of them, not really. Not true love, exactly, you know what I mean?"

Elder signaled the waiter for another espresso. "These fears of Maddy's, that she was being watched. Spied on. You think they were real?"

Taylor smiled. "Or was she just paranoid like the rest of us?"

"If you like."

"No, I don't think so. Not Maddy. I mean, it might have got a bit exaggerated inside her head, but no, there was something behind it, I'm sure."

"According to what you said, it all started round about the time of the Grant business."

"More or less, yes. I suppose it did."

"This officer who was killed, Draper . . ."

"Paul, yes."

"Maddy was there when he was shot, in the same room . . ."

"Standing right next to him, close as I am to you now." She leaned in to the table, as if to make her point.

"It must have shaken her up pretty badly."

"It did, you could tell. Draper's wife and little boy, she was upset about them too. Went round to see them quite a few times."

"And she didn't talk much about it, other than that? It didn't seem to be preying on her mind?"

"No. Not really, no. Though she did mention it, must have been the last time I saw her, last time we went out together, at least. About the enquiry, you know, into the shooting."

"What exactly did she say?"

"Just they'd given her a pretty tough

time, sounded like. Questions, you know. Maddy thought they were going to have her in again."

Elder made a mental note to check whether that had been the case. He should read the report of the enquiry, certainly, maybe go and talk to the investigating officers.

His espresso arrived, the waiter smiling at Taylor, making conversation.

Elder eased back his chair and loosened his tie. "The night Maddy was killed, d'you think she could have been meeting someone?"

Taylor chewed on a strand of hair that had found its way into the corner of her mouth. "I don't know who. And, besides, why there?"

"Perhaps it was convenient. Possibly, whoever it was, they didn't want to be seen."

"Married, you mean?"

"Either that or someone she worked with."

"No," Taylor said. "No way."

"Why ever not?"

"It's something she was always hot on. God! She slagged me off for it enough times. Messing around on your own doorstep. Only leads to grief, she said.

Course . . ." Looking at Elder now. ". . . how far that was based on personal experience, I've no idea. But she was dead right anyway." Taylor treated Elder to a salacious grin. "Disaster every time. And besides, if it was serious, she'd have said something. A little hint, something. She wouldn't have kept it to herself."

"She seems to have played her cards pretty close to her chest where her ex-husband was concerned."

"That's different, though, isn't it?"

"Is it?"

"Yes. You know, husbands, wives, someone you're trying to pretend never existed." Taylor looked at her watch. "I'm due back."

"Okay." Elder pushed back his chair as she got to her feet. "If you think of anything else . . ."

"I'll call you," she said.

He remembered the number of his cell phone at the third attempt and she wrote it down. She glanced back through the window from the street, red mouth and dark hair, a quick smile and then gone.

Elder sat a few moments longer, collecting his thoughts, before heading toward the station.

Chapter 18

Karen Shields was less than happy. Ferreting for a lost spoon that morning, she'd discovered a patch of damp the size of two large dinner plates on the wall between the stove and the sink. Several shades of mottled gray, bubbling out from the plaster like an infection on the lungs. Then, when she'd poured milk from the carton into her coffee, instead of merging, it had floated in sour globules on the surface. And, as if to cap it all, she'd gone outside to find someone had keyed her car. All this before eight o'clock.

All she needed was the assistant commissioner, of all people, to summon her to his office, which of course he did, within fifteen minutes of her arrival. Only to keep her waiting for another five minutes outside. Shields standing there in a blue-black trouser suit, the toes of her boots pinching slightly, one heel starting to rub. If she ever got as much as an hour to herself, there was a pair of red leather Camper boots she was longing to try, and bugger the expense.

"Karen. Excellent, excellent." When Harkin finally ushered her in, he was in one of his annoyingly affable moods, all smiles and cliché. "Just wanted to check, you know, how things were going."

Patronizing was another word for it. She preferred him when he was in a temper; she found it easier then to respond.

"Yourself and Elder, everything sorting itself out?"

Shields undid the center button of her jacket and did it up again.

"No friction?"

She thought she'd better say something. "No, sir. None."

"You're sure? Because if . . ."

"To tell the truth, sir, we've hardly noticed he's here."

"Stepping quietly at first, I expect. Tactful."

"Yes, sir."

"Because if there is anything, I expect you to bring it in here. Nip it in the bud before it takes hold."

Gardeners' bloody *Question Time*, Shields thought. "Yes, sir," she said.

"Though I'm sure there'll be no need."

She could just see herself running into the AC's office, like some snot-nosed kid, the kind that was always telling tales. *Please, sir, Billy Bang's stolen my pencil case. Please, sir, Frank Elder's stolen my murder investigation.* Don't even think about it. Anything that wanted sorting out, she'd sort it out herself.

Mike Ramsden was at his desk, chair hiked back onto its rear legs, using the end of a straightened paper clip to clean his nails.

"Any sign of him?" Shields asked.

"Who's that?" Ramsden said.

"Mike, don't play silly buggers. I'm not in the mood."

When are you ever? Ramsden thought. "Okay, okay," he said. "He rang in, left a message. Wants us to get together this afternoon."

"What time this afternoon?"

Ramsden shrugged. "Didn't say."

Shields swore and looked at the ceiling. What did Elder think? She was going to sit around till he condescended to grace them with his company?

"Where the hell are Furness and Denison?" she asked.

"Chasing down one of that last set of possibles the computer spewed out. Ealing somewhere. Some poor sod living in a bloody hostel. Waste of time, if you ask me."

"One of the last. How many does that leave?"

Ramsden leaned across far enough to snag a sheet of paper. "Two to go. Cricklewood and Dalston."

"Okay." She tossed him the keys to her car. "You can drive. We'll do Cricklewood first."

Change at Camden and go back on the Edgware branch to Belsize Park and walk. The hospital was up the hill and then down again at the end of a roughly cobbled lane. Elder remembered these things without being able to recall precisely when he'd been there before or why. Not his part of London, after all.

The pub on the corner was advertising its New Year's Eve party. Tickets in advance, only a few remaining.

Inside the hospital the corridors were broad, the ceilings low; posters warning of the dangers of smoking and obesity hung on the walls, along with artwork, bright and gestural, from a local primary school.

The pathologist was suitably cadaverous, with slender, reedy fingers and bifocals perched on the bridge of his nose; not for the first time, Elder wondered whether we chose our professions or whether they chose us.

"It's Maddy Birch you're interested in?" He spoke a precise, educated Scots that Elder associated, perhaps wrongly, with Edinburgh.

"It is."

"You know the body's been released for burial?"

Elder nodded. "Like I said on the phone, I'm reviewing the investigation. I thought if you could spare me some minutes of your time."

"Fire away."

"You didn't find a trace of the attacker anywhere. No stray hairs, no skin, saliva, blood, nothing. That's right?"

"Absolutely."

"How usual is that?"

"What's usual?"

"In your experience, then."

"In my experience, it's surprising. Unexpected."

"And does it suggest anything? About the attacker, I mean?"

"Aside from the fact that he was scrupulous, meticulously careful?"

"Aside from that."

One of the overhead lights was buzzing slightly; barely diluted, the smell of chemicals permeated the room.

"Anything I say would be purely speculation. If anything, this sort of conjecture is far more your field than mine."

"Feel free to speculate away."

"Very well. It might suggest someone who, by instinct or by training, is highly methodical. Who, even though capable of great anger, is, nonetheless, able to exert an unusual degree of self-control."

"You're thinking of the rape, the nature of the wounds?"

"Indeed."

"The rape itself, it took place while the victim was still alive?"

"I've no reason to believe otherwise. All the signs of nonconsensual intercourse were present, bruising, tearing. No semen, of course. Presumably a condom."

"And the weapon that killed her?"

"Let's just take a look." He pulled a set of photographs from a drawer. "Some of the wounds, here on the arm, for instance, are slash wounds. Quite long, you see, but not so deep. Look at the tail there, indicating the angle of the blow, from above."

"Tall, then? Whoever this was? Taller than her."

"It's possible. But far from certain. She could have been falling, have been on her knees, he could have been standing above her. A host of permutations, I'm afraid."

"And these?" Elder asked, pointing to the torso.

"Stab wounds. Quite different, almost certainly fatal. Both of them deep. And see here, where the opening of the wound is wider than the blade, the knife has been levered forward and back before being withdrawn."

"What about the knife itself?"

"The blade was single-edged, you can tell from the square termination on the underside of the wound. To achieve this degree of penetration, almost certainly sharp at the tip. I should say a minimum of twenty centimeters in length, a good couple of centimeters across at the widest point."

"A butcher's knife?"

"That sort of thing."

Elder looked at the photographs. Extreme anger and control. The ability to switch between the two. Facility, maybe that was a better word. He talked with the pathologist for perhaps ten minutes more without anything new surfacing.

"Good luck, Mr. Elder." When he bade Elder good-bye, the pathologist's hand was smooth and cold like porcelain.

On his way back down the hill, Elder stopped outside one of several charity shops and browsed through two boxes of books. Tom Clancy. Jeffrey Archer. Several women called Maeve. No matter, he still had another hundred or so pages of his Patrick O'Brian to go.

Chapter 19

There was a photograph of Maddy Birch on the wall, staring back at the camera, unsmiling; recent, Elder assumed, lines on her face she'd not have liked, the odd gray hair.

Neither Karen Shields nor Mike Ramsden were on the premises; the message Shields had left was vague; they might be back, they might not.

A detailed map showed where Birch's body had lain, where her clothing, her possessions had been found. Elder remembered standing there that morning, the relative quiet in the midst of so much inner-city activity and noise; imagined it again as it would have been that night, that evening. Maddy waiting, shifting her sports bag from one shoulder to the other, glancing again at her watch, the hands luminous in the half-dark.

Elder looked at the photographs once

more, Polaroids taken at the scene. Maddy's arms were bare. No watch.

DS Sheridan was ensconced behind several hundred megabytes of PC.

"Sherry," Elder said, "disturb you for a minute?"

Sheridan pressed SAVE, removed his glasses, and blinked. "Go ahead."

"Her watch. Maddy's watch. Was she wearing one that evening? Do we know?"

Sheridan shook his head. "Nothing listed as far as I can remember. I can check, but no, I'm pretty certain."

"How many officers do you know," Elder said, "who don't wear a watch?"

"Not to say she wore one off duty."

"In which case she'd have left it at home. The stuff that was in her flat, where's it all now?"

"As far as I know, everything was packed up and sent to her mother."

"But there'll be an inventory?"

Sheridan nodded toward the computer. "On here somewhere."

"Check it out for me, would you? And maybe you could pass a message to double-check with the mother?"

"Will do."

"Oh, and Sherry, one other thing. Maddy's arrest record. Anyone who's been inside and recently released. That's been checked, I suppose?"

Sheridan nodded. "One of the first things we did. Not sure offhand how far back we went, though. I can get you a list."

"Thanks. Let's make sure we looked at Lincoln as well. Someone she put down for a long stretch, maybe, who might have had reason to feel aggrieved, bear a grudge."

"Okay."

"Thanks, Sherry." Elder rested a hand briefly on his shoulder. Get on the wrong side of the office manager, he knew, and you were pushing a boulder uphill from day one.

Steve Kennet was four stories up, sitting astride a roof beam atop one of those late-Victorian semidetached houses that, in Dartmouth Park, fetched upward of a million and a quarter pounds, a million and a half. Elder shouted up, raising his voice above the distortions of a small transistor radio that was dangling from the scaffolding. After several moments of misunderstanding, Kennet came down cheerfully enough, wiping his hands on a piece of towel hanging from his belt.

"How's it going?" Elder asked, nodding back up.

Kennet's smile was honest and open. "Should've been finished before Christmas. Would have been if not for the weather. Two blokes I work with've already started on another place up Highgate Hill. Part of the old hospital. Turning it into flats."

"You don't mind if I ask you a few questions about Maddy?"

"Still got nobody, huh?"

"Not yet."

Kennet cleared his throat of dust and spat neatly onto the side of the road. "Go ahead."

Before sitting on the low wall outside the house, Kennet took a slender pouch of tobacco from the back pocket of his jeans, a packet of papers from the top pocket of his plaid shirt. His face and the backs of his hands were streaked with dirt and dust.

Elder sat down beside him.

On the opposite side of the street, a young au pair went by pushing an empty stroller, a small child walking unsteadily beside her, holding on to her hand. With her other hand, the au pair held her cell phone to her ear, talking excitedly in a language Elder didn't recognize.

Methodically, Kennet began to roll a cigarette.

"Maddy, how did you meet her?" Elder asked.

"Usual way, in a pub. Holloway. She was there with that pal of hers. Vanessa. To be honest, that's who I was interested in first off. Vanessa. You've met her?"

Elder nodded.

"Then you'll know what I mean." Kennet wet the edge of the paper with his tongue. "Upfront, I s'pose that's what you'd say. Not shy about coming forward." When his lighter didn't work the first time, he gave it a quick shake. "I was with a mate. We went over and sat with them. His idea, really. After a bit, my mate drifted off. Vanessa, she was dead lively — she'd had a few, I daresay — whereas Maddy, mostly she was just sitting there, smiling a little, you know, not unfriendly, but not — what could I say? — obvious. What she was after."

"And you liked that?" Elder said.

Kennet grinned. "S'pose I did. What bloke wouldn't? End of the evening I got both their numbers, but it was Maddy I called. She seemed surprised, I remember that. Thought I'd made a mistake, got the numbers mixed up."

"And you went out with her for how long?"

"Few months. Three. Couldn't've been more." He clicked his lighter again with no response. "Haven't got a light, have you?"

" 'Fraid not."

Kennet crossed the pavement to the car parked at the curb, unlocked it, and reached inside the dash for a box of matches.

"You didn't get on as well as you'd thought," Elder said.

Kennet dropped the spent match toward the gutter and drew deep on his cigarette. "No, it wasn't that. We got on fine. Least I thought we did. It was just — oh, I don't know — what would you call it? — circumstances, I suppose. And, to be honest, I think she lost interest. We were supposed to meet a few times and she called up, more or less last-minute, and canceled. Got so every time the phone rang I knew that's what it was going to be."

He looked at Elder and then down the street.

"So you broke it off?" Elder said.

"Yes."

"You did?"

"Yes." More emphatically this time.

"Not Maddy?"

"No. Look . . ."

"It's okay. I'm just trying to get a clear picture of what happened."

"Why?"

"What do you mean?"

"Why is it so important? Why d'you need to know? I've been through all this before, you know."

"I know. It's just right now I don't know what's important and what's not."

"And you think this might be?"

"It's possible, like I say."

Kennet shook his head in disbelief. "Glenn Close, right?"

"I'm sorry?"

"Glenn Close in *Fatal Attraction*. Can't stand being dumped. Attacks Michael Douglas with a knife. You think that's me."

"Michael Douglas?"

"Glenn Close."

"Is it?"

"Did I go after Maddy with a knife?"

"Did you?"

"No, I did not."

"Of course not."

Kennet's roll-up had gone out and he got it lit again on the second attempt.

"Do you know if Maddy was seeing anyone else?" Elder asked.

"While she was seeing me, you mean?"

"Then or later."

"Then, I don't think so; later, I wouldn't know."

"You didn't keep in touch?"

Kennet shook his head. "Clean break. Besides, once I'd said, you know, I thought we should stop seeing one another, she agreed it was for the best. I certainly didn't want to mess her around."

He got to his feet and glanced toward the roof.

"I really should be getting back to work."

Elder held out a hand. "Thanks for your time."

Kennet's grasp was firm. "Catch him, right?"

"Right."

"And, hey!"

"Yes?"

"Happy New Year."

Elder watched as Kennet climbed back up the scaffolding without taking a wrong step, without missing a beat.

Chapter 20

The first Friday of the new year, a gray cold day, the sky the color of aging slate, ice slick on the surface of untreated roads. Maddy Birch's funeral: Hendon Crematorium, eleven-thirty sharp. The flower beds a picture of turned earth and once-green leaves blackened by frost, spindly rosebushes cut back almost to the root. Maddy's mother sat hunched in the long black car as it followed the coffin around the slow curves of Nether Street and Dollis Road, her sister, whom she'd scarcely seen in twenty years, sitting pinch-faced by her side. Crowded in the car behind, disparate cousins and aunts sat with their hands clenched in their laps. Those who'd thought her mother would want the funeral near the family home in Lincolnshire had been swiftly disabused. "She'd turned her back on all that," Mrs. Birch had said, "on us, a long time since." Blame, at that moment, easier than regret.

Elder had arrived early and stood a little to one side. As befitted the last rites of a fellow officer, the police presence was somber, manifest. Near the entrance, a surveillance team, unobtrusively as possible, videoed the assembled company, in case the hoary myth that murderers were drawn to the funerals of their victims bore any truth. Lawns, sparse and dry, stretched away toward a high boundary hedge and the municipal golf course beyond.

Alighting from the car, Mrs. Birch lost her footing, and only the outstretched hand of Detective Superintendent Mallory prevented her falling to the ground.

Inside the chapel, a CD of uplifting music played, courtesy of Classic FM. Karen Shields, wearing a black pantsuit, hair pulled sternly back, slid, long-legged, into a pew across the aisle from Elder and began leafing through the small hymnbook resting behind the seat in front.

The coffin stood in full view: solid, real.

The minister cleared his throat.

The last time Elder had seen Maddy alive, he'd been standing at the foot of the cobbled street leading down from Lincoln Cathedral, watching as she walked away. "Good night, Frank. Take care." Waiting for her to turn and smile. She never did.

The hymn was mumbled tunelessly, voices falling silent till only the echo of the prerecorded organ wheezed out the last few lines.

"Let us pray."

Clad in a black corduroy coat, black skirt, black boots, Vanessa Taylor began to cry and, turning, Shields pushed a tissue into her hand.

Given the occasion, the assistant commissioner was in full dress uniform. He spoke of Birch as a model officer, a dedicated servant of the public, a brave young woman whose life had cruelly been snuffed out. George Mallory, a pale carnation somewhat incongruous in the buttonhole of his gray wool suit, testified to the honor it had been to have such a resourceful officer as Birch under his command, if only for so sadly short a time. Referring to the operation to arrest James William Grant, he recalled with pride the moments of extreme danger when she had stood, unflinching, at his side.

Maddy's mother sat at the front, bent forward, head down.

Vanessa Taylor continued to cry.

The congregation stood reluctantly and labored through another hymn.

With a slight jerk, the mechanism that

would carry the coffin forward clanked to life.

As the coffin passed through the heavy curtains and disappeared from sight, Elder felt Maddy's breath pass, cold, across his face.

Desperate for a cigarette, Karen Shields stepped between the wreaths and floral tributes that had been spread out on display at the rear of the building. Feeling for the roll of mints at the bottom of her bag, she pulled out with it an old shopping list and a ticket for the tube. New Year's Eve just gone. Drink don't drive. She had spent the evening with three old school friends, a tradition stretching back more years than any of them liked to remember. Two of them were married now with growing kids; one, finally out, was living with her female partner in leafy Letchworth Garden City and enjoying the frisson they caused whenever they elected to walk the length of the main street hand in hand. Shields had got used to showing up and leaving alone.

Seeing Elder standing on his own, she walked across to join him.

"I used to think I preferred this to burial," Shields said. "Now I'm not so sure."

212

"When it comes down to it, I doubt there's much to choose."

"Soulless, though, isn't it?"

Elder didn't see how it could be anything else.

"You went to see Kennet," Shields said, changing tack.

"That's right."

"What did you think?"

"Seemed straightforward enough."

"That's pretty much what Mike said. Besides, his alibi seems to hold up. On holiday in Spain with his girlfriend. Didn't get back till the day Maddy's body was found." Despite her best efforts, the mint had fragmented between her teeth. "Sherry said something about a watch?"

Elder nodded. "Maddy's watch. Yes. Seems to be missing."

Over Shields's shoulder, he could see Mallory and a shorter, sharp-faced man in earnest conversation.

"Who's that? With Mallory?"

"Maurice Repton, his DCI."

As if realizing they were being watched, both men turned their heads and Mallory, smiling, raised a hand in cheery greeting.

"This Grant business Mallory mentioned," Elder said. "No mileage in it for us?"

"I don't think so."

"Might be worth taking another look, just the same. In the absence of anything else." Seeing Maddy's mother leaning on her sister's arm as she bent toward one of the wreaths, Elder excused himself and walked over to express his regrets.

Taylor stubbed out her cigarette with the low heel of her shoe and began to walk toward the exit. She hadn't reckoned on the service affecting her so badly, embarrassed almost by the fuss she'd made, the way she'd drawn attention to herself. But all the way through she'd been unable to suppress the images of Maddy that had played out across her mind: Maddy laughing, listening, pretending to be shocked by Vanessa's ribaldry, her good humor laced, toward the end, with traces of fear Vanessa had failed to take seriously. *You're not getting weird on me, are you? Freaking out?* Hearing the car approaching behind her, Taylor moved closer to the side.

Instead of driving past, the car slowed to a halt.

"Where you heading?" The gray hair on Mallory's head seemed to have been recently brushed or combed.

"Down to the tube."

"It's a long walk. Hop in, we'll give you a lift."

While Taylor hesitated, the nearside door swung open and Mallory, welcoming, slid back along the rear seat, leaving room.

"All right, thanks."

"Excellent. Drive on, driver." Though the carnation had disappeared from his buttonhole, the detective superintendent was still in an expansive mood. More wedding than funeral.

"Police Constable Taylor, isn't it?"

"Yes."

"Vanessa."

"Yes."

"You and Maddy, bosom pals."

"We were good friends, yes." Tears pricked again at the back of her eyes.

"Go ahead," Mallory said. "Let it out. Bit of genuine emotion. No need to be ashamed."

"No, it's all right . . ."

"Maurice, let the lady have a handkerchief, there's a good chap."

One of the last men in the twenty-first century to carry a handkerchief, washed and ironed, Repton swiveled around in the front passenger seat and passed it to Taylor with a manicured hand.

215

"Thank you." Taylor sniffed and dabbed her eyes.

"See those women weeping and wailing on the news," Mallory was saying. "Iran, Iraq. Can't help but wonder sometimes if they haven't got the right idea. Better than keeping it all bottled up inside like the rest of us. Eh, Maurice, what d'you think? Vanessa, eh?"

Taylor said she wasn't sure. Maurice Repton didn't seem to care.

They were marooned at a junction between an au pair struggling to get an Isuzu Trooper into first gear and an articulated lorry on its way to the nearest ASDA.

"You were close, you and Maddy," Mallory said, moving a little closer himself.

"Yes, I think so."

"No secrets, that sort of thing."

"Pretty much."

"Friendship between two women, it's a wonderful thing. Nothing held back. Open, honest. Not like me and Maurice here, cheek by jowl the best part of twenty years and what gets his withers in a turmoil is still a mystery. And just as well."

The engine of the SUV was flooded and, with the au pair watching, several men were trying to push it out of the way.

"That awful business, Grant going down, the boy Draper being killed, she'll have talked about that, I daresay."

"A little, yes, not much."

"Confided, though."

"It upset her, yes. What happened to Paul Draper, especially."

"And Grant? Did she say much about that? The shooting." For a moment, Mallory's hand was on her knee.

"No, not that I remember."

"If there was anything . . ."

"Really, there's not."

"Of course." As if he'd suddenly lost interest, Mallory shunted across to his own side of the car, and a few moments later they were pulling up to the curb.

"Your stop," Repton said, without turning around. "Hendon Central."

"Camden Town and change," Mallory said. "It is Kentish Town you're stationed?"

"Yes."

"Marvelous thing, London Underground. Where would we be without it, that's what I want to know."

"Thanks for the lift," Taylor said, pushing open the door.

"Anytime," Mallory said, with a generous wave of the hand. "Anytime."

Watching as the car eased out into the

traffic, pedestrians spilling around her, Taylor held her hands fast down by her sides, her legs weak and her guts churning without quite knowing why.

Chapter 21

If there was one thing guaranteed to make Elder feel he was getting old, it was a pub in Camden on a Saturday night. The tables, square and heavy, were crammed with empty bottles and glasses, awash with beer and the language of the brag. Not a spare seat anywhere. A scrum, three deep, at the bar. A large television screen showing continuous music videos, nobody listening, nobody watching. Tobacco smoke laced with the scent of cannabis. Voices raised, loud, above a mixture of reggae and some kind of stripped-down sledgehammer rock. White Stripes, did Elder but know it. "Seven Nation Army." "Stop Breaking Down." Age aside, Elder stood out for not having some part of his body studded or pierced, for not wearing black.

"Over here," Taylor said, seizing his arm.

With a fast smile and judicious use of

her elbows, she found them a haven of sorts, squashed up against the window, which faced out on to High Street, smoke and condensation blurring the pane.

"Sorry," she said.

"What for?"

"Bringing you here."

Elder summoned up a smile. "I've known worse." He just couldn't remember when.

"Of course," she said, "it might be nothing." Her words all but lost in an upsurge of sound.

"I'm sorry?"

"I said, it might be nothing."

"Try me."

He had to lean forward to catch every word. What Mallory and Repton had been playing at, he wasn't sure, but one thing was certain, they'd got Taylor truly rattled.

"And you weren't holding anything back from them? Something Maddy might have said?"

"God, no."

"You said they gave her a pretty tough time at the enquiry."

"Yes. Said they were likely going to have her back in, but I don't think they ever did."

Elder had obtained a copy of the Hertfordshire team's report and had still to get around to reading it.

Taylor's face tilted up toward his, perspiration on her upper lip. "It did make me think of something Maddy mentioned, about the Grant thing, something I'd more or less forgotten. There was this guy, SO19, Firearms, you know? Coming on to her. Not just the once either. Didn't like no for an answer."

"You know his name?"

"Don't think she ever said. But ginger, she did say that. Ginger-haired. No wonder she never fancied him."

"You think he might have persevered? Chanced his arm again?"

"You never know, do you? What some blokes will do."

A bottle broke near the far end of the bar and Elder slipped down from his seat. "Let's drink up and get out of here, okay?"

The street was busy with the slow passage of cars; rain dithered in the air and glossed the headlights. Young men and women trawled the pavement in threes and fours, the occasional couple arm in arm or hand in hand. Oblivious, a girl of no more than sixteen or seventeen sat cross-legged on the ground, tears raking her face. An elderly black man, dreadlocks streaming out from under his beret, pantomimed a sinuous shuffle to a tinny song from a boom box on the ground.

Always the intermittent sound of police sirens, some little distance off.

"I'm hungry," Taylor said suddenly. "How about you?"

"I don't think so," Elder said, realizing as he spoke that it wasn't true.

They bought falafels from a stall and ate them leaning against the wall.

"How's it all going, anyway?" Taylor said. "The investigation."

"Oh, you know."

"Still stuck?"

"Pretty much. But something will open it, it usually does."

She smiled. "I don't think I've exactly been a great help."

"No. You were right to tell me. Ginger, we'll check him out. Besides, it's good falafel. Can't get this in Cornwall, you know. Pasties, that's about it."

"Cream teas."

"That too."

A youth wearing an England soccer shirt and little else, despite the cold, lurched against them, apologized, and staggered on his way.

"I'd best be making a move," Elder said, stepping clear.

"Okay."

"How d'you get back from here, tube?"

"Bus."

They walked together toward the station.

"Take care," she said at the entrance. "Good luck."

"You too."

The streetlight shone bright on her face.

When Taylor sidestepped the usual coterie of druggies and near-drunks on her way to the bus stop, it's doubtful that she noticed the dark blue sedan illegally parked near the crossroads, the man watching her carefully from behind the wheel.

Elder slept fitfully, disturbed by dreams in which his daughter, like a dragonfly, sloughed off one skin to reveal another, her face and body becoming those of Maddy Birch, only to be replaced, as easily, by those of someone he didn't recognize, so that, when he woke, his hair was matted to his scalp, the quilt, sticky with sweat, tangled between his legs.

Clambering from the bed, he stood for fully five minutes under the shower, warm water washing over his head and shoulders as he soaped himself clean; a final burst of cold, face raised, as if to purge himself before stepping clear.

Coffee, toast, a white shirt more or less uncreased from the hanger, navy blue trousers, the same comfortable, well-worn shoes; yesterday's shirt and boxer shorts he stuffed into the washing machine, along with the quilt cover and pillowcase.

When he dialed Joanne's number, hoping to speak to Katherine, all he got was an automated voice, requesting that he leave a message.

Someone in the flat below was treating him to Capital Gold and he countered with Radio 3. Haydn, probably. Wasn't it usually Haydn? Mozart or Haydn. Maybe Bach.

A chapter of Patrick O'Brian — enemy vessel at four o'clock on the horizon, run out the guns, run up the flag — and he was ready for something altogether drier. Scooping up his cell phone just in case, he slipped it into his pocket; the Grant Enquiry Report, notebook, and ballpoint pen were all ready to go. The *A-Z* he checked in the car.

No space in the small parking lot close to Kenwood House, he parked on Hampstead Lane. Most of the tables outside the café were taken, Sunday newspapers spread wide. The weather was kind. He found a space toward the rear corner, broke off a corner of his almond croissant, tasted his coffee, and began to read. Somehow, the hum of other voices around him made concentration easier.

Ashley and his team, it seemed, had gone about their task with thoroughness if not inspiration; reading between the lines, it was clear certain sections of the Met had not made their task any easier than was necessary. The report's conclusions, which lay down a modicum of organizational blame but nothing else, were unexceptional. In the matter of James William Grant and the second gun, Detective Superintendent Mallory had been given the benefit of any possible doubt.

Elder thought a few words with Trevor Ashley might not be out of place.

Taking out his cell phone, he tried Joanne again with the same result.

The residue of his coffee was cold.

When he had been an officer in the Met and stationed in West London, he and Joanne had driven to Hampstead Heath with Katherine one Sunday afternoon and flown her kite from the top of Parliament Hill. Katherine — five then, or was she six? — had lost patience and run down the slope toward the children's playground and the paddling pool, Elder scrambling after her, laughing, while Joanne reeled in the kite's thin line.

Had she already been sleeping with Martyn Miles by then?

Some truths it was better not to know.

Chapter 22

Gray Monday. The previous day's wintery sunshine had flattered to deceive. Karen Shields was at her desk, advancing a batch of circulars and memos toward the shredder. Elder had stopped at the coffee machine on the way.

They sat on either side of Shields's desk, the hubbub of the day ringing around them.

"How was your Sunday?" Shields asked.

"Nothing special. You?"

"Much the same." Shields had slept in as long as she could before meeting one of her friends on Upper Street for brunch, followed by a so-so movie at the Screen on the Green. In the evening, she'd watched TV, washed clothes, ironed, spoken to her sister in Stockwell, her mother in Jamaica.

"One thing I did do," Elder said, "was read through the report on the Grant shooting."

"Anything there for us?"

"Not that I could see right away. Pretty straightforward, really."

"Dead end, then?"

"Probably." Elder sipped his coffee through a hole in the lid. "Might be worth contacting Ashley, the Herts Super who ran the enquiry. Just for a chat. Talk things through."

"A little help reading between the lines."

Elder grinned. "Something like that."

How he could drink his coffee that hot, she didn't know. "Mike and I checked out the last couple of possibles from the Sex Offenders Register."

"Anything?"

Shields shook her head. "Could have saved ourselves the trouble. Elderly rapist with diabetes and a dodgy hip, and a twice-convicted sexual predator incapacitated by the onset of AIDS."

"Oh, well. Tick 'em off and move on."

"Where to?"

Elder set his cup on the edge of the desk. "Vanessa Taylor?"

"What about her?"

He gave Shields the gist of what Taylor had told him on Saturday evening.

Shields gave it a few moments' thought. "Mallory and Repton, what do you think?

They were just winding her up for the sake of it? Playing games?"

"It's possible. But, no, I think there's more to it than that."

"And it goes back to Grant?"

"So it would seem."

"Grant and Maddy."

"Yes. Somehow."

"Which is why you want to talk to Ashley."

"Correct."

"A little more than just a casual chat, then?"

Elder smiled. There was a sudden flurry of telephones in the middle distance. Raised voices. Someone urgently, repeatedly swearing.

"What about this other thing she mentioned?" Shields said. "This ginger lothario from Firearms?"

"Tracing him shouldn't be too hard."

"You don't think it's clutching at straws?"

"I think right now we clutch at anything we can."

Shields knew he was right. "I'll get Mike and Lee onto it." When she tried her coffee again, it was just okay to drink. "By the way, Maddy's missing watch, I had the inventory double-checked in case there'd been some kind of clerical error. But no, no sign."

"I asked her mother about it at the funeral," Elder said. "Apparently her father gave her the watch years ago. A Lorus. Nothing fancy. Water resistant. Stainless steel. Maddy's name engraved on the back. And the date: fifteenth of the seventh, 1981."

"Her twenty-first," Shields said, doing the sums in her head.

"Yes."

A brief image of Katherine flickered behind Elder's eyes.

"Vanessa confirmed," he said, "that was the watch Maddy still wore."

"In which case," Shields said, "where is it now?"

They both turned toward the map on the wall, the area around the old railway line where Birch's body had been found. Thick scrub, bushes, trees.

"It's been searched once," Shields said.

"It could be searched again."

"You think it's that important?"

"If it isn't there, there's a possibility whoever killed Maddy took it with him."

"A souvenir?"

"Maybe."

For several moments neither spoke. If

that were so, it told them something about the killer, something a profiler could work with.

Shields leaned across the desk and dropped the polystyrene cup and what remained of its contents into the waste bin. "Getting enough bodies out there's going to be a problem. We may have to rely on volunteers. But I'll make the case as strongly as I can."

"Good." Elder was on his feet. "Just one other thing."

"Go on."

"Kennet. That alibi of his. I assume it all checked out?"

Shields shot him a look. "I thought you didn't fancy him for this?"

"I know. It's just hard to get away from the idea that whoever did this, Maddy knew him, maybe knew him well."

"I wouldn't exactly say Kennet knew her well, would you?"

"They'd had a relationship."

"If you can call it that."

"They'd slept together."

"Half a dozen times in — what? — three months?"

"That isn't a relationship?"

"You tell me."

Elder held her gaze. "I'd like to get

Sherry to make a few more checks into his background. If you've no objection."

Shields thought it would be pretty much a waste of time.

"Go ahead," she said.

"Thanks."

Graeme Loftus adjusted his position, feet apart, arm extended, sighted along the barrel of his pistol, and fired into the center of the stenciled figure that was menacing him from the target by the far wall. Eighteen holes clustered around the heart.

By the time he'd signed out and left the building, the rain that had been threatening off and on again had set in with a vengeance. Mike Ramsden intercepted him on his way across the car park.

"Graeme Loftus?"

"Who wants to know?"

"DS Ramsden, Homicide."

"What's this about?"

"Few minutes of your time. Won't take long."

"I'm getting soaked standing here."

"That's my Sierra over there. Let's get in out of the rain."

Lee Furness was in the backseat and, with Ramsden holding the door open, Loftus grudgingly slid in alongside him.

"Bloody weather, eh?" Furness said with a grin.

Loftus said nothing. His red hair was darkened by the rain.

"Maddy Birch," Ramsden said.

Loftus blinked. "Who?"

"Maddy Birch."

Loftus shook his head.

Furness took a photograph from his pocket and held it up between them.

"Oh, yes." Loftus blinked again and wiped something, real or imaginary, from his mustache.

"You remember her now," Ramsden said.

"Of course I bloody do."

"Knew her well, then?"

"No."

"You're sure."

"Course I'm sure."

"Not for want of trying."

"Look, what . . ."

Ramsden smiled. "All over her, what I've heard. Like a dog in heat."

"That's bollocks."

"Pig at the fuckin' trough."

Alongside Loftus, Furness laughed. Outside, the rain showed no sign of easing.

"Listen," Loftus said, man to man. "I gave her a bit of chat, offered to buy her a

233

drink, you know how it is."

Ramsden grinned encouragingly. "Sure. Good-looking woman, out on her own. Few pints down. You were on the pull."

"If you like, yeah."

"Leg over at the end of the evening, only natural, right? Where's the harm?"

"Yeah."

"Except she didn't want to know. Maddy."

"Yeah, well . . . Can't score every time, you know?"

"And when she told you no deal?"

Loftus shrugged. "That was that. End of story."

"You walked away."

"Yes."

"And then?"

"Then nothing."

"Had to smart a bit, though, getting the big no in front of everyone. Slinkin' away with your dick between your legs. Not so good for the old ego."

Loftus shook his head. "Happens, doesn't it?"

"Often? To you, I mean?"

Loftus bridled. "No, not often."

Ramsden glanced across at Furness and winked. "Lover man. Cock of the walk. Just see him, Lee, can't you? Strutting his stuff. Rutting around."

"All right," Loftus said, coloring, "that's enough."

"Temper, too. Quick to rouse. Redheads, of course, what you expect. True to type." Ramsden's fingers executed a little paradiddle along the back of the seat. "Didn't take your temper out on Maddy, I hope? When you saw her again? You did see her again, didn't you?"

Loftus pushed open the car door. "All right, we're through. Anything else you want to say to me, make it official. Federation solicitor, the whole bit. Otherwise, stay out of my way."

Leaving the door wide open, he strode off into the rain.

"Touchy, isn't he?" Ramsden said.

Chapter 23

The drive north to Hertford was slow and
rendered slower by a broken-down lorry
and two competing road crews, cable com-
panies digging for gold. Close to where the
A10 met the M25 near Waltham Cross, the
rain started to fall for the second day running. Light at first, but by the time Elder
had turned off toward the center of town, it
was thrashing down with such force that he
had the windshield wipers working double
time. The only space into which he could
shoehorn the Astra was at the extreme edge
of the car park, about as far from the entrance as it was possible to be. Running,
collar up, he was soaked by the time he
pushed his way inside and reported at the
enquiry desk.

A uniformed constable took him up to
the small office with Detective Superintendent Ashley's nameplate on the door.

Ashley shook Elder's hand affably and

commiserated about the weather.

"If you want to take off that coat, put it on the radiator."

"Thanks, I will."

Ashley was wearing an aging tweed jacket with patches on the elbows and around the cuffs; Elder half-expected him to take out a pipe and begin the ritual of striking match after match, trying to get the damned thing to light.

"You're one of Framlingham's cronies, then? The old geezer brigade."

"Is that what they call us?"

"Among other things. Mind you, they already call me that and worse."

Elder thought they were probably the same age.

"Helps supplement the pension, I daresay," Ashley went on. "Prevents the joints from seizing up."

"Something like that."

"What was it in the old days? Taking over a newsagent's. Running a pub. Now it's security. Guarding some posh enclave where they expect you to touch your cap and call them 'sir' and 'madam.'"

"You don't see yourself doing that?"

"Would you?"

Ashley grinned and eased himself back in his chair. "Herefordshire, me. Best fishing there is. Outside Scotland, of course. Got a little place all staked out."

Elder had heard it, or similar, many times before, and wondered if it would ever come to pass.

"You wanted to talk about Maddy Birch," Ashley said.

"Yes."

"What happened to her, that kind of mindless violence, like those women in London, out running in the park, well, you know the statistics as well as I do. No matter how much you massage them, violent crime, crime against the person, it's up — what? — fifteen percent last year. And there's that pillock of a Home Secretary, fannying about with fancy schemes for tracking offenders by bloody satellite, telling people on council estates if they want decent policing they've got to pay for it themselves. Talk about the blind leading the poor bloody blind."

He raised his hands, palms outward.

"I know, I know, I'm ranting, but that man, this government, they get my bloody goat."

Elder smiled and waited for the other man to calm down. The rain continued to lash against the windows outside.

"You think there might be some kind of

connection? Between the Grant shooting and Birch's murder?"

"I'm not sure. I think it's possible, without really seeing how. Just casting around, I suppose."

"I'll tell you what I can."

"You interviewed her yourself, you and DCI Mills?"

"That's right."

"How did she strike you?"

Ashley gave it a few moments' thought. "A little on edge, maybe. But no more than most in that situation. Wary of being criticized. Found in the wrong."

"And was she?"

"Not as far as I can see."

"And her version of events, the shooting . . . ?"

"Basically the same as everyone else's. Detective Superintendent Mallory shot and killed an armed man in the line of duty; the circumstances didn't leave him any alternative."

"Mallory's version of events, though, the business with the second gun, it depends to a large extent on Maddy Birch's testimony."

"Not really. Even without it, there's no real alternative. No reason for Mallory to open fire without due cause."

"You didn't ever consider bringing her in again?"

"We thought about it, yes, at one time. DCI Mills was pretty keen. But then . . . Well, you know what happened then. We'd lost our chance." Ashley pushed an uncapped pen across the papers on his desk. "I can't see it would have changed anything."

Elder thanked him for his time, and not so many minutes later he was back in his car, the one o'clock news just starting on the radio, the sky lightening to the south where the rain was easing.

Shields had always thought going after Loftus would lead nowhere, and from what Mike Ramsden had said there was little to make her change her mind. In some instances, the haste to employ a lawyer might be seen as an admission of guilt, but with Loftus it seemed to be short temper and little else. Earlier that day, she'd had a word with his immediate superior in SO19 and all the indications were that, being a little prickly aside, he was a good officer with a near exemplary record. Another blind alley, Shields thought. But maybe worth exploring a touch longer, just to be sure. She would get young Denison to poke around a little, see what, if anything, he could find.

More, maybe, than the half-dozen officers and twenty volunteers who'd been searching the woods along the railway line for any sign of Birch's watch.

Whether Elder was still up in Hertford or not, she wasn't sure. Possibly back at his flat by now, she thought, smiling, taking an afternoon nap. In retirement that's probably what you got used to.

It was somewhat short of three when Sheridan bustled toward her, tie akimbo, excitement palpable on his face.

"Sherry, what's up?"

Shields listened, not quite believing. "How come we didn't know this before?"

"Never made it onto the computer."

"Fuck!"

Grabbing her coat from the back of the chair, she brushed Sheridan aside. "Tell me about it on the way down. Everything you've got."

She called Elder from the car. "Kennet, eleven years ago his then-girlfriend applied for a restraining order against him."

"And we've only just found this out?"

"This afternoon. When she didn't follow through with the application, any record was wiped clean. Sherry found out by chance, asking around, tracking back."

"The girlfriend, any idea where she is now?"

Shields allowed herself a smile. "Write down this address. I'll meet you there, thirty minutes' time."

Chapter 24

Shields drove fast: roundabouts were a test of nerve, traffic lights a starting grid. After weeks of dead ends and disappointment, she was pumped up. Friern Barnet, Totteridge and Whetstone, Hadley Wood. The roads narrowed, then broadened, then narrowed again. All those questions, statements, searches leading nowhere. Trees, some recently pollarded, lined the pavements; houses, mostly detached, stood back from the road behind tall hedges, neat gardens; small blocks of flats sat on the edge of curving drives clustered with BMWs and Jaguars, SUVs. Slow down, she told herself, slow down.

Despite her speed, Elder was there before her.

"The restraining order," he said, "just stalking, or more?"

"More." Shields's face, he noticed, had taken on a definite glow.

The house was brick-built, slate-roofed, the windows on the first floor a crosshatch of small squares that would have made the window cleaner curse inwardly and add another fiver to the bill. A near-mint Mini Cooper, gray with silver trim, stood outside the two-car garage.

When she rang the bell, Karen half-expected it to be answered by a maid, not the cap-and-frilly-apron kind, but someone overqualified and underpaid from Croatia or Brazil. In fact, it was Estelle Cooper herself, Estelle Robinson as she'd been when Kennet knew her; Mrs. Cooper now, alone at home with the *Mail* and daytime TV until the school run, parents sensible around here and taking it in turns so as not to clog up the roads; Jake and Amber were being collected today by Tara's mom from number thirty-five.

"Mrs. Cooper? I'm Detective Chief Inspector Karen Shields. This is my colleague, Mr. Elder."

They followed her through a parquet-floored hallway into a long living room at the rear of the house, French windows leading into a diamond-shaped conservatory, large tubs of geraniums brought inside to protect them from the frost. There were photographs of the children above the fireplace and on an oval table at the side of the room, mostly those school photos in pristine uniform with artificial lighting that had always seemed to Elder, where Katherine and her friends were concerned, to transform them into distant cousins of the kids they really were.

Estelle Cooper sat small in the center of a wide high-backed settee, the print dress she wore in danger of getting lost among the busy flowers of the upholstery. She had a sharp face with a down-turned mouth and faded eyes, like a doll that had been played with, discarded, and left, most of the life and stuffing gone.

"Would you like some tea?" she asked. "I wasn't sure . . ."

"It's fine, Mrs. Cooper, thanks," Shields said. "We won't take any more of your time than's necessary."

"Estelle," she said, "please call me Estelle."

"Very well, then. Estelle. Estelle, you had a relationship with Steven Kennet . . ."

Elder thought she flinched at the sound of his name.

"That was a long time ago," she said.

"I know. I wonder, can you tell us a little about that relationship? How it ended, for instance?"

"Ended?" She made a sound somewhere between a laugh and a sigh. "Badly. But then I suspect you know."

"Please tell us in your own words."

"All right." Her eyes rested on Shields, then slid away till she was looking at the floor. "I started going out with Steven in nineteen eighty-nine. I was working in central London, Holborn, as a legal secretary. I hadn't gone to university . . . well, I had, at least I'd started, but somehow, I don't know, I just hadn't seemed to be able to get on. Anyway, I was working for this firm and I started seeing Steven. I met him through a friend, a mutual friend, and he was . . . well, it was wonderful at first. He was considerate, you know, and kind and — this sounds a terrible thing to say — but for someone who did what he did, building work, you know, working with his hands, he was, well, not intellectual exactly, but interested in things, cultural things. We'd go to the theater occasionally, foreign films, galleries."

"When all this was happening," Shields said, "you were living together?"

"Yes. Steven wanted me to move in with him more or less from the start. And finally, well, he was . . . he could be very persuasive."

"And how was that? Living together."

"It was fine at first. At least, at least I thought it was. I'd never lived with anybody before. I suppose you could say I was a bit naive." She was fidgeting with the material of her dress. "Sometimes he got angry when I wouldn't . . ." She looked at Shields again as if looking for some kind of understanding, sympathy. "He asked me to do things . . ."

Her voice slid away.

Shields glanced across at Elder; waited. "On these occasions," she said, her voice soft, almost a croon, "on these occasions when he got angry, did he ever hit you?"

Estelle Cooper's eyes were closed.

"Did he hit you, Estelle?"

"Yes."

"Often?"

Eyes still closed, Estelle turned her head aside.

Shields looked across at Elder again.

"Did you ever talk to anyone about what was happening?" she said. "Ask for help?"

"I tried to, but I didn't know . . . it wasn't easy. In the end I plucked up my courage and spoke to my mother, but at first she just wouldn't, she wouldn't listen. She stood there with her hands clasped over her ears and then, when I persisted, she said, 'You silly little cow, why don't you stop complaining and just do what he says.' "

She was sobbing now, her arms locked tight across her chest, rocking slowly forward and back. Shields went over and leaned toward her and at the first touch of a hand on her shoulder, Estelle stiffened and gasped.

Elder went in search of the kitchen, and when he returned with a glass of water the two women were sitting on the settee side by side.

Estelle drank the water in small sips, like medicine.

"Take your time," Shields said quietly.

Her hand not quite steady, Estelle gave Elder back the glass.

"When finally I found the courage to tell him I was leaving him," she said, "he just said no. As though there wasn't any room for argument. 'I'll change,' he said. 'I won't do it anymore, you'll see.' And for a long time, months, almost a year, that was what he did. It was like it had been before, when we started going out together, and then, suddenly, without reason, it happened again, he hit me, so badly I had to go to hospital, in the middle of the night, to accident and emergency, and I said, 'Right, this time I am leaving you, I really am,' and he said, he said, 'I'll kill you if you do.' "

There was a clock ticking somewhere that Elder hadn't noticed before.

Shields reached across and took one of Estelle's hands in hers. "You believed him," she said.

"Yes. Of course."

"What did you do?"

"I told my father this time. I hadn't dared tell him before. And he was wonderful. He came round when Steven was out and helped me pack my things, and then he went with me to the police. They asked me if I would make a formal complaint about Steven, apply for a restraining order against him, and I tried to say no, just tell him to keep away from me, but my father said you've got to sign a complaint, and in the end I did."

"But, in the event, it never went that far?"

"No."

"It never got to court."

"No, I . . . I changed my mind. The thought of standing up in front of a magistrate, other people, and having to talk about . . . I couldn't go through with it. And besides, by then I thought Steven would have calmed down, found somebody else."

She laughed nervously, as if something had suddenly struck her as amusing.

"I lived with my parents for six months or so before finding a flat of my own and that's when he started to turn up again. Just once or twice at first. I'd see him, you know, in the supermarket, or across the street, but then it was more and more. He'd be waiting there when I finished work, wanting to give me a lift home, things like that, and I told him it had to stop, I didn't want to see him again, and then one evening I came back home and he was there, in the flat, he'd got in somehow, I don't know how he'd got in . . ."

Pulling away from Shields, she pressed both hands hard against her face.

"I went back to the police and they said if I wanted anything done I would have to go through the whole process again, and this time I said I would. I'd had enough. My nerves were in tatters. But then — I don't know if Steven knew about the police, I mean, but he just stopped. Following me. Coming round. I didn't see him again. Not after that. Not once." Her eyes lowered. "I assumed he'd met someone else."

"I'm sorry," Shields said, "to make you go through all this."

"It's all right," Estelle said. And then: "Steven, has he . . . has he done something?"

"We don't know," Shields said.

"He has, hasn't he? He's done this to someone else."

"We really don't know."

Estelle looked toward the window; it would soon be dark outside. "The children will be home soon."

Shields got to her feet, Elder following suit.

"I'm sorry for bringing all that back," Shields said at the door. "I really am."

Estelle smiled the best smile she could. "I hope it's done some good."

"I'm sure it has. Thank you again."

Shields stopped alongside her car, keys in her hand. Her face had lost its glow. "I need a drink and I don't want to sit in a pub on my own. Maybe we could stop and pick up a bottle of Scotch?"

"How about Irish?" Elder said. "I've got some back at the flat."

"Okay, I'll follow you."

They drove along Whetstone High Road toward North Finchley, the traffic congealing around them, Elder wondering why Estelle's story had affected Shields as much as he thought it had.

Chapter 25

"Jesus!" Shields said. "Don't you have any heating in here?"

Elder smiled. "It's that underfloor thing. Comes on automatically, as far as I can tell."

"No thermostat? Override?"

"What looks like a thermostat in the bedroom. Doesn't seem to work."

Shields looked at him, eyebrow raised. "How about the living room? Is it any warmer in there?"

"I doubt it, but I'm not sure. I seem to spend most of my time in here."

The kitchen held a dining table and two chairs and little else. Shields wandered off to check the living room, while Elder rinsed two glasses and wiped them dry. Still wearing her coat, she returned and looked idly along the kitchen shelves.

"This is how it works, then? They set

you up in one of these places, what, rent free?"

Elder nodded.

"Plus salary?"

"Some kind of daily rate."

"Overtime?"

"We didn't discuss it."

"Maybe I should apply for early retirement."

"What? Before you make superintendent?"

"Yeah. And hell freezes over."

Elder was holding the bottle of Jameson over Shields's glass. "Say when."

"Say it for me."

He poured them both a good shot, considered, then poured a little more.

"Cheers."

They clinked glasses and stepped back.

"You want to sit?"

"Why not?"

The chairs were made from some kind of molded plastic, less uncomfortable than they looked, though it was close.

"It really got to you, didn't it?" Elder said. "This afternoon."

Shields shrugged. "Kind of thing you hear all the time."

Elder thought there was more to it than that, but he let it ride.

"How come you drink this?" Shields said. "And not Scotch?"

"Habit, I suppose."

Karen tried a little more. "If you had to drink it blindfolded, you think you could tell the difference?"

"I doubt it."

"Kennet," she said a few moments later. "What do you reckon? You reckon he's our man?"

Elder made a face. "We've got no forensics, nothing that places him at the scene."

Shields nodded. "Plus the little matter that he was still in Spain when Maddy was killed."

"You said that had been checked?"

"We saw a printout from the airline — electronic ticketing, isn't that what it's called? But did we go rifling through flight manifests and so on? No, I don't think so." She sighed and shook her head and drank some more whiskey. "We fucked up, right?"

"We don't know that."

"No," laughing despite herself. "Not yet. But chances are looking pretty good."

"Like I say, we don't know it was Kennet at all."

"We know what he does when someone tries to walk away."

"That was different; they were living together."

" 'I'll kill you,' that's what he said."

"Situations like that, stakes are raised, people say that all the time. Doesn't mean they're going to follow through."

Shields looked at him. "Have you?"

"Ever said, 'I'll kill you'?"

"To someone you were involved with, yes."

"No. No, I honestly don't think I have." But he'd thought it, more than once, Joanne. Martyn Miles. When he'd first learned the truth.

"Kennet didn't just say it," Shields said. "He beat her up. Put her in hospital."

"That doesn't mean he killed Maddy."

"You're backing away from this now?"

"No. Not at all. I just think we shouldn't get too . . ."

"What? Too excited?"

"Yes."

"I should be so lucky." She drained her glass and slid it across the table toward him. "Tunnel vision, that's what you're supposed to guard against, isn't it? When you're leading an investigation. I've been to bloody lectures on it, for God's sake."

"It isn't easy," Elder said. "Everything starts to point one way, you get dragged along."

"Frank," pointing her finger, "don't you fucking patronize me."

"I'm sorry, I wasn't. I didn't mean to."

Shields held his gaze.

"I held on to an idea for a dozen years once," Elder said. "Case I'd been working on. Girl who'd disappeared. Sixteen. So certain I was right about who'd murdered her I almost got my own daughter killed in the process. And I was wrong. Couldn't have been more so."

Shields didn't speak right away. "Whoever it was, killed the girl, you found them in the end?"

"She's wasn't dead. She was alive. On the other side of the world."

"And your daughter? How's she now?"

Instead of an answer, Elder slid the bottle back in her direction. "You ever had any kids?"

She shook her head.

"Before Katherine was born, when Joanne was pregnant, people would tease us, you know, half joking, about sleepless nights, how your life's never going to be your own. What they don't tell you, how the minute they take their first step, kids, away from you, on their own, you've got this fear about what's going to happen to them. I don't mean pedophiles, things like that, just ordinary everyday things like stepping off the curb at the wrong moment, falling off the top of the slide and cracking their head open. And then you start to worry about yourself. Mortality. Dying. Stuff you'd hardly thought about before. Like what happens if you're running up this hill, pushing them in the buggy, just the two of you in the park, and suddenly you have a heart attack and they're left alone."

Shields topped off Elder's glass and then her own. She'd pretended not to notice the tears that had come momentarily to his eyes.

"She is all right, though? Your daughter? Katherine, is that what you said she was called?"

"Katherine, yes."

"And she's okay?"

"That depends."

"Something like that, it can't be easy. Not for either of you."

"I don't know how to talk to her. Not now. Perhaps I never did. No. No, that's not true. I think we got on pretty well. Even after Joanne and I had split up. We could talk to one another then. But, now, I don't know what to say to her, how to be with her even, and as far as she's concerned, the less she has to do with me the better."

Shields smiled with her eyes. "You know what, Frank?"

"No, what?"

"You're feeling sorry for yourself."

"Probably."

"More so than you are for her."

"That's not true."

"It's the way it comes across."

"Too bad." Angry, he pushed back his chair and went toward the window.

Shields sat where she was, head down, then went to join him. "I didn't mean to upset you."

"You didn't."

Her breath was warm on his face.

"I think I'm a little drunk, Frank."

"Most likely."

"How about you?"

"Me? I'm fine."

"Earlier, when you asked about this afternoon. Letting it get under my skin . . ."

"You don't have to tell me, you know."

"No, it's okay." She took another taste from her glass. "When I was younger, not long out of school, doing some part-time college thing, I started going with this guy. Older than me. Quite a bit. He was a musician. Well, not even that. More a hanger-on, you know. Scarcely played at all. Did a bit of deejaying, nothing special. But me, I was just a kid. What did I know? There's all my mates, you know, 'want to watch out, he's just out for what he can get.' Well, he had that, didn't he, and we still carried on seeing one another. I'd go round, sleep over, stay weekends. My parents — I was still living at home — they were going ballistic, but I didn't care. 'Get your nose out of my business, let me live my own life,' all that bullshit. Course, they were right. I turned up late one night, somewhere I was supposed to be meeting him, this club. All right, I was fifty minutes, nearly an hour, late. He smacked me round the mouth, right there in front of everyone. Smacked me round the mouth and made it bleed. Next day he came round, all apologies, bought me this bracelet. Expensive, you know, not cheap. Talked about moving in together, getting engaged."

A wan smile crossed Shields's face. "Was a whole month before he hit me again. At a party this time. In front of all these people we knew. As if he needed to show he could."

"You stopped seeing him," Elder said. "After that."

"Not soon enough."

"I'm sorry."

259

She shook her head. "That poor woman, in that huge great bloody house."

"She got away," Elder said. "Started a new life."

"Did she?"

"People do," Elder said, knowing, even as he spoke, he was wishing that, for Katherine, it was true.

"I'd better phone for a taxi," Shields said. "Pick up my car tomorrow."

"I could drive it in for you."

"Okay."

Neither of them moved.

His arm was not quite touching hers. And then it was.

Leaning forward, she kissed him softly on the mouth, then stepped away. "This isn't going to happen, Frank. I'm sorry."

A slow release of breath. "Okay."

Fishing her cell phone from her bag, she punched in a number, spoke and listened, broke the connection. "Twenty minutes."

"I'll make coffee."

"Good."

Twenty minutes was fifteen. "Kennet," Shields said at the door. "Tomorrow morning we'll see his girlfriend. The one he went with to Spain."

For some time after she had gone, Elder could smell her scent in the room, recall the warmth of her arm, the slight pressure of her lips, barely opening. Foolish to pour himself a nightcap before turning in, but who was to know?

Chapter 26

Taylor had been thinking about Maddy. Oh, not constantly, far from it. Too busy for that. A gang of twelve- and thirteen-year-olds, bored by the school holiday, had been entertaining themselves by chucking stones from the pedestrian bridge between Churchill and Ingestre roads onto the trains below. On the last occasion they had shattered the windshield, injuring the driver seriously; twenty-seven fragments of glass had to be removed from his face and neck. Then there were the two fifteen-year-olds who, three times in a week, had robbed a local newsagent of the contents of his till, once making their getaway on stolen bikes, twice on skateboards. To say nothing of a plethora of burglaries that needed checking into and logging, crime numbers to be assigned, anxious or angry people to reassure, the whole tedious and largely pointless business set in some kind of motion.

Still, through it all, there were moments, unbidden, when she would remember Maddy's laugh, Maddy's smile, Maddy's fear. *It's not funny. It's not some bloody joke.* No joke at all in the end, no joke at all. A statistic, a tragedy, a headline for as long as it was news; the object of an enquiry going nowhere, an absence, a pall of blue-gray smoke rising into the winter air.

Even at that time of the evening, too late for the last stragglers returning home from work, too early for the raucous and the semi-drunk on their way back from the pub or off for a night's clubbing, she had to push her way through to the doors when the tube pulled into the Archway. An elbow at her back. A face along the platform she half-recognized. Nobody.

Coming up out of the station, uncomfortably aware of the smell of her own sweat, she walked through the usual congregation of beggars and *Big Issue* sellers colonizing the sidewalk and joined the small crowd of people waiting at the lights. Sometimes she took her life in her hands and crossed against the red, traffic bearing down from several directions, but tonight, after a split shift and a couple of hours of unpaid overtime, catching up on paperwork, she lacked the energy.

On the opposite corner, someone pushed out of the pub just in front of her, and for a moment she jumped, startled, and then, music and voices spilling through the door, considered a quick half-pint before going home, maybe a rum and Coke. But the moment passed and she walked on, crossing the road again, lower down, much the same path, much the same steps Maddy would have taken so many evenings before.

A chill moved inexorably along Taylor's arms.

You're not getting weird on me, are you? Freaking out?

Turning past the bollards at the top of her street, away from the noise and the traffic, she laughed. *Stupid mare! Silly tart! For God's sake, get a grip!*

Lights showed behind a good number of the windows, blinds on the upper floors left open. The overlapping sounds of TV sets and stereos, indistinct and comforting. A dozen houses shy of her own, she started feeling around in her bag for her keys. Stopped to disentangle them from her notebook and the charger for her cell phone, something made her look across the street.

Someone was standing in the half-shadow a short distance down the street. A silhouette and little more. Broad and tall against the overhanging hedge. A shape. A man. Though she couldn't make out his face, she knew his eyes were focused on her. Watching her.

Fear froze her, her legs, her voice, and then she hurried, half ran the short distance to her door; key in the lock, she swung her head around and there was nothing there.

An empty road, an empty street.

Dark on dark.

Inside, she slammed the door closed and leaned back against it, catching her breath, her thoughts, slow, slow, slow, before climbing the stairs toward her flat on the second floor.

Without switching on the light, she crossed to the window and looked out. A couple were walking along now, arms around one another's shoulders, heads close; farther along, a man, smaller, not the one she'd seen, was watching his dog defecating at the side of the road. Her breathing was almost back to normal, her blood ceasing to race. Already she was thinking of what she should have done, how she should have stood her ground, challenged him. She was a police officer, for God's sake. But police officers, she knew all too well, could be victims, too.

It was some while before she left the window, drew the curtains, switched on the light. What had she said to Maddy? *Report it, why don't you? You should.*

There was a bottle of white wine half-empty in the fridge.

Half-empty, or half-full?

Tomorrow she would report it to the local station, even though she could see already the bored officer, hear his questions. *This man, what exactly did he do?* Maybe she would even phone Frank Elder, mention it to him. Or Karen Shields?

She could see the expression on the other woman's face, sympathetic but matter-of-fact: after what happened to Maddy, you're bound to be jumpy for a while. Apprehensive. Imagination in overdrive. Wouldn't be natural otherwise.

The wine tasted thin and bitter in her mouth and she poured the remainder down the sink. In bed, she moved the small reading lamp down onto the floor to lessen the glare, but left it switched on throughout the night.

Chapter 27

Wednesday morning. A fine fall of rain. Elder had driven Shields's car to Hendon early, left it parked, and passed time in the canteen. In the queue, tray in hand, Frank felt his stomach rebelling at the sight and smell of sausages and bacon and he'd settled for two slices of toast. There was a copy of the *Mirror* lying around and he thumbed through it, not really paying attention. After a while he saw Mike Ramsden come in and he raised a hand in greeting.

Ramsden carried over a breakfast plate full to overflowing. "Best meal of the day."

"Your boss in yet?" Elder asked.

"Just arrived." Ramsden grinned. "Like a bear with a sore head this morning. Don't know what she was up to last night, but it's left its mark, I'll tell you that."

"See you in a while," Elder said.

Ramsden mumbled something through a

mouthful of egg and beans.

Shields was sitting at her desk, a large carton of orange juice close at hand. Elder said good morning and gave her back her car keys.

"What are you looking so smug about?" she said.

"I didn't know I was."

"The girlfriend," Shields said, "she's called McLaughlin. Jennifer McLaughlin. Twenty-seven. Works in a chemist's, Muswell Hill Broadway. But not every day."

"Today?"

"That's what I'm waiting to find out."

Another fifteen minutes and they were on their way.

Jennifer McLaughlin was neat in her white uniform, buttoned and belted, reddish hair pulled back in a barrette, pale freckles across her face. If Kennet had a type, it wasn't easy to discern what it was.

Shields showed her ID card as discreetly as she could.

The manager agreed to let them use his office.

"What's this about?" Jennifer McLaughlin said, but the way, even in that enclosed space, she contrived to look neither of them in the eye suggested that she knew.

"November just gone," Shields said, "you went to Spain."

"Málaga, yes. Winter break."

"You and Steve. Steve Kennet."

"Yes. Why? What's wrong?"

"When did you come back?"

"Twenty-eighth. End of the week."

"Jennifer."

"What?"

"This might be important."

Jennifer slid both hands up her neck, fingertips against the roots of her hair. "We had a row. Stupid, really. About nothing. Where we were going to eat, which café. Steve, he lost his temper. Really lost it, you know?"

"He hit you?"

She looked at the floor, guilty; as if she had something to be guilty about. "I said I didn't want to stay, not anymore. He could stay if he liked, but I was coming home. He said if I was going, we both were. I phoned the airline to change the flights. Cost a fortune. We didn't talk all the way back, sat in separate rows. Soon as we got back to Stansted that was that."

"You've not seen him again?"

"No."

"Which day did you fly back, Jennifer?"

"The Tuesday. Tuesday morning. The twenty-fifth."

"All right. Thanks." Shields doing her best to keep any excitement from her voice.

"Steve," Jennifer McLaughlin said. "He hasn't done anything, has he?"

"Not necessarily." Shields opened the office door. "Thanks for your time."

Out on the street, the rain had just stopped, leaving the paving stones slippery and dark.

"Didn't waste any time, did he?" Shields said. "Flies back on the twenty-fifth and a day later Maddy Birch is dead."

"We still don't have proof."

"We've got enough to bring him in for questioning."

Elder nodded.

With a broad smile, Shields hit Ramsden's number on her phone. "Okay, Mike. Bring him in."

Kennet had finished in Dartmouth Park and moved on. One wing of the Whittington Hospital was slowly being transformed into luxury apartments with views over London, Waterlow Park on their doorstep, a ten-minute stroll to Highgate Village, five more to the Heath.

Kennet was sitting on a platform two-thirds of the way up the scaffolding, time out for a smoke and a drop of tea from a thermos. One of his colleagues alongside him, stretched out, the *Sun* open across his face.

Situations like that, people panicked, even innocent people, tried to do a runner, but Kennet, Ramsden thought, where could he go? Besides, he'd seen them coming, sure enough, and not made a move.

"Steve," Ramsden called up, keeping it friendly. "A word, eh?"

Kennet shook out what remained in his cup, screwed it back on top of the thermos, put the thermos in his backpack, said something to his friend, who was sitting up now, wondering what was going on, and began to climb down.

"DS Ramsden. This is DC Furness."

"Yes, I remember."

"Not altogether defective then."

"What?"

"Your memory."

"Sorry, you'll have to explain."

"At the station."

"What? Oh, come on."

"No, you come on."

Kennet's body tensed and his eyes narrowed just a little and Ramsden readied himself in case, but then Kennet relaxed and said, nodding back toward where he'd been working, "Give me a few minutes," and Ramsden said, "Go ahead," and then, to Furness, "Go with him."

Ramsden lighting a cigarette and pacing easily up and down, wanting to believe they had him, but not letting himself, not quite, preferring to believe in what they said about when the fat lady sings.

They kept him waiting the better part of an hour, trying his patience, the young uniformed constable as inscrutable as one of the Guardsmen on sentry duty on Horse Guard's Parade. When Karen Shields entered, Ramsden and Elder close behind her, the PC stepped outside.

"You know you can have a solicitor present if you wish?" Shields said, sitting down.

Kennet smiled. "No need for that."

"And you realize you can leave at any time?"

Kennet made a play of getting up, then sat back down.

"You don't mind if I tape this interview?"

"Be my guest." Leaning back now, enjoying it.

We'll see, Shields thought. "I'd like to

ask you some questions," she said, "about your recent holiday in Spain."

"Great food, lovely weather, iffy hotel."

"You stated previously that you and Ms. McLaughlin returned to this country on Friday the twenty-eighth."

"That's right."

"According to Ms. McLaughlin, you came back early on the twenty-fifth."

Kennet drummed his fingers on the table. Broad fingers, nails cut short. Shields was remembering Maddy Birch's former husband. Workingman's hands.

"Mr. Kennet, is that the case?"

"Sorry, what?"

"That you flew back to this country on the twenty-fifth?"

A slight movement of the shoulders. "If she says so."

"What do you say?"

"All right, yes. Yes, the twenty-fifth."

"Then why, when you were asked before, did you claim it was the twenty-eighth?"

Kennet threw up his hands, rocked back his chair. "God, woman! Why d'you think?"

Shields leaned, almost imperceptibly, toward him. "Tell me."

"It's obvious, isn't it? She was killed on the Wednesday, wasn't she? Maddy. And you were going to be going round, all the blokes she'd been out with. Friends. Anyone who knew her. Asking questions, poking into their lives. Easier to stay out of it, right? No harm done either way."

"Unless you've got something to hide."

"Who hasn't?"

"Where were you on the evening of Wednesday, the twenty-sixth?"

"See. There you go, right there."

"Where were you?"

"Went to see this film. *The Medallion.* Jackie Chan. Holloway Odeon. Absolute bloody rubbish. Don't often go and see stuff like that, but sometimes that's what you want, right? Rubbish. Give your brain a rest. But can I prove it? No. Who keeps cinema tickets? No one. Afterward I went to the pub up the road, set back, past the traffic lights toward the Archway. I don't even know what it's called. Had a couple of pints, went home."

"And then what?"

"Then nothing. Up at six-thirty next morning. Off to work, same as usual."

"You didn't go out again?"

"No."

"You're sure?"

"Course I'm sure."

"Like you were sure you flew back to

274

England on the twenty-eighth?"

"I've explained that."

"This pub you say you were in, did you talk to anyone?"

"Bloke behind the bar."

"Think he'd remember you?"

"I doubt it."

"No witnesses to support what you say you did or where you were."

"That's right."

"As an alibi, it doesn't begin to stand up, does it?"

Kennet smiled. "Now you know why I lied."

"So what do you think?" Shields asked.

They were in her office, she, Elder, and Ramsden. Late afternoon, early evening. Furness was babysitting Kennet in the interview room.

"I'd like to smack him in the face," Ramsden said.

"Frank?"

"Would he be that sure of himself if he were guilty? I don't know."

"You don't think he's covering up something?"

"Probably."

"Well?"

"I don't know if it's what we want it to be."

"Half an hour alone with him," Ramsden said, "I'd bloody find out."

Shields laughed despite herself. "Mike, you're such a sweet old-fashioned thing."

"Bollocks," Ramsden said. Adding a mock-deferential, "Ma'am."

"Well, I'd like to have another go at him, ask him about his relationship with Maddy. See if there isn't something we can shake him on there."

Elder was just about to say something when his cell phone started to ring. Turning away, he listened briefly. "Five minutes. I'll call you back."

"I'm sorry," he said to Shields, "something I have to deal with. You carry on."

As he turned away, she wondered what could have brought the concern so clearly to his eyes.

Chapter 28

Elder had recognized Maureen Prior's voice instantly, her tone preparing him for something bad, but not for this.

"It's Katherine."

For an instant Elder's heart had seemed to stop.

"She's been arrested."

Of all his fears, not the one he would have most suspected, not the worst.

"Okay, Maureen," he said now, standing close against the parking garage wall. "Let me have the details."

"She was arrested for possession."

"Cannabis? Ecstasy? Out clubbing and . . ."

"No, Frank."

"What then?"

"It was heroin."

"Jesus!" The word expelled with a hiss of air.

Elder closed his eyes and brought his

head forward against the corner of the wall. He could hear Prior's breathing at the other end of the line.

"How much?"

"Five grams."

"They're charging her with intent to supply?"

"Not yet."

"Not yet? Either they have or they haven't, I don't see . . ."

"It's not so straightforward, Frank. There's someone else involved."

"Okay, I'm coming up."

"It's not my case, Frank. They're holding her at Canning Circus. I could put you in touch if you want. Perhaps if you just had a word . . ."

"No. I'm coming up." Stepping back, he checked his watch. "I can be there in a couple of hours."

"All right. You'll call me?"

"Sure. If not tonight, tomorrow, first thing."

"Good. And Frank . . ."

"Yes?"

"If you're driving, take care."

Elder grunted and broke the connection. At least where he was, he was close to the M1, though by now the volume of traffic would be building steadily.

Sweating a little, he dialed Joanne's number.

"You've heard?" he said before she could speak.

"Of course."

"Why didn't you call me?"

"Frank . . ."

"Why in God's name didn't you call me?"

He heard the clink of a glass. "I'm sorry, Frank, I . . ."

"What? You didn't think I'd find out? You didn't think I wanted to know?"

"It's not that, Frank, it's . . ."

"How is she?"

"She's all right. I mean, I suppose she's all right. It's difficult, Frank, you don't . . ."

"I'm driving up, leaving now. I just wanted you to know."

"Don't, Frank."

"What else d'you expect?"

"She won't talk to you, you know."

Elder wanted to hurl the phone into the far-flung reaches of the car park. Instead, he pocketed it carefully and made himself stand for some moments, perfectly still, controlling his breathing, before reaching for his keys.

The first fifty miles of the motorway

were nightmarishly slow; after that the lanes cleared enough for him to pick up some speed, only to close down again beyond Leicester Forest East. Finally turning off at the exit for Nottingham South, he skirted the river and then drove along Maid Marian Way onto Derby Road, turning left again just past Canning Circus and into the police station car park.

There was a small fracas going on outside the entrance, a beleaguered PC standing among a group of angry women, doing his best to calm things down. Inside, a balding man with blood on his shirt was standing with his back against the wall, pressing a square of bandage against the gash on his head.

Elder identified himself to the officer on duty. "I believe you're holding my daughter, Katherine."

"Just one moment, sir."

Elder caught the wounded man's eye.

"What the fuck you starin' at?" the man said, his accent raw from north of the border. "You askin' for a fuckin' kickin', you."

The noise from the street abated as the PC walked in off the sidewalk. "Kenny, we can't have you hiding yourself in here all evening. You'd best get yourself off to Accident and Emergency, get that seen to."

"No wi'out an escort, I'm not. Those are wild women out there."

"Mr. Elder?" The duty officer had returned. "If you'll come through. The inspector would like a word."

Elder had met Resnick once in the past four years, and then briefly. By reputation, he was a bit of an odd duck, a good thief catcher nonetheless; not so many years before he had astonished all and sundry by taking up with a young woman from the force, some twenty or more years his junior.

"Frank."

"Charlie."

Resnick's grip was warm and strong, the smile quick to his face and gone; his expression as he sat back showed concern.

"You're working late," Elder said.

"It's a poor business, Frank. Your girl. I'm sorry. Especially after what happened before."

"Thanks."

"I didn't know how to get in touch with you direct. I thought you and Maureen were probably still in touch."

"She rang me as soon as she heard."

Resnick nodded, awkward in the situation the Drug Squad had left him to sanitize.

"Katherine," Elder said, "how is she?"

"Fine. Fine, Frank, all things considered."

"I'd like to see her."

Resnick scraped a speck of something from the cuff of his shirt, real or imaginary, "All in good time."

"Christ, Charlie. That bastard Keach kept her locked up . . ."

"I know, I know."

"And now you . . ."

"Frank, it's not so straightforward. Hear me out."

Elder sat back with a slow release of breath. "Is it ever?"

Resnick resettled himself in his chair. "The car she was traveling in was stopped on Forest Road East. There'd been an incident, Cranmer Street; a firearm discharged."

"And they thought she was involved?"

"Not really. Just stopping everyone. Routine. They'd've been off and away if Katherine hadn't been giving the officer a piece of her mind. Bored standing around, got up his nose, I daresay."

"She'd been drinking?"

"Maybe just a little."

"She wasn't breathalyzed?"

"She wasn't driving."

Now we're getting to it, Elder thought.

282

"Officers hoiked them out of the vehicle," Resnick said, "the pair of them. ID, the usual palaver. Phoned it all in."

"The driver," Elder said, "he was known to you."

"Rob Summers. Two priors. Nothing too serious. Possession of cannabis. Public order. Some kind of argy-bargy at the university. Demonstration."

"I've met him. Briefly. I didn't know he had a record."

"Drug Squad, they've had their eye on him for a while now. Suspected him of handling a little cannabis, spreading it around, friends mostly. Not worth the aggravation of bringing him in."

"And now?"

"Some consideration he might be moving up, apparently. Different league."

"They'd like a reason to squeeze him."

"Something of the sort."

"And that's where my Katherine comes in."

"When the vehicle was searched there were a little over five grams of heroin in a small leather bag in the dash."

"You're saying it was hers?"

"Her bag, Frank. Her stuff inside."

"She was holding it for him."

"Likely."

"No way he's putting up his hand?"

"What do you think?"

"And Katherine?"

"Beyond the fact that, yes, the bag's hers and she hasn't the foggiest how the drugs got inside, she hasn't said a thing."

"And you reckon holding her overnight might make her think twice, drop him in it, this Summers, change her mind?"

"Somebody does."

"Somebody?"

"Bland. Detective inspector."

"Then he doesn't know her very well."

Resnick held Elder's gaze. "How well do you, Frank? Driving round in broad daylight with a suspected drug dealer, sizable amount of a class A drug in her possession."

Katherine lay curled on the narrow bed, knees drawn up and pressed against the cell wall, the collar of her oyster-colored sweater pulled up close to her neck. If there had been a belt with her tan jeans it had been punctiliously removed. Her feet were bare.

"Kate?" His voice was loud in the fetid, airless room. "Katherine . . ."

A slight tensing of her muscles and nothing more. A tray of food, uneaten, lay nearby on the floor.

"Talk to me."

A silence, unbroken, and then, muffled by her arm, so that Elder had to strain to hear: "What for?"

"I want to help."

She laughed then, a harsh sound that raised her head and broke into a jittering cough. Elder moved closer and sat, perched, near the end of the bed; when his leg inadvertently touched her foot, she pulled it, sharp, away.

"You want to help," she said, not looking at him, her voice small and dry.

Times he had sat like that when she was a child, four, almost five; his hand would touch her cheek and, as he spoke and said her name, she would slowly stroke his lower arm, her fingers smooth and warm and small. His eyes smarted with the beginnings of tears.

"Of course I do," he said.

The laugh again, harder this time. "You mean like you did before?"

Elder flinched as if he had been hit.

For an instant he must have looked away, because suddenly he was aware of her staring at him, her gaze, the awful flatness of her eyes.

"Katherine . . . ," he began.

But by then she had turned again toward the wall, head buried in her arms.

Elder stayed where he was, not moving, awkward, listening to her breathe. When the custody sergeant called time, Elder bent over her once more, stopped short of kissing her, stood, and turned aside, the sound of the door closing behind him like the clenching of a fist.

She's alive, Frank, and you're some great hero, your picture all over the papers, all over the screen every time you turn on the bloody TV.

Joanne's words.

Chapter 29

Martyn Miles answered the door. "She's in a bad way, Frank. Shaky at best."

Joanne was sitting at one corner of the settee, legs pulled up under her, face drawn, a half-empty wineglass in her hand. A cigarette was smoldering in an ashtray on the floor. "You've seen Katherine?" she said.

"Yes."

"How was she?"

"Confused, angry, upset. Take your pick."

"When I went to see her, she kept her face to the wall. She wouldn't tell me a thing."

"The drugs they claim she had in her bag," Miles said. "Planted, like as not."

"Martyn," Joanne said. "Please stay out of this."

He carried on as if she hadn't spoken, as if he hadn't heard. "No offense intended,

Frank, not to you, but the police, you know what they're like, some of them."

"Martyn," Joanne said. "I'm warning you . . ."

"All right, okay. Calm down, why don't you? Just calm down."

Ash spilled down the front of Joanne's dress and she brushed it casually away. "Heroin, Frank," she said. "What would she be doing with heroin?"

"These days . . . ," Miles began.

"Don't get to thinking she's like those skinny models you're so fond of," Joanne said, her voice shrill. "Doing cocaine and God knows what else every five minutes of the day."

"One of your fantasies, sweetheart, not mine."

"Fuck you," Joanne said, swigging down what was left in her glass.

"All I'm saying is, Frank," Miles went on, "these days you can never tell. Well, you'll know that yourself, better than anyone."

"For Christ's sake, Martyn, stop trying to get him on your side."

"I didn't think it was a matter of sides."

"No?"

"No."

"Because if it is, why don't you tell him

what you told me when you heard Kate had been arrested. See how far he's on your side then."

"Oh, for Christ's sake, leave it out, Joanne . . ."

"Why? Because it doesn't suit you now? For Frank to know what you really think?"

"Now you're being stupid."

"Am I?"

Miles gave Elder a look as much as to say, you see how unreasonable she's being.

"I think," Elder responded, "I might like to know what it was you said."

"He said it was no more than she deserved."

"What I said was, it might not be such a bad thing."

"Why was that, Martyn?" Elder said. "I'm not sure I understand."

"You know, Frank. These past months, the way she's been. And now it seems drugs as well."

"And you think being locked up in a police cell will make her see the light?"

"It might scare some sense into her, yes."

"Don't you think she's been scared enough?"

"That was a year ago, Frank. She can't keep hiding behind that forever."

"Listen to yourself," Joanne all but

screamed. "Just bloody listen to yourself. You don't understand a bloody thing."

"And you do?"

"Yes, I fucking do."

"That's it. That's it. Get hysterical," Miles said. "Great help all round."

Tears welled in Joanne's eyes.

"Martyn," Elder said. "Maybe you should let Joanne and me talk."

"Fine."

The lanterns on the patio shone small candles of light through the window, their reflections doubled and redoubled in the glass. Nursing a fresh glass of wine, Joanne stood close against the window, staring out, and Elder wondered if in some way it made her feel invisible. Or was it something to do with how she felt, what might happen at a touch? He could see her face, its contours in the glass, not quite real, white against the dark. The small triangle of skin where the hair parted at the nape of her neck.

It was past midnight by now, Elder thought, closer to one.

The reflection of his face slid over hers and merged. Slowly, he touched her shoulder with his hand.

"Frank."

When she said his name a small circle of mist blurred the glass before her face. She said his name again and turned, and when she turned it was into his arms. Eyes closed at first, he held her close, her head beneath his chin, feeling her heart race against his chest.

Minutes passed and her breathing steadied and she lifted her face toward his. "I'm sorry," she said.

With a slow shake of his head, he stepped away.

"I need a cigarette," she said and crossed the room.

Elder went into the kitchen and ran the tap, drank water from a glass. Whoever Joanne had in to clean had worked hard on the bottoms of the burnished pans hanging in perfect order from a polished metal rail high on the wall.

In the living room, Joanne was sitting at one end of the settee, and he sat opposite her on a pale curve of cushioned chair that gave a little with his weight.

"What will happen?" Joanne asked.

"To Katherine?"

She looked back at him as if to say, what else?

"They could charge her with possession with intent to supply, in which case she'd

291

almost certainly be released on police bail. But I don't think they will."

"Because of you?"

"That wouldn't matter one way or another."

"What then?"

"I don't really think it's Kate they're interested in. It's him. Summers. I think they were hoping if they pressured her, she'd give them something they could use against him."

"And she won't?"

"It doesn't look that way."

"God." Joanne took a last drag at her cigarette and ground it out in a hollow globe of glass.

"How long has she been seeing him?" Elder asked. "Summers? D'you know?"

Staring at the floor, Joanne shook her head. "I don't know who she's been seeing, Frank. Not recently. She won't talk to me. About anything. And if I ask her, she just flies off the handle and storms out. Martyn's right, she's been running wild and I don't know what to do." She looked at him then. "She's our daughter, Frank."

"I'll talk to her. If I can."

Joanne pulled a folded square of tissue from a pocket in her dress, dabbed her eyes, and lit another cigarette.

"You'll stay, Frank."

"I don't think so."

"This time of night . . ."

"I'll go to a hotel."

"There's no need."

He shook his head. "It's easier."

"Martyn won't be back, not tonight."

"It isn't that." He crossed toward her and aimed a kiss at the top of her head. "I'll see you tomorrow, okay?"

"Okay." She reached for his hand but he was already on his way toward the door.

Outside any wind there'd been had dropped off and the air, as he walked back down through the winding crisscross of roads toward the city center, was heavy and still.

Chapter 30

Against all odds, Elder slept like a stone. The radio alarm on the small bedside table woke him with inane chatter, slightly off station. In the bathroom mirror his face looked tired and drawn; a thin scar, where Adam Keach had cut him with a knife, ran from the center of his forehead down along the bridge of his nose, stitch marks like tiny perforations to each side.

The hotel dining room was busy with businesspeople in dark suits, enjoying the full English breakfast behind the *Telegraph* or the *Mail.* In the buffet, the scrambled eggs were congealed and the catering tomatoes swam in a sea of their own juice. The toast, brought to the table too soon, was scarcely brown and almost cold.

"Coffee or tea?" the waitress said with a charming smile, her heavily accented voice, to Elder's ears, from South America or Spain. Though he asked for coffee, she brought him tea, and he had neither the heart nor the energy to complain.

He met Maureen Prior in the Starbucks on Lister Gate, close to the entrance to the Broad Marsh Center. She was seated at a table in the rear when he arrived, unobtrusively dressed in brown and beige. He might have seen her in bright colors once, but couldn't easily remember when. Her hair, medium-length, medium-brown, softened the sharp oval of her face.

"Good to see you, Frank."

"You, too."

He went to the counter to pick up the coffee he'd ordered, carried it back, and sat down.

"I'm sorry about Katherine," Prior said.

"Thanks."

"She's been charged?"

"No, thank God."

"Special pleading then."

"Not on my part. No favors asked."

"She's your daughter, Frank. Five grams in her bag. Difficult to see her walking away otherwise."

Elder told her what had happened, what little he knew, and she listened carefully, breaking off pieces of a muffin almost absentmindedly with one hand.

"They think she's lying, obviously," she

said when Elder was through. "Covering up for Summers."

"You know him? Anything about him?"

Prior shook her head. "Drug Squad, any idea which officers are involved?"

"Resnick mentioned a name. Bland."

Prior smiled. "Ricky Bland."

"You know him?"

"By reputation."

"Which is?"

"Bit of a chancer. Gets results. One way or another. Came up from the Met, oh, good few years back now."

"You don't like him."

"I said I don't know him."

"You know what I mean."

Prior ate some of her muffin. "What I've heard, let's say he sails close to the wind. Came under investigation once, him and a partner. Eaglin? I'm not sure of the name. Quantity of crack cocaine confiscated and then disappeared. There was some rumor Bland and whoever had sold it back to the dealer they'd taken it from in the first place."

"Nothing proved?"

Prior laughed. "Answer that for yourself, Frank. They're still out there, working. Putting the bad guys away. Some of them, at least."

"You think they were guilty?"

The laugh transposed into a smile. "You know me well enough, Frank. Everyone's guilty in my eyes."

Watching Prior eat had made Elder hungry and, seeing him eyeing the plate, she pushed it toward him. "What about you, Frank?"

"What about me?"

"How's it going in London?"

"Not so badly."

She looked at him seriously. "When it's over, you ought to consider coming back up here."

He shook his head. "It's too complicated. Besides, if I wanted more there's plenty where I am. Devon and Cornwall have just brought four detectives out of retirement and they're scoping round for more."

"Sheep rustling at a premium, is it?" The smile was back on Prior's face. "Someone playing fast and loose with the mackerel fleet?"

"Six murders in eight days. One of them specially nasty, couple in a garage badly beaten then shot."

"You're not tempted?"

"Not what I went down there for."

"If you were up here you'd be near Katherine."

"Not where she wants me to be."

"You think she means it?"

"I know she does."

Prior resisted the temptation to say more. "Ricky Bland, you're going to see him? I could come with you if you like."

"It's good of you, but no, it's okay. An address though, just in case he isn't pulling overtime."

Prior was already reaching for her cell phone. "Just let me make a call."

The house was in Mapperley Plains, a once-new development near the golf course, UPVC windows and frosted-glass aluminum-framed doors. A blue Audi A6, dented, stood outside the garage. The front lawn was in need of a final mow, the grass already beginning to clutter up with leaves.

Elder knocked on the door and rang the bell.

Nothing seemed to happen.

An arthritic Honda sedan came cautiously along the street, slowed down almost to a halt, then continued on its way. Neighborhood watch, Elder thought.

He rang the bell again.

This time there was movement within, an inner door opening and then bolts being released, locks turned. The man who appeared was in his mid-forties with a thick stubble and close-cropped hair, a V-neck sweater hastily pulled over an otherwise bare chest, patterned boxers and bare, muscular legs.

"Richard Bland?"

"Who the fuck are you?"

"Frank Elder. I used to be on the job."

He looked at Elder keenly, squinting a little into the light. "This better be good, pal."

"Katherine Elder, she was arrested yesterday. Possession of heroin. She's my daughter."

Bland looked at him again and pulled the door wider. "Come on in. Tryin' to get some kip. Three late nights on the fuckin' trot. Thought you were one of them bleeding-heart collectors, famine in fuckin' Sumatra or somewhere."

Dust had gathered in small circles in the corners of the hall. The room Bland led Elder into was almost bare, crumpled clothes and cans and empty take-out boxes on the floor. The venetian blinds were two-thirds closed.

"Cunt took all the furniture when she left. Had a van come round when I was out. Sleeping upstairs in a fucking sleeping bag." He pointed toward the kitchen door. "There's beer in the fridge, help yourself."

When Bland came back down, blue shirt outside his jeans, he grabbed some beers for himself, lit a cigarette, and instructed Elder to get hold of the pair of plastic folding chairs that were leaning up against the wall.

They sat outside on a small patio, looking out over a rectangle of unkempt lawn, bare borders, a line of recently planted saplings. In among the hum of traffic, children cried and dogs set off a chain of barking. January notwithstanding, there was some warmth in the sun.

"Get shot of this fuckin' place," Bland said, "soon as I fuckin' can. Get back into the city. One of them new flats, by the canal. Only thing, minute I sell it, the bitch gets fuckin' half."

Elder said nothing.

"You married?"

"Not anymore."

"Know what I mean then."

For a while they swapped war stories about life on the force, Bland quizzing Elder a little about his time with Serious Crime, elaborating on the spread of drugs, the steady influx of guns.

"Fuckin' noddies out patrolling St.

Ann's in body armor with Walther P990s holstered at their fuckin' hips like Clint fuckin' Eastwood. Me, I can walk into a crack house or down some alley in the Meadows and all I've got is a finger to stick up their arse, always supposing they'll bend over and oblige." He coughed up phlegm and spat it at the ground. "Every kid dealing out there on the streets has got a Glock or some converted replica stuck down the back of his designer fuckin' underwear. Niggers driving round in thirty-thousand-plus of motor with their fuckin' rap music blaring out and an Uzi under the fuckin' front seat. All very well to say it's one another they're killin', only problem with that they're not killin' one another fuckin' fast enough."

He dropped the butt of his cigarette into the empty Heineken can and lit another.

"Your kid," he said, "she was carrying for the bloke she was with, Summers, no fuckin' doubt. Thought a night in the cells might get her to turn him over, but it didn't. No worries, we'll get him another way."

"And Katherine?"

Bland popped another can. "Needs to reconsider the company she's keeping."

"Tell me about Summers," Elder said after a moment.

"Rob Summers. Robert. Early thirties. Moved here from Humberside twelve or thirteen years back to go to university. Hung around ever since the way some of 'em do. Too idle to get up off their fuckin' arses and move somewhere else. That or too fuckin' stoned." Bland swallowed some beer. "Started selling a little dope when he was still a student, nothing too serious. Carried on ever since. Low-level, just below the eye-line, you know the kind of thing."

"So why the great interest?"

"While or so back, six, nine months maybe, his name started cropping up. Heavy hitters now. Not round the estates, either. Clubs and the like. Upmarket."

"You've had him in?"

Bland sneered. "Clever bastard, isn't he? Loves the sound of his own voice. Reckons he can talk his way out of fuckin' anything. Get the Red fuckin' Sea to part if he's a mind. Talk soft tarts like your Katherine into carryin' for him, carryin' the can."

He could see the anger rising in Elder's face and eased forward on his chair, one officer to another, man to man.

"Listen to what I'm saying, Frank, don't go wading in, doing your indignant father thing. Okay? Don't rock the boat. Not

302

now, now we're close. Someone coming in from outside, making him jumpy when there's no need. There's too much at stake."

"You're asking me?" Elder said.

"Asking you, yes, that's right."

"And Katherine?"

"She can walk. I'll make the call. Go and get her if you like. After this."

"All right," Elder said, getting to his feet. "Thanks for that at least."

"We're all right about Summers?"

"Won't lay a hand on him, you've got my word."

Bland swallowed some more lager, belched, and wiped his mouth with the back of his hand. "Need a lift back into town?"

Elder shook his head. "It's a nice enough day, I'll walk."

Bland followed him through to the front door. "Where did you get this address?" he asked.

Elder hesitated. "Maureen Prior."

"Wasting your time there," Bland leered. "Had it sewn up when she was seventeen. I can put you in touch with several blokes counted the stitches, if you like."

Elder had to restrain himself from thumping him hard.

Chapter 31

The custody sergeant made Katherine sign for the contents of her pockets and her purse. As soon as she and Elder were outside, she began to walk away.

"Wait. Katherine, just wait," Elder said.

"What for?"

"We need to talk."

"I don't."

He took hold of her arm and she shook him off. " 'You need to talk, phone the Samaritans. See a shrink.' " Anger blazed in her eyes. "I did. See what a lot of bloody good it did me."

He stood and watched as she strode toward the far sidewalk, forcing the traffic to swerve and brake: one moment she was walking past the corner of the Circus and then she was lost to sight.

He had a good guess where she would go.

Don't rock the boat, Bland had asked him, *leave Rob Summers alone, leave him to us.* The curtains at the front of the house in Sneinton were drawn again, the same ginger-and-white cat sitting on the window ledge alongside the door. When Summers answered it, Elder pushed him back into the hall.

"Something you forgot to tell me," Elder said. "Left off your CV. Teaching, writing poetry, the odd story. Somehow you left out the fact you deal drugs on the side."

"She's not here," Summers said, "if that's what you're thinking."

"Of course she's bloody here."

"All right. But she's upstairs, lying down. She's exhausted, right? Worn out."

"Whose fault's that?"

"She's taken something to help her sleep."

"No need to ask where she got that from."

Summers shook his head. "Come through here and sit down. Or do you want to stand yelling in the hall?"

The room was the same jumble as before, the same sweet afterwash of cannabis in the air. Summers switched on the stereo, but turned the volume low.

"Okay," Elder said, "start talking."

Summers retrieved a packet of Rizla papers and a tin of Old Holborn from one of the shelves and began rolling himself a cigarette. "When I was Uni I traded a little dope, right. Mostly to friends. It's no secret."

"You were arrested. Charged."

"Someone ratted me out."

"Some honest citizen."

"Some creep."

"You were found guilty."

"Of possession."

"Still a crime last time I looked."

"Come on," Summers said. "A few ounces of cannabis resin. These days all that'd get you would be a nod and a wink, keep it out of sight."

"And you got what? A suspended sentence? Probation?"

"Something like that."

"But that's not all."

"I don't . . ." For a moment, Summers seemed genuinely confused. Then, shaking his head, "Jesus, you're dredging that back up?"

"Assault, wasn't it?"

"Affray. A demo on the university campus. Some arsehole American right-wing Christian antiabortionist coming to speak at the Student Union. I'm just sorry

I didn't get in a few good punches while I had the chance. He's probably in some think tank now, advising Bush on social policy."

"And you're what?"

"We've just been through all that."

"As much as five grams of heroin, more than enough for personal use."

Summers shook his head, more emphatically this time. "Not mine."

"You saying it was Katherine's? Is that what you're telling me?" Elder's voice reverberated in the confines of the room. "You're saying she's on heroin now?"

"Of course she's not."

"Because if she is, I'll know who turned her on."

"Relax, she's not. She won't go near the stuff."

"Then how did it get into her bag?"

"I don't know. We were at a party the night before."

"And this was what? Somebody's idea of a joke? A party bag? Smarties and a piece of cake, three balloons and a stash of H?"

"I don't know. Maybe it was a mistake."

"A mistake?"

"All right, all right. More likely, someone trying to set me up."

"And why would they do that?"

"Look," Summers said. His roll-up had gone out and he lit it again. "Believe this or not, it's up to you. Eighteen months or so ago, I was stopped in the street. Stop and search, right? Coming down through Hockley. Late at night. Happens all the time. Well, you know. You should. Two blokes in plainclothes, Drug Squad or so they said. Of course, they didn't find anything, there wasn't anything to find." A few stray ends of tobacco flaring up from his cigarette. "Maybe I was a little mouthy, I don't know. Whatever reason, it put a hair up their arse. Been on my case ever since. Oh, not all the time, every day. Just once in a while, when they've got nothing better to do. Pull me over, pat me down. 'Reason to believe' . . . you know the drill."

"That's why you take precautions."

"That's why I'm clean."

"The reason you make sure you're not caught carrying your own stuff."

"There is no stuff."

"No?"

"No."

"This place stinks like a café on some back street in Amsterdam."

Summers threw back his head and laughed. "I'll have to take your word on that."

Elder reached forward quickly and took hold of Summers's arm between elbow and wrist. "I don't give a damn what you do, how much skank and scag and shit you shift. But you get my daughter involved once more, any way at all, and I'll see you pay. That understood?"

"Let me fucking go," Summers hissed.

Elder increased the force of his grip and then pulled his hand away.

"I mean it. If Katherine ever gets into trouble again because of you, I'll be back. And you'll regret you ever saw the light of day."

An hour later, he was on the motorway, heading south.

Chapter 32

Shields woke before the alarm and lay there listening to the wind rattling the windows and the occasional vehicle going past on the wet road outside; once, twice, she turned over, pulling the covers higher, trying for another ten minutes' sleep, but it wasn't to be. Sooner or later she would have to brave the first cold journey to the bathroom, the shower.

"What's the matter with you, child?" her father had said when he'd visited. "All this promotion, chief inspector now, and you're still content to live like this."

Child! She wondered if she would ever reach an age when he stopped automatically calling her that. Only when and if, she supposed, she had a child of her own. But there was some truth in what he said; she could afford to move, a bigger flat, bigger mortgage, but where would she move to? And why?

She was happy here. The damned cold aside. What she should do, she told herself for the thousandth time, was pay to have those old windows, which had been there since the days of Methuselah, taken out and new, double-glazed ones put in. Take care of the damp. Get the central heating overhauled, radiators with individual thermostats attached. Radiators, for God's sake, that worked.

In the bathroom she splashed cold water onto her face, shivered, and squeezed toothpaste onto her brush.

One reason she didn't do these things, she knew, was the inevitable hassle and disruption. Finding a construction firm that wasn't going to mess with her or, worse, rip her off, was the first thing; workmen who would actually turn up on time and do the job until it was finished, instead of the usual two days here, two days there, now you see them, now you don't; the place left looking like a sty while they juggle jobs all over half of London. Someone you could trust.

Shields rinsed her mouth, spat, wiped her face on the towel, and sat down on the closed toilet lid.

Someone you could trust.

Someone who would have access to your

home, your things; who was adept at climbing in and out, gaining entry, scaling walls and scaffolding.

She was thinking of Steven Kennet, broad-faced, smiling.

Now you know why I lied.

No, she thought, standing up and switching on the shower. Not yet they didn't.

As the water ran over her, bouncing off her shoulders and the back of her neck, she ran her mind over what she had learned about the possible break-in of Maddy Birch's flat. Nothing taken, barely disturbed, just a sense that someone had been there.

She reached for the shower gel.

Yesterday there had been a message saying that Vanessa Taylor had called, but she'd been too busy to call back. She would try this morning before the day took hold. A short while later she was dry and partly dressed and spooning coffee grounds into the pot. Not so many minutes past six o'clock.

Elder had contacted Shields from Nottingham, explaining the reason for his absence in as little detail as possible, the bare bones. Back inside the building now, he opted for the stairs instead of the lift and was puffing slightly by the time he reached the fourth floor.

"How is she, Frank?" Shields asked immediately. "Your daughter?"

Elder hunched his shoulders. "Good as can be expected."

He looked tired, she thought; heavy around the eyes.

"How did it go with Kennet?" Elder asked.

"We pushed him back and forth about Maddy; this most recent woman, Jennifer. Nothing. Nothing we could use. Oh, sometimes you got the feeling he was close to showing us a little, giving something away, but then he'd clam up. As if he was teasing us almost. Enjoying it." She shook her head. "By the time we kicked him loose I was with Mike, wanting to smack him in the face."

"Not enough to hold him?"

"Not really. No."

"No chance of a search warrant then? Turn his place over, see what we can find?"

"Not without something more solid. Conjecture, that's what the magistrate would say. Supposition. No reasonable grounds."

"And what do you think?"

"I think he's still our best shot."

"Denison's not been able to shake any-thing out about Loftus?"

"Not a thing."

Shields unwrapped a mint and offered one to Elder, who shook his head. "I spoke to Vanessa Taylor earlier," she said. "A couple of nights ago, she thinks there was someone hanging around outside her flat."

Elder sat forward sharply. "She thinks, or she knows?"

"She can't be certain, it was dark. One minute he was there, the next he'd gone. No chance of a description, anything like that. If it hadn't have been for what hap-pened to Maddy, I doubt she'd have even bothered getting in touch. Her flat, it's not far from where Maddy Birch used to live."

"You've informed the local nick?"

"Vanessa had done that herself. I checked. They've promised to have a car drive by at intervals through the night, in-crease foot patrols."

"How did she sound? Vanessa?"

"A little nervous. Concerned not to be wasting my time."

"You think one of us should go and talk to her?"

"I'm not sure what she could tell you that's any different. My guess, in the circumstances, it's her imagination working overtime."

Shields pushed her chair back away from the desk and stretched her long legs. "I thought I'd drive out and see Estelle Cooper. Talk to her on my own this time. See if I can't get her to loosen up a little. Might learn something useful."

"Woman to woman," Elder said.

A smile passed across Shields's face.

"What?"

"Shirley Brown. Stax. Seventy-four. I used to play it all the time."

Elder had no idea what she was talking about.

When Shields arrived in Hadley Wood, Estelle Cooper wasn't at home. The children, according to one of the neighbors, were having a day off school. An inset day, isn't that what it was called nowadays? Estelle had taken them out for the day. Somewhere in London. The Science Museum?

Shields returned to her car. She would try again after the weekend; no sense trying to talk to Estelle when there was a chance her family were around. What she wanted was Estelle Cooper alone.

Maybe, Taylor thought, she just hadn't

315

been in the mood. Coke and a bucket of popcorn. The Odeon, Camden Town. Wind down. Relax. *Love, Actually.* They had to be kidding, right? And of course, sitting there on her own hadn't helped. She remembered when she'd been to see *Bridget Jones's Diary* with Maddy. How they'd loved it, every minute, right down to the slushy ending. Practically wet themselves with laughter.

Poor Maddy. God, she missed her!

Somehow she didn't fancy the tube home and waited fifteen minutes for a bus instead, she and a couple of dozen others, half of them hungry from the pub and scarfing their way through burgers or chicken chow mein, the stink of onions, kebabs, and hot sauce, fast-food litter swirling around their feet. She was just about to give it up as a bad idea, walk back to the tube station after all, when there it was at last, veering toward them from the lights, a 134.

The lower deck was crowded and she went up top, a spare seat beside the window near the back, and as she sat down a man sat next to her, leaning for a moment quite heavily against her as the bus lurched away.

"Sorry," he said, and then, "Vanessa? It

is Vanessa, isn't it? Almost didn't recognize you." A quick, apologetic smile. "Miles away."

He was holding out his hand.

"Steve. Steve Kennet. I used to . . ."

"I know, I know."

"Haven't seen you since . . . must be ages. Couple of years, at least."

Taylor nodded and said nothing. One of the last times she'd seen Steve Kennet, one evening in the pub, when Maddy had gone to the loo he'd leaned across and said, "How about meeting up one night, just the two of us? What d'you think?" Afterward he'd tried to pass it off as a joke, but she'd never been sure.

"Terrible, wasn't it?" he said now. "What happened to Maddy. Couldn't believe it at first. You don't think, do you? Someone you know."

Taylor shook her head.

"So, anyway, where've you been?" Perkier now. "Tonight, I mean. Not working, I hope?"

"Cinema."

"Anything good?"

"Not really."

"*Pirates of the Caribbean*," Kennet said. "You seen that?"

"No."

"It's good. A laugh, you know?"

"That what you saw tonight?"

"Me? No. Just out for a drink, few beers."

Taylor looked out of the window. They were moving slowly along Kentish Town Road, passing close to where she worked. Superimposed on the upper stories of buildings she could see Kennet's reflection, the thickness of his hair, the collar of his leather jacket turned up against his neck, his eyes watching her. At Tufnell Park she made as if to get up.

"This isn't your stop," Kennet said.

"Isn't it?"

"Not unless you've moved."

"How do you know where I live anyway?"

"We walked past there one night, remember? You and Maddy and me. Going back to her place. 'That's my street,' you said."

"Well," Taylor said, standing. "Not anymore."

He swung his legs out into the aisle, leaving just enough room to let her pass.

"I'll get off if you like. Walk you home."

"Don't bother."

She just made it down the stairs before the doors closed. She stopped herself from looking back up at the bus as it drew away, knowing she would see his face at the window, looking down. She had bought herself a good twenty-minute walk, and why? Because she'd been uncomfortable sitting pressed up next to him, certain that any moment he would say something she didn't want to hear, a proposition of some kind?

Two-thirds of the way along Junction Road, she turned right down St. John's Road, cutting through. At the end of her street, she hesitated, then quickened her pace; it was only as she neared the short path leading to her front door that it occurred to her that Kennet might have been the man standing in the shadows outside her house a few nights before.

The keys slipped from her hand.

Her skin froze.

Only with the door finally open did she turn.

Nothing, nobody there.

Vanessa, she said to herself, *for God's sake get a grip.*

In bed less than fifteen minutes later, she lay listening to each sound; it was almost another hour before she finally drifted off to sleep.

Chapter 33

The early rain clouds had disappeared, leaving the sky above Primrose Hill a clear, crystal winter blue, the light glinting off the roof of the mosque at the edge of Regent's Park below. From his vantage point near the top, Elder watched Robert Framlingham striding up from Prince Albert Road like a landowner out to survey the vastness of his acreage and his EC subsidy. Framlingham was wearing his Barbour jacket and a pair of softly polished, hand-stitched brogues.

"Frank, good to see you." His grip was firm and warm. "Sorry if I'm a couple of minutes late."

"Sit or stroll?" Elder said.

"Oh, stroll I think, don't you? You can fill me in as we go."

For the best part of a lap Elder talked and Framlingham was mostly content to listen, the Hill busy with dog walkers, young mums and the ubiquitous au pairs, students and bums and OAPs, all making the most of the morning sun.

When Elder had finished, they continued to walk for a while in silence, Framlingham running it all over in his mind.

"Kennet, your mind's pretty made up then?"

"Not necessarily."

"And Shields? What about her?"

"There's not a lot else for her to latch on to."

"So far, Frank. So far." Framlingham paused to ease something off the sole of his shoe. "That business with Mallory and Repton, that young PC in the car. I wonder if I'd let that go for nothing, after all."

Elder fixed him with a look. "You know something that I don't."

Framlingham allowed a smile to spread slowly across his face. "A good deal, Frank, a good deal. And much of no conceivable use to man nor beast." He rested his hand for a moment on Elder's arm. "All I'm saying, don't lose sight of the bigger picture."

They shook hands.

"Your daughter, Frank. I heard just a little. I'm sorry. If ever there's anything I can do."

A wave of the hand and he was on his way.

The Brent Cross shopping center was just off the North Circular Road, no more than ten minutes in the car from where Elder was staying. By mid-morning, the car parks were close to full.

Vicki Wilson was standing in the center aisle, between Next and Hennes, in front of a brightly colored stand promising tomorrow's cell phone today. Makeup picture-book perfect, Vicki was smiling her best professional smile and glad-handing leaflets extolling the virtues of a technological marvel that allowed you to text, take, and transmit photographs, download video clips from current movie releases and the top ten singles, watch the latest Premiership goals, surf the Internet, and, if time allowed, make the occasional phone call. She was wearing a short pencil skirt and a T-shirt with the manufacturer's logo snug across her breasts.

She'd been there since ten, the best part of an hour, five more to go, and her feet in those stupid shoes were aching already.

Oh, Christ, she thought, when Elder approached. *Another sad bastard, can't take his eyes off my tits.* Elder had walked past her once slowly, turned, and come back around. When he got closer, she revised her opinion. *Shit. It's only the fucking law.*

"Vicki Wilson?"

"If you're asking that, you already know the answer." Her voice was sharp, east London–edged, Goodmayes or Dagenham.

"Frank Elder."

"Here." She pushed a leaflet into his hand.

"What time d'you get a break?" Elder asked.

"Not soon enough."

"How about a cup of coffee?"

"Now?"

Elder tried a tentative smile. "Why not?"

"Just hang on a minute."

She fanned the leaflets out across the table behind her, lifted a shiny green jacket from the back of the chair and slipped it across her shoulders, picked up her bag, and walked with Elder toward the lift by the corner of Marks and Spencer.

They sat at the end of a row of small tables overlooking one of the aisles; below, shoppers wandered past oases of green-leaved plants, plastic and real, prospering equally beneath a glass roof.

With a small sigh, Vicki eased off her high-heeled shoes. Touch a fingernail to her face, Elder thought, and it would glide like a skater on fresh ice.

"How d'you know where I was?" she asked.

"Your agency."

"Wonder they didn't give you my address and chest measurements while they were about it." ꞁ

"They did."

"You're fuckin' kidding."

"Maybe not the chest measurements."

Vicki tossed her head. "Coppers, you're all the bloody same."

Elder held his tongue.

"Jimmy, i'n it? That's what you want to talk about."

"Jimmy?"

"James William Grant. Jimmy. It was what he liked to be called. By his friends." Vicki stirred some of the chocolate from the top of her cappuccino into the froth and brought the spoon to her mouth. "Come to make sure I've done what I was told, I suppose."

"What you were told?"

"Keep my mouth shut, of course."

"What about?"

"I don't know, do I? Fuckin' everything."

"Who told you this?"

"I don't know, do I? Some copper, plain-clothes."

"Describe him."

Vicki leaned back in her chair. "Forties, maybe. Sharp. Bit old-fashioned, but sharp. Joking with it. Not heavy. But all with that look in his eye. Like it wouldn't pay to cross him, you know?"

"He have a name?"

"Not for me. I'd seen him, though. Seen him before. After what . . . after they killed Jimmy. Talking to the one who shot him. That bastard."

"How do you know he was the one?"

"Came over and told me, didn't he? That morning. Right after it happened. I was sitting in the back of this police car, right? Didn't really know what was going on. 'Cept I knew Jimmy was dead. I knew that. Anyway, he come over, pointed his finger, right in my face, and made this sort of popping sound. Like a little kid, you know, pretending he's got a gun. That's the finger, he said, pulled the trigger. Put him away. And then he laughed and wandered off. Mallory. I asked this copper in the car and he told me. Detective Superintendent Mallory."

"And this detective, the one who came to see you, him and Mallory, they were together?"

"Yeah, I said so, didn't I?"

"Tell me again what he said to you."

"I already told you."

"Tell me again."

" 'Anyone comes round asking questions, anyone, you don't know a thing.' " She lifted her cup from its saucer but didn't drink. "No one has. Till now. And if they had, I don't know anything anyway. Jimmy, he never talked about . . . you know . . . what he did. Not really. Joke about it sometimes, bragging I suppose. This big score or that, but that was all. Nothing more. Just, sometimes he was there, sometimes he wasn't. Besides, I hadn't known him very long. And I liked him, you know. He was fun." She looked at Elder, moist-eyed. "Why did they have to kill him?"

"I don't know."

"He always said whatever he did, he'd be okay. Said they wouldn't touch him, you know?"

"They?"

"The police, I suppose."

"He didn't say any more? Give any names?"

"Said he had someone looking out for him, that's all. All-round protection. Like garlic. You know, keeping away vampires." She shook her head. "Wasn't true, was it? Not in the end."

Elder drank the rest of his coffee.

Vicki renewed her lipstick, leaving a near-perfect impression on a folded napkin. "I'd better be getting back to this sodding job."

"Here. Take this." Elder took a notebook from his pocket, wrote down his cell phone number, and tore out the page. "If you do think of anything, call me."

Vicki hesitated, then pushed the piece of paper down into the side pocket of her bag. "Thanks for the coffee."

"Any time."

Elder walked with her back to her stand, where a covey of small kids, having strewn half of her leaflets across the floor, was misspelling obscenities on the white spaces of the painted board.

"Fuck off!" she shouted. "The lot of you."

While they jeered and whistled and offered her the finger, Elder helped retrieve the leaflets from the ground. Then he wished her well and walked away to where he'd parked his car.

"I could be back over your way Sunday evening," Framlingham said in response to Elder's call. "Whitestone Pond. Near the old Jack Straw's Castle. I'll be parked on the north side. Seven, give or take?"

It was dark when Elder arrived, Framlingham sitting with the car window wound partway down, listening to a broadcast of *Idomeneo* from the Met.

At the aria's end, he turned the radio down to listen, Elder sitting in the passenger seat alongside him.

"Of course," he said, when Elder had finished, "he could have been lying to her. Vicki, is that her name? Mouthing off."

"Why would he do that?"

"Wanting to impress?"

"I don't think so."

"Grant had someone in his pocket, is that what you're thinking?"

"Either that or the other way round."

"He was an informer, you mean?"

"It's possible."

"He'd be high-grade if he were. Top-drawer. Not some sniveling menial of the toe rag variety."

"How easy would it be to find out?"

A smile passed across Framlingham's face. "How difficult you mean. That stature of informant — covert human intelligence sources, as we're supposed to call them nowadays. CHIS, can you believe that? If it hasn't got a fucking acronym, it doesn't exist. But that's by the by. All that information's kept in a closed file at the Yard. Strictly need-to-know. Senior officers only. And I mean senior."

"That would include you, surely?"

"Given good reason, Frank, it might."

"You'll try then?"

"It may take a day or two, but I'll try."

The moon broke through the clouds as Elder skirted the pond, heading back the way he had come.

Chapter 34

There were times when Estelle thought it was only the garden that kept her sane. If sane was what she was. Her friends, of course, had she really had any friends, would have said, *Darling, you've got the children,* and while it was true they still accounted for a large part of her life, they were no longer hers in the way they used to be. Jake acted and sounded more like his father every day, and Amber, at five and a half, was lost much of the time in a world of ballet shoes and tutus and the right shade of pink for her cardigan, the right shade of blue for the band that held back her hair.

As for Gerald, he was, of course, the perfect gentleman, so polite at times it was as if he'd forgotten who she was and imagined her some distant cousin come to stay. He left early each weekday for the city and often returned late, occasionally phoning to say he was sorry but he'd have to miss dinner, and if that happened sometimes he'd bring her flowers and a little note. Once she found in one of his pockets a card advertising a members-only gentlemen's club in Soho and she'd been careful to put it back, pleased that he'd found somewhere to relax and unwind. If he asked her for sex now it was once a month at most, the light always out beforehand; when his leg slid over hers in the way she recognized, she would put her bookmark carefully in place and excuse herself to the bathroom; quite often, by the time she returned, he was asleep and snoring.

Estelle stood now by one of the rose beds, late morning, wearing an old green woolen coat, slacks tucked down inside calf-length Wellington boots, a pair of scuffed brown gardening gloves on her hands. The trouble with January, it was too late to plant more bulbs, too early for much else; all she could usefully do was tidy up the beds, cover the mess left by one or another of next door's cats, nip off the odd brown leaf with her pruning shears.

She thought how ugly the rosebushes were, pruned back, their hard green stems poking up blind into the air.

Somewhere in her mind she heard the car approaching, then a silence, then, faint, the front doorbell. If the door to the conservatory had not been open, it was unlikely she would have heard it at all. Not that it mattered: whoever it was, another of those sharply dressed Mormons or someone collecting for the church swap meet, they would soon lose patience and go away.

Nearer the bottom of the garden a sparrow was giving itself a dirt bath, its wings spraying up a film of loose soil. Helped by the cold air overnight, the ground had dried out quite well; the sky today was a washed-out blue-gray smeared with cloud and the temperature in single figures, eight or nine at most.

The side gate clicked open and when Estelle turned she saw the black detective who had, for a moment, held her hand. Tall, she hadn't remembered her as quite so tall; as tall as Gerald she could swear, the heels of her boots making sharp indentations in the lawn.

"Mrs. Cooper. Estelle. How are you this morning?" Smiling, smiling, smiling. "I rang the bell, but I suppose being in the garden, you didn't hear. I hope you didn't mind me finding my own way round?"

"No, of course not. Not at all." What else was she supposed to say?

"You do all this yourself?" Karen Shields

said, looking around. Though in all probability meant as praise, to Estelle's ears it came out more as accusation. *Is this all you do with your life?*

"Gerald helps with the heavy work sometimes, that is, he used to. And Jake, now he's older, he . . ." Abruptly she stopped: why was she saying this?

"Estelle?" Shields asked gently. "Are you okay?"

Estelle looked up at her, that large commanding face with those red, red lips. Beautiful, was that the word?

"Estelle?"

"Mm? Yes, of course." Of course what? She didn't know.

"Why don't we go inside?" Shields said. "That cup of tea you offered last time. Something to keep out the cold." Walking back toward the house, she took Estelle's arm.

They sat in the conservatory, the door now closed, the corners of glass beginning to mist over. Here and there a flower, brick red or butterfly white, still clung to one or another of the geraniums, their upper leaves healthy and green, those gathered around the base shriveled brown and paper thin.

Tea was in broad-brimmed white cups with a gold line faded around the rim; the china teapot in its cozy sat on a tray with a matching milk jug and sugar bowl, though the sugar remained untouched. Rich tea biscuits fanned out on a plate. Paper napkins.

Shields took her time, listening while Estelle pecked at conversation like a bird, waiting for what might be an opportune moment. In the end she dropped her question into the silence, like a pebble falling slowly into the well.

"Estelle, I know this will be difficult, and if there was any way I could avoid asking you I would, but when you said there were things Steven Kennet wanted you to do, things you felt uncomfortable with, I need you to tell me what they were."

Estelle's hand shook and tea spilled from her cup into her saucer and from there into her lap. "How silly of me," she said, dabbing at it with her napkin. "I'm sorry, what was it you said?"

When Shields left an hour and a half later, her face was rigid with anger and hurt, her mind alert. During the course of their relationship, Kennet had persuaded Estelle to take part in a number of scenarios in which they played out the act of rape. Sometimes where they were living, sometimes in cheap hotels, and sometimes, after dark, on Wimbledon Common and Hampstead Heath.

In those instances, what he had her do, against her will, was walk along the path pretending to be lost, whereupon he would appear as the apparently kind stranger, offering to show her the way. Or sometimes, wearing a mask, he would jump out at her, grab her arms, and throw her to the ground.

Toward the end of the relationship, when she wouldn't agree to play along, he raped her for real.

Shields called Mike Ramsden from her car before switching on the ignition and slotting the seat-belt buckle into place.

"Mike? I want Kennet back in for questioning. ASAP. Drag him down off a roof if you have to."

One last glance back at the house before she drove away.

Steven Kennet was nowhere to be found. He had failed to show up for work that morning, no reason, no excuse. His home address was a flat off Seven Sisters Road, between Finsbury Park and the Nag's

Head. No reply. One of the couple who lived above said they didn't think he'd been home last night. Came in and drove away. A five-hundredweight Ford van, dirty white. They hadn't seen him that morning, either.

"Keep looking," Shields said. "Keep a watch on the flat. Let's get a description ready for circulation, details of the van."

When Tara's mother delivered Jake and Amber back home just before four and there was seemingly no one in, she simply bundled them back into the Toyota and drove them along to number thirty-five with Tara, where she gave them all chocolate biscuits and juice and then, after they'd played together and the Cooper telephone remained unanswered, some pasta with M & S tomato sauce.

As far as Jake and Amber were concerned, it was an unlooked-for treat.

Tara's dad went to the house as soon as he came home and knocked loud upon the door; he let himself into the garden by the side passage and found the conservatory locked, the whole house in darkness. Shouting yielded nothing.

They thought of phoning the police, but decided to wait until Gerald Cooper arrived from work. At least he would have a key.

Gerald, as it happened, caught the early train and was back by seven, to find a note from Tara's parents pinned to the door. He thought he'd have a quick G & T before going to the fetch the kids. God knows where Estelle had gone off to, silly cow.

He found her in the living room, hanging from the chandelier, the kitchen stool she'd brought in to stand on kicked away.

Chapter 35

Elder read bad news in Karen's face before hearing the words.

"Shit," he said. And then, "Poor woman."

"Yes."

"How are you feeling?"

"How am I? What difference does that make? She's dead, for Christ's sake."

"You went to see her yesterday? Spoke to her?"

A laugh choked from Shields's throat. "Yes, I spoke to her."

"How was she?"

She looked at him as if he were some kind of fool. "How do you think she was? I cozied up to her and calmed her down and made her tell me about that arsehole Kennet raping her."

"He raped her?"

"He raped her. Sometimes in some kind of sick game she went along with and sometimes for real."

"She told you this?"

"She told me this and then I left her alone in that house with her gardening gloves and her fancy fucking teacups and her fake fucking chandelier." There were tears running freely down Shields's face. "And yesterday afternoon when I wanted that bastard brought back in, he'd fucking disappeared."

Elder eased her chair away from the desk. "Sit down a minute."

"I don't want to sit down."

"Sit down, have some coffee, let's talk this through."

"I don't want any fucking coffee either."

"Karen."

"What?"

"Sit down. Come on." Firmly but gently, he took hold of her arm. "Let's sit."

Shields sighed and did as she was told; she found a tissue in her bag, wiped her eyes, and blew her nose. Elder pulled another chair around from the other side of the desk and sat opposite her, close enough to have held her hand.

"It's not your fault, you know."

"Oh, no. Yes, it is. Of course it is."

"You didn't do any of those things to her."

"I made her talk about them, think about them."

"You were doing your job."

"My fucking job."

"Besides, you think they weren't on her mind, all the time? You think she could forget? Ever?" He was thinking of Katherine, standing in Rob Summers's house, back before Christmas. *Dad, I'm never going to be like I was before.* "It's Kennet," Elder said. "That's who's to blame. What we've got to do is make sure he doesn't do it again. Make sure he pays."

Jennifer McLaughlin was serving a customer something for a sore throat and sympathizing: a lot of it going around this time of the year. Elder went in and begged ten minutes of her time. Together with Shields they walked along Broadway, Jennifer taking the opportunity for a cigarette, Shields doing her best to inhale but getting only petrol fumes instead. Starbucks was full so they went on past the circle to Pizza Express.

Shields began her questions as delicately as she could, but Jennifer, a good decade and a half younger than Estelle Cooper by age, and several generations by attitude and experience, was largely unfazed.

"We quarreled about it, yes, course we did. All that play-acting stuff. Don't know

now why I went along with it as long as I did." Pausing, she looked Shields in the eye. "Except, well, it was exciting at first. You know? You know what I mean? It's only afterwards you think, God, what was going on there at all?"

"And when you fell out on holiday," Shields said, "is that really what it was about? More of the same?"

Averting her face, Jennifer slowly released a wavering line of smoke. "Yes," she said.

"We'd like you to come in and make a statement," Shields said. "I presume that's okay?"

"Now? You don't mean now?"

"Later this afternoon would be fine. When you finish work. We can give you a lift both ways if that would help."

"All right." She looked at them again, first one and then the other. "He has done something this time, hasn't he? Something serious."

"It's possible," Elder said.

"Dear God," Jennifer whispered and crossed herself.

"If it were necessary," Shields said, "you'd be prepared to give evidence in court?"

"Oh, yes."

"You don't know the names of anyone Steven went out with before, do you?" Elder asked. "We'd like to talk to as many as we can."

Jennifer reached for her pack of cigarettes. "I don't know, I might. If I think about it, you know. Names he's mentioned. Not above a bit of bragging, as you might imagine. But offhand there's only that . . ." The cigarettes slipped from her hand. "Only that policewoman, the one who was killed. Oh, God. Oh my good God!" A sudden shiver running through her, every vestige of color bleached from her face.

In the end, Jennifer McLaughlin came up with three names, going back, she thought, a good few years. One might have been working in Waitrose, another a nurse. All were — or had been — north London–based.

"You and me then, Frank," Shields said. "Bit of old-fashioned legwork. What do you say?"

Chapter 36

Elder picked up the CD box and glanced at the front: a round-faced black man with short cropped hair, saxophone balanced over one shoulder, hands together as though in prayer. "Stanley Turrentine," Elder called toward the kitchen. "Should I have heard of him?"

No reply.

Saxophone and what? Organ?

"Sorry," Shields said, carrying two newly rinsed glasses and the bottle of Aberlour she'd spotted on sale on their visit to Waitrose. "You said something but I couldn't hear what."

"Turrentine, is he famous?"

"Celebrity-famous or the jazz cognoscenti kind?"

"Either."

"Maybe a little bit of the latter." She poured two quite generous measures of Scotch, handed one to Elder, and raised her own. "Cheers."

"Cheers."

"I saw him a few years back at the Jazz Café." Shields smiled. "Back in my clubbing days."

"Now you sit around in the evenings knitting and doing crochet."

"Something like that."

The whiskey was good, warm on the back of the throat. They'd eaten at a place on Upper Street, Turkish; had to stand on line twenty minutes or so for a table, but it had been worth it. Lamb kebabs and rice, hot sauce, a bottle of red wine.

"He played this," Shields said, listening. "You know it?"

Elder shook his head.

" 'God Bless the Child.' " She sang a few bars.

During the course of a long afternoon, they'd managed to track down and talk to two of the three women whose names Jennifer McLaughlin had remembered.

Maria Upson, a nurse working in orthopedics at the Middlesex, had confirmed pretty much everything they either knew or suspected about Kennet; she'd gone out with him for nine months and now regretted almost every minute of the last six.

"Men," she said, with a not totally disparaging glance toward Elder, "get to know them, or think you do, let them slip under your guard and they either turn into five-year-olds who want cuddling and cosseting or else they're Fred West." She didn't need to add whom Kennet resembled.

Lily Patrick was a trainee manager at Waitrose, and the picture she painted was different: Kennet was kind, funny, considerate. Okay, he did once climb through her second-floor bedroom window in the middle of the night and scare the wits out of her, but that was to deliver a dozen red roses and some red balloons on her birthday. "You know, like the Milk Tray man."

"And sexually," Shields said, "he didn't ever suggest anything you felt uncomfortable with?"

"No." Blushing, but just a little. "What kind of thing?"

"Games, acting out fantasies. That kind of thing."

"We did act out a bit of *Romeo and Juliet* once. You know, the balcony scene. After we'd seen the movie."

"I was thinking of something a bit less romantic."

"I don't understand."

"Rape fantasies, perhaps."

"Rape?" Lily wiped her hands down the front of her Waitrose apron, as if they were suddenly dirty. "You're joking, right? This is some kind of a joke?"

"No."

"You've got to be."

"It's something people do, Lily. Fantasies like that. Ordinary people."

"Not people I know. Not Steve."

Elder had been thinking about a song by Dire Straits that Joanne had played over and over. He was trying to recall their fantasy life, his former wife and himself, if they ever had one.

"If it was so good," he said, "the relationship with Steve, how come you stopped seeing him?"

"He went away, didn't he? The Middle East somewhere. For work. This big project, rebuilding a hospital I think it was. Kuwait, maybe. Somewhere they couldn't drink, I know that. No alcohol. I remember Steve joking about it, how he'd have to be careful which airline he was flying with, in case, you know, it was dry. 'As much free booze as I can get,' he said, 'before the drought.'"

"He liked a drink then?" Shields said.

"No more than anyone."

"And you haven't seen him since then? What was it? Eighteen months ago?"

"Two years nearly. No. He's still there, isn't he? Living there."

"You've heard from him then?"

"No. Not really. Not since Christmas, Christmas before last."

They'd thanked her for her time and left her looking wistful and not a little sad.

The third — Jane Forest — they were still waiting to track down.

Shields was sitting on a low-backed love seat, orange with purple and red cushions; Elder sat opposite in a gray wicker chair. The music was still playing over sounds of traffic and muffled voices from the street.

"Eighteen months ago," Shields said, "according to Lily Patrick, Kennet went out to Kuwait." She shook her head. "I don't think so. Eighteen months ago or not so long after, he started seeing Jennifer McLaughlin."

"During which time he was also seeing Maddy Birch."

"And, presumably, shopping at Tesco instead of Waitrose."

"Seems to be a pattern," Elder said.

"So what's the betting that while he was

going out with Miss Waitrose, he was seeing someone else then too?"

"Somebody whose fantasies ran on the rougher side of Cadbury's Milk Tray and *Romeo and Juliet.*"

"Most likely. Though even Juliet died in the end."

"So did Romeo, remember?" Elder sipped his Scotch. "If I knew my Shakespeare better, I could probably come up with someone more like Kennet than Romeo."

"Othello," Shields suggested. "No, Iago."

Elder had seen it once, *Othello.* When he was in the sixth form. The Grand in Leeds. A matinee. He could remember the teacher forever shushing them, then reading the riot act when they got back to the coach; could also remember the name of the girl he'd sat next to but not a lot about the play. Desdemona? A handkerchief?

"Wait, wait," Shields said. "*Titus Andronicus.*"

"Who?"

She laughed. "I don't know. I just know there was a lot of blood."

Stanley Turrentine seemed to have come to an end. It was comfortably quiet.

"I'm sorry about the other night,"

Shields said after a while.

"The other night?"

"At your place. You must have thought I was being a bit of a tease."

"No."

"You didn't think I was coming on to you and then backing off?"

"I didn't think you were coming on to me at all."

She threw back her head and laughed. "God! I must be losing my touch."

"No, it's me. Forgetting how to read the signs."

"A little rusty?"

"Something like that."

"Well," she picked up the bottle of Scotch and tipped some into his glass, "what you need is a little lubrication." And then, aghast. "I can't believe I just said that."

"You didn't."

"No, you're right."

But he was smiling, smiling with his eyes, and though she wasn't certain, having got this far, she kissed him anyway. Once would have been okay, acceptable, within the limits of the situation, a point of some return, but it was more than once: his mouth, his neck, his cheek, his eyes. His hands on her body, her back, her thighs, her breasts. She pulled him toward her from the chair onto the floor. Oh, God, they weren't going to do it on the floor? His fingers warm across her shoulder blades, his leg between hers. Some part of her mind flashing warnings. Her diaphragm was in its box in the bathroom, no condoms, and the chances of his having one were less than nil. As his thumb brushed her nipple she repositioned herself. Buttons and zippers. She unbuckled his belt. Salt and sour in her mouth. Grabbing one of the cushions from the love seat she raised herself up and touched herself between her legs. He kissed her there and there. Her heels drumming on his spine. If screams could wake the dead.

Afterward, they lay side by side. Somehow Shields had contrived to turn the music back on again. "More Than You Know." Elder was amazed at the colors of her skin, everything from dark chocolate to iron gray.

"I'm going to have a shower," she said eventually, scrambling to her feet.

Elder lay there wondering what the time was, whether he'd be expected to stay the night. Whether he wanted to.

She came back five minutes later wearing a cotton robe, glass of water in hand, broad smile on her face.

"What?" Elder said.

"Wasn't so long ago, I could have got dressed up, really fit, put on my face, got myself down to the Funky Buddha, Sugar Reef, Chinawhite. Pulled some rising rap star or a brace of Premiership wannabes. And what do I end up with?" She laughed. "Tired white meat."

"Thanks. Thanks a lot."

"My pleasure."

"You've got a mouth on you, you know that."

"You should know."

Elder shook his head. "Look, I should go."

"Okay. You need a hand up off the floor?"

He looked at her to see if she was being serious and couldn't tell. When he was in the shower his cell phone rang, and Shields answered it.

"Here," she said, handing it to him as, water off, he reached his hand around the shower curtain. "A woman. Young."

He knew it was Katherine before he heard her voice. "Dad. I need to see you. It's important."

"What about?"

"When I see you, okay?"

"All right, but I'm not sure when . . ."

"Dad, if it weren't urgent, I wouldn't have asked."

He knew it was true.

"Tomorrow morning then," Elder said. "Nine-thirty, ten?"

"Make it ten. The castle. I'll meet you in the grounds."

"Katherine . . ."

"Tomorrow." And she ended the call.

"Trouble?" Shields asked once he was dressed. She was in the process of making coffee.

"I've got to go up to Nottingham tomorrow. My daughter again. I'll be back down as soon as I can."

"Don't worry. We'll keep after Kennet. See if we can't trace this Jane Forest. Meantime, it's my turn to call you a cab, okay?"

Elder nodded. "Okay."

She kissed him at the door, nothing lingering. "Not so tired," she said, grinning. "Just very white."

Chapter 37

It was a peerless winter's day. Elder had considered driving, but in the end had opted for the train. Not so much over an hour and a half, an hour and forty minutes, and he was in the center of the city, walking past the canal and then the bus station, one edge of the Broad Marsh Center taking him on to Lister Gate, Castle Gate, and Maid Marian Way. The castle sat on rock, not a child's idea of a castle with turrets and narrow windows and now-crumbling arches, the castle of Robin Hood and King John, sword fights and bows and arrows, but something more recent, more four-square and municipal.

The grounds were as neat and cared for as Elder remembered, the earth in the flower beds newly turned, the wood of the bandstand looking as if it might have been given a fresh coat of paint, or maybe that was just the untrammeled winter sun, pale but warm enough to lift the chill.

Katherine was standing by the lower wall, leaning against the parapet, staring out. She turned her head as Elder approached, what looked like a man's fleece zipped up almost to the neck, sneakers, baggy jeans.

Elder hesitated, bent to kiss her cheek and, as she turned her head aside, kissed the ragged crop of her hair instead.

"Not a bad morning," he said, needing something to say. "Nice coming up on the train. Bright, you know. Quick too. No sooner've you glanced at the paper, had a cup of that dreadful tea than you're here."

He was babbling.

There were the same dark patches around her eyes that he'd noticed before. The oversized fleece made her look undernourished and small. Unwell. Not so much more than a year ago she'd been running for her county, she'd been . . . he stopped himself, stopped the thought.

"Last night," he said. "You sounded worried."

"Yeah, well . . . Let's walk. Can we just walk?"

They set off slowly along the path that would wind them, eventually, up to the castle itself.

"You've got to promise me," Katherine eventually began.

"Promise what?"

"You've just got to promise, that's all."

"What?"

"That you won't snap your rag, get angry. Just let me . . . let me finish, okay?"

"All right."

It was a while more before she began again. "You know that time I was arrested, when you came up, the heroin. It was Rob's, you were right. Well, not his exactly, he was holding it for someone. No, wait, wait. Remember what you said. Calm down, okay? Chill." Katherine stopped, head down, arms hanging loose by her sides. "I knew this was a bad idea."

"No, it's fine," Elder said. "Go on, go on."

They set off again, walking slowly.

"It was my fault, really stupid; if I'd kept my mouth shut we'd have got away with it, nothing would have happened. But once we were at the station and that bastard from the Drug Squad got involved . . ."

"Bland?"

"Yes. Him. He'd been on Rob's case for ages, picking him up for this and that, you know, threatening him. How they were going to find him with this huge stash in his possession, get him sent down for a long time. Never actually doing anything — I mean, he could have arrested him plenty of times for little things, but all he ever did was keep on needling him."

Katherine stopped on the curve of the bend, looking back down toward the gate and over the town.

"Then, after last time, when you came round, he was there next day, half-six in the morning, him and some pal of his . . ."

"Eaglin?" Elder interrupted, recalling Prior mentioning his name.

"I don't know. They didn't stop for much in the way of formal introductions. Turned the place upside down. Rob, he tried to stop them and they punched him, knocked him down and kicked him."

"They had a warrant?"

"So they said."

"You didn't see it?"

"I didn't see anything. Just crashing and shouting from upstairs while I was trying to see to Rob. He was bleeding from a gash to the head."

"And this was when?"

"Two days ago. Monday."

"What happened then?"

"They came back down, grins all over their rotten faces, waving this bag of crack cocaine. 'Got you, you bastard. Talk your way out of this one.' Claimed they'd found it under the boards in the bedroom."

"Is that where he kept it?"

"They'd planted it. It wasn't his."

"Like the heroin in the car wasn't his."

"No."

"No? It's no use covering up for him, Kate . . ."

"I'm not. Not this time. Not about this. I mean . . ." Angling her head up toward the sky, down toward the ground, avoiding his eyes. "I mean, that was where he kept stuff, yes, all right, sometimes, but not crack, he didn't deal crack, not ever, hardly ever, and honestly it wasn't his. It wasn't."

There were tears running into the hollows of her cheeks. While Elder fumbled in his pockets for a clean tissue, Katherine wiped her face with her sleeve.

"What happened after they arrested him?" Elder said.

"That's it, they didn't."

"Why not?"

"Because they wanted him to make a deal."

"What kind of deal?"

"They wanted him to give them information."

"About what?"

"What do you think?"

"Who was supplying him. Other dealers, maybe. I don't know."

Katherine had started walking again. "Suppliers, yes. If there was a safe house they used. That was what they seemed to want more than anything."

"And he told them?"

"There wasn't a lot else he could do."

They were at the high wall overlooking Castle Boulevard, the canal, and the Meadows. A small flock of birds, six or seven, almost too white to be pigeons, took off from the rock below and scattered in a random curve before alighting on the roof of the Brewhouse Museum below.

"Rob gave them the address of this flat in Forest Fields, he didn't think they were still using it, it was all he could think of to do. Turns out they were. Bland and his mate went round just as it was getting dark. What we heard was they got close to nine thousand in cash and God knows how much crack. H too. If they ever find out it was Rob who gave them away, they'll kill him."

"Where is he now?"

"In hiding."

"As well as the money and drugs, Bland and Eaglin, did they make any arrests?"

"Not as far as I know."

For a moment she let him hold her hand.

"Where are you staying?" he asked.

"At Rob's, why?"

"Go home. Go home to your mum's."

"No."

"Do it, Kate."

"But if he wants to get in touch with me . . ."

"He'd be stupid coming there. He can ring you on your mobile, surely?"

"I suppose."

"Is there anything you need to collect?"

"No, not really."

"Then go now, I'll walk along with you."

"And then what?" Her face thin and pleading. "Is there anything you can do?"

"I don't know. I can try. What I can't do is promise. Okay? You understand?"

She nodded, sniffing, hands in pockets, so forlorn she was a child again, agonizing over a broken toy, a favorite doll lost, her friends had refused to play with her at break time or she had lost a glove, grazed her knee. He'd never come to terms with loving her as much as he did, never would.

"Come on," he said. "Let's go if we're going."

Chapter 38

The sun persisted behind a thin skim of cloud, but close to the Trent the air bit sharp into unprotected skin. Prior wore a scarf and gloves, her parka zipped and buttoned. She had met Elder on the south side of the bridge, near County Hall, and they had set out along the river toward Wilford, the City Ground at their backs.

A few runners and the occasional dog walker aside, they had the path pretty much to themselves.

"You believe her?" Prior said.

"I believe her, yes."

"Not Summers?"

"Without speaking to him face-to-face, it's difficult to know. He was obviously lying to me before."

"Come on, Frank. His girlfriend's father and an ex-copper, what do you expect?"

"It doesn't help me to accept his side of the story at face value, that's all."

"Katherine, though. She saw what she saw."

"Yes, I suppose so."

They continued walking. Nearing the pedestrian bridge that led to the Memorial Gardens, a pair of swans and assorted ducks swam toward them, hoping for bread.

"Bland and Eaglin, taking down the safe house and pocketing the proceeds, you think it's possible?"

"Anything's possible, Frank, you know that."

"But likely?"

"Drug Squad, you know, a few of them, old school, pretty much a law to themselves. And these two, they're both known to sail pretty close to the wind. But this . . . I don't know, Frank, I'd need proof."

"Yes."

"Not easy."

"If something like that went down, word would get around."

"I know. It's a matter of who to talk to, who to trust."

"Nothing different there then."

Prior smiled. "Nothing at all."

At Wilford Bridge they crossed to the embankment and followed the curve of the river back around.

"What time's your train, Frank?" Prior asked.

"Quarter past."

"I'll nose around, see what I come up with. Let you know."

"You'll be careful."

She gave him a look.

"Thanks, Maureen."

They shook hands.

"How's it going down there in the smoke?" Prior asked.

"Three steps up, two back."

"Better that than the other way round."

At the station he bought a paper and sat on an empty bench to make some calls. Katherine's phone was switched off and he left a message: "Great to see you, don't worry. Love, Dad."

Elder phoned Shields on his cell phone as the train was nearing St. Pancras: still no sign of Kennet, but they'd got a line on Jane Forest and Shields was hoping to talk to her later that afternoon.

The scar that began just below Jane Forest's right ear and continued past her jaw was visible only when she turned into the light. When her hair swung back from her face. Self-conscious, most days she wore a turtleneck sweater or a scarf inside the collar of her shirt or blouse.

"Why didn't you report it?" Shields asked.

"I was frightened."

"Of him?"

"Yes, of course. But not just that."

"What then?"

"What people would say."

"People?"

"When it got out. Whoever I had to explain it to. The police. You. My parents. Everyone."

"You were the victim. There's no blame attached to that."

"Isn't there?" Jane Forest twisted the cap off a bottle of Evian and lifted the bottle to her mouth. They were standing in a small yard at the rear of the florist's where she worked, one of a small parade of shops at the bottom of West Hill, adjacent to Parliament Hill Fields. Jane was wearing a green apron that tied at the back, the name of the shop embroidered in small yellow letters on the front.

"You know the north end of the Heath," she said, "up past the Vale of Health?"

Shields shook her head.

"We used to go up there, one or two in the morning. Park round the back of Jack Straw's Castle. Not that we were the only ones. That time of night it's mostly gays, lots of black leather, chains, that kind of thing. Real bondage stuff. Anyway, we'd go out into the middle of the heath; up there it's mostly bracken, trees, really overgrown, but there are these paths running through. Quite high up, you know. And I'd walk along as if I were on my own, pretending I didn't know Steve was there. And I didn't. I mean I never knew exactly where he was."

She took another swig at the bottle and wiped one edge of her mouth with the back of her hand.

"Sometimes he'd keep me waiting, just wandering up and down, for ages. Twenty minutes, more. These blokes every now and then staring out at me from behind bushes, wondering what on earth I was doing."

"You weren't scared?" Shields said.

"Of course I was scared. That was the point."

"Go on," Shields said.

"Well, sooner or later Steve would jump out at me and I'd — I don't know — pretend to fight him off, try to run away."

"And he'd catch you?"

"Oh, yes." There was a certain light in Jane Forest's eyes, blue-green eyes.

"And then?"

"Then we'd have sex."

"Consensual?"

"Sorry?"

"He didn't force you?"

"Yes, of course."

"Against your will?"

"Yes. No. I mean not really. But in the game, the game we were playing, yes. He'd hold me down, tear, you know, some of my clothes . . ."

"Hit you?"

"Not usually, no. Not hard."

"Nothing more?"

"What do you mean?"

Shields was looking at the scar on Jane Forest's face. Jane turned her head away and touched the tips of her fingers faintly to the pale, raised line.

"Sometimes, not often but sometimes, he would have a knife. It was big, broad, a sort of carving knife. This black handle with — what do you call them? — rivets through it. 'My butcher's knife,' he called it. 'Want to make good and sure I don't butcher you.'"

She was starting to shake now, first her arms, the upper half of her body, and then the rest. Shields took the bottle of water from her hand before it fell.

"One night, it was my birthday, he said,

'I've got something special for you, a celebration.' He tied my hands behind my back. He . . . he put the point of the knife . . . inside me . . . and when, when I started to scream, really scream he punched me in the face and when that didn't make me stop he cut me. Cut my face."

"Here," Shields said, moving an upturned crate away from the wall. "Here, sit down. There. Now put your head down towards your knees. That's it. That's right."

A blue tit alighted for a moment on top of the gate that led out from the yard into the alley behind, yellow beneath cobalt-blue wings.

"Afterwards," Jane said, barely raising her head, "as soon as it had happened, he was so upset, he really was. Almost beside himself with worry. And really gentle, caring, you know? He took me to the hospital, the Royal Free. Casualty, A & E. We said I'd been sleepwalking and stumbled over something, fallen against the window breaking the glass."

"They accepted that?"

"They seemed to. They stopped the bleeding and then stitched me up. Steve, he held my hand the whole time." She looked at Karen. "He was so sorry, genuinely sorry. He knew he'd let it get too far, out of hand. He said he wouldn't blame me if I never wanted to see him again."

"And did you?"

"At first I thought, yes, it would be okay. Him being so nice and everything. But after that night, I don't know, it was different. I mean, we never . . . it wasn't just that we stopped, you know, those games, we never had sex at all. He didn't . . . he wouldn't even touch me. And then, after a while, he told me he was seeing someone else."

She looked away.

"It's happened again, hasn't it?"

"We think so."

"Has he . . . did he . . . Oh, Christ!" She let her face fall forward against Shields's waist and for several minutes Shields held her, stroking her hair, touching once, inadvertently, the ridge of scar tissue running across her neck.

Together with another officer, Vanessa Taylor had spent two hours that afternoon interviewing a cocksure, snotty-nosed nine-year-old about throwing stones and doing serious damage to trains and train staff. With him were his father and his social worker, neither of them speaking to one another but both quick enough to interrupt and intercede. The boy's mother had left home eighteen months before, taking two of his younger siblings with her and leaving the boy and an elder sister behind. The father's response had been to go running to social services claiming that he couldn't cope. As a result, the boy was taken into care, the girl went to live with an aunt. Sometime in the following months, she drifted back, and then, after almost a year and two bouts of short-term fostering, the boy followed. Social services, meanwhile, were worried that the relationship between the dad and the thirteen-year-old daughter was inappropriate, to say the least.

Shortly before Christmas, the boy was expelled from school and a week later stabbed his tutor in the back of the hand with a ballpoint pen, alleging the man had tried to molest him.

Taylor began the interview feeling sympathy for a young person whom life had dealt a raw hand, but thirty minutes later wanted to use the same hand to slap the smirk off his ratty face. Sullen, even tearful when it suited him, he was quick as a trained solicitor to proclaim his rights and privileges, taunting them with their relative powerlessness over him.

By the time the interview was over, the boy released back into his father's care, the social worker chewing her way through a roll of mints as she wrote up yet another report, Taylor was more than ready for a drink.

Two pints and a vodka tonic later, she wandered into Nando's with a beat sergeant she vaguely fancied and devoured peri-peri chicken and rice while listening to him babbling on endlessly about Thierry Henry and the glories to come once Arsenal had settled into their new sixty-thousand-seat stadium at Ashburton Grove.

Scratch him off the list.

Nine-fifteen. Too late to catch a movie, too early to go home.

There used to be music, she knew, at the Bull and Last. Sometimes it was jazz but sometimes it was okay. Tonight, when she pushed the door open into the bar, it was nothing, just the electronic jingle of a few brightly lit machines and a television mumbling to itself above the bar. Fairly busy all the same, mostly men. A trio of clearly underage girls wearing next to nothing, more skin than clothes.

She could have turned around and walked out, but instead she asked for a vodka tonic and carried it over to an empty table near the middle of the room, a few faces turning to watch her progress, but not many.

She hadn't been there more than a few minutes before she was aware of someone leaning over her from behind.

Steve Kennet, smiling, a drink in his hand, jeans, checked shirt, and short leather jacket, still trailing the faint scent of aftershave. He was sitting down next to her almost before she could react.

"Regular bad penny," he winked. "That's me."

Chapter 39

Taylor didn't move. Didn't return Kennet's smile. "What are you doing here?" she said.

Kennet shrugged. "Same as you." Affable enough.

"Why here?"

He glanced around. "Not a bad pub. Quiet. Except on music nights. Or when there's some band on at the Forum. Packed out then."

"You come here a lot then?"

"Wouldn't say a lot, but yes, once in a while. Steady."

"You're not following me?"

When he laughed, his head jolted back, Adam's apple pushed out against his skin. "That what you think?"

"I don't know. The other night on the bus, now this."

Kennet shrugged. "Small world."

"Not that small."

"Coincidence, then."

Taylor held his gaze a few moments longer, then picked up her drink.

"I'll move on if I'm troubling you," Kennet said. He made no move to go. "You've had a bad day, maybe. Want to be alone."

"I have, as it happens. A shitty day."

"Keeping the street safe."

"Yes, if you like."

"Okay, I just thought, you know, see a friend, share a drink, a chat . . ."

"I'm not your friend. We're not friends."

"All those times . . ."

"I was Maddy's friend. Not yours." Her voice was loud enough to turn a few heads in their direction.

"All right. Okay." Kennet on his feet now, still smiling, backing away. "Just thought you might appreciate the company, that's all."

Hands raised, as if in surrender, he retreated toward the bar, pulled out a stool, and sat down, quick to exchange a few words with the barman, who looked over in Taylor's direction and laughed.

Taylor closed her eyes, picked up her glass, and lowered her head toward it, resting the rim against the bridge of her nose. When her breathing had steadied, she leaned back and finished her drink in two swallows.

"You know there's a law," she said to the barman, nodding toward the trio of girls nearby, "serving alcohol to kids under eighteen."

Kennet didn't as much as glance in her direction, but one of the girls stuck out her tongue and called her a name. The two others gave the finger to Taylor's back and giggled loudly.

There was a bus coming and she caught it to the Archway, thinking as they stop-started along about the boy they'd interviewed, what kind of a life he had, his sister, too, wondering how much truth there was in the social worker's concerns, doing her best not to think about Kennet at all.

It was a nice enough night, not cold, not nearly as cold as it had been, and, getting off the bus, she loosened her scarf and unzipped the front of her coat. At the far side of the lights, she bought a copy of the *Big Issue*, though she knew, in all likelihood, it would end up in the trash unread. On Holloway Road she lengthened her stride. More exercise, that was what she needed, either that or it wouldn't be too long before she couldn't even squeeze herself into a thirteen. Swimming. Why didn't she leave for work an hour early, do a few lengths in the Prince of Wales pool?

At the corner of her street she slowed her pace and looked around, but it was a bright night, as well as relatively warm, and there were no shadows lurking in dark corners. As usual, it took her a few moments to locate her key and she was just slotting it into the lock when an arm wrapped itself tight around her neck and she felt something cold and sharp pressing fast against the underside of her chin.

"Don't scream," Kennet hissed in her ear. "Don't make a fucking sound."

Elder had phoned Prior in Nottingham, not once, but twice.

"It's difficult, Frank. Seen asking too many questions too soon and the whole thing might slip away. Give me another day or so, okay? As soon as I know anything definite, I'll be in touch. You've got my word."

At least Katherine was at home where he wanted her to be. After a desultory five minutes of conversation, more silences than words, she asked him if he wanted to speak to Joanne and he said, no, it was okay, another time.

In the silence, Elder reached for the bottle and the glass.

He was drinking too much, spending too much time alone. Why had that been fine when he was down in Cornwall — perhaps the thing he relished most — but not here, in the city?

Difficult, too, not to let his mind slip back to the previous night, the taste and touch of another's skin. He was midway through dialing Shields's number when he stopped: what had happened between them, it was a one-time thing, a collision of need and circumstance, no more. Tired white meat, was that what she'd said? Sipping a little whiskey, he clicked the switch on the radio, a special report from our correspondent in Dafur.

In the hallway, Kennet kicked the front door closed. It was dark: not black but muted dark. Free newspapers and unwanted mail lay all down one side and underfoot. The air was stale and cold. When Taylor opened her mouth to shout, Kennet narrowed the angle of his arm against her throat and a choking sound was all that emerged. The knife was steady against the curve of her chin.

"Up!" he hissed. "Up, up. Upstairs."

Something seemed to have happened to Taylor's eyes. The contours of everything — stairs, banisters, the electric cord that hung down to a bare bulb — were blurred. And then she realized she was half blinded by tears.

Kennet's knee nudged against the back of her thigh.

Again, harder this time.

"Get moving. Go on."

On the first landing she slipped and her footing almost went, but he held on to her, hauling her back upright. His breath, smelling of beer and tobacco and something else she couldn't make out, was warm and raw against her skin.

"Move. Come on, come on."

The television was on in the first-floor flat, the sound of laughter muffled and brief. One of the things she'd always liked about the building was that people kept to themselves. If ever she did bump into one of the other tenants, a quick nod was all that usually passed between them, occasionally a brief word. Some bland remark about the weather or a complaint about the trash cans was the most any of them had ever exchanged.

She knew she had to get away from him

before they reached her apartment and he got her inside. Get away or raise the alarm.

On the final landing, she dug her elbow into his chest as hard as she could and wriggled as she kicked her heel back against his shin, but he only laughed and increased the pressure on her neck until she was afraid the flow of blood might stop and she would faint.

"Inside. Come on, inside."

Her fingers couldn't fit the key into the lock until he withdrew the blade from her face and his hand slid smoothly over hers. "There." Steadying her until the key slipped in and turned.

"Good girl."

Taylor's eyes closed tight.

They were inside.

"Don't switch on the light," he said. "Not yet."

His arm was no longer at her neck and she moved a few stumbling steps away, her hand against her throat. Heard him turn the key in the lock and slip the safety catch down.

The curtains were open, and when she turned there was light enough to see the shape but not the details of his face. The knife was back in his hand, held low against his side. She thought he was smiling but she wasn't sure.

"Anything to drink?" he said, the ordinariness of the question taking her by surprise.

"What?" A croak of sound and little more.

"A drink. You know, wine, some beer. Vodka, that's your thing." As if this were normal now, some kind of date. Calling around after the pub. Want to come in for coffee, both knowing what that meant. The features of his face were clearer now and, yes, there was a smile playing at the edges of his mouth and around his eyes.

"Look," Taylor said, her voice no longer recognizable as her own. "Why don't you just go. Leave. We'll forget about it, okay?"

"Forget? I don't think so. Not until we've finished. Not until we're through." He was tapping the knife against his leg. "Now, what about that drink?"

The bottle was on the shelf unit in the alcove to the left of the stove. Stolichnaya, four-fifths gone. A couple of shot glasses next to it. Books, not many. CDs. David Grey. Damien Rice. Norah Jones. Magazines. The telephone was on a low table to the right; her cell phone in the inside pocket of her coat. She could hear her own breath reverberating inside her head, against, it seemed, the inside of her skull.

"Just a small one for me," Kennet said, a smirk just visible on his face.

Unsteady, Taylor poured vodka into the glass and it spilled over the rim.

"Nerves," Kennet said. "Don't worry. Soon take the edge off those."

She was thinking about Maddy, about what had happened to her. She knew she had to do something now, before it was too late. The vodka bottle still tight in her hand, glass cold and smooth against her palm. Her eyes flicked back toward the door, the key still in the lock.

"Here," Kennet said, leaning forward. "Why don't you let me put that somewhere out of harm's way?"

And he lifted the bottle clear and, with a smile, returned it to the shelf.

"That's better," he said. "Now we can relax a little. Get to know one another better. What do you say?"

How long they had been sitting there, Taylor didn't know. Sitting opposite one another, the small table pushed aside. Knees touching. Fifteen minutes? Twenty? More? Kennet talking about this and that, about his work, his holiday in Spain, and all the while easing his hand between her legs, slowly, slowly, forcing them apart, his fingers pressing hard then soft, before switching his attention to her breasts, and all of this happening almost casually, without remark. When he squeezed, finger and thumb, her uncovered nipple, she cried out with a start.

"Sorry," he said with an apologetic smile. "Hands too cold. Warm them up a little, eh?" And slid both hands between his thighs, legs closed tight.

Taylor threw what was left of her vodka in his face, aiming for his eyes, and as she did so lurched sideways, reaching for the bottle on the shelf.

"You bitch!" he said, grabbing at her arm.

Shaking him off, she swung the bottle as hard and fast as she could against his face. The base struck the temple, just above the eye, and as he staggered back she swung again, teeth gritted, full force, and the bottle shattered against his cheek, driving him sideways through a quarter-circle, left leg folding beneath him, blood streaming from below his eye.

Taylor dropped the bottle and dashed for the bathroom, feeling for her cell phone as she ran.

Two bolts, top and bottom, and she slid

them across, leaning her weight back against the door as she dialed 999.

"Emergency. Which service do you need, caller?"

She gave the details as precisely as she could, waiting all the while for Kennet to hurl himself against the door and break it down.

When it didn't happen she began to cry, and when she heard the sirens, distant at first, then closer, closer, and then feet loud and heavy on the stairs, she cried louder and couldn't stop, not even when the first officers to respond had convinced her it was safe enough to unbolt the door; not even when she saw the glass, some of it smeared with blood, on the floor; not till a fresh-faced young PC, barely out of training, so young he looked more like a boy, led her firmly, not roughly, over to an easy chair and sat her down, sat with her holding both her hands and telling her it was all right, it was okay, they'd just gotten the bastard, hadn't they? Legging it across the Holloway Road and he'd run smack into the side of a bus and cannoned off. On his way to A & E now, most likely, cuffed inside an ambulance. That's it. Go on, cry. Let it out. This kid with peach fuzz on his cheeks, still holding her hand while other officers secured the scene.

"The knife," Taylor said. "He had a knife."

"We'll find it. Don't worry."

And they did, an hour later, where Kennet had thrown it, in the front garden of the house closest to the main road, hard up against the wall.

Chapter 40

The doctor had checked Taylor over, pronounced her bodily sound, waited while an officer took Polaroid photographs of the marks on her neck, then given her something to help her sleep. But of course she'd hardly slept at all. For half of what remained of the night she lay in bed, knees pulled up close to her chest, trying to blank out the sound of Kennet's voice, the coarse warmth of his breath. For the rest, she'd sat up in her old dressing gown, a blanket pulled around her, staring at the images that moved across the television screen. *ITV Nightscreen. Skiing on 4.* A signed edition of the *Antiques Roadshow.*

"You're a lucky girl," one of the officers had said. "Dead lucky." And then tried to swallow back his words.

"You did brilliant," said another. "Fucking brilliant."

Taylor was not just thinking about herself; she was thinking of Maddy. Had that been him? Kennet? Had he done those things to her? She had never seen the photographs of the body, only spoken to someone who swore he knew someone who had, but she knew that, as well as being raped, Maddy had been cut badly with a knife before she died.

Lucky girl.

She was, she was; she pressed her face against the rough material of the blanket and wept.

Alerted by the senior officer at Kentish Town, Shields had arrived shortly after midnight and spoken to Taylor briefly, enough to get an abbreviated version of what had happened, and arranged to take a proper statement in the morning. She'd considered phoning Elder and waking him with the news, but decided to let him slumber on.

At the hospital, Kennet had taken eleven stitches to the face and an X-ray of his chest had shown three broken ribs. Now he lay in a side ward, sedated with painkillers and handcuffed by one wrist to the bed, an officer sitting outside reading the *Mail* and trying to catch the eye of one of the nurses and scrounge another cup of tea.

Elder was finally put in the picture at seven and met Shields outside the hospital at eight. Ramsden and Denison were already there, the uniformed officer having been gratefully relieved.

One of the lifts was out of order and an orderly was carefully positioning a patient on a gurney in another, so they took the stairs.

"Has he been charged?" Elder asked.

"Not yet."

"Possibilities?"

"As it stands? Aggravated assault. Possession of an offensive weapon. Enough to hold him."

When they got into the room Kennet was on his side, sheet pulled level with his chin, eyes closed. A nurse had just finished checking his temperature and blood pressure and was entering the results on his chart.

"Is he asleep?" Shields asked.

The nurse shook her head.

"Kennet," Shields said, moving closer. "Mr. Kennet."

No movement; no response.

Ramsden seized hold of the sheet and tugged it sharply back.

"Mr. Kennet," Shields said, "there are questions I need to ask."

Kennet's eyes remained closed.

"Is there any reason," Shields asked the nurse, "why he shouldn't answer questions?"

The nurse shook her head. "The painkillers might have made him slightly woozy, but other than that, no."

"I'll give him fuckin' painkillers," Ramsden said.

Shields shot him a warning look.

"Listen, Kennet," Elder said, leaning toward the head of the bed, "why don't you sit up? The sooner we get this done, the better."

Nothing.

"Nurse," Shields said. "I wonder, could you help to sit him up?"

"I suppose so, I . . ." She faltered, for a moment uncertain. "Mr. Kennet, come along." When she touched his shoulder, he shrugged her off.

"What seems to be the problem?" the doctor said, walking toward them. He was tall and bearded, mid-thirties, his accent from north of the border.

"These police officers," the nurse said, "they want to question the patient."

"All right, nurse. Thank you."

She wheeled her equipment cart away.

"Detective Chief Inspector Shields," she

said, holding out her hand.

The doctor's grip was strong but brief.

"This man is charged with a serious crime," Shields said. "And we have reason to believe he can assist us with several more. It's important that we talk to him."

"Now?"

"Now."

The doctor lifted the chart from the end of the bed and gave it a cursory look. "He seems to have been well medicated to control his pain . . ."

Ramsden snorted.

"If I might suggest, an hour or so might allow the more soporific effects of the medication to wear off and you'd likely get clearer answers to whatever questions it is you need to ask. Besides . . . ," with a glance toward the handcuffs, "he's not exactly going anywhere, is he?"

Outside, Shields spoke to headquarters on her cell phone, while Ramsden lit a cigarette.

"Right," she said, hanging up. "We've got a warrant to search Kennet's flat. Mike, you get over there. Lee'll meet you there. Paul can stay here at the hospital. I'll arrange for him to get spelled by someone from the local nick."

Grinning, Ramsden was on his way.

"How far's Vanessa Taylor's place from here?" Elder asked.

"Not far. She should be up to making a statement by now. Come on, I'll call her from the car."

The traffic approaching the Archway roundabout was solid in all directions, and they were stuck alongside an articulated lorry that was heading back to Holland and behind a people carrier ferrying half a dozen kids to school, half of whom were making faces out of the rear window. Shields fiddled with the radio, then switched it off.

"I don't suppose there are any witnesses?" Elder said.

"To last night? No."

"Vanessa's word against his."

"Pretty much."

"And there are no injuries?"

"To her? Some bruising to the neck. Little else. Not a lot to pass round in front of the jury."

"Maybe it'll look more spectacular this morning."

"Maybe."

"And the knife?"

"Forensics are checking it for prints.

Hopefully he wouldn't have had time to wipe it clean."

"You'll try and match it to the wounds on Maddy's body?"

"You bet."

They slid forward another couple of feet. "I thought Livingstone had sorted all this out," Elder said.

"So he has."

"I don't know how you put up with it."

Shields smiled. "I suppose the most you get's the occasional tractor?"

"Cattle. Sometimes a herd of sheep."

"I don't know how you can do it, Frank."

"What?"

"Live like that. Cut off from everything."

"Everything?"

"Don't be obtuse. You know what I mean."

The lorry turned off into the left-hand lane and Shields accelerated into the space, swung hard right, cutting off not one vehicle but two, then left again and down through the first set of lights, pulling wide around a 43 bus.

"You enjoy this?" Elder asked.

"Love it." She grinned.

Taylor was pale-faced and puffy-eyed.

The bruises around her neck had indeed intensified in color. She made them coffee without bringing the water properly to a boil and the granules floated around the surface, only partly dissolved. Her account of the attack and what had led up to it was flat and emotionless, as if she were describing something that had happened to a distant friend. Only when she spoke of the moment Kennet had first jumped out at her, the knife to the side of her face, did her voice falter and break. Elder could see a faint red line traversing the skin.

"The man you reported seeing across the street," he said, "you think that was him as well?"

Taylor waited a moment before answering. "No, I'm not sure."

"It hardly matters," Shields said. "From what you've said, it looks as if he was stalking you. Building up to last night."

"Agreed," said Elder. "But if it was him, it suggests a pattern. Watching. Following."

"You're thinking of Maddy, aren't you?" Taylor said. "What happened to her?"

Both Shields and Elder looked back at her.

"You think he killed her."

"In the circumstances," Shields began,

"we have to consider . . ."

"Oh, come on!" Taylor almost shouted. "Don't give me that crap."

"It's a possibility," Elder said.

"It's more than a bloody possibility."

"Maybe."

"Sod maybe!" Flushed, Taylor went toward the door, stopped, and turned back. Nowhere to go. "Kennet, what's he saying?" she asked.

"So far, nothing."

"He threatened me with a knife; half-choked me. He was going to rape me."

"I know," Shields said. "I know."

"He was going to kill me."

Shields reached for her hand, but Taylor pulled away, crossed to the sink and turned on the cold tap, and then nothing, simply stood there, watching it run.

After a few moments, Elder went over and switched it off. When he brushed her shoulder accidentally, she jumped.

"We ought to go," he said quietly.

"Then go."

"Vanessa," Shields said at the door, "you should arrange to see somebody."

"Somebody?"

"You know what I mean. A counselor. They'll sort it out at the station, I'm sure."

Taylor stared back at her hopelessly.

"Don't let him get away with this."

"Don't worry. We won't."

Kennet was sitting up in bed, propped up against a number of pillows, his recent stitches standing out like tiny bird tracks along the plane of his face. Seeing Shields and Elder he actually smiled.

"Back in the land of the living," Elder said.

"Just about."

"Luckier than some."

"There are questions," Shields said, "about last night."

"You mean when I was attacked?"

"You were attacked?"

"Of course." Kennet touched his fingertips to his coming scar. "Bloke who stitched me up reckoned I was lucky not to lose an eye."

"And Vanessa, what was she lucky enough to escape with?"

"Anything that happened to her, self-defense."

"Wait," said Shields. "Wait. You're claiming she attacked you?"

"Of course. Asked me up, started fooling around, everything going along fine and then — wham! — swung at me with the bloody bottle. Out of nowhere." He shook

392

his head. "I knew she'd been drinking, but not that much. Not like that. Out of control. If I'd known that I'd never have agreed to go back with her after the pub."

"She invited you, that's what you're saying?"

"Yes, of course. What else?"

"The knife," Elder said. "What about the knife?"

Kennet looked back at him, all wide-eyed astonishment. "What knife?"

"The one you threw away just before you ran full-pelt into the bus."

"I don't know anything about any knife."

"We'll see."

Ten minutes later Elder and Shields were standing in the corridor outside. Kennet had persevered with his story: Vanessa had been the one to attack him, breaking a bottle across his face, and any injuries she might have sustained had been a result of him trying to restrain her. In the end he'd left her swearing and screaming and headed home, so stunned by what had happened that he had not been thinking where he was going when he stepped out into the road and got side-swiped by a bus. No hard feelings, he hoped she was okay, nothing much more than a thick head.

"How long d'you think he'll stick to that?" Shields said.

"As long as he can. Any prints on the knife?"

"We can hope," Shields said.

Elder was looking at his watch. "Another twelve hours before he has to be charged."

"Time enough."

The doctor agreed there was no reason Kennet couldn't be released from the hospital that afternoon. By which time they would not only have heard back about the knife, but also have the results of the search of his flat. Time enough, Shields thought, was probably right.

Chapter 41

When Elder's cell phone rang, not so many minutes after leaving the hospital, Maureen Prior was pretty much the last person on his mind. Her train was due in at St. Pancras in forty minutes. It was important they meet. No more than an hour of his time.

The café was French, a small patisserie set back from the main road that ran immediately south from the station. There were a few tables on the pavement, maybe half a dozen more inside. Croissants, baguettes, and a gleaming espresso machine. Two women of a certain age, smartly dressed, sat near the rear window drinking coffee; a silver-haired man, camel coat folded over the back of his chair, was reading *Le Monde* and eating a *croque monsieur.* Elder, who had used St. Pancras enough over the years, had had no idea the place was there.

It was warm enough, just, to sit outside.

Jet trails crisscrossed overhead and the sun was a rumor behind a screen of gray.

A young man, white-aproned, brought them coffee.

"How did you know about this?" Elder said, looking around.

"Charlie told me about it."

"Charlie?"

"Charlie Resnick. He said it would be a good place to meet."

"You've been talking to him."

Prior smiled. "About London cafés?"

"About Bland. And Katherine."

"I had to talk to someone. Someone I could trust."

That would be Resnick, Elder thought. "What did he say?"

She smiled again. "Not a lot. He's a great listener, Charlie."

"He wasn't surprised?"

"About Bland? No, not really. Rumors aside, he'd never liked him overmuch. Too much time down in the smoke. Infects the lungs, rots away from the inside. His words. Reckons the only reason Bland left the Met when he did was to keep a step ahead of CIB."

"He was never actually charged?"

"With corruption? No. Allegations, unproven. Usual story. Had his card marked a few times, apparently, but that was it."

"So," Elder said, "is there a plan?"

"It's what I wanted to talk to you about. And I thought in person. Rather than risk a call." She lifted her cup of coffee from its saucer. "Getting paranoid in my old age."

"Careful," Elder said. "No harm in that."

"How about you, Frank? You taking care down here?"

"In the big city? Yes, I think so."

"Near a result?"

Elder's turn to smile, just with his eyes. "I think there's more than one game."

"There always is, Frank. There always was."

The coffee was perfect. Strong, not bitter. Elder listened attentively. As a plan it was simple enough, straightforward; the chances of success all the more certain for depending upon Bland's greed.

"Summers, he'll play along?"

"I think so. Further in over his head than he's comfortable with. Might see this as a way out."

"And Katherine, it won't put her in any danger?"

Prior thought a little before answering. "No more than she's in already."

Elder nodded. "You want me to talk to her?"

"Later, Frank. When it's over."

"You'll let me know when it's going down?"

"Better still," Prior said. "I'll let you know when it's done."

Steve Kennet left the hospital handcuffed to a uniformed officer the shape and size of a small tank, Paul Denison walking closely behind. The one call Kennet had been allowed, to a firm of solicitors, had yielded up Iain Murchfield, left holding the fort that Thursday afternoon. Any wetter behind the fucking ears, as Ramsden was to remark, and he'd fucking drown.

Shields had corralled Elder the instant he reappeared and from her expression he knew the news, some of it at least, was good.

"See why he was cocky about the knife. Must have wiped it off on his clothes as he ran. But not as thorough as he thinks. Thumbprint on the base of the blade. Partial, but clear."

"And it's a match?"

"Waiting for confirmation now."

"How about his place? Anything interesting there?"

"Not a lot. Few borderline videos. Clothes, shoes, usual stuff. I told Mike to go back, try again."

"Kennet's here?"

"With his lawyer. Deciding strategy." Shields grinned. "Kid just out of college. Looks as if he'd need a strategy to tie his laces in the morning."

At a little after four the call came through from Forensics. The partial print was a match. But partial, nonetheless.

They ushered Kennet into interrogation ten minutes later, the exact time noted scrupulously by Shields at the beginning of the interview. In Ramsden's continued absence Paul Denison, slightly nervous himself, sat alongside her. Elder sat in an adjacent room, watching the proceedings through a two-way mirror, listening on headphones.

Kennet leaned forward, forearms resting on the table edge, faint signs of strain beginning to show around his eyes. Beside him, seated a little way off, Iain Murchfield had a notebook open on his knee, pen in hand.

Shields's hair was pulled back, the front of her suit jacket buttoned, her gaze rarely leaving Kennet's face.

"I'd like you to tell me," she began, "what happened last night, from the time you met Vanessa Taylor in the Bull and Last pub until you both went back to her flat."

In a monotone, Kennet repeated, with a few additions, the version of events he had given in the hospital.

"You still maintain that PC Taylor hit you with the bottle without cause or reason?"

"Other than that she was pissed out of her head, yes."

"And the injuries that she sustained . . ."

"Were on account of me trying to stop her taking my eye out, yes. Going crazy, wasn't she?"

"And that includes the marks to the side of her face?"

"I don't know. What marks?"

"Cut marks."

"I don't know. Glass from the bottle, I suppose. Glass bloody everywhere."

"This injury was a caused by a knife."

Kennet leaned away from the table. "I don't know about that."

"You didn't attack PC Taylor with a knife?"

"No."

"Hold it against her throat?"

"No."

"Hard enough to break the skin."

"Look, look." Kennet agitated now. "I've said. I know nothing about a knife. Okay?"

"No?"

Kennet replied in capitals, a space between each word. "There was no knife."

"Really?" Shields said, slightly amused.

Kennet turned toward his solicitor. "How much longer have I got to put up with this?"

"Detective Chief Inspector," Murchfield said, dredging up what little gravitas he could find. "I must complain about the degree to which you are harassing my client."

Shields looked at him with a mixture of sardonic amusement and contempt. "The knife I'm referring to, Mr. Kennet," she said, "is the one you threw away as you were trying to make your escape."

"That's bullshit. That's untrue. Sheer bloody fabrication."

A line came to Elder, watching; something about protesting too much.

"In that case," Shields said, "I'd like to hear your explanation of how your print came to be on the blade."

"What blade? What bloody print?" His chair scraped back as he swung around toward Murchfield. "You. Do something, will you? Sitting there watching them fit me up."

Murchfield flipped his notebook closed.

"I must object again to the manner in which you are questioning my client."

"Objection noted."

"And remind you, should it be necessary, that the time remaining in which you must decide to charge my client or else release him is running down."

"Fine," Shields said. "You're right. Let's get him charged. How about inflicting grievous bodily harm for starters? Offenses against the Person Act, 1861. Paul, take him down to the custody sergeant, make sure he's properly charged and cautioned. We'll see if that changes his perspective on things. This interview halted at four twenty-three." She got to her feet. "Thank you, Mr. Murchfield, for your welcome advice."

"What do you think?" Shields asked.

Elder made a face. "With all the testimony we can bank on as to Kennet's past behavior, if it comes down to his word against Vanessa's, most juries are going to take hers. But in terms of hard evidence, one partial print looks pretty sad."

"Mike'll come up with something, don't worry."

But by seven that evening, that's exactly what they were doing.

Kennet had been duly charged and was

preparing to spend his first night in the cells; on Monday morning, he would appear before the magistrate and bail would be vigorously opposed. But when Ramsden and Furness returned, it was with long faces and bad news.

"Unless you include a stack of Brentford programs going back ten years, nothing iffy in sight."

"You searched the van as well?" Elder said. "The one he uses for work."

"What d'you think I am, a fucking amateur?"

"Sorry."

"No problem."

But Elder's mind was suddenly elsewhere: the first time he'd seen Kennet, spoken to him, outside the house he was working on in Dartmouth Park, Kennet with a roll-up, wanting a light.

"He's got a car," Elder said. "As well as the van."

"You're sure?"

"Sedan, four-door. Dark blue. Ford, I think, but I couldn't swear."

"Lee," Ramsden said, "check it out. As long as it's registered to him, we're quids in."

"Well done, Frank," Shields said. "Well remembered."

"We'll see," Elder said. "We'll see."

Chapter 42

Elder got back to Finchley at about seven. The morning, when Shields had first phoned him with the news of Kennet's arrest, seemed a long way off. A couple of aspirin, he thought, and a long soak in the bath.

His cell phone rang before he could turn on the taps, adrenaline pulsing at the sound of his daughter's voice.

"Katherine, are you okay?"

"Yes, why?"

"Nothing. Just, you know . . ."

"You sound worried."

"Not specially, no. Bit of a headache. Busy day."

There was a brief silence and then, "I wanted to ask you, Dad, this business, the police, you do know what's going on?"

"I think so, yes."

"Only Rob . . . well, what they're asking him to do . . . he's not sure who he can trust."

404

"Who's he been talking to?"

"This woman, policewoman. Maureen. Her mostly."

"Maureen Prior. You can trust her, believe me."

"I don't know."

"When's he meeting him, Rob? When's he meeting Bland again?"

"Soon, I think. The next couple of days."

"As soon as that's done with, maybe you should get away for a bit. Just till things calm down."

"Rob's got friends up Hull way. Family too."

"Why don't you go up there then? Just for a week or so."

"You don't mind?"

"Mind what?"

"Me and Rob, being together like that."

"It's not what I'd choose."

"But you don't mind?"

"You're old enough to make your own decisions."

"Make my own mistakes, that's what you mean."

A pause. "Maybe."

There was a man's voice, just audible in the background, Rob's, Elder thought, and then Katherine saying, "Look, Dad, I'd better go."

"All right. Just be careful. The two of you. And keep in touch, okay?"

"Okay."

"I love you," he added, but the line was already dead.

Elder took one swallow of whiskey and then another. He remembered how she had been when he had found her, a prisoner in the jerry-built hut sheltering against rock, high on the North York coast. The stench of rotten fish and drying blood. The bruises discoloring her face and back. Was this something else he was helping to draw her into, some new danger? Or had she chosen that herself when she started hanging out with the down-and-outs in Slab Square, going out with someone who, in no matter how small a way, dealt drugs? It was difficult to care and not judge.

While the bath was running, and despite her assurance she would contact him, he rang Maureen Prior.

"Falling into place, Frank," she told him. "Another couple of days, that's all we need."

"Katherine said."

"You've spoken to her then?"

"She rang earlier."

"She's a good kid, Frank."

"Not a kid."

"You know what I mean. She's strong."

"She's had to be. She'd have gone under otherwise. I thought she had."

"I'll keep an eye out for her, you know that. Do any more, put someone baby-sitting her, there's a good chance Bland'll catch wind."

"I know."

"I'll be careful. Do what I can."

"Thanks, Maureen."

"Look after yourself, Frank."

"Do my best."

He topped up his glass and carried it into the bathroom. No message from Shields yet about Kennet's car, which probably meant they were still chasing it down. At ten to-morrow, Kennet would go before the magistrate. That would buy them time. And tomorrow he would talk to Sherry, go over what it was he'd been able to unearth. The water was a touch too hot and he ran a quick burst of cold, whisking it around before lowering himself in. When Katherine was a baby, eighteen months or less, he would lift her into the bath with him and she would splash and laugh, slippery like a fish between his hands. Times like that, they never came back. Had he said "I love you" knowing she was no longer on the line?

"I love you, Katherine," he said aloud, tears in his stupid eyes.

Chapter 43

The car was a Ford Mondeo four-door Estate, S reg, with a little over 18,000 on the odometer. It was found parked on Tollington Way, close to the back of the old Royal Northern Hospital. There were a pair of Kennet's work boots in the back, speckled with plaster and paint, overalls and a woolen checked shirt folded around one another alongside them. Old copies of the *Sun* and *Mail*. A spiral-bound *London A-Z*, well-thumbed. Parking tickets. Snickers wrappers and a half-eaten roll of mints. Several audiocassettes in the side compartment, driver's side: Queen, David Lee Roth, U2, Springsteen's Greatest Hits. A box of matches with only five remaining. A pair of worn leather gloves. A red and black thermos flask that still smelled faintly of coffee. A paperback Patricia Cornwell novel, turned down on page 121. Jump leads. A screwdriver. A chamois cloth, stiff and darkened with use. A rusted can of WD-40; a plastic bottle of Holt's concentrated all-seasons nonsmearing Screen Wash and another of Comma Xstream Deicer. An empty two-liter container that had once held engine oil. And in the wheel space, snug beneath the spare wheel, a small metal box that contained, carefully wrapped in a piece of material that looked to have been torn from an old denim shirt, a single earring, green and gold and in the shape of a moon; a plain silver bracelet; a pendant necklace with a fine silver chain; and a watch with a medium-brown leather strap, a Lorus with a plain face and the name Maddy Birch engraved on the back, together with the date, 15.07.81.

Shields drank a large cup of black coffee in the canteen and then splashed cold water on her face in the locker room. "Take it easy," she told herself. "Easy. Chill."

At a little after ten, Steven Kennet had been remanded in custody until the twenty-seventh at a specially convened Magistrate's Court, his application for bail denied. Now he was back in the interview room, throat dry, looking as if he had barely slept. Beside him, his solicitor fiddled with his pen, removing the cap and then replacing it, the same action over and over again.

Ramsden thought if he carried on like that he might just reach across and grab the pen, then stick it up his bony arse.

"This interview," Shields began, "timed at eleven forty-seven . . ."

Steadily she led Kennet through the same events as on the previous day, the same denials, letting him dig himself into a deeper and deeper hole.

"Mr. Kennet," Shields said nonchalantly, almost an afterthought, "do you own a dark blue 1998 Ford Mondeo Estate?"

Even from where he was watching, through glass, Elder could read the apprehension that flickered across Kennet's eyes.

"Mr. Kennet?"

"Yes."

"Do you own . . ."

"Yes, I said yes."

"My client," Murchfield intervened, "would appreciate a break at this time. It's now very nearly . . ."

But Shields cut him off with a brusque, "I'm sure he would," followed by, "I wonder, Mr. Kennet, if you could identify this?"

Ramsden held up the necklace, secure

inside a plastic evidence bag.

Kennet paled. "No," he said, "I've no idea."

"Or this?"

The earring.

"No." A vigorous shake of the head.

"Or this?"

The bracelet.

"No."

"Mr. Kennet, these items were found in the boot of your car."

Recovering, Kennet shifted heavily in his seat and shrugged. "Nothing to do with me. I've never seem them before."

"Secure in your car, carefully wrapped and hidden away."

Kennet stared back at her, silent, sullen.

"Where you left them."

"Jesus, I just told you . . ."

"You've told me nothing."

"Okay, I'll tell you again. These things, they're nothin' to do with me. I've never seen 'em before, okay?"

"You've no idea how they came to be in your possession?"

"They weren't in my fucking possession."

"They were in your car."

"Says who?"

Ramsden smiled. "Says me."

"Then you fucking put 'em there."

Shields leaned back from the desk. There was sweat accumulating in the palms of her hands and she wiped them against her pant legs. Sweat in the air, too: hers, his, everyone's.

"A little over an hour ago," Shields said, "one of my officers showed this bracelet to Jennifer McLaughlin and she identified it as hers."

A pulse, Elder noticed, had begun to twitch in the corner of Kennet's left eye.

"This earring," Shields said, holding up the evidence bag, "was identified by Jane Forest as belonging to her."

"So?"

"Jennifer McLaughlin and Jane Forest, both women with whom you have had relationships."

Kennet stared back at her, unblinking.

"So can you explain how these items came to be hidden away inside your car?"

"No. I can't. Except that someone put them there."

"And that someone, Mr. Kennet, was you."

Kennet swung around on his chair, his knee knocking against Murchfield's leg, the impact jarring the pen from the solicitor's hand.

"You," Kennet said, "when are you going to do something instead of just sitting there while they do me fucking over?"

Murchfield stammered, blushed, reached down to retrieve his pen.

"There is one further item," Shields said, almost succeeding in keeping the tone of virtual triumph from her voice as she dangled the watch, in its bag, in front of Kennet's face.

"This watch. Maddy Birch's watch. You can see her name clearly engraved, there on the back. You see? You see the name, Mr. Kennet? The name and date? Mr. Kennet, for the tape recorder please. Do you agree that the name on the back is that of Maddy Birch?"

"Yes."

"That this watch belonged to her?"

"Yes."

"Can you then tell me how it came into your possession?"

Kennet looked back at her and shook his head.

"Mr. Kennet?"

"No. No, I can't."

"Well, I suggest to you that she was wearing it the night she was killed."

"I don't know."

"And that is when you took it from her body."

"No."

"After you had raped her."

"No."

"Murdered her."

"No." The sweat on Kennet's forehead was clearly visible now, his upper body rolling a little, side to side, as if he were being punched.

"Mr. Kennet, I put it to you, on the night of Wednesday twenty-sixth, Thursday twenty-seventh of November, in the vicinity of Crouch End Community Center, you attacked and raped Maddy Birch, then stabbed her repeatedly with a knife until she was dead."

"No."

"She was wearing this watch, wasn't she? That evening?"

Kennet raised both hands, clenched, and as Shields sat quickly back out of range and Ramsden threw out an arm to ward off a possible blow, brought them down full force on the center of the desk.

"She couldn't have been wearing the watch. Not then. I'd already taken it, weeks before."

Shields brought her breathing back under control. "Say that again."

"The watch, I'd already taken it. Weeks before."

"And how did you do that?"

"I broke into her flat. When she wasn't there."

"When was this?"

"End of October sometime. Tuesday, Wednesday, I don't know. Middle of the week."

"And had you done this before?"

"Broken in? Yes, but not there. Not Maddy's place. Others. Jane. Jennifer." He almost smiled.

"And each time, you take away what? A souvenir?"

"Yes. I mean, not always, no."

"Nothing else?"

"How d'you mean?"

"You don't take anything else?"

"Not take, no."

"What then?"

"I don't know, I . . . sometimes I just stand there. Not doing anything. Sometimes, you know, look at things."

"What kind of things?"

Kennet shrugged; now that he was talking he was more at ease. "Depends. Clothes. Diaries, sometimes. Anything."

"Panties," Ramsden suggested scornfully. "Knickers. Underwear."

"Sometimes."

"Jerk off into them, do you?"

"No."

"Mr. Kennet," Shields said, "when you're alone in these places, these rooms, do you ever indulge in any kind of sexual activity?"

He looked at her carefully before answering, her eyes, her mouth. "Sometimes," he said, "I masturbate. Into a condom. Take it home. That the kind of thing you mean?"

"I think, Mr. Murchfield," Shields said, "your client can have a break. Twenty minutes, no more. This interview suspended at twelve nineteen . . ."

"What do you think, Frank?"

They were standing outside, the sky overcast but the temperature a good five degrees warmer than the day before. Shields had come close to snagging one of Ramsden's cigarettes and was munching her way through a Bounty instead.

"You had him sweating, no doubt about that."

"Like a Turkish bath in there."

"All that stuff about the murder really had him in a state. Once he'd copped to the break-ins, though, different again. Proud of it, almost. Relieved, certainly."

"You think I let him off the hook?"

"I don't see what else you could have done."

"You said yourself. It was as if he'd got away with something."

"You'll keep on at him. If there's anything else there, you'll make him crack."

Shields stuffed the last piece of Bounty into her mouth, screwed up the wrapper, and pushed it down into her jacket pocket. Black today, funereal black.

"Frank, the other night. At my place. We've never really talked about it."

"Maybe there's no need."

"Not worth remembering, then?" Just a hint of a smile.

"That's not what I meant."

"I just don't want you to think . . ."

"What?"

"You know, that it meant anything . . . anything special I mean, between us."

There was an amused look in Elder's eyes. "You mean we're not engaged?"

She punched him, quite hard, on the arm.

"I don't want you to expect . . ."

"Believe me, I don't expect anything."

"You're sure? Because if . . ."

"Listen, listen. It was great. I had a great time. A total surprise. But one off, okay? I understand."

"Okay." With a quick glance around to make sure no one was looking, she kissed him on the cheek.

"Though of course if I go back inside with your lipstick on my face . . ."

She went to punch him again, but this time, laughing, he dodged out of the way.

Chapter 44

Elder had barely parked outside his flat when his cell phone began to ring. Katherine, he thought. Maureen. Instead it was Framlingham's familiar burr. "That place of yours, Frank. Presentable, is it?"

"You should know."

"Twenty, thirty minutes. I'll be there."

He arrived within fifteen, bearing gifts. Scottish oatcakes, a chunk of Mrs. Kirkham's Lancashire cheese, a bottle of wine.

"Thought you might be peckish, Frank. Must have been a busy day."

"Busy enough."

"This Kennet, enough to hold him at least?"

"I think so."

Framlingham unwrapped the cheese and set it on a plate. "Your thought that Grant might be an informant, protected that way, doesn't seem to pan out. But as a line of enquiry, not without its worth." He was ferreting for a corkscrew in the kitchen drawer. "Aussie plonk, Frank. Garlands Shiraz. Family winery near Mount Barker."

The cork came free with a pleasing pop.

"Mike Garland, he's the cellar master, knows what he's about."

Framlingham brought the glass to his nose to sniff the bouquet, then drank, holding the wine for a long moment in his mouth before swallowing.

"Lovely stuff, Frank. Tobacco, spice, licorice, plum."

Elder cut off a piece of cheese and it crumbled against the knife.

"This whole business," Framlingham said, "Grant and Mallory, unraveling that makes reading *Ulysses* like Harry bloody Potter. Key thing is this, though. For years now, going back to when he was a DI, Mallory's registered informant was Lynette Drury. Former prostitute, more recently brothel keeper and, more importantly, before that, shacked up with a known villain named Ben Slater."

Framlingham broke an oatcake in two and set cheese deliberately on each half.

"The contact between Mallory and Slater seems to have come first. As much as twenty years ago. Eighty-four. Along with three others, Slater was up on trial for a payroll robbery out at Romford. Five days in, the judge ordered a mistrial. Slater and the rest walk free."

"And what's Mallory's connection to this?"

Framlingham smiled. "Mallory was in the Special Patrol Group called in by the team on the ground. This is a couple of years before it was disbanded."

"And he'd be what then? Thirty? A little more?"

"Twenty-nine."

Nodding, Elder tried the wine.

"So now," Framlingham said, "we move on two years later to eighty-six. There's a series of armed robberies in the Home Counties, all of them within a thirty-mile radius of London. Post offices, building societies. By this time Mallory's moved on to the Territorial Support Group with the rank of sergeant. Slater's put under surveillance, his phone bugged, everything. Finally arrested on one charge of robbery after a raid on building society offices in Colchester. Thanks to a tip-off, the TSG are there in force. At the trial, however, one of the officers crucially fails to identify Slater as being present. No need to tell you which one. Slater walks free. Begins proceedings against the Met for harassment and wrongful arrest, which he later drops. For a while, things go quiet. Then in eighty-nine there's an armed robbery, appropriately enough at Shooters Hill. Securicor van rammed into on the edge of Woolwich Common. Four men got away with eighty thousand in used banknotes. Slater and another man called Warland were questioned but not charged."

"Mallory's involved?"

"Not yet. Eighteen months later, this bloke Warland's stopped for speeding going north out of the Blackwall Tunnel. Turns out he's got half the proceeds of a supermarket robbery in the car with him, a sawn-off shotgun in the boot. Plus a quantity of illegal drugs on his person. Of course, he rolls over. Coughs to the Woolwich Common job, names names. Slater for one."

"Slater's arrested?"

"Arrested and charged." Framlingham ate some more cheese, drank some more wine. "When he comes up before the magistrate, the police case against bail's not as strong as it might be. Surprise, surprise. Slater skips the country, probably to Spain. Looks as if he stays away until sometime in ninety-two. By which time Mallory's a detective inspector in the Flying Squad."

"The Sweeney."

"Absolutely. With Maurice Repton his DS, holding his hand. It's around here Ben Slater's former girlfriend, Lynette Drury, is registered as Mallory's informant. What connection there was between them before that it's impossible to say. But my guess is they'd been close for years. The pack of them."

"Where exactly does Grant come in?"

"Not so much later. Slater stays clean as a cat's arse till ninety-five. Then he's suspected of a bullion raid at City Airport. Gold ingots. Three-quarters of a million pounds. And this is the first time Slater's name is linked with Grant. Familiar story. They're both arrested and charged but the case falls apart when it comes to court. The evidence of one of the principal witnesses is tainted and the jury's directed to ignore just about everything she's said."

"She?"

"Drury. Lynette Drury." Framlingham's smile lingered longer this time. "Rumor has it her relationship with Mallory went well beyond the terms regarding informants laid down by the Yard."

"They were lovers?"

"The way you put it, Frank, it sounds old-fashioned, almost charming. For all I know, she was still shtupping Ben Slater at the same time. Grant, too, for that matter."

"And there's nothing more recent, linking them all together?"

"Until Mallory kills Grant. No, apparently not. But who knows?"

"Someone," Elder said. "Somewhere there's someone."

"How about Lynette Drury? What she knows would fill a book and a half."

"Have we got an address?"

"Funny you should ask." Framlingham took a slip of paper, folded, from his breast pocket. "There. Blackheath. Two years old; she might have moved on since then."

"Surely you'd know?"

With a lazy movement, Framlingham's arm snaked out toward the wine. "Best finish this off, Frank. Can't abide the waste."

Not long after Framlingham had left, Elder's cell phone rang again. "Bland," Prior said. "He's taken the bait. This weekend maybe, Monday at the latest."

Chapter 45

The house was off the southern edge of the Heath, a tall Victorian villa set well back from the road behind high hedges and an iron gate. The gate complained a little as Elder raised the latch and pushed it back. In the edge of dark earth, between shrubs and grass, a pair of blackbirds searched for worms. Heavy curtains hung across the upstairs windows, the lower ones covered in patterned net. What looked to be the original stained glass was still in the front door. He could imagine the house on a different day, under different skies, seeming forbidding and grim; but this morning, pastel blue overhead and church bells ringing down in the Vale, it was anything but.

Elder rang the bell, and a dog barked and then was still.

Footsteps on the stairs and along the hall.

"At least," said the man who opened the

door, "you're not the Jehovah's Witnesses. Unless they've taken to dressing down."

The man himself was wearing a black T-shirt and off-white cotton trousers that left little to the imagination; his hair was fair and cut short — not as short as a soccer player or a supporter of the British National Party, but short enough to be fashionable. The dog was an off-white wirehaired terrier, which the man nudged out of the way with his foot.

"Frank Elder."

"Don't tell me, you're standing as an independent in the local elections. For sustainable resources and the recycling of waste, against gay marriages."

"Is that an issue?"

"Gay marriages? Not for me. Unless you're about to make me an offer."

"For fuck's sake, Anton," came a woman's voice from inside, "stop the second-rate cabaret and let the man in."

She was a slim figure in a wheelchair, a shawl around her shoulders, blanket across her knees. The chair was battery operated and she eased the toggle forward to bring herself to the door. Her face, Elder saw, was deeply lined, the skin twisted tight around her unaligned left eye, as though she had suffered a stroke.

"I'm Lynette Drury," she said, her voice a harsh rasp.

"Frank Elder."

"Is this official, Frank? Should I be calling my lawyer out of mass?"

"I don't think so."

She stared at him with her good eye, as if making up her mind. "I don't get that much company these days, Frank, I can't afford to turn it away."

Adroitly, she maneuvered her wheelchair around and back into the house.

"Anton, do you think you could demean yourself long enough to find us something to drink?"

Anton peeled off to the right, the dog at his heels. Elder followed Lynette Drury into a high-ceilinged room with windows to the back and side, the garden at the rear largely lawn surrounded by shrubs and small, spiny fruit trees, rosebushes pruned well back.

"You're not the usual kind, Frank, but you've still got the smell about you."

"Takes a while to wash off," Elder said.

"Ben didn't send you?"

"No."

"George Mallory neither."

Elder shook his head.

"Thought not." She gestured toward the

dark, polished table near the window. "Get me a cigarette, will you, Frank? Light it for me?"

She inhaled deeply enough to bring on a coughing fit and summon Anton from the other room to pat her back and wipe spittle and dark lipstick from her mouth.

"What?" she said. "No lecture?"

Anton shot her a look over his shoulder as he left.

" 'You've got to stop, you're killing yourself,' " she mimicked, then laughed. "Does it look like I'm alive, Frank? Is that what this looks like?"

She coughed again, more controlled this time. "Anton," she called toward the doorway, "where's that fucking drink?"

The answer was the popping of a cork and Anton, moments later, reappearing with two glasses of champagne, the bottle in an ice bucket, on a silver tray.

"Cheers, Frank. Your good health. Got to be some little perks, eh? Otherwise what's the point?"

"Cheers."

"All right," she said to Anton, "you can get back to your Game Boy or whatever it is you get up to in the servant's quarters. Polishing the silver."

"I've sold it already."

"That and your skinny arse."

Elder sipped some champagne; if it was high-class or six-ninety-nine from Tesco, he had no idea. The bells seemed to have stopped ringing. Presumably all the good people of Blackheath were already on their knees.

"Each month," Lynette said, "Ben sends a case of champagne. Saves him coming round in person. Rubs a little Vaseline over his conscience. And he pays for Anton, of course. Though he's probably knobbing him as well. Not that he's queer, don't get me wrong. Ben, I mean. Just doesn't care what he fucks as long as it's tight."

She coughed again and some of the champagne spilled across the purple veins at the back of her hand.

Elder lifted away the glass.

Anton appeared for a moment at the door, then, reassured, went away again.

"But my guess," she said, "it's George Mallory you're more interested in. More than Ben. Am I right?"

"Maybe."

"Georgie-Porgie, kissed the girls and made them cry. He did that all right. And now he's running scared, isn't he? Not that he'd ever admit it, of course. He could be standing in the middle of a fire, flames up to his armpits, and swear blind everything was hunky-dory. But he sent that creep Repton round, didn't he? A sure sign. Maurice Repton smarming up to you in one of those neat little suits he likes to tell you are custom made by some tame tailor out at Winchmore Hill, used to be a cutter in Saville Row.

"Maurice with all those questions. Anyone been to see me, sniffing round. CIB or whatever they're called nowadays. Change their fucking names as often as a whore's knickers. No, I says. Number of visitors I get these days, anyone'd think I've got the fucking plague. HIV. If anyone does, Maurice says, you will give us a call? Let us know. 'Us,' like they're husband and fucking wife."

She paused, collecting her breath. Ash fell from the end of her cigarette.

"Course, like I told him, no one ever came near. Till you."

Elder took what remained of the cigarette from between her fingers and replaced it with the glass of champagne.

"Should I tell them about you, Frank? Maurice and George. What do you think?"

"I think it's up to you."

"We'll see, we'll see. See how you behave, what it is you want. What you want

430

to know. What do you want to know, Frank?"

"What it is that's got Mallory rattled, that would do for starters."

She looked at him lopsidedly across the top of her glass. "Wouldn't it, though? Just wouldn't it."

After several moments' thought, Lynette swung her chair around and repositioned it close to the rear window.

"Bring that over, would you, Frank?"

"That" was a small rosewood table with an ashtray and a coaster for her glass, which Elder refilled before lighting her another cigarette. He carried across a curved-back wooden chair and set it down close by.

There was little sign they were a relatively short drive from the heart of London, a short walk down the hill to the noise and bustle that was Lewisham. Or that visitors, on this fine January morning, would be strolling across Greenwich Park to the Observatory, then down the sloping paths toward the Maritime Museum and the *Cutty Sark*.

Out in the garden nothing moved. The faint shadows of bushes, cast by the winter sun, seemed to have been painted, soft gray, upon the grass.

Lynette coughed before she spoke. "I had a card from Ben a few days back, Cyprus. The Turkish Republic of Northern Cyprus, to be exact. Sort of New Year's card, I suppose. He did have a place in Paphos, down in the south. Had it for years. Went there every winter, didn't we, for a while. Ben and me. A few others, sometimes. Friends. George and Maurice, for instance, they came out a few times, early on."

She released a slow stream of smoke toward the glass.

"Got too busy, Paphos, too many tourists. Too many fucking ex-pats. That was why Ben sold up, moved across the island. Kyrenia. Lovely spot. And besides, no extradition, is there? Turkish Republic." She laughed, a short breathless sound. "What they gonna do, send in the fucking SAS, drag him out?"

Elder turned the stem of the glass between his fingers. How far to let her take her own time, go where her own mind took her? When to push?

"Why aren't you there with him?" he said, gently as he could.

Another laugh that she washed down with a shaky gulp of champagne. "Me? Why doesn't he want me? What sort of a stupid fucking question is that? What the earthly fuck would he want me for? Like this?"

"He obviously cares for you."

"He what?"

"You said yourself, someone to look after you, the champagne."

"And that's because you think he fucking cares?"

"Why else?"

She grasped his arm, just above the wrist. "To keep me fucking quiet, that's why. Buy my fucking silence. Buy me off." Elder thought she would let go, but she tightened her grip instead. "We had it planned, didn't we, Ben and me? Agreed. More or less from the first. All the time I was with George, even, that never changed a thing. We were going to go off there one winter, Cyprus, and never come back. Retire. Enjoy the rest of our lives in the sun. Look, over there. Above the fireplace."

The photograph was in a filigreed silver frame. A younger, almost beautiful — striking, certainly — Lynette Drury lit up by the sun; beside her, a handsome, dark-haired man with a strong, almost aquiline nose and dark eyes that stared out while the rest of his face attempted a smile.

"That's what it was going to be," Lynette

433

said, "the rest of our fucking lives. And no matter how . . . how filthy it all became, that was what I clung on to. The rest of my life in the fucking sun."

Her nails were digging deep into Elder's arm, close to breaking the skin.

"Well, I'm not, am I? Not going fuckin' anywhere. I'm going to die here in this place with just a poof for company while him and Mallory are out there living the life of fucking Riley after all . . . after all the . . ."

A fresh fit of coughing doubled her forward and Elder pried her hand from his arm, then patted and rubbed her back, low below the shoulder blades. He thought Anton might reappear, but there was no sign; perhaps he was content to listen outside the door.

"Ben and I, we were living together. Not married, not official, but it had been a long time. I was running this place in Streatham, girls, you know, young some of them, almost as young as they looked. That was when I met George Mallory. One of the girls, she had a bit of trouble with this punter. Went for him with a knife. Panicked. Next thing you knew, emergency services everywhere. Ambulance. Police. George was there. Promising to make it all go away. And he did. Only there's payback. Wants me to be his snout, doesn't he? No way, I tell him, I'm not turning Ben in, not for anyone, but he says no, that's not what he means. Play this right, and we all stand to gain. 'Your Ben, he knows what's going on, got his nose in the trough. Have a word with him, see what he says.' So I do, and Ben says fine.

"Couple of months later there's this robbery, Hatton Garden. Diamonds. Big reward. Ben knows who took it down. He tells me, I tell George, they're caught cold, most of the stuff recovered. The Yard only passes on five grand to me, right? Reward money for giving the information leading to the arrest. George and me, we split it down the middle. Lovely. Six months later, more of the same. Next thing I know he's coming on to me. Wants to set me up in a flat somewhere. I told Ben, thinking he'll tell him to fuck right off, but instead he says, yes, why not? Not going to do us any harm is it, you and me, having someone like Mallory in our pockets?"

She stared out of the window, sipped more champagne.

"That's how it was, for years. Favors going back and forth. Little celebrations. Parties. Pop singers and second-rate movie stars. Yanks, some of them. Hollywood, you know. Rubbing up against real villains, loved that, didn't they? LSD, horse, cocaine. Boys and girls, all handpicked, paid for. And George, he was in the thick of it, wasn't he? Lapping it up. Girls, especially; he liked girls, did George. Two or three at a time. Young girls. Not, you know, really young, he's not some bleeding pedophile. That kind of thing I won't go near it, won't touch it, makes my skin crawl; but young, you know, fifteen, sixteen, not been around the block too many times. In the end it all went too far. You don't want to know how and I'm not telling you. Not ever."

Elder was about to ask anyway, but Lynette didn't give him the chance.

"Things settled back down," she said. "Went on pretty much as before. Ben got hooked up with Will Grant and they pulled off a couple of tasty scores. Tasty himself, Will Grant, I'll say that for him." She gave Elder what would once have been a coquettish glance. "Once or twice the law got too close and George had to straighten things out, make them go away. Then, a few years back, there was this big falling-out after they done this job at Gatwick. Law comes sniffing round, as per usual, and someone's only dropped Grant right in it, name and number, and of course he thinks I've grassed him up. Reckons George has persuaded me to roll him over. It's not true, not for a bloody moment, but Grant's not having any, real paranoid by now, thinks they're both out to stiff him of his share of almost a million, Ben and George both. Won't be persuaded. No way to turn him round. Oh, when the case fell apart and they all walked free, he let on it was okay, all pals again together, forgive and forget. But no, whatever trust there'd been had gone. George, especially. Always figured Grant for a loose cannon after that."

She stubbed out her cigarette.

"Grant had threatened him, that was the problem. 'I know where the bodies are buried, George, remember that.' Said he had something could put George inside for life."

"You know what that something was?"

"Me? No, no idea. Just talk, more'n likely. But George, he believed him, I know that. I'd not often seen him worried, really worried, but that's what he was."

"Worried enough to kill Grant if he got the chance?"

Lynette looked at him with her good eye. "George would kill his own mother if he thought she might turn against him."

Anton had come back into the room. "Time for your nap before lunch."

Lynette swore and smiled and brought the wheelchair back around. "Nice to have met you, Frank. Come and see me again sometime."

"I'd like that." He placed a card on which he'd written his London address and cell phone number down on the arm of her chair.

"Lying bastard."

Elder smiled and raised his glass.

Chapter 46

Karen Shields and Mike Ramsden were gradually wearing Kennet down, chipping away at the carapace of half-truths and denials he'd constructed around himself, teasing out each incident in which he had broken into the flats or houses of various women living alone, some whom he knew well, others whom he scarcely knew at all. They persuaded him to talk, sometimes haltingly, sometimes, despite his own best interests, almost with relish, of the sexual life he had persuaded, cajoled, or bullied the women in his life to share: fantasies of forced sexual activity and rape that were often played out in public places where the risk of discovery added an extra frisson.

But on Maddy Birch's murder, they could not shake him. He remained adamant that he was not involved. And as long as there was nothing more than circumstantial evidence to link him to the crime, they were stymied.

"Bastard keeps it up," Ramsden said, "he'll have me halfway believing he's telling the bloody truth."

"About Maddy? Maybe he is."

"You reckon?"

"In here, no. I think he's guilty as hell. But unless we can prove it, break him down."

"Yeah."

"We've got to find out what he was doing, Mike. The night she was killed. If he wasn't watching Jackie Chan and downing a few pints on the Holloway Road, what was he doing? Maybe he was drinking somewhere else? Somewhere closer to where Maddy was killed. Filling in the time till she was through with her yoga. Getting himself up for it, who knows? Let's have Lee and Paul back round the pubs with a photograph, Tottenham Lane, Crouch End, Hornsey Rise."

"Okay."

"And Mike, another thing. That story of his about getting up early the next morning to go to work — if he was, to all intents and purposes, still off on holiday, why was he going to work? And where?"

"Self-employed, isn't he? Work when you feel like it."

"Even so. Let's nail it down."

"That's a joke, right?"

"What?"

"Nail it down. Building. Kennet's job . . ."

"Mike?"

"Yes?"

"No time left for jokes."

Attention to detail, Shields thought, check and double-check. That's what brought most cases to a satisfactory conclusion. That and sheer luck. She hoped their luck hadn't run out.

Meanwhile, the process by which Grant's assets would be claimed by the Crown had begun its slow and tortuous progress. His bank accounts had been traced and were being examined; the sale of his penthouse flat would eventually be negotiated. There were no records of him having had a safety deposit box.

The clothes and paraphernalia that had been removed from the flat itself were sitting in a succession of cardboard boxes, which it took two officers a good half hour to locate and transfer to a room where Elder could examine them, article by article, piece by piece.

Suits, jackets, shirts, shoes. Toiletries, gizmos, histories of Stalingrad, Berlin, and both the First and Second World Wars, some, as far as Elder could tell, unread, their spines uncracked. A few vinyl albums with bent and ragged sleeves: the original *Dusty in Memphis*, Otis Redding's *Otis Blue*. CDs that mixed Phil Collins and Simply Red with pop singers from the sixties, more Dusty, Lulu, Sandie Shaw. Some Aretha Franklin. The Temptations. A couple of DVDs. *Titanic. Pearl Harbor.* And videos: *The World at War* in a box set, *Cross of Iron, Apocalypse Now, Das Boot.* A slew of old musicals: *Funny Girl, Top Hat, Follow the Fleet, An American in Paris, Singing in the Rain, Carousel.* A stationery box that had once housed A4 paper and now held photographs.

Elder spread them out across the table. Holiday snapshots, beaches, umbrellas, tanned bodies, exotic plants; celebrations, faces mugging for the camera, champagne, cigars. Three men standing outside a nightclub, slightly the worse for wear, dressed to the nines, startled by the sudden flash of light: Grant, Mallory, and a man Elder recognized from the framed picture in Lynette Drury's house as Ben Slater. There were photographs also of

Grant and Slater in the changing company of others: in restaurants and bars, relaxing round the pool, the racetrack, the dogs, a hospitality box at Chelsea, the departure lounge at Heathrow.

Elder shuffled them around.

Grant and Mallory ringside at a boxing match — Elder lifted it up and turned it toward the light — Maurice Repton in the background, almost edged out of the frame.

Grant and Mallory.

I know where the bodies are buried, George, remember that.

Something could put Mallory inside for life.

How far did it go? How thick the stew?

Elder tapped the photos back into piles and replaced them in the box.

Close to two hours later it was all being resealed and replaced.

Vicki Wilson was sharing a flat near Gloucester Road with two other women. Andrea was a makeup artist, working mostly on corporate videos and the occasional pop promo for MTV; Didi, real name Deirdre, was a dancer at a Revuebar in Soho. When Elder called, Andrea was out filming and Didi in bed sleeping.

Vicki didn't look as if she'd been sleeping much at all.

She was wearing baggy sweatpants and a loose cotton top and she was letting her hair grow out; the only traces of makeup were at the corners of her eyes where she'd failed to wipe them away. In some strange way, Elder thought she looked more attractive than before.

"You're not working," Elder said.

"Can't be arsed. Besides, Didi, she's thinking of chucking it in, going to Australia. This mate of hers, she's got a job dancing. Sydney. Says it's great. Thought I might tag along. Why not? Nothing to keep me here."

"You'd work as a dancer?"

"Oh, yeah. Just see it, can't you? That'd be faking it and no mistake. Five minutes, they'd have me good and sussed. Out on my ear."

"What then?"

"Same sort of stuff I do here, I suppose. Demonstrations, sales. Bit of modeling maybe. Catalog stuff, you know? Got to be something, hasn't there? Better'n this." She coughed and fidgeted a tissue out from her sweatpants pocket. "Bastards like that Repton, sneaking round."

"He's been to see you again?"

"Oh, yeah."

"Tell me."

Vicki pushed a hand up through her hair. "First it was like before, right? Wants to know if anyone's been to see me, asking questions. 'No,' I said, 'course not. Why would they? I never mentioned you. Didn't want to drop you in it, did I?' Then he changed tack, didn't he? Come out with all the smarm. 'Why don't we go out for a drink, something to eat, enjoy ourselves?' All the while he can't take his eyes off my tits. Tongue hanging out so far he could practically lick his own dick."

Elder smiled. "It was a no, then?"

"Too bloody right."

"And you've not seen him since?"

"Be feeling sorry for himself, won't he?" She snorted dismissively. "His sort, they can never get it up anyway."

"His sort?"

"Something about them, blokes like him, you can see it in their eyes. Get off on watching. Or that business, you know, where they stuff oranges in their mouths and pretend to hang themselves — what's that called?"

"Self-asphyxiation."

"Yeah, that's it. Sad bastards."

"And you think Repton's one of those?"

"Yeah. Wouldn't be surprised." Suddenly her face brightened. "Maybe I could get a job as one of them sex therapists, what do you think?"

"Maybe you could."

"Bet you need qualifications though, even for that. Some bloody degree. Nonvocational qualifications."

Elder was looking at the framed photograph across the room.

"Lovely, isn't it?" Vicki said, following his gaze.

It showed the two of them, Grant and Vicki, standing together in front of a low stone wall, the sky behind them a tremulous blue.

"Mykonos," she said. "Last year."

Elder nodded.

Vicki blew her nose. "He was a good bloke, you know? Straight."

"Are there any others?" Elder said. "That I could see."

There were only a few that she'd been keeping flat in the back of a book, mostly shots of her and Grant, one of him on his own.

"Any idea where this was taken?" Elder asked.

Vicki shrugged. "Cyprus, I think."

He handed the photographs back.

"He never talked about Mallory, I suppose?"

"Jimmy? Talk about the copper? Why would he do that?"

"I don't know — some history between them. Bad blood."

Vicki shook her head. "Never as much as mentioned him. Never heard of him, had I? Not till the bastard shot poor Jimmy dead."

Chapter 47

St. Ann's was one of those areas in the inner city that had, amidst much protest, been largely demolished in the 1960s at the expense of new, more modern housing; now some of it was being knocked down and replaced again. The flat that Summers had fingered as a dealer's safe house was on the upper floor of a block of twelve, six and six. Only one of the lights in the central stairway was still functioning; the narrow walkway stank of sour piss and vomit and excrement. More than half of the flats were boarded up, and several of the others had old sheets or blankets draped across the windows in place of curtains. One, close to the top of the stairs, had a small light shining above the doorbell at the center of the door, artificial flowers inside a plastic holder next to it, a sticker proclaiming JESUS LOVES YOU, a mat on the ground, worn but clean.

Bland came up the stairs first, Eaglin behind him. Both men were wearing leather jackets, jeans, and sneakers. For heavy men they were soft on the stairs. Bland's Audi was parked a street away. Both men were armed. Eaglin was holding a heavy-duty flashlight in his left hand.

The flat they were looking for was at the far end, black material taped across the windows.

Hip-hop beats drifted up from the floor below.

Bland stood with his ear pressed to the door, listening, before stepping back.

"Police!" he shouted through the mail slot. "Open up!"

No response.

With a look at his partner, Bland took one step back and then another, swung his leg, and drove the underside of his foot against the side of the door, close to the lock. As the door splintered open and swung back, Eaglin ducked inside, Bland following, both with pistols drawn.

"Police!" Eaglin shouted in the darkness. "Armed police."

He switched on the flashlight.

The room was bare, save for a few posters still on the walls; save for Resnick sitting in a lopsided easy chair, trying not to smile.

"What the fuck!" Eaglin said, rooted to the floor.

"Ricky," Resnick said pleasantly. "Dave."

"Charlie," Bland said, recovering, "what are you doing here?" But inside he already knew.

Eaglin too. Dropping the flashlight, weapon at his side, he spun around and went back fast through the door, and, as he did, a searchlight hit him full on. Two armed officers were on the walkway opposite the stairs, one kneeling, one standing with legs slightly apart. Both were aiming their MP5 rifles at Eaglin's chest.

"Drop the gun!" came the instruction. "Drop it now."

Eaglin dropped the gun.

"Now kick it away. Over here. Over here."

Resnick and Bland were still staring at each other inside the flat.

"We got a tip-off," Bland said. "Some scum using this as a safe house. Drugs stashed. Money too."

"This is official?" Resnick said.

"Of course. What else?"

"You'll have a warrant then?"

"Charlie, come on. We just got word, less than an hour ago. There wasn't time."

450

"I know just when you got word," Resnick said. "And who from. What you promised him, too, his share of what you took down. I'll play you the tape later, Ricky. Refresh your mind."

Outside, Eaglin was facedown on the concrete, arms cuffed at his back.

When the call came, Elder was sitting with a glass of Jameson, reading, the radio doodling in the background.

"It's done," Prior said. "Safe in custody, both of them."

"Talking?"

"Not yet. But they will."

"Okay, Maureen. Thanks."

Elder walked to the window and looked out, not really seeing anything, thinking about Katherine. Relieved that it was over, that part of it at least.

Rob's got friends up Hull way. Family too.

Wondering if she were truly safe, for now at least.

You're old enough to make your own decisions.

Make my own mistakes, that's what you mean.

Happy even, what chance was there of that?

Framlingham woke him a little after six-thirty.

"Coffee on, Frank? I'll bring the croissants. My treat."

Elder was just out of the shower, still toweling himself down, when the buzzer sounded. He let Framlingham in, switched on the kettle, and went into the bedroom to get dressed.

"Knew if I didn't get to talk to you first thing," Framlingham called after him, "we'd likely be looking at day's end. Maybe even tomorrow."

"Busy, then?"

"Meetings, Frank. Forward planning. Position papers. Targets. Bloody government's target mad." He got two plates out of the cupboard. "When this country finally goes under, it's not going to be invasion or revolution or even some godforsaken plague; it's going to be paper, the sheer weight of bloody paper, committee after committee, report after report, commission after commission. It'll sink us, Frank, between the North Sea and the bloody Atlantic, you mark my words."

Elder came back into the kitchen wearing dark pants and a faded blue shirt.

"Hard to get better than these," Fram-

lingham said, setting down two fat croissants, one on each plate. "Picked them up
in Hampstead on the way through. Bakers
in South End Green. Bloody marvelous."

"How strong?" Elder asked, before spooning coffee into the jug.

"Strong."

Elder switched off the kettle and waited
a few moments before pouring in the
water. What Framlingham, with a wife and
house the other side of London, was doing
this far north in the relatively early hours
of the morning, he didn't ask.

"So," Framlingham said, "something important you said in your message."

Elder barely touched his coffee or croissant as he recounted in detail his conversation with Lynette Drury, while
Framlingham ate, drank, and listened.
When Elder had finished, Framlingham sat
a short while longer, thinking.

"Any chance she'd stand up in court?"

"Doubtful."

"Not even to shop Mallory?"

"I really don't know. No love lost between them, that's pretty clear. Maybe if
there was a way she could shop him
without taking down Slater at the same
time, but who knows?"

Framlingham reached across and appropriated a piece of Elder's croissant. "Shame you weren't wearing a wire."

"Likely inadmissible anyway."

"Stick with it, Frank. Something about Grant put the wind up him and whatever it was, it hasn't gone away. And we need to find out what it was. Could haul him in, of course, face him with some of those allegations, but I'm not sure that's the best way to go."

He steepled his fingers together and pressed hard enough for the blood to drain from the tips.

"Keep pushing, Frank. We're getting close."

Chapter 48

Elder caught up with Graeme Loftus early: Loftus already pumped up, rumors of something major about to go down, striding out across the car park, wearing his red hair like a flag.

"A word," Elder said, stepping out.

Loftus had either to barge into him or stop short.

"What the fuck about? No, wait. Wait. I didn't recognize you at first. It's that murder again, right? Maddy Birch? Look, I've already answered all your questions about that. I mean, don't get me wrong, I hope you get the guy, right? But just get out of my face, okay? It's nothing to do with me. *Nada*. Nothing."

Elder didn't move.

Several other officers, passing, turned their heads and slowed their pace but nobody stopped.

"It isn't Maddy Birch," Elder said. "Not exactly."

"What then?"

"A few more questions about the shooting."

"Shooting?"

"Come on, Loftus."

"Christ! What is it with you people? Grant, you mean? The same bloody stuff over and over again."

"It's called police work. At least it used to be."

Loftus half-turned away, shaking his head. "All right, okay. Let's get it done."

"Here?"

"Here."

"After the two shots, the ones that killed Grant, you were the first one in the room, yes?"

"Yes. I mean, just seconds maybe. But yes, I was first through the door."

"And you saw what? Exactly."

Loftus released his breath slowly, keeping himself in check. "Like I told you before. Detective Superintendent Mallory's standing with his back to me, right arm raised, pistol in his hand. At least that's what I assume. From where I'm standing I can't actually see the weapon, but Grant, he's down and wounded. Dying if not already dead. And Birch, she's sort of crouching, head down, between the two of them." He looked Elder square in the face. "There. That's it."

"When you described the incident before, you said Maddy had blood on her face."

"So?"

"So now you're saying she was facing away from you, away from the door."

"That's right."

"Then how did you see blood on her face?"

"God! Does it matter?"

"Everything matters."

"All right, then I suppose I must have seen it later, the blood I mean."

"You suppose?"

For a moment Loftus closed his eyes. "Yes, I saw it later. I must have. She had her head down, facing away."

"You could only see what? Her back? The back of her head?"

"Yes."

"And she was positioned between you and Grant?"

"Yes."

"Shielding him?"

"Partly, yes."

"You could see what? His head?"

457

"He was sort of kneeling, leaning forward. I could see he'd taken a shot to the head."

"Nothing more?"

"Not really, no."

"So, just to be clear, from where you were standing inside the room, you could see Detective Superintendent Mallory but not his weapon; you could see Maddy Birch from behind, crouching down, and the head and maybe the shoulders of the wounded man."

"Yes."

"You couldn't see Grant's hands?"

"No, I just said . . ."

"Neither hand?"

"No."

"Nor anything he might have been holding?"

"For fuck's sake, no!"

"You didn't see him with a gun?"

"No."

"You didn't see the gun?"

"Not then, no."

"Not in his hand and not on the floor?"

"How many more fucking times?"

"Then how did you know it was there?"

"What?"

"You heard me, how did you know it was there? It's in your testimony, to the enquiry. A .22 derringer, on the floor beside Grant's leg. You saw it, or so you said."

"Then I did."

"But now you've just said . . ."

"I couldn't see it when I very first went into the room. Not from where I was. That's what you asked."

"Then you saw it when?"

"When the detective super stood away. He was pointing at it, showing it to Birch, I imagine."

"Then the only person who could have seen the derringer in Grant's hand and then on the ground, because of the way she was facing, was Maddy Birch?"

"Yes, I suppose so."

"Yes, definitely, or yes, you suppose?"

"All right, yes. Definitely yes. Now, can I go?"

Elder stepped aside. "Be my guest."

Loftus pushed past and then turned. "And tell that little prick who's been sneaking round asking questions about me, trying to get someone to dish the dirt, that if I see his face again, I'll take it off."

The Merc was parked with its offside wheels on the pavement, outside Elder's flat. Maurice Repton was sitting behind the wheel, George Mallory alongside him.

The windows on either side had been lowered several centimeters and both men were smoking. Mallory got out of the car as Elder approached and dropped his cigarette to the ground.

"Frank Elder?"

"Yes."

"You know who I am?"

"I know."

He was older than he looked in his photograph, Elder thought, heavier too. Ash down the front of his three-piece suit. His eyes were tired, his face a little gray, as if, maybe, he hadn't had the best day.

"I thought," Mallory said, "it was time we met."

"Why's that?"

A smile leaked around Mallory's face. "Don't play dumb with me, Frank. Act the fool. Oh, you might be a puppet of some kind, I realize. Framlingham's toy. His Spring-Heeled Jack."

He pronounced each syllable of Framlingham's name distinctly, separately, each segment more dismissive than the last.

"Robert Gentleman Farmer Framlingham. Or so he'd have us believe. Streak of piss in his country tweeds. Behind you somewhere is he, working your strings? Well, we've got history, Robert and me, did he tell you that? Came after me once before, when he was with CIB. The Ghost Squad." Mallory laughed. "Difficult being invisible when you're seven foot tall with green Wellies and a shooting stick. Five charges he brought against me and each and every one of them refuted. Denied. Dismissed. Case fucking closed. Except he doesn't like that, your Robert, so he's got you weaseling about, sucking the puss out of every dirty little rumor, every little half-baked mendacious lie. And you'll do his bidding, won't you, Frank? Have been up to now. Suborned, that's what you are. What you've been. Fucking suborned. Play the cards whichever way you can, as long as what? As long as my hand comes down with the ace of spades? Forget it, Frank. There's nothing there. Just jism floating in the fucking breeze. Fairy dust, Frank. Nothing real."

He poked his finger hard against the center of Elder's chest.

Repton chortling in the car, enjoying the show, the boss going off on a rant. Ian Drury crossed with Laurence fucking Olivier. Sir Larry to you. Poor old bastard turning in his grave. Both of them, come to think of it.

Mallory wasn't through. Home-going

commuters stepped around them with no more than the odd word, the odd glance.

"Going back through my records, Frank, past arrests. Villains I've put down. Those that've walked away. That fucking anorak Sheridan. Searching for a pattern. Something to hang me with, hang me out to dry. Maddy Birch, you even figured me for that. Come on, Frank, don't deny it, don't be shy. What did you think? I'd climbed into my Ripper kit one night, just for the fun of it? Just for the crack? How you must have been disappointed now it's turned out to be someone else. Wouldn't have been winding young Loftus up this morning, else."

Mallory took a step closer: no farther to go without Elder stepping aside.

"No, Frank. Not my style that kind of thing. Messy. Too much risk. Here . . ." He pressed his index finger, once, twice, against Elder's body. "Head and heart, Frank, head and heart. Ask Grant. He'd tell you if he could."

Mallory laughed in Elder's face, mint and nicotine on his breath. "You've got a daughter, Frank. Up north. No better than she should be by all accounts. Drugs, wasn't it? Heroin? Cocaine? I'd look to her, if I were you. Something nasty happened to her once. A shame for it to happen again."

Elder leaned back and punched him in the face, Mallory forewarned enough to turn his head aside and ride with the blow. A stumble back and blood at the side of his mouth, a smile alive in his eyes.

Repton was out of the car.

"A mistake, Frank," Mallory said. "When you look back, if you can, that's what you'll think."

He spat at the ground between Elder's feet and turned away again.

Moments later, smooth as grease, the Mercedes slid out into the traffic and away.

"Beautiful, Frank," Framlingham said, when Elder told him. "Beautiful. Didn't I tell you we were getting close?"

Elder could still feel the hard bone of Mallory's jaw against his knuckles.

"Repton, that's who we'll go for," Framlingham said. "That's the route we'll take."

"We?" Elder queried.

"Not going to let you have all the fun, Frank. Meetings with the junior Home Office minister or no. Time, I think, for a convenient bout of flu."

Even over the phone, Elder could sense the broadness of Framlingham's smile.

Chapter 49

Repton was wearing a three-button charcoal gray suit with a faint red stripe, narrow lapels, and a single vent at the back; seven years old now and just beginning to take on a little surface shine around the elbows and the behind. His black Oxfords he'd buffed for fully five minutes while listening to yet another foolish politician digging the ground from under himself about Iraq. Why hadn't Blair and his cronies realized all they had to do was say we want to go in with the Yanks, kick the shit out of Saddam, secure the oil, and give our boys a good workout into the bargain? Sixty percent of the population would have said fine; a few thousand others would have marched up and down waving banners, but no more than did anyway, and once the initial push was over and we were in without too many casualties, that sixty percent would be up around seventy.

Of course, he thought now, lighting a Benson's for his trudge across the car park, go in alone next time, instead of waiting for the bloody Americans, and the number of our casualties would be cut by more than half.

Friendly fucking fire!

At the door, he nipped the half-smoked cigarette, blew on the end carefully, and dropped it into his side pocket for later. Waste not, want not. Any luck, he'd be at his desk before George put in an appearance. Stuff been hanging around his in-box long enough to have grown whiskers.

As soon as he pushed open the door to the long, open office, he saw his luck was in. And out. No George Mallory, but that long streak of piss Framlingham, and Frank Elder along with him.

What the fuck was this all about? Payback for last night?

"Maurice, good to see you." Framlingham's voice could have been heard three fields away, never mind between those walls. "Frank and I thought it was time for a little chat."

"What about?"

"Oh, you know, this and that. Loose ends. I don't doubt we'll go into details later."

"Bollocks," Repton said, shaking his head. "I'm not going anywhere. You've got no jurisdiction. You . . ."

Framlingham lowered a friendly hand onto Repton's shoulder. "Maurice, Maurice. No need to be hostile. Whatever this is, I'm sure we can work it out to the best of your advantage." He gave the shoulder a squeeze. "Yours at least."

Repton glanced around: several heads turned in their direction, others bent judiciously over their desks, everyone listening.

"Come on, Maurice. We'll take my car, what do you say?" And then, as they were walking toward the door, "Nice suit, Maurice. Good cut. You must let me have the name of your tailor."

Up in Nottingham, Dave Eaglin was still stonewalling, self-preservation uppermost in his mind. Sooner or later, his interrogators would slip one through his defenses and that would be that.

In another similarly airless and anonymous room, Ricky Bland was playing a different game. More attacking, more imaginative, but mired in risk.

"Wait, wait a minute, Charlie. Wait. That tape, the conversation you claim I had with Summers . . ."

"Claim? It's your voice, Ricky, clear as day."

"Maybe, maybe."

"No maybes about it."

"Okay, for the sake of argument, let's say it could be me."

"Ricky."

"Could be, okay?"

"We've got photographs of you and Summers talking, timed. We've got the tape, timed. What do you think? Right. They coincide. It's you on the tape, tapping Summers for information, offering him a deal."

"Come on, Charlie. Wise up. Get your head out of the sand. What d'you think? We get what we need out of this scum without offering them something in return? What d'you think's going on out there, Charlie? It's not helping old ladies across the fucking road. There's a serious fucking drug problem that we're just about keeping the lid on. Just. And never mind the odd handgun, there's thirteen-year-old kids out there riding round with grenades and fucking rocket launchers. It's a war, Charlie, a fucking war."

"With rules."

"Fuck the rules!"

"Exactly."

"Fuck the fucking rules!"

"Exactly."

Bland lurched forward. "Okay, listen. You know how long I've been out there, on the streets. Down in the smoke and then up here. You know how long?"

"Too long?"

"Not so fucking long I'm losing my fucking brain. What? You think I'd let that creep Summers cut some kind of a deal in his favor? Let him run rings round me? I was out there doing this stuff when he was still crapping his fucking nappies, for fuck's sake. You know that? Promise him stuff, of course I promise him stuff. Promise him whatever he fucking wants. Ten percent of cash? Okay, finder's fee. Half the drugs to go back out on the street? Why not? It's all baloney, Charlie, you know that. Use your common sense. Use your brain. It's not real, it's never gonna happen. Summers, he's gonna get fuck-all. It's just what I need to say to bring him along, make sure he plays ball."

"Like in Forest Fields, just over a week ago."

"What?"

"Crack, heroin, nine thousand in cash. Another tip-off from Summers, I believe."

Bland angled back his head and laughed.

"There was never nine grand, nothing near. A few hundred, as I remember. Enough crack to keep you and me and a couple of others happy for the rest of the day. Whoever told you anything else's a fucking liar."

"You didn't give Summers some of the proceeds of that raid?"

Just for a moment, Bland hesitated. Front foot or back?

"A few grams of H, that's all. Keep him sweet."

"You knew he'd sell it back on the street?"

Bland shrugged.

"What if I told you instead of selling it, he handed it over to the police?"

"I'd say someone was lying or Summers has lost his fucking mind."

"And the rest of the proceeds from that raid, Ricky, the rest of the drugs, the cash, they're where? Logged somewhere? Evidence? Search and seizure?"

"They're safe; that's all you need to know."

"Safe? Safe where?"

Bland leaned back and tugged his tie even looser at his neck; the front of his shirt was dark with sweat. "Hot in here, Charlie. How about a fucking drink?"

The pub was at the bottom of Hornsey Rise, set well back from the sidewalk, a signboard promising hurling and Gaelic football on large-screen TV. Its wood-and-glass facade had seen better days. A ratty dog, tied to one of several outdoor tables, barked at Furness and Denison and nipped hopefully at their ankles as they approached the door.

The interior was dark and smelled of disinfectant and stale beer.

At a round table close to the window, an elderly black man was playing solitaire with a dog-eared pack of cards. A woman of similar age and classic dimensions, the kind Furness thought still existed only in old seaside postcards, was sitting on a patched mock-leather seat near the fire, nursing a small drink in a tall glass.

It was the kind of pub, Furness thought, people meant when they said, admiringly, "It's a real old-fashioned local, not been tarted up like the rest." Said that and then headed off for the bright lights and shiny wood of a Pitcher and Piano, an All Bar One.

The barman had his shirtsleeves rolled back and tattoos snaking up both arms, a silver ring piercing the corner of his left eyebrow and a stud through the center of his lower lip.

"Get you?" he said, affably enough, glancing up from a well-thumbed copy of *Love in the Time of Cholera*.

Furness nodded at Denison, and Denison took out the photograph, showing Kennet full-face and profile.

"Don't suppose you've seen him?"

The bartender barely gave it a second glance. "Not for a good while now. Other side of Christmas, certainly."

"You know him then?"

"Used to come in here quite a bit. After work like, you know. Pint of Guinness, maybe two, and then he'd be on his way. Lived around here, that'd be my guess."

"The other side of Christmas, you said. You couldn't be more specific?"

The barman folded down a corner of a page and let his book fall closed. "Time and date, you mean? I don't think so. Early December, maybe? No, wait, wait, it was November, the end of the month. I know because . . ." He looked past them, toward the man playing cards. "Ernest, your seventieth, when was that exactly?"

Ernest placed a red jack on a black ten. "Tuesday, the twenty-fifth day of November, two thousand and three."

"We had a bit of a party for Ernest, got some food in, dug out the Christmas decorations early. Picture of Ernest in his prime here over the bar. Full uniform — what was it, Ernest?"

"Second Royal Fusileers." Black king on red queen.

"What's all this got to do with Kennet?" Furness said.

"Who?"

"Kennet." Tapping the picture. "Him."

"Oh, right. He came in, didn't he? Later than usual. Eight-thirty, nine? Asked me about the photograph, I remember that. Still up, you see. Started to pour him his Guinness, but no, whiskey he said. Doubles, two of them. Standing there, where you are now. Quite chatty he was, more than usual. Bit hyper I thought. Just back from Spain, he said, holiday."

"He didn't say anything about meeting someone? Later?"

"Not to me, no. Not as I recall."

"How about where he was going? After this, I mean."

The barman shrugged. "Home, I suppose."

"Thanks for your help," Furness said.

"Drink before you go? On the house."

Furness gave Denison a glance. "Yes, why not? Small Scotch, maybe."

"Lee," Denison said.

"What?"

"Better not."

Furness shook his head and stood away from the bar. "Another time," he said.

"Suit yourself." The barman opened his book.

"Blessed are the pure at heart," Furness said, as he followed Denison through the door. "Blessed and thirsty, too."

"What the flying fuck," Mallory said, "is going on?"

"Not here," Repton said.

"Not here? Not fucking here? Farmer fucking Framlingham and that deadbeat Elder come waltzing in without so much as a by-your-leave, and next thing you're going off with them in Framlingham's fucking four-by-four. Nice little drive, Maurice? Giving the motor a spin? Got the picnic basket out later? Spot of lunch? Hamper in the fucking boot?"

"Not here," Repton said again.

Mallory's face was puce, fingernails digging deep into his palms.

"Then you better say where, Maurice, and soon."

★ ★ ★

Shields's call tracked down Elder at his flat, late afternoon.

"We've placed Kennet near the scene of the murder, the day after he came back from Spain. Had a drink in a pub on Hornsey Rise, close to the time. Right between his flat and the place Maddy was killed. He could have walked from there to the community center in five minutes, ten tops."

"Good work," Elder said. "I mean it. Really good work." And then he excused himself to go answer the entry phone. There was a parcel downstairs waiting for collection.

Chapter 50

By the time he had arrived downstairs, whoever had delivered the package was nowhere in sight. A padded envelope the size of a hardcover book, with his name printed on the front. Elder shook it, prodded it, carried it back upstairs. Inside the envelope the contents were swathed in Bubble Wrap, a videotape with a title handwritten on the edge. *Singing in the Rain.* Just that and a date.

Who, Elder wondered, was sending him home-taped movies, and why?

Not certain when he'd last eaten, Elder thought he'd do it right; he phoned out for a pizza and some garlic bread and, when they arrived, opened a bottle of Beck's from the fridge.

A mouthful of pizza, and he slotted the tape into place, pressed PLAY, and leaned back. For a copy, the picture quality wasn't too bad. Fine, in fact, until the scene, maybe a quarter of the way through, when Debbie Reynolds, in her pink cap and little pleated skirt, pops up out of the cake. Then the image twisted abruptly, caught and jarred, and changed to black and white. An interior, blurred and poorly lit. Some kind of party scene. Men in dinner jackets, black tie; others with jackets discarded, white shirts, suspenders. Women in low-cut dresses. Champagne. And, as if on cue, a face Elder knew. Like watching a veteran actress in her heyday, cigarette in one hand, glass in the other, wearing a pale dress that reached to the floor, Lynette Drury crossed the room and, for one moment, looked directly at the camera, as if she were the only person present who knew that it was there.

Elder pressed PAUSE and searched the screen for someone else he recognized, but no. When he moved on, the picture changed: the same room later. Kneeling at the low table in the center of the room, a young woman, naked save for a bracelet in the shape of a snake on her upper arm, snorted cocaine through a rolled-up banknote, while a man, trousers around his knees, fucked her from behind.

A starburst of static and what had to be another camera, six people sitting around another table in another room, a poker game. And among them faces Elder knew: Mallory, Slater, Grant, and standing just behind Mallory, at his shoulder, Maurice Repton. Younger, all of them. A decade ago, Elder guessed. Possibly more.

The image broke again and re-formed.

A bedroom, sparsely lit. Elder adjusted the brightness with the remote control but to little effect. Shapes moved naked across the bed, arms, legs. Three bodies, intertwined: two women and a man. One of the women detached herself and stood beside the bed. Not a woman at all. A girl, slim-hipped, no breasts to speak of, long fair hair. The man reached out for her and she evaded his hand, turning away. Surfacing from the bed, he seized her arm and pulled her back. As his arm tightened around her neck, the other hand pulled at her hair. Silently, head swiveling toward him, she shouted or screamed.

Elder could see her mouth, opening wide, but heard nothing.

He moved closer and peered at the screen.

The man had the girl in his grasp, increasing pressure, and now the other girl, similar but with shorter, darker hair, started hitting him, pummeling his back and shoulders, trying to get him to stop, but to no avail.

Suddenly, without warning, the man released one girl and swung around toward the other, smashing his forearm into her face with such force that her head was jolted back and around and she tumbled over the edge of the bed toward the floor.

Imagining that he heard the impact, the clash of bone against brittle bone, Elder held his breath.

Now the man caught hold of the girl's ankles and dragged her back onto the bed, legs spread, and lifted himself above her.

The fair-haired girl gouged her nails down his back and, spinning, his elbow struck her full in the face so that blood shot from her nose. Grabbing her, he forced her down. His hands at her neck, squeezing, as he leaned down with all his weight.

Elder stopped the tape, rewound and watched again, looking for the moment when the fair-haired girl's body went limp and Mallory pushed her to the floor and she lay, lifeless, as no unbroken body could have lain.

Mallory.

If there'd been doubt in his mind before, it was no longer there.

The dark-haired girl was just visible in the far corner of the room, mouth slightly open, silent, staring, one arm tight across her breasts. And for a second, possibly two, a shadow fell across her, followed by the partial figure of a man, fully dressed, walking into the room, the frame. Then nothing.

Fade to white.

To black.

To nothing.

Treasure trove.

Elder went into the kitchen on less-than-steady feet and poured a shot of whiskey, the neck of the bottle rattling against the glass.

His call to Framlingham was rerouted to Hampstead, a terraced cottage in the Vale of Health, a hop, skip, and a jump from the Heath itself. The woman who let Elder in was in her late forties, tall, wearing a generous green needle-cord dress. Dark hair turning gracefully gray. "Imposing" was the word that came to mind.

She made no attempt to introduce herself and neither did Framlingham when he appeared, stooped, in the doorway, slippers on his feet.

They sat in the small living room, not much more than an arm's length from the television screen, sipping twelve-year-old Macallan and watching as the girl fell, again and again, to the floor.

"This is what Mallory was afraid of? What Grant had threatened him with?"

"I assume so."

"There has to be more."

"You think so?"

"We need more than just the tape, Frank. We need a place, we need names. If there are bodies buried, we need to know where they are."

"There's a date," Elder said, "written on the label, along with the name. *Singing in the Rain.* Fourteenth May, 1996. Could be when the film was recorded, we could check the schedules, but I doubt it. If you look at them carefully, date and name, I'd say they were written at different times."

"Then that's the date of the video, the party?"

"It's a good bet."

"The raid at Gatwick, the one which linked up Grant to Slater, that was when?"

"Ninety-five."

"And the case was thrown out of court?"

"A year later."

Framlingham smiled. "Celebration party, then."

"Could well be."

"For Mallory, too. Thanking him for his assistance. Let him win a few hands of poker, throw him a couple of girls."

Elder shivered inside, remembering. "When I was talking to Lynette Drury, she said that was what Mallory liked, young girls."

"And that was her, Drury, at the party? You've no doubt?"

"None."

"We should talk to her then."

"Sooner or later."

"Where the bodies are buried, you think she's the one to know."

"If they're buried."

"If."

Elder was thinking of Lynette Drury's face, the pain behind her eyes. *That was what I clung on to, no matter how filthy it all became.* "Yes," he said. "I think she knows."

"You think she sent you the tape?"

"It's possible, yes."

"She'll deny it."

"Of course."

Framlingham wound back the tape again.

"There, Frank — the man who comes into the room at the end — what are the chances that's Repton?"

"You think have another go at him first?"

"Why not?"

Framlingham rose, slightly awkwardly, to his feet. These chairs, this room, they weren't intended for a man his size. "I'll see if I can't organize some coffee. Don't want you falling asleep at the wheel."

Chapter 51

Framlingham's office was dominated by an oil painting of his yacht, a Mistral-class twenty-footer with white sails and green trim. Framed alongside it were three small watercolors of the Blackwater estuary by St. Osyth Marsh that Framlingham had made as a young man.

Framlingham looked comfortable behind his desk, chair eased back, one leg crossed lazily across the other. Elder stood by the side window in front of drawn blinds, feet apart, hands lightly clasped behind his back. Both men were looking at Maurice Repton, and Repton did not look comfortable at all.

The faint ticking of the clock on the shelf opposite the window was just audible beneath the ragged edge of Repton's breath.

The phone on Framlingham's desk rang unanswered and then was silent.

"You're hanging me out to dry," Repton said.

"Maurice, nonsense. Another little chat is all."

"A fucking summons, your office, eleven sharp."

"You weren't expecting coffee?"

"Fuck your coffee!"

"Tea, then. It might be possible to arrange tea."

"You're a cunt," Repton said.

Framlingham slowly smiled, as if this were indeed a compliment. Perhaps, from Repton, it was. "We just thought," he said, "you might appreciate the privacy. Rather than resume discussions in the full public view."

"There's nothing to discuss."

Framlingham leaned lazily forward. "I think if there's a problem it may be rather that there's too much. A matter of where to start. Though Frank and I think what we've seen on the video might be the place."

"What fucking video?"

Framlingham and Elder exchanged smiles.

"*Singing in the Rain*," Framlingham said. "Always a favorite."

Watching Repton's increasingly ashen

face, Elder thought about the call he'd received from Maureen Prior earlier that morning. Up in Nottingham, Bland was coming around to making some kind of a deal, the best in a bad set of circumstances that he could. In the end, Elder thought, that was what they all did. Bland and his kind. Aside from the ones who chose a gun to the head or a rope knotted tight about the neck, the ones who went silent to the grave.

Repton sat watching the tape with scarcely a movement, scarcely a word. Now, faced with a blank screen, a nerve twitched arrhythmically above his right eye, hands knotted in his lap. Elder eased open the blinds and light seeped back into the room.

Framlingham spoke into the silence. "Only two ways to go, Maurice."

Repton said nothing.

"Try saving your pal Mallory, it isn't going to happen. Isn't going to work. Besides, you've watched his back long enough. Wiped his backside. Time to save yourself, if you can."

Repton looked at him quickly, then away. There was something troubling him about the crease in his trouser leg and he straightened it carefully with index finger and thumb.

"I need to think about it," he said.

"Of course." Framlingham rose to his feet. "I need to take a slash, anyway. Five minutes, okay? Frank will be just outside the door. And no calls, Maurice, eh? In fact, Frank, why don't you relieve Maurice of his mobile, just in case?"

Sour-faced, Repton handed over his phone.

"Not armed are you, Maurice?" Framlingham said. "Carrying a weapon of some kind? Dereliction of duty if I left you alone with enough time to put a bullet through your brain pan."

"Fuck off," Repton said.

"Frank," Framlingham said.

Elder carefully patted Repton down: no weapon.

"Five minutes," Framlingham said, opening the door. "Don't let them go to waste."

When they came back into the room, Repton seemed not to have moved.

"I'm going to need assurances," he said.

"Of course," said Framlingham, repositioning himself behind his desk. "That's understood. Your assistance, a case like this. Minimum sentence, open prison.

Back outside in eighteen months, I shouldn't wonder."

"No," Repton said. "No jail time. None at all."

"Maurice, be reasonable. You know I can't promise that."

"Then there's no deal."

"Oh, Maurice, Maurice. What am I going to do? You want me to fetch CIB in on this? Here . . ." Reaching for the phone. "I can call them now. If you'd really feel more comfortable talking to them than me."

"Listen," Repton said. "Everything you want to know George has been into, going back what? The best part of twenty years?" He tapped his fingers against his temple twice. "It's all in here. Names, places, amounts, everything. And that stuff on the tape . . ." He laughed. Not a pleasant sound. "You want to know where the bodies are?" He tapped his head again. "But I want guarantees. One, no time inside. Two, protection, before the trial and after. Twenty-four hours, round the clock. And then I want a new identity, new address the other side of the fucking world."

Framlingham set the phone back down, unused. "Maurice, I'll do what I can, you know that. But there's only so much, in good faith, I can promise."

"Then make your calls," Repton said. "Firm it up. You know what I need." He got to his feet. "And don't try fobbing me off with any witness protection scheme bollocks, either. I don't want to spend the rest of my life looking over my fucking shoulder, waiting to see who's going to come through the fucking door. You handle this differently. Handle this your-self. Close to your chest."

Framlingham sighed. "All right, Maurice. I'll do what I can."

"This time tomorrow," Repton said. "And not here. I'll contact you. Okay?"

"Okay."

"My mobile," Repton said to Elder, holding out his hand.

Elder gave him back his phone.

"How do we know," Framlingham said, after Repton had left the room, "he isn't calling Mallory right now?"

"We don't."

"In which case, let's hope self-preservation beats in his heart a shade more strongly than loyalty."

Chapter 52

Nayim had worked with Steve Kennet for five years, on and off, himself and Victor, sort of a team. Turn their hand to anything, building-wise, except for real specialist stuff. Simple electrics, plumbing, all that was fine, but something like installing underfloor heating, they'd call in the experts, stand aside. Renovation though, new flooring, windows, stairs, outside work, repointing, replacing tiles, new roofs, there wasn't much they couldn't handle. Put in a loft not so long back, West Hampstead, architect designed. Some woman writer. Photos in the local paper. Signed one of her books for him, nice that. Not that he'd read it, mind.

Nayim sat next to Karen Shields on a bench in Waterlow Park, crows making a racket in the trees. A small boy was being pushed on the swings. The former hospital building Nayim and Victor were working on was clearly visible, a short way down the hill.

It was cold; too cold to sit comfortably for long.

When Nayim took out his cigarettes and offered one to Shields, she shook her head. He was what, she thought, Spanish, maybe? Portuguese? Something of an accent, olive skin.

"Back in December," Shields said, "close to New Year. One of my officers came to that place you and Steve Kennet were working on in Dartmouth Park Road."

Nayim nodded.

"You must have been quite a while on that job."

"Too long. Landlord going crazy, but it's not our fault. Weather, you know? Rain. Always rain."

Shields smiled. "Winter in England. That's what it does. It rains."

Nayim grinned.

"And you were what?" she said. "Fixing the roof, stuff like that?"

"New roof, yes. Brickwork, guttering. Wood round the window frames, rotted away."

"So you must have started when? Back in November sometime?"

"Earlier. October, must have been."

"Steve Kennet going off on holiday in the middle of it, that couldn't have helped."

Nayim hunched his shoulders. "Steve cut short his holiday, come back to work early."

"And this was when?"

"November. Last week."

Shields willed herself to slow down. "When he came back," she said, "how did he seem?"

"Sorry, I don't . . ."

"His mood, I mean. Was he chatty, friendly, glad to be back?"

Nayim shook his head. "At first, he hardly say a word. I go, hey Steve, good you're back, but he just grunt and go straight up to the roof, start work."

"You didn't happen to notice if he had anything with him? Out of the usual, I mean?" Shields hoping against hope.

But Nayim was shaking his head. "Just his bag of tools. Like always."

Shields stood and brushed the seat of her trousers. "If we wanted to take a look up there, where he was working — would that be difficult, do you think?"

Nayim looked up at her, uneasy without knowing why. "Easy enough, I think. You

491

can get into the roof space through the top-floor flat if you wish. If owner give permission."

Shields nodded, smiled. "Thanks for your time."

As she turned, something quick and brown scuttled through the leaves that had gathered between path and pond, either a squirrel that had emerged early from hibernation or a rat. On balance, Shields thought, a rat.

The leaseholder was away and not answering his cell phone. Shields wasted the best part of an hour being shunted between the landlord and the management company, much of it either being asked to choose from the following options or being left on hold listening to Vivaldi's "Four Seasons." Finally, out of frustration, she slammed down the phone, jumped in her car, and drove the few miles to the company's offices in Edgware. Once there, dark suit, stacked heels, taller than all of the women and most of the men, she got the attention she needed. The right permissions, the right keys. No more delay.

Forty minutes later, she and Ramsden, Furness and Denison in attendance, were passing the reservoir on Dartmouth Park

Hill, turning right across the traffic and looking for a place to park.

The entrance hall and stairs had recently been recarpeted; the usual plethora of unsolicited mail and restaurant fliers sat neatly piled on a small table just inside the front door. Someone in the first-floor flat was practicing the violin. On the floor above, the washing machine lurched into its spin cycle as they passed. A bicycle, presumably belonging to the owner of the upper flat, was on the landing outside his door.

Shields exchanged a quick glance with Ramsden before turning the key in the lock.

The entrance to the roof space was easy to find, through a drop-down door set into the ceiling between the kitchen and bathroom.

"Mike?" Shields said, looking at Ramsden.

"Paul," Ramsden said, "up you go."

Furness fetched a chair and held it steady. Denison pushed at the wood and slid it aside, hauling himself up and out of sight.

"What's it like up there?" Ramsden called.

"Dark."

Furness handed him a flashlight.

"You know what you're looking for?" Shields called.

"I think so."

Not so many minutes later, he'd found it, taped to the side of one of the beams, snug against the angle and the roof itself. Thick dark tape and, Denison guessed, plastic or paper underneath.

It was both.

He passed it down and, using gloves, Shields pried away the tape, folded back the plastic, and then unwound several pages from the late-night edition of the *Standard*, dated November 26, 2003.

It was a butcher's knife with a twenty-centimeter stainless steel blade firmly bolted all the way down the handle. Black haft, shiny blade, the tip not broken but bent very slightly to one side, as if it had been driven against something hard, like bone.

"Let's get this off to Forensics, first thing," Shields said. "Almost certainly he'll have wiped away any prints, but we need to check. Then compare it to the photographs of the wounds to Maddy Birch's body."

Ramsden grinned a wolfish grin. "That'll be sharpish, then."

Chapter 53

Under as high security as he could muster, Framlingham had set the technicians to work on the videotape: after enhancing the picture as much as they could, they had transferred it onto disc. From this they printed off a number of digital images, and it was these that Elder carried with him as he walked across Blackheath. Past six and the sky had already taken on that luminous orange glow; there were stars faintly visible above, though compared to Cornwall, precious few. One of them, he remembered reading somewhere, was some kind of satellite station and not a star at all.

Anton's T-shirt was white today instead of black; otherwise he looked exactly the same. The same sardonic, slightly camp look in his eye.

"She's in what we laughingly call the breakfast room, watching the snooker. Can't be doing with it myself. All that hushed commentary, as if they were in church. He's just kissed the ball up against the baulk pocket. Well . . ."

If Lynette Drury was indeed watching the snooker, she was doing so with her good eye closed.

The room smelled fetid and warm.

"Don't tire her," Anton said.

Elder brought over a chair and sat at an angle between the wheelchair and the screen. He sat there silently while one of the players made a break of forty-seven.

"I didn't think you'd be back so soon," Lynette said.

"Even after you sent the video?"

"What video's that?"

"*Singing in the Rain.*"

"I never took to Gene Kelly much. More of a Fred Astaire fan, myself. Lighter on his feet I always thought. More debonair."

"Something missing in the credits," Elder said. "My copy, at least. Nothing about the locations. The party scene in particular."

Lynette watched as a balding man with a cummerbund barely holding in his beer gut skewed the cue ball in off the black and looked heavenward for forbearance. "Manningtree," she said, still staring at the screen. "Ben had a place out there. Not

496

just him. Him and a few others. Country club, that's what they liked to call it. Gone now."

"Gone?"

"Sold to some foundation. Don't know what they're called."

"How long ago was that?"

"Three or four years, must be. Around the time Ben bought the place in Kyrenia."

Elder took the photographs from the envelope and spread them across her lap. The pace of her breathing quickened and then slowed. They showed, in bare bones, the story of what had happened in the bedroom. It didn't take any great imagination to fill in the gaps.

"I assume," Elder said, "there was a camera hidden in the room."

"In every room. Whenever there was a party, Ben had them on all the time. Some years he'd make a Christmas tape, you know, highlights. Send 'em round to his friends."

"Not this particular year," Elder said, indicating the photographs.

"No, not that year." Then, "Watch what you're bloody doin'!" as the balding man's opponent clipped the yellow attempting to pot the green.

"The two girls," Elder said. "Do you

know what happened to them?"

She took her time answering. "I know there was a problem. It got sorted."

"Sorted?"

"Yes. I don't know how. Didn't want to know."

Elder leaned forward and tapped one of the photographs, showing the girl on the floor beside the bed. "This girl, she's dead. Neck broken, that would be my guess."

"If you say so."

"And this girl?" He was pointing at a young, dark-haired girl cowering, terrified, in the far corner of the room. "What happened to her?"

Lynette's good eye flickered between the photograph and Elder's face, and then back to the screen in time to see one of the reds slide gracefully into the top pocket, the cue ball skewing back to cover the black.

"I said, they got it sorted. Ben and George between them. Made it go away."

"Between them?"

"Fucking yes! Have I got to repeat every fucking thing I say?"

The anger in her voice brought on a fit of coughing, raising spittle to her lips.

Elder waited until the coughing had subsided. "How exactly did they make it go away? Pay her off? What?"

"I'm trying to watch this," Lynette said. "And you're doing sod-all for my concentration."

"Who were they? The two girls? What were their names?"

Lynette started to cough again. "Call Anton for me, will you? I need a fuckin' drink."

"You used to get him girls, Mallory. Young girls. You must know who they were."

"I need a fuckin' drink!"

Anton showed his face around the door.

"Out," Elder said.

"A drink."

Anton hesitated, uncertain.

"Get out," Elder said.

He went.

"You've helped us so far," Elder said. "Help us with this."

"I've done nothing."

He touched her hand and she pulled it away, turning her face toward the wall. Only gradually did he realize that she was speaking, the same sounds over and over, low, barely audible, the same names. "Judy. Jill. Judy and Jill. Judy and Jill."

He took hold of her arm, gently, and felt skin slip loose across bone.

"Judy and Jill," he repeated. "Those were their names."

She looked into his face.

"They were twins."

Long after Elder had gone, long after one frame of the snooker had finished and another begun, Lynette propelled her chair out of that room and into another, guilt and uncertainty jostling against one another in her brain. She thought she might still have Mallory's number somewhere. Perhaps she owed him that much at least.

Chapter 54

Repton saw the police vehicle approaching from the opposite direction and checked his speed, lifting his foot from the accelerator and easing it down on the brake. Being stopped for driving under the influence was just what he didn't need. Not that he'd drunk a lot, not by some standards.

Checking the mirror to make sure the police car had continued on its way, he grinned. Not by some fucking standards! Christ! Times he and George had laid one on! Practically paralytic at five in the morning and still they'd turned in at their desk three hours later, ready for a day's graft, a day's hard sodding work. Not like today's bunch of puerile wankers! Binge drinking! They didn't know what a fucking binge was, didn't know how to fucking drink!

Shit! He'd only gone too far, hadn't he? Too far down the fucking road.

Catching sight of his reflection as he readied to make a U-turn, he laughed out loud. *Metaphors, Maurice? Fucking metaphors. Who the fuck d'you think you are? Too far down the fucking road, all right, and no mistake.*

He nudged into a space between a worn-out Escort and a white van, front wheel striking the curb and maybe shaving the van's paint with the rear end, but good enough all the same.

Twenty past fucking two.

There was a half-bottle of Scotch in the glove compartment and he unscrewed the top and took a quick belt.

His breath came back at him off the inside of the windshield. Like something out of a dog's arse, he thought.

Poetic, Maurice, he thought as he got out of the car. *Fucking poetic.*

Green Lanes Sauna and Massage was spelled out in electric light above the curtained glass. Except close to half the letters were missing, bulbs gone or bust, and you had to be a regular or one of those sad shits who did the *Times* fucking crossword in five fucking minutes to know what it said.

Reaching for the handle and not finding it, he wondered for the umpteenth time why, when the place had had a new front door fitted a year or so back, they'd hung it the wrong way around, the handle on the wrong fucking side.

Fuck!

When finally he'd pushed it open, it sprang back too fast and he almost collided with the facing wall. Hallway the size of a toilet for fucking dwarves.

Immediately to his right, a curtain of colored beads hung from the ceiling almost to the floor, and he parted this with both hands and stepped into the room. Rosie, as usual, was seated at a stool behind her desk, peroxide hair black at the roots, makeup half an inch thick sandblasted into place. Hundred and thirty years old, God bless her, and as ugly as the day she was born. Nothing else to do, twelve hours a day, other than work the puzzle books, watch her pocket-size black-and-white TV, drink cup after cup of instant coffee, and smoke endless cigarettes.

"Maurice, how's tricks?"

The times he'd told the stupid cow not to use his name.

There were three girls occupying the chairs opposite the desk, two he vaguely recognized, one that was new, not one of his favorites in sight. Busy, maybe. Each of the girls in button-through white overalls and bare legs, two of them flicking lazily through magazines, *Now* or *Hello!* or some such bollocks, scarcely bothering to glance up when he came in.

The third girl, the one he didn't recognize, was leaning back, legs pulled up, bottom two buttons of her overall undone, one high-heeled shoe on the floor, the other dangling from her toes. Toenails painted alternately red and blue.

"This all there is, Rosie?" His voice sounded slightly blurred to him, but who was going to give a shit? No one there.

"Veronica's upstairs."

"That fat cow!"

"That's Edie over there. She's new."

Edie, Repton thought, what kind of a name was that? Not that they used their real names anyway, most of them. He'd always reckoned Rosie picked them out of a hat.

"Knows what she's about, does she?"

Repton stared at the girl as he spoke and she looked back at him, holding his gaze, mouth opening in a smile. New, right enough, he thought, out to make an impression.

"Edie's from Slovenia," Rosie said.

Heaven fucking help us, Repton thought.

He followed her up the stairs, a nice enough arse on her, the last door along the corridor standing ajar and in they went.

Repton removed his jacket as Edie closed the door behind them, reaching out to take it from him and laying it folded across the foot of the bed. Repton waving his hands and saying, "Not like that. Not like that. Put it on a fucking hanger, for fuck's sake, you soft Slovenian cow. No offense."

The girl taking a thin metal hanger from inside the rickety wardrobe and fitting Repton's suit jacket on it, even smoothing down the shoulders, he liked to see that, before hanging it from the double hook behind the door.

It was going to be okay, Repton thought, as he took a handkerchief from his pocket and spread it over the pillow — well, you never knew — and lay down with Edie standing alongside him and bending to unbuckle his belt, slip it through the loops, and then attend to the buttons on his fly. Buttons, that was what he'd always insisted on, none of your fucking zips. Disaster waiting to fucking happen.

He felt himself hardening and closed his eyes.

Concentrated on the slip slip slap of

massage oil on Edie's hands.

First time he'd done this, he remembered, had this done, he'd been a young DC, green around the gills, the other lads putting him up to it, pulling a freebie on his behalf, some scrubber from Swansea with more than a touch of the tar brush about her and dirt under her fingernails. The minute she'd touched him, he'd shot his load. Caught himself in the fucking eye.

Laughing at the memory, he glanced at Edie, solemn-faced, concentrating, he thought, chuckling, at the job in hand.

"Come here," he said. "Here, closer, here."

Reaching up, propping himself on one elbow, he unfastened the remaining buttons of her overall. Bit of lace around the top of the bra, nipples standing firm. White knickers not much larger than your average postage stamp. No pierced navel for a change. Well, thank God for that.

Feeling himself close, he lay back and closed his eyes once more.

First thing tomorrow he'd find Framlingham and tell him to go fuck himself up the arse.

Breath accelerating, he arched his back as the girl's hand moved faster. Firmer. Faster.

He failed to hear the door open, then close.

"Maurice." The voice was soft, almost a caress.

Repton's eyes opened in time to see Mallory's face; the ugly bulge of the silencer at the end of the gun.

"Come again, Maurice," Mallory said and fired.

The girl screamed and, without moving his feet, Mallory slapped her with his free hand, slamming her, mouth bleeding, heavily against the wall.

Raising the gun, Mallory fired again.

Bone and tissue littered Maurice Repton's Irish linen handkerchief and the cheap pink polyester pillowcase beneath it, stained permanently by a hundred heads and now darkening pink to red.

Chapter 55

Elder was talking to Karen Shields, still a few minutes short of eight o'clock, the day not really under way, when Framlingham phoned, more of an urgency in his voice than Elder was used to.

"It's Repton. He's been shot."

"How bad?"

"Bad as it gets."

Shields read the concern on his face.

"How did it happen?" Elder asked. "Where?"

"Green Lanes. Early hours of the morning. Someone walked into a massage parlor and shot him twice. Why don't you get yourself down here now? Midway between Manor House and Turnpike Lane."

"Okay, I'll be there."

"Serious?" Shields said.

Elder nodded. "Good luck with Kennet. I'll phone in when I can."

The traffic was the usual morning nightmare, especially after he'd taken what looked, on paper, to be the most direct route, through the middle of Wood Green. He promised himself, once this was over, never again to curse the ten-minute wait to get down into the center of Truro on Saturdays.

Police vehicles were parked near the scene, half on the road, half off, loops of tape keeping the sidewalk closed for forty meters on either side of the building where the incident had occurred.

Elder left his car illegally parked on a double yellow line, a hastily scribbled note under the windshield. Framlingham was inside talking to a DCI from Homicide and the DI from the local Wood Green unit. He continued his conversation for several moments more, introduced Elder, and then drew him off to one side.

"Worst nightmare, Frank."

"What do we know?"

Framlingham steered him outside. There were knots of people staring from the far side of the street, men in bright African-style robes or with their hair cut according to the Hasidic style; women encased almost entirely, head to toe, in black. Produce outside the various Greek and Turkish shops shone purple, red, and green in the winter sun.

Framlingham lit a cigarette. "We know Repton was shot twice, once in the head, once in the chest. Nine-millimeter rounds." He breathed smoke out into the air. "Trousers round his ankles, poor bastard. What an inglorious bloody way to go."

"Anything on the shooter?"

Framlingham nodded. "Made no attempt to disguise himself. The woman running the place gave us a pretty good description."

Elder read the look on Framlingham's face.

"Mallory," he said.

"Yes."

"No room for doubt?"

Framlingham shook his head. "The girl who was with Repton when he bought it — here illegally, terrified out of her life she's going to be sent back to whatever godforsaken place she comes from — she swears he called him Maurice. Before he shot him. Maurice."

"You've got a call out for him? Mallory?"

"Oh, yes."

"Any sign?"

"Not as yet. Not a trace. This aside, no one seems to have seen him since around nine last night. Making his travel arrangements, I shouldn't wonder. Passport's missing. Description's gone out to all the airports, ferries, Eurostar terminal, but I'm not holding my breath. He had a good two hours clear, maybe more. By this time he's probably checking into his hotel on the Costa del Sol, looking forward to his first tapas of the day."

Or Cyprus, Elder thought. Or Cyprus.

In the interview room, Kennet looked even more tired, anxiety evident in his eyes and the way his hands were rarely still.

"This knife," Shields said, holding up the evidence bag, "it was found in the roof space of the house in Dartmouth Park Road where you were working."

Kennet looked back at her and said nothing.

"You were working in that building?"

"You know I was."

"At the time of Maddy Birch's murder."

"No."

"Think again."

"No, I told you. I was on holiday."

"You came home early. We've already established that."

"That doesn't mean I went back to work. I was still on holiday."

"But you did go back, didn't you? On

511

the Thursday morning. The morning after Maddy was killed."

"Did I? Who says I did?"

"The man you work with."

"He could be mistaken."

"I think not. I think you went to work that morning at eight o'clock sharp. Scarcely gave anyone the time of day. Straight up the scaffolding and into the roof, taking your tool bag with you."

"I'd hardly leave it behind."

"Then you were there?"

"Sometime, yes. If you say so, yes."

"Thursday, twenty-seventh of November."

"I don't know."

Shields leaned closer. She could smell the sweat seeping through his pores. "Come on, Steve, you've had a bust-up with your girlfriend, you're back early from Spain, no need to go in to work, you could sit at home with your feet up, watch TV, wander down the bookies, out a few quid on the three-thirty, but instead there you go, first chance you get."

"There was a job wanting finishing, we were way behind. It's called having a sense of responsibility, maybe you've heard of it?"

"Big on responsibility are you?"

"I like to think so, yes."

"Taking responsibility."

"Yes."

"Then why don't you take responsibility for this?" Shields had picked up the knife again and was holding it in front of Kennet's face.

"I tell you what," Kennet said. "You show me some proof that says conclusively that knife is mine, I'll take responsibility for it. Fair enough?"

Without taking her eyes from him, Shields leaned back against her chair.

Nearing four in the afternoon, just before dark, Elder had two brief telephone conversations with Katherine, both interrupted, neither satisfactory. Except that she was okay. Rob Summers was okay. He was still with the police, talking, sorting things out. She didn't know what was happening to Bland and his mate, except that she hoped they'd be put away for a very long time.

"I'll come up and see you," Elder said at the end of the second call.

"When?"

"I don't know. As soon as I can."

How many times had he said that when she was growing up? *Not now, Katherine.*

Not now, okay? But soon.

Framlingham had been in and out of a string of meetings, some of which Elder had also been involved in. During others he had been left to kick his heels. There had been sightings of Mallory, unconfirmed, on the ferry from Folkestone to Calais, boarding a flight at Heathrow bound for Miami, buying a Frappuccino in Starbucks on the avenue de l'Opera in Paris.

"Go home, Frank," Framlingham said eventually. "Go home and get some rest. We've done all we can for today."

Chapter 56

It was a gray late-January day: one of those days that promise nothing except that, sooner or later, it will end. Elder had lain awake since five, thinking, trying not to think. By six-thirty he was showered and dressed, had drunk orange juice and two cups of coffee, and had walked down the street to buy a paper and bought three; he read slightly differing versions of Repton's murder, more wishful thinking than factual statement, the few known certainties spun together with fantasies involving gangland executions and Turkish drug barons exacting revenge. Only one report, as an aside, mentioned that Repton had been one of the officers involved in the police operation, three months before, in which a high-profile criminal, James William Grant, had been shot and killed. Enough to leave a taint of retribution hanging in the breeze.

Head and heart, Elder thought, as he shrugged on his coat.

Head and heart.

He was at Framlingham's office well before eight and Framlingham was there before him, silver thermos on his desk. Elder suspected he had been there all night.

"Take a look at this, Frank," he said, handing Elder a fax.

The blurred image of two girls stared back up at him: school uniform, white blouses, striped ties not quite tight to the neck, faked smiles.

"Jill and Judy Tremlett. Disappeared from home, May seventeenth, ninety-six. Last seen at a nightclub in Colchester, friend's eighteenth birthday. Some reports have them leaving with an older woman, never been identified. According to others, one of the girls, Judy, complained of feeling sick and went outside for some fresh air. Jill went after her. When their father arrived to pick them up, just before midnight as arranged, they were nowhere to be seen.

"Usual procedure followed. Everyone at the club was questioned, the route home searched in case they'd started walking, thumbing a lift; drivers checked. It seems as if for a time the father was in the frame, but it came to nothing. No personal belongings were ever found, no shoes, no clothing, nothing. No sign. They were seventeen."

Elder was seeing again the grainy video images, remembering Lynette Drury's words. *Boys and girls, all handpicked, paid for. And George, he was in the thick of it, wasn't he? Lapping it up. Girls, especially; he liked girls, did George. Two or three at a time.* An older woman, Framlingham had said, never identified.

"There are better pictures," Framlingham said, nodding toward the fax. "I'm having them biked across. In case you're not sure."

Elder shook his head. "I'm sure. It's them."

Framlingham sighed. "Slater's old place out at Manningtree. I've spoken to the secretary of the Foundation. Seems they use the place for courses mainly. Alternative medicine, holistic therapy, that kind of thing." He looked at his watch. "Should have a search warrant within the hour."

"You think that's where they are?" Elder said.

"It's a start, Frank. It's a start."

Karen Shields had spoken to her boss, urged, pulled strings; the technology was there but not everyone had the same access, not every case was given the same priority, justified the same expense.

"She was one of ours," Shields kept saying. "Remember that. One of ours."

By mid-morning what she needed was up on the computer: a three-dimensional reconstruction of Maddy Birch's body, in outline, showing the extent and depth of the stab wounds to both arms and torso. Sheridan, operating the program, introduced the exact dimensions of the knife found in the roof. Zoom in on one of the wounds, the deepest first, and then move the image of the knife across and down. Some contraction of the skin around the exit point, no more than you would expect, but otherwise as perfect a fit as you could wish. In and out. Clean.

Shields swallowed and the sound seemed unnaturally loud.

She watched as Sheridan repeated the process with a second wound, lower in the torso, left-hand side. Another match. This knife, or one identical in every aspect, had almost certainly been the cause of Maddy Birch's death. Almost. Shields could see the defense barrister arguing the odds in court. Computers are like statistics; you can maneuver them to prove anything you need.

"Mike," she called across the room. "Anything back from Forensics yet?"

Ramsden shook his head.

"Get them for me on the phone."

The officer at the other end never stood a chance. "What do you mean," Shields said, her face tight with anger, "you're still processing my fucking request? And don't tell me to watch my fucking language, just do your fucking job. And fast."

When she put the phone down, the office gave her a small round of applause.

Two minutes later, she called back. "Look, I'm sorry about just now. I had no right to talk to you that way and . . . Yes, yes, yes, that'd be great. Fine. Just as soon as you can. Yes. No. I do understand. Of course. And thanks again."

Ramsden looked at her enquiringly.

"Patience," Shields said with a grin. "Patience. All in good time."

Out here closer to the coast, the wind was keener, the sky the gray of blue-gray slate. Magwitch, Elder thought. *Great Expectations.* The Essex marshes. He wondered if Jill and Judy Tremlett had been given the book at school. What expectations they'd had themselves. Seventeen. The same age as Katherine.

A pair of magpies hopped down from the branches of a nearby tree and played desultory chase across the grass. The place looked as if it had been given a face-lift since it was sold, the exterior painted blue and gold.

Framlingham was walking around the perimeter of the grounds with the chair of the trustees. Framlingham in greenish tweed, the chairwoman wearing a pale suit with a full skirt, hair pulled back from her face, nodding as she listened, interposing the occasional question, then nodding again.

At the end of their third circuit, the woman went back inside and Framlingham cut across to where Elder was standing.

"Coffee in the lounge," Framlingham said. "Ten minutes. Decaffeinated, I don't doubt. She's going to get hold of the surveyor's report they commissioned before the sale. Might give us a clue where to look first."

Elder looked toward the line of trees and beyond. *They got it sorted. Ben and George between them. Made it go away.* "They don't have to be here," he said. "They could be anywhere."

"Think, though, Frank. It would have been the middle of the night. Party going on, plenty of people still around. Two kids picked up not so many hours before, promising them God alone knows what. I doubt they'd want to go far, risk discovery." Framlingham pushed his hands down into his jacket pockets. "No, you're right. They could be anywhere. But what me water tells me, they're somewhere here."

With a sudden rattling cry, one magpie followed the other back into the trees.

Forensic Services rang back at twenty past one. Shields was eating a chicken salad sandwich at her desk, drinking from a bottle of mineral water.

It was the same officer as before.

"Detective Chief Inspector Shields?"

Shields gave a wary yes.

"I'd just like to hear you say you're sorry, ma'am. One more time."

"You serious?"

"Yes, ma'am. Quite serious."

Shields cast her eyes toward the ceiling and crossed her fingers. "I'm sorry."

"Very good, ma'am. Now you can have your reward."

As Shields listened, a smile spread wider and wider across her face.

Rising from her desk and crossing the office, she waited until she was close enough to Ramsden that her voice could remain a whisper. "Kennet. Get him in the interview room, soon as you can."

After setting the tape rolling, she let Ramsden ask the first few questions, teasing away again at Kennet's alibi as if that was all they had. Ten minutes in, Kennet relaxed, she produced the two knives: the one found near Taylor's flat, the one from the roof in Dartmouth Park.

"What do you think, Steve?" she said, almost offhand. "Similar, aren't they? Don't you think?"

"Kitchen knives," Kennet said. "So what?"

"They are similar, though?"

"If you say so."

"Part of a set."

"Yeah?" As if it didn't matter; as if he didn't care.

Shields held them closer, almost within reach. "Take a good look. Same kind of handle, same rivets, same carbonized steel. Good knives, professional."

"Fell off that Jamie Oliver's lorry," said Kennet with a smirk.

"Whoever bought these, Steve," said Shields, not to be deterred, "they cared about their utensils. Cared about their tools. Wouldn't you say? Someone who knows the value of a good blade."

Kennet shrugged and shifted a little on his seat.

"I asked Jane about them."

"Who?"

"Jane Forest. You remember. She says she was there when you first brought them home. Says you were really proud."

"You can't believe her. Not a bleedin' word."

"Why's that?"

"Mental, isn't she? Doctors, pills, the whole bloody time. Mental."

"I wonder why that is?" Shields said, looking at him hard.

Kennet held her stare but not for long.

"Come on, Steve," Shields said. "Save us all time. Admit it, they're yours."

"Prove it."

Shields leaned back in her chair and smiled. "This," she said, "is the part I like." For a moment, her tongue touched the edge of her lips. "This knife, the smaller one, the one with which you attacked Vanessa Taylor, has your thumbprint clearly on the handle, in addition to being identified by PC Taylor herself. And this, the knife you attempted to hide . . ."

"I did no such . . ."

"The sample taken from the blood found on the blade matches your DNA profile exactly."

"There was no blood!" Kennet swayed to his feet, kicking back the chair. "There was no fucking blood!"

"Not much," Shields acknowledged quietly. "Microscopic, but enough."

"It's a fucking lie!"

"Sit back down," Ramsden said, advancing on Kennet from the desk. Two uniformed officers had come through the door.

"You might suggest to your client," Shields said amiably to Kennet's solicitor, "that calming down would be a good idea."

Kennet took a step toward her and then stopped, shoulders slumped.

"You'll be taken to the custody sergeant," Shields said, "and charged with the murder of Maddy Birch. Now get him out of here."

She remained sitting there for fully fifteen minutes, alone, until the sweat had dried on her skin and the smell of adrenaline had all but faded from the room.

Chapter 57

They'd taken a table in a side room, a bit of a hike to get served, but it was a small price to pay for privacy and a little elbow room. Shields had left her credit card behind the bar and a clear maximum that, the way Mike Ramsden was throwing down large Scotches with beer chasers, wasn't going to last a whole lot longer. Sheridan had wandered off and found a quiz machine and was busy testing himself on Sports Trivia 1960–1990. *Which non-league player, coming on as a substitute in extra time, scored a hat trick in the F.A. Cup Quarter Final of . . .* Furness was prepared to swear he'd seen Denison say a Hail Mary in the Gents and then cross himself before sticking two fingers down his throat and throwing up so that he could carry on drinking.

"I owe you one, Frank," Shields said. She was wearing a pale lavender suit with a soft short-sleeved purple top, the suit jacket back at the table, her arm brushing his as they stood jammed up against the bar waiting for another round.

"Nonsense," Elder said, raising his voice above the general clamor.

"You were the one who made us look at Kennet again after I'd dismissed him out of mind."

"You'd have got back around to him sooner or later."

"Later, most likely."

Elder shook his head. "Don't do yourself down. You did a good job. All of you did."

She smiled. "Do you always find it this hard to take a compliment?"

He found himself smiling back. "Probably."

"Anyway, I'm buying you dinner by way of saying thanks. And no arguments."

"Okay. When's this?"

Shields glanced at her wrist. "In about an hour's time."

"You're serious?"

"Table's booked."

Elder looked back across the room. "People will talk."

Shields smiled again. "Look at me, Frank. I'm an almost six-foot-tall black woman of African-Caribbean descent, who's got herself promoted to quite a senior position on Homicide. You think people don't talk?"

They got away shortly after nine, the taxi driver, for once, leaving them to their own devices.

"Where are we going?" Elder asked.

"It's a surprise."

He smiled. "I'm a country boy, remember. Anything much beyond a trip to the local Wimpey's a surprise to me."

"Okay," Shields said. "We've got a table at Moro."

"Sorry?"

"Moro. It's a Spanish restaurant. Not a Wimpey Bar. And you're supposed to be impressed. You have to book weeks in advance to get into this place. Even on a Monday."

"What did you do? Offer to arrest the chef?"

"Something like that."

The cab dropped them at the corner of Clerkenwell Road and Roseberry Avenue, and they walked past a succession of closed shops and small cafés until they came to a restaurant on the right-hand side of the narrow street. Nothing auspicious from the outside.

Shields hesitated before pushing open the door. "I should have said. It's not a table exactly. The best they could do was two seats at the bar."

However, when Shields gave her name there'd been a cancellation and they were shown to one of several small tables close to the window facing out onto the street.

"Wine, Frank? Red or white?"

"Red's fine."

After a little hesitation, she picked out a Bobal Tempranillo '01 on the list.

Elder settled into his seat and looked around. The interior was crowded, busy; a steady buzz of overlapping conversations, interrupted by the odd raised voice, the occasional guffaw. Toward the rear of the room, a clutch of thirty-something men in dark suits, who looked as if they'd been there since finishing work, were making more noise than most. On either side of their table, handsome couples gazed into one another's eyes, out on a first or second date.

Elder hadn't been sure what to expect from the menu, his knowledge of Spanish cuisine not stretching far beyond paella or chorizo, and neither appeared to be there. Shields ordered a starter of broad beans and Serrano ham and he followed suit.

"Tell me about the forensics on the knife," he said.

"You really know how to woo a girl, Frank."

"Is that what I'm supposed to be doing?"

"God, no." A smile creased the corners of her eyes.

"So tell me."

"I'd been busting this poor guy's balls. In Forensic Sciences. Dickenson? Dickerson? Finally he tells me they've found a microscopic sample of blood, right at the base of the blade, close against the handle. Only reason, I suppose, it didn't get wiped away. Anyway, when he says this I'm thinking okay, fantastic, it's got to be Maddy Birch's blood. Put that with what we've got from the computer simulation and we've got this nailed as the weapon for sure."

"Is everything all right?" the waiter asked, leaning toward them.

"Fine," Shields answered, not looking up.

The waiter went away.

"So," she continued, "there I am getting all excited and I ask him, assuming I know the answer, but just to hear him say it, the blood, it's a match with Maddy Birch, right? And he says, no. I could have shouted at him down the phone, really lost it, but I'd done that already."

She took a sip of her wine.

"So," Elder said, "you asked him whose blood it was."

"What I actually said was, who the fuck does it belong to then?"

"And he said . . . ?"

"And he said it's Steve Kennet's blood. I could have kissed him. Probably would have if he'd been there."

"Just as well he wasn't. You know, work colleagues, station intrigue."

Shields leaned back in her chair, as if to focus on him more clearly. "That what you are, Frank? A work colleague?"

"Not for much longer."

"The business with Mallory and Repton?"

Elder nodded.

"Where are you up to with all that?"

He told her over their main course, Shields having opted for sea bass with roast mixed squash, Elder the lamb with spicy chickpea purée and spinach.

"So what do you reckon the chances," Shields said, setting down her knife and fork, "of tracking Mallory down and bringing him back?"

"Tracking him down, I'd say pretty good.

But if he's joined his buddy Slater in the TRNC . . ."

"The what?"

"TRNC. Turkish Republic of Northern Cyprus. There's no extradition treaty."

"Asil Nadir. I remember."

"Exactly."

"You want some more wine?"

"Have we finished this?"

"Just about."

"Best not."

"You fancy something else? Brandy? Whiskey?"

"Maybe later."

Shields raised an eyebrow, amused. "Don't count too many chickens, Frank."

Elder drank a double espresso, watching her eat her way through a largish helping of chocolate ice cream with cardamom. Despite his protestations, she paid the bill. The restaurant had ordered them a taxi.

"You're going to have to be careful," Shields said, settling back against the seat.

"What of?"

"Getting a reputation."

"I don't know what you mean."

"Twice now, isn't it? That you've pulled cases out of the fire. Last year and now this."

"Luck," Elder said, "that's most of it.

That and the people I've been lucky enough to work with."

Shields laughed. "You old charmer, you!"

It made sense, she said, for the cab to drop him off first. They stood on the pavement outside the small block of flats, his home but for not much longer, the driver keeping his engine idling, the meter ticking.

It was a surprisingly mild night for the time of year.

She looked beautiful, he thought, the way the light shone in her eyes.

"Say good night, Frank."

"Good night."

She kissed him on the mouth.

Elder stirred, waking in the darkness, not knowing if he'd been asleep for minutes or hours. Not knowing what had woken him, other than the smell, the scent of mint and garlic clear in the room.

His eyes focused on Mallory standing just beyond the end of the bed, pistol in hand.

"Sometimes you can delegate," Mallory said, "off-load. Sometimes there's so much shit been spread around, you just have to clear it up yourself."

His eyes narrowed marginally as he raised his arm.

"Should've stayed in Cornwall, Frank. Safer by far."

As his finger touched the trigger, he heard a sound at his back and spun around. On her way back from the bathroom, Shields had picked up the kettle from the kitchen counter. She swung it fast and hard into Mallory's face, the edge striking his nose full on, the flesh splitting open like an overripe plum.

Elder jumped at Mallory from behind, struggling to wrench the pistol from his hand.

Mallory struggled and swore and Shields swung the kettle a second time to the crack of splintering bone.

Elder forced Mallory to the ground and, one foot firm in the small of his back, brought first one arm and then the other around tight behind him.

The sound Mallory made, forced between broken teeth, was not a word at all.

"Hang on," Shields said, stepping into a pair of panties before fetching the handcuffs from her bag. "Any emergency," she said, with a grin.

Elder was still far too shaken to smile back.

"Keep an eye on him," Shields said. "I'll phone it in."

Elder said okay and lowered himself to the edge of the bed. Another moment, another second, and he would have been dead. Heart and head.

As his breathing steadied, he listened to Shields's voice from the other room, concise and clear. He already knew he would never forget the sight of her, stepping stark naked into the room, preparing to swing an aluminum kettle at Mallory's head.

Chapter 58

Katherine had arranged to meet Elder in the Arboretum, near the center of the city. He made his approach down through the park from the North Sherwood Street end, looking for signs of early spring. It was almost a month since the attempt on his life; three months since the murder of Maddy Birch; a shade over three weeks since the remains of Jill and Judy Tremlett had been unearthed beneath the house in Manningtree. Ash and bone.

There were crocuses, Elder saw, yellow and white along the flower beds and here and there haphazardly among the grass; snowdrops also, a few, still showed pale against the dark earth.

Rob Summers was sitting with Katherine on a bench near the corner of the rose garden and when he saw Elder he stood and walked away, giving them time to talk alone.

Katherine had allowed her hair to start growing back and there was some small color in her cheeks, though Elder thought a good meal or two wouldn't go amiss.

"Dad."

"Kate."

Her skin felt like newsprint against his lips.

"Did you drive up?"

He shook his head. "Train."

"All the way from Cornwall?"

"Came up to London yesterday. One or two things I needed to do."

"What's her name?" Katherine said, close to a smile. "Karen?"

"Since when has my private life been such an interest?"

"Since you had one."

Elder's turn to smile. Two small boys, who should certainly have been at school, went by on skateboards. A girl wearing the High School for Girls uniform stopped and asked for a light; Elder couldn't oblige, Katherine could.

"You are seeing her, though?" Katherine persisted.

Elder hesitated; he wasn't even sure. "It's not that straightforward," he said eventually. "Kind of job she has, it doesn't leave a lot of time for much else."

"Like you used to be, then."

"I suppose so, yes."

He reached for her hand, but she pulled it away.

"You think that's all it takes, don't you? You always did."

"What?"

"A quick cuddle, a hug, a kiss on the cheek. As if that made it all okay."

"I'm sorry. I was only trying . . ."

"It doesn't. Make up for everything, you know."

"Everything?"

She looked away. "All the times you weren't there."

There were tears in her eyes neither of them wanted to see.

"Are you saying it's my fault?"

"What?"

"I don't know. Everything. This."

She looked at him then, held his gaze, then slowly turned her head away, reaching into her pocket for her cigarettes.

"Kate . . ."

"What now?"

"Nothing." The admonishment frozen on his lips.

"You want to take a walk?" he said several long moments later.

"Not specially."

They continued to sit. Summers appeared lower down the path, walking in the direction of the bandstand, circling around.

"You and Rob, you're still . . . ?"

"We're going to back off a little. Just, you know, chill for a while. Rob needs some time to sort himself out, get his shit together." She smiled. "He comes out with stuff like that from time to time. 'Getting your shit together.' Like it was the sixties or something."

"What's happening to him?"

"With the police, you mean?"

Elder nodded.

"He'll be charged with possession. Then probation, most likely. That's what they're saying. Get a — what is it? — Community Punishment and Rehabilitation Order. A hundred hours of community service and a couple of years in a drug rehab program."

"He's happy with that?"

"He doesn't have a lot of choice."

"And you?"

"What about me?"

"What are you going to do?"

Katherine held the smoke in before releasing it slowly into the air. She was going to give it up. She was. Maybe for Lent. "I've started seeing my therapist again."

"You have? Katherine, that's great. I'm pleased. That's really good news."

"Okay, okay. Don't go crazy."

He knew he shouldn't ask, but went ahead anyway. "I don't suppose you've thought any more about college? School?"

"One thing at a time, Dad, right?"

"Okay, I'm sorry." Something about her expression reminded him of when she had been ten or eleven, scarcely grown, and he felt his breathing change, his chest constricting close above his heart.

Katherine stubbed out her cigarette. "I did go and talk to someone at Clarendon. There's an open-access program for AS level that didn't look too bad." She sprang to her feet. "Come on. Before you get all gooey and overcome. Let's catch up with Rob."

"All right."

Summers was sitting in the center of the bandstand, leaning back against the wrought iron railings, writing in a notebook.

"Just look at him," Katherine said. "He's such a poser sometimes."

"If you did go to Clarendon," Elder said, "start studying again, where would you live?"

Katherine grimaced. "Mum's threatening to redecorate my room."

"Maybe come summer you might even feel like running again."

She shot him a quick sideways look. "Not before I can walk, okay?"

Elder called on Resnick before catching his train back down to London. Both Bland and Eaglin were trying to outdo the other in apportioning blame, offering information in exchange for a better deal.

Framlingham had asked him to attend a meeting with the Chief Crown Prosecutor about the case against Mallory, which was under continuous review. While the circumstances of Maurice Repton's death were straightforward, at least as far as the Crown was concerned, those surrounding what had happened to the Tremlett twins were less so.

The bodies of two young females had been found beneath one of the cellars, covered by quick-setting concrete. Both corpses were badly burned. It looked as if they had been placed down there and then set fire to, using petrol, presumably in an effort to destroy them beyond recognition. But even as the fire had blackened and torn apart some of their skin, other parts it had preserved. Several fingerprints were still partially clear. Moreover, a comparison of their teeth with their dental charts made identification.

Pinpoint hemorrhages behind Judy Tremlett's eyes suggested that she had died from strangulation; a subdural hemorrhage around her sister's brain led the pathologist to conclude that she had died from a fractured skull. In neither girl was carbon monoxide present: they had been dead when the fire had been started. Small, small mercy.

Mallory was still denying responsibility for both deaths or any knowledge of how they occurred.

Officers from CIB were continuing to question him about a number of investigations in which he had been involved, prosecutions that, for various reasons, had failed; also several robberies that had so far remained unsolved. And Mallory, of course, was happy to string things out, feeding a little information here, a little disinformation there, all the while playing the system, delaying what was still, in all probability, inevitable.

When the meeting with the Crown Prosecutor was over, Framlingham insisted on buying Elder a drink and Elder was happy to accede. He was catching the sleeper back down to Cornwall later that evening and a call to Shields's cell phone had been diverted to her office voice mail, where he had failed to leave a message.

"I'm not asking you," Framlingham said, "to move back lock, stock, and barrel. Start another career. You're through with that, I understand. But what I'm saying is, be flexible. Give us four months of the year."

"No way."

"Come on, Frank. The winter, for God's sake. You don't want to spend that down there, surely?"

"Don't I?"

"Frank . . ."

Elder smiled and shook his head. "Look, no promises, okay? Nothing definite, nothing set. We'll stay in touch. If there's anything you think I might be really interested in, suitable for, give me a call. I'll say yes or no."

Framlingham held out his hand. "Can't say fairer than that, I suppose."

On the curb, he fished into his pocket and took out an envelope with Elder's name on it. "Had a call from that Shields woman this morning. Heard I was seeing you. Biked this over. Asked me to be delivery boy."

Elder stuffed the envelope out of sight.

"Safe journey, Frank. Take care."

There were still a good twenty minutes to go before boarding and Elder bought a cup of coffee from the Costa by platform one, sat down at one of the tables outside, and took out the envelope. When he opened it, a ticket slipped loose onto the tabletop. Dee Dee Bridgwater at the Jazz Café. A Saturday in March. Shields had written on the back. *A bit of a long shot, but if you happen to be in town . . .*

Elder drank some coffee, stuffed the ticket back inside the envelope, and tore them both in half, regretting it the instant it was done.

"Idiot," he said, and an elderly woman, going past with a suitcase on wheels, turned her head and smiled.

Taped together the ticket would probably be okay. He pushed the halves down into his top pocket, just in case.

There were still ten minutes before his train.

Acknowlegments

Special thanks are due to my editor, Susan Sandon, for reading the manuscript with her usual sagacity and for suggestions without which the finished book would be a lesser thing. My thanks also go to my agent, Sarah Lutyens; to Justine Taylor at Random House (UK) for holding a more than steady fort; to Mary Chamberlain for precise and sympathetic copy editing; to Mark Billingham for providing the answers to certain crucial questions at crucial times; to Sherma Batson and Sarah Boiling for reading earlier versions of the manuscript; and finally to everyone at Random House for their friendship and support.